3 9082 11277 0212

3/30/09

D1515940

Salty Like Blood

AUBURN HILLS PUBLIC LIBRARY 50
3400 EAST SEYBURN DRIVE
AUBURN HILLS, MI 48326
(248) 370-9466

DISCARD

HARRY KRAUS, M.D.

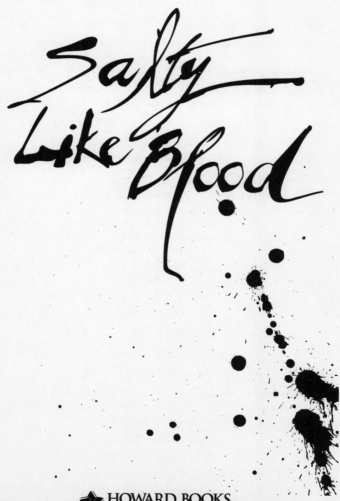

Salty Like Blood

 HOWARD BOOKS
A DIVISION OF SIMON & SCHUSTER
New York   London   Toronto   Sydney

Our purpose at Howard Books is to:
• *Increase faith* in the hearts of growing Christians
• *Inspire holiness* in the lives of believers
• *Instill hope* in the hearts of struggling people everywhere
Because He's coming again!

Published by Howard Books, a division of Simon & Schuster, Inc.
1230 Avenue of the Americas, New York, NY 10020
www.howardpublishing.com

Salty Like Blood © 2009 by Harry Kraus

All rights reserved, including the right to reproduce this book or portions
thereof in any form whatsoever. For information, address Howard Subsidiary
Rights Department, Simon & Schuster, 1230 Avenue of the Americas,
New York, NY 10020.

In association with the Natasha Kern Literary Agency

Library of Congress Cataloging-in-Publication Data

Kraus, Harry Lee, 1960—
Salty like blood / by Harry Kraus.
p. cm
Includes bibliographical references and index.
ISBN 978-1-4165-7789-8 (tradepaper : alk. paper)
1. Missing children—Fiction. 2. Kidnapping—Fiction. 3. Man-woman
relationships—Fiction. 4. Triangles (Interpersonal relations)—Fiction.
5. Maryland—Fiction. 6. Virginia—Fiction. I. Title.
PS3561.R2875S35   2009
813'.54—dc22
2008037527

ISBN-13: 978-1-4165-7789-8
ISBN-10:   1-4165-7789-0

1 3 5 7 9 10 8 6 4 2

HOWARD and colophon are registered trademarks of Simon & Schuster, Inc.

Manufactured in the United States

For information regarding special discounts for bulk purchases,
please contact: Simon & Schuster Special Sales at 1-800-456-6798 or
business@simonandschuster.com.

Edited by Lissa Halls Johnson
Interior design by Davina Mock-Maniscalco

This novel is a work of fiction. Names, characters, places, and incidents either are
the product of the author's imagination or are used fictitiously. Any resemblance
to actual events, locales, organizations, or persons, living or dead, is entirely
coincidental and beyond the intent of either the author or publisher.

For Joel
With admiration and love
Dad

Acknowledgments

Thanks to my editors, David Lambert and Lissa Halls Johnson, for valuable suggestions that have sharpened this work. Great writing is first a gift from God, and my editors are an avenue of this grace to me. Thanks to Kris, my first reader, who always catches the little stuff. Her eyes provide the polish.

Mostly thanks to God. His love makes all the difference.

Salty Like Blood

RACHEL AND I tumbled into the tall grass at the bottom of the hill, having survived yet another Daddy-just-one-more sled ride from the edge of our front porch. I collapsed on my back, trying to find oxygen between gasps of laughter, and looked up at the summer sky. My daughter, with limbs sprawled in a wide X and her head against my foot, shouted her delight toward the house. "We did it! We made it!"

Seconds before, airborne and soaring toward record distance, Rachel reached for an octave above the normal human voice range, squealing a note that rang on in my head, and I suspected invited half the neighborhood's canine population to play. I laughed and put my fingers in my ears, rolling them in an exaggerated twist as if she'd deafened me.

She moved to lay her head upon my chest and quieted herself there, listening to my racing heart.

I stroked her hair, inhaled the scent of mown grass, and nestled my head back into the tickle of green.

"Is it okay?" she asked.

"It's okay."

"It's too fast," she said, raising herself up and pushing a bony elbow into my gut.

"Oh, so now you're the doctor."

She smiled. "Someday," she said. "For now, you're the doctor."

"Don't worry. I'm okay." I scowled at my seven-year-old. "Really."

We rested together, staring at the sky full of clouds of hippopotami, horses, rockets—whatever Rachel imagined. Mostly I gasped and oohed. In a moment I found myself blinking away tears, overwhelmed with the enormity of it all.

It was so ordinary. A summer Saturday morning without an agenda. It's hard for me to describe beyond the sense I had of emerging, as if I'd been submerged for so long, and now, just to play and laugh and roll in the grass seemed a joy that would burst my heart. I smiled, taking it in, gulping in ordinary life as if I'd never have a chance again.

As Rachel chatted on with her running commentary of sky castles, fiery dragons, and fairies, other images drifted through my mind, pictures of painful chapters that set my current joy into sharp contrast. Traveling with Joanne through the dark tunnel of postpartum depression. My mother's battle with cancer. Memories of an intensive care unit visit while I was the too-young patient, watching my own heart monitor and wondering if life would be cut short.

Joanne's voice swept me into the here and now. "What's going on?"

I looked up to see her standing on the covered porch, eyeing a bottle of vegetable oil that was set on the white railing.

Rachel lifted her head, her blond hair dotted with grass seed. "We're sledding, Mommy."

Joanne's hands rested firmly on her hips. "It's July, David." She picked up the bottle. "And I've been looking for this." She was serious, but her eyes betrayed her attempt at scolding me. Her happiness at my delight in our little Rachel couldn't be spoiled by my summer antics.

I exchanged a mischievous glance with Rachel. She betrayed me in a heartbeat. "It was Daddy's idea."

"Women!" I said, grabbing my daughter by the waist and swinging her around in a circle. "You always stick together!"

As I trudged up the hill with Rachel folded around my back, I grunted exaggerated puffs. "You're getting so big."

I set her on the top step and kissed her forehead. She started pulling away. "Wait." I picked at the seeds in her hair. "You'll need to brush this out."

She opted for the shake-it-out method. "I'm a rock star."

I smiled. *My star.* For Joanne and me, Rachel had been the glue that helped us stick together through a valley of misery.

Joanne reappeared, carrying lemonade in tall, sweaty glasses. She handed me one and kissed me. She had thin lips to go with sharp, elegant features, dark eyes alight with mystery, and hair the color of caramel. She could have been a model before big lips became the rage.

I'd been to hell and back with Joanne, but the last six months, I'd sensed a real change in her. She seemed settled, somehow. Content. More romantic toward me—the way she had been back in my medical school days. Our relationship, once teetering on the precipice of divorce, was now solidly a safe distance from the edge. I'd seen significant pieces of my life's puzzle fall together in the last few years. When the marriage one finally clicked into place, everything else brightened with it. It was as if I'd been living my life in black-and-white and someone just invented color.

I kissed her back, trying to discern her mood. There seemed a surface calm, but I sensed a deeper stirring. I'd become a champion at reading her. I knew the quiet of her bitterness, the bubbly way she prattled on when she felt guilty, and the aloofness that dared me to pursue her into bed. For a moment our eyes met. It was only a flash, but in that instant, I felt the foreboding that threatened my wonderful ordinary-life euphoria.

I took her hand. "What's up?"

She lowered her voice, but even at that volume, sharp irritation cut at the edges of her words, clipping them into little fragments. "Your father."

I raised my eyebrows in question.

"His neighbor called."

I waited for more, but it seemed the silence only uncapped her annoyance. In a moment she was on the verge of tears.

"He always does this. Every time we have plans, he has a crisis."

Plans. The practice was dining at the country club tonight.

I started to protest, but she interrupted, pushing her finger against my lips. "You know they're going to announce that you've made partner."

I smiled. *Partner.* A year early. Just reward for the practice's highest revenue producer nine months in a row. Another puzzle piece in my wonderful life about to connect.

"Which neighbor?"

"That Somali family," she said, flipping her hand in the air. "A woman. She has an accent. She said his place is a wreck. He's ill." She seemed to hesitate before adding. "He's asking for you."

It was my father's way. The crab fisherman wouldn't pick up the phone and let me know he needed me. He sent word around the block and expected me to show. "Define 'ill.'"

Joanne imitated the neighbor's accent. "Mister Gus isn't eating. He toilets in the bedroom."

I groaned. Whatever the neighbor meant, I knew it couldn't be good. I walked into the house to my study and picked up the phone. I was listening to the endless ringing on the other end when Joanne entered. "Not a good sign," I said. "He doesn't pick up."

"What are we going to do?"

I looked at my wife. Petite. Strong. And so able to read my thoughts.

She threw up her hands. "We're going to the shore," she said. "Just like that."

I nodded. I was predictable. Family first. We had to go.

She glared at me. I read the silence, loud and clear. *That's why I love you . . . and hate you.*

"I'll call Jim. The practice will understand."

Joanne shook her head. "This is your night, David. The moment you've been waiting for. And you throw it away because of family."

I couldn't say anything. She had me pegged.

"I'll see if Kristine will take Rachel for the weekend."

"Let's take her with us."

Joanne's face hardened. "With us? That place is so . . ."—she paused, apparently mulling over adjective options—"crusty."

It was the gentlest description of several other options that came to mind.

"We'll take care of the crisis and stay at that seaside bed and breakfast. It will be fun. A chance for her to see her grandfather." I let a hopeful smile tease at the corners of my lips. "Even if he is crusty, he does adore her."

Joanne sighed in resignation. "Yes, he does." She tipped her glass against mine. "As long as we don't have to sleep there," she said, shivering as if that thought was horrifying. She gave me a don't-even-try-to-cross-me look. "You're driving."

I walked out onto the porch and into the humidity we Virginians call summer. As I called for Rachel, I followed the border of the house, my prize lawn soft beneath my bare feet. From her perch on the back deck, my daughter ambushed me with open arms.

"Can we sled some more?"

I looked at the blue sky and my *Southern Living* home, and I pushed aside a fleeting presence. A ripple beneath the calm.

I'd been through too many hard times to trust the peace. *Nothing this great can last forever.*

"We're going to Grandpa Conners'," I said, trying my best to sound excited.

Rachel wrinkled her nose. To her, the shore meant stinky crabs and everything smelling fishy.

I poked her nose with a finger. "You're too much like your mother."

She poked me back. "You're too much like your father."

A sudden breeze lifted Rachel's hair against my face. I stopped, looking east. In the distance, a small thundercloud hung over the horizon. *Not today. I don't want to travel the Chesapeake Bay Bridge-Tunnel in the rain.*

My daughter squeezed my neck, bringing a smile to my face and pushing my anxieties aside. I nestled my face into her hair, trying to find an earlobe. She giggled, and everything seemed right again.

2

JOANNE PACKED IN a rush, throwing in enough clothes for one night. I added my medical bag and swimwear for myself and Rachel, slipping in her little fishing rod and reel on the sly, hoping to escape from family obligations with Dad long enough to hear Rachel's delight over reeling in a croaker or if we were lucky, a catfish or two.

With our sights set on the Eastern Shore of Virginia, we left our suburban home west of Richmond by eleven. By noon we were sitting at a picnic table outside Pierce's Pit Barbeque near Williamsburg.

Joanne wiped Carolina Red sauce from Rachel's chin. "I don't like those clouds."

To the east, fluffy popcorn clouds darkened the sky above the pines. I grunted a response and shoved the last of a shredded pork barbecue sandwich home. The clouds bothered me, too. I'd seen the tenacity of storms coming off the Chesapeake, and I didn't like the idea of being over the water on the lonely twenty-three mile bay bridge-tunnel between Norfolk and the Eastern Shore. But my job, as chauvinistic as it sounded, was to offer a rock solid reassurance to my women. "Not to worry," I said. "They come up fast and burn out fast. We'll be fine."

A distant rumble punctuated the end of my sentence. Joanne raised her eyebrows at me and stayed quiet for Rachel's sake.

"Jim says they'll miss us for dinner," I said.

Joanne smiled. "I'm sure he'll drink enough to make up for all of us."

I chuckled. She was right, though. My senior business associate was a savvy businessman and a competent physician, but I worried that his liver would die before he did. When I told him this, he joked it would likely last forever, as often as he'd drowned the organ in pickling juice.

I remembered the uncomfortable moment like it happened yesterday. I had put my hand on his shoulder. "Are you really okay?"

His face reddened above his silk tie. "Mind your own business," he'd said, ending the conversation.

Joanne gathered our trash and looked at Rachel. "Let's use the ladies' room. Last stop before Grandpa's house."

Rachel closed her lips around a straw and pulled noisily at the last of her soda.

I watched them go and stood to take a better look at the sky. Having grown up in a small fishing town on "the shore," as we called it, I turned my eyes constantly to the horizon. It was second nature, something I still did, in spite of my indoor occupation as a family physician.

Moments later we were on our way again, east on Interstate 64 and moving shoulder to shoulder with a steady flow of Virginians escaping to the beach.

Joanne fretted in heavy traffic and liked it even less when the rain started. Soon the isolated plunk, plunk, plunk, closed together into a steady rhythm. I turned on the wipers and glanced at my wife. She needed something else to think about. "Why don't you call ahead to the Bayside Bed and Breakfast?"

I squinted through the windshield and frowned, noticing a fraction too late that I was about to pass my exit. I changed lanes quickly, a maneuver that rocked my Ford Explorer and prompted an expletive from Joanne. "Look out!" she screamed.

A horn blared. An old red convertible with the top down pulled up beside us, all occupants screaming. Three angry white men, with their hands in the air, lifted a redneck welcome with middle fingers flying. A lone occupant in the backseat, a tattooed man seated beside a surfboard, clasped his hands together as if carrying a handgun and jerked his arms back and forth as if experiencing a handgun's recoil.

"Idiots," I muttered. "Don't look at them." I bolstered my bravado by laughing at their predicament. "Looks like they can't put the top up because of the surfboard."

"You almost hit them."

"I know." I hesitated. "Blind spot." Inside, I cringed. I didn't enjoy being the cause of conflict. I glanced in the rearview mirror and wished for a Rolaids.

We exited toward the Chesapeake Bay Bridge-Tunnel, a man-made wonder crossing above and below miles of open water near the mouth of the Atlantic Ocean. Behind us, the red convertible followed. From the front, the bumper and grille heaved forward with menacing shiny braces exposed in a snarl of chrome. I watched as he nestled in behind me, thankful that Joanne was busy with her cell phone. I tapped the steering wheel and shifted my eyes from the road to the mirror, fighting the churning anxiety in my gut.

I glanced at Joanne. At least for the moment, she ignored me. I wished I hadn't eaten that second barbeque.

The red car hugged my bumper. He followed for two blocks, then pulled off, engine revving, likely seeking refuge from the pounding rain.

I took a deep breath and turned to see that Rachel had fallen asleep. *Oh, to be that trusting,* I thought.

Joanne folded her flip phone. "No service."

"Maybe it's the storm."

She sighed.

I squeezed her hand. *I love you.*

She didn't squeeze back.

The rain picked up again before the first tunnel. The bay churned white beneath us. I suspected the water gushing onto my SUV was at least half bay, half rain, a miserable recipe for corrosion.

In the tunnel there was peace.

A few minutes later we exited the tunnel, and my alarm grew as we began to cross the open water. I squinted ahead, looking for the safety of the next island. Just before the start of the second tunnel, the storm accelerated, and wind gusts forced me to a crawl. Once on the man-made island, with my wipers set to frantic, I pulled into a parking lot with the others seeking safety off the open bridge.

Five minutes later the red convertible reappeared, top up, surfboard jutting from the trunk. The three angry men stopped directly behind me, at a right angle to us, hemming us in. Faces to the windows, they leered at us through the downpour.

My eyes studied the rearview mirror. Joanne turned around and cursed under her breath. I double-checked the locks and waited.

There we sat, each second stretched unmercifully by our circumstance. My chest tightened. I wiped my forehead and forced a smile at Joanne, an implant I was certain she saw through.

Five minutes passed. The rain slackened. I wanted the license plate number but couldn't get it since I had only a view of the side of the car. I studied the vehicle, wishing I knew cars. It was old. Beautiful and restored. High back fins bordered the trunk. I guessed late fifties, a Chevy perhaps, with paint too new for its owner to tolerate a dent.

I started the SUV, flashed my brakes, and put it in reverse to warn the driver I meant business.

The red car sat there. I backed up an inch. Then two.

"What are you doing?" Joanne whispered.

"I want him to move."

I backed a total of two feet, until my bumper must have been nearly kissing his car. He sat there, unmoving, daring me to continue.

Joanne pleaded, "Stop."

I looked ahead, judging the distance between the front of my Ford and the concrete wall—a secure barrier that separated the parking lot from the boulders that provided the foundation for the man-made island. "Hang on."

I shifted into drive, cut hard to the left, and gunned the accelerator, hopping over a concrete wheel stopper intended to keep me from parking too close to the wall. My front bumper scraped the wall, but my momentum was enough. We completed the turn and fishtailed into the wet parking lot.

My evasive move took my nemesis by surprise. I sped across the parking lot and onto the bridge road, with lightning flashing and the red convertible dead on its wheels. Inside the tunnel I pushed the accelerator, rocketing past the speed limit—pushing eighty, ninety, and then one hundred miles per hour. Fortunately, traffic in the tunnel was sparse. Changing lanes in the tunnel was illegal, but I was jazzed and afraid. I had no idea what kind of drug or psychosis was driving the man in the red convertible, and I had little interest in finding out.

Weaving around slower traffic in the tunnel, I was soon out in the rain again and tangled in traffic. I made four passes, one around a large delivery truck emblazoned with a large blue crab. In the mirror there was no sign of the red convertible.

I slowed the SUV, dared my heart to do the same, and glanced at Joanne. She was pale, eyes closed and knuckles whitened around the shoulder strap. "It's okay," I said. "He's not following us."

Joanne uncurled her fingers from their death grip on the seatbelt harness.

The storm slackened, with the rain soon a nuisance drizzle. I glanced around at Rachel. She slept with her arms around Bobo, her little stuffed Pound Puppy. I was amazed that she could sleep through such craziness. I stole a second look, savoring the air of peacefulness around her. My eyes landed on Bobo. He struck me as a bit scary. With one missing eye, the remaining one seemed to stare blankly ahead, boring into me, chilling me with unreasonable dread. *It's just the storm and those crazy men in the red convertible.*

We drove in silence, exhausted from the rain or rednecks or both. I tried to recapture some optimism about my wonderful life, but my earlier mood had been destroyed. The suddenness of our trip, the storm, the inoperable cell phone, and the red convertible all combined forces against us.

It was weird in a heavy sort of way. I'm not suspicious by nature, but I felt weighted by our experience. I couldn't admit it, but I knew Joanne sensed it, too. "I want to go home," she said, gripping my hand.

"We'll be fine," I said, unconvinced. "The storm's over." I pointed up the road. "Look, here we are. Wake up Rachel."

3

NORTH OF OYSTER, Virginia, nestled in the fingers of the Chesapeake, is the town of Tippins, a town that slept through winter and opened its eyes each April, rising and falling with the fate of the blue crab harvest. Life was slower on the shore, and I needed to get back there two or three times a year to clear my head of mainland busyness. In August mainlanders from Baltimore, Norfolk, and Virginia Beach would crowd the Tippins Crab Festival, consuming bushels of steamed crabs, eating on newsprint paper and picnic tables beneath open-air tents and washing it all down with gallons of bottled beer. They listened to the high school marching band, laughed at the Crabber mascot, and whistled as the local girls paraded down a sawdust runway in search of the coveted title of Miss Crustacean.

Such were the memories of my childhood. I loved this place, which seemed, on this side of my medical education, to be another world. I was a mainlander now, on foreign soil.

I stepped out of my SUV and let my foot scuff the sandy driveway. I took in a deep breath. Salty. I could almost taste it. I was home.

Dad's place sat at the end of a cul-de-sac in a grove of pines adjacent to Nimble Creek, a muddy finger that insinuated itself from the bay through thick marsh like a snake in no hurry to go anywhere. It was a brick ranch, built in the seventies. He had an acre, mostly in the back, where he had two outbuildings, flanked by stacks of wire crab pots. Extending into the creek was a fifteen-foot wooden pier bordered by wood pilings that smelled of creosote.

I lifted Rachel from the backseat. "Come on, sweetie. We're here."

Rachel brightened and wanted to walk. She squirmed from my arms and ran toward the three steps leading to a small stoop. The house was dark, curtains and drapery over the windows. Dad's old pickup was parked in the yard with a flat rear tire. The grass, spotted over bare sandy clay, stood bedraggled and uncut, soldiers unprepared for battle.

I followed my girls across the sandy lawn, pausing to touch the wound on the front bumper of the Explorer. I lifted my eyes to the horizon, where lightning still danced across the churning stage of the Chesapeake. I shivered once, swallowed my foreboding, and put on a smile for my girls.

I knocked on the door. No answer. I twisted the handle. No one in Tippins locked the doors. Pushing open the door, I called, "Dad?"

The stench of stale urine greeted us. "Dad?"

To say that the place looked lived in was an understatement. A plate laden with bread-crust edges sat on a coffee table strewn with magazines. A peanut butter jar was open on the kitchen counter, unwashed dishes overflowed the sink, and the back door stood ajar. I sidestepped a cereal box and an empty Coke can on my way to the concrete patio.

I felt Joanne's hand on my elbow. "David." She pointed to the pier. There, fifty yards away from us, my father sat on the edge of the pier, feet dangling toward his crab boat, the *Beautiful Swimmer*.

I walked across his scraggly lawn and stepped onto the pier. "Dad."

He looked over at me.

"Dad, it's David. What are you doing?"

"What's it look like? I'm trying to get on my boat." He paused. "Thank God you've come. I'm in a horrible mess."

He reached for me, and I pulled him to his feet. He'd lost weight since I'd seen him. His skin was shiny, with a yellow hew. I bet he didn't weigh much more than 120 pounds, much too light for his six-foot frame.

He collapsed into my arms, hugging me, close to tears.

"Dad," I said. "What's going on?"

"I was just about to take the *Beautiful Swimmer* out for a final voyage." His eyes met mine. I understood what he meant. "I'm dying, David."

"Come on inside," I said, hoisting him up with my arm under his shoulder. "Let me look at you."

He started crying. Embarrassing sobs. "I was afraid you wouldn't come."

"Why didn't you call?"

He shook his head, muttering as we walked. "Children are supposed to check in on their parents."

I left it alone. *Whatever.*

He smiled at Joanne and Rachel. "My son's come to rescue me."

I walked him to his bedroom. The smell of urine was stronger there. Bath towels littered the floor. The bed was unmade. I was suspicious that it was the source of the odor. I sniffed the mattress. Bingo.

"Your neighbor called. She said you were toileting in your bedroom." I looked at him. "Exactly what does that mean?"

He chuckled. "Amina struggles with her English." He looked down. "It dribbles constantly."

"Your pee?"

He nodded.

"Don't make me ask every detail. Tell me what's happening."

"It's my back. It's killing me. Then my urine started losing its strength. Finally, five days ago, it stopped completely. I can't go at all." He shook his head. "Just drips out uncontrollably all the time."

I nodded and turned to leave.

"Where're you going?"

"To get my bag."

I returned a few minutes later, carrying my black medical bag with K-Y Jelly, a urinary catheter, and latex gloves. I started by laying the items on his dresser. "I'm going to have to examine you."

When I came out to the kitchen a few minutes later, I found Joanne staring into the refrigerator. "Doesn't this man eat anything besides peanut butter?"

I shrugged. Apparently his diet was worse than I thought.

"How is he?" she said.

"Not good. I think he has prostate cancer. His urine flow was nearly completely closed off. I was able to get a catheter in."

Joanne put her hand to her mouth. "He let you—"

"He wouldn't let me do anything." I raised my eyebrows to her. "Morphine is a wonderful thing."

"You drugged him so you could treat him against his will!"

I returned her stare. "Don't look at me like that. I made him relax so I could do what he needed."

"You arrogant—"

I shrugged my shoulders. "I could feel his bladder above his belly button. I drained off a liter and a half. He's not too happy about the catheter."

"You forced him to have treatment against his will."

I started running water in the sink for the dishes. "He won't go to the hospital."

"Stubbornness runs in the family."

I let it go. "I'm afraid his kidneys are failing."

"What will you do?"

I turned away from her. "I can't just let him die."

Joanne slipped in behind me and laid her head against my back, wrapping her arms around my waist. "Yes, you can. Love doesn't insist on its own way."

"He doesn't know what's best."

"He's your father. You owe him the respect of letting him choose."

I looked at my hand, knuckles whitened around a dishcloth. *What do you know about prostate cancer? I'm his blood. I'm a doctor. I can help him fight this.*

I felt her sigh against me. "How is he now?"

"Sleeping."

She grabbed a towel hanging from the counter and held it to her nose. It must have passed inspection. "I'll dry."

Rachel walked in from the den, dragging her Pound Puppy. "Can I play outside?"

"Stay off the pier," I said. "Maybe we can go fishing after we get this placed cleaned up."

She scampered off, leaving me with Joanne.

Joanne stayed quiet. I couldn't read her. After the last dish was put away, she spoke. "I want to go home."

"Joanne, we can't just——" I stopped when I saw her expression.

"Let's leave tonight. I want to be in my own home. Not in this place, not on this shore. I want to be home."

A panic attack? Not now, I thought. *Joanne, it's been two years.* "Honey," I started softly. "We can't run home like that. I need to take care of my father."

"This whole trip has been wrong. Everything——"

I took her in my arms. "Shhhh. Talk to yourself, Jo. Tell yourself the truth. We had some bad luck with the weather, that's all."

"The weather, those horrible men in the red car, the phone, your father——"

"Shhh," I said, pulling her close. "I'm here. Why don't you call the bed and breakfast now? I brushed her cheek with mine. "Just one night. I have to stay for Dad."

I studied her face for a moment. Eyes closed. Expression hard. I knew she was whispering to her soul, trying to rein in her runaway emotions. After a minute she took a deep breath. "I'll be okay," she whispered.

The noise of an engine accelerating touched the edge of my consciousness. *Probably some high school kids cruising their way through summer vacation.*

I gave her a squeeze. "I'm going to take Rachel to the pier for a minute. Then let's get this place aired out."

I opened the back door and walked into the yard. Coming home was like going through a time warp. Everything seemed the same. The creek, the marsh, the *Beautiful Swimmer*, the smell of the marsh after a rain, the squawk of the gulls. Exactly like I remembered it when I'd left fifteen years before. And in spite of my determination to escape the life of crab pots and the pungent fish we used for bait, a peace settled on my soul when I was near the bay. I knew I was, and always would be, a waterman.

"Rachel," I called, walking toward the shed. "Rachel-honey."

After circling the house, I felt my pulse quicken. "Rachel!" I picked up my pace and walked quickly to the water's edge.

No Rachel.

I glanced toward the pier and Dad's crab boat. *She wouldn't dare.*

I jogged onto the pier and checked the *Beautiful Swimmer*. No Rachel.

I walked back toward the house, imagining Rachel hiding behind one of the tall pines. "Rachel, come out!"

I poked my head in the back door, glancing around the clutter for my little girl.

Joanne looked up from her position straddling Dad's old

Electrolux vacuum and blew a rebellious strand of hair from her face. "Why don't we hire the man a maid?"

I walked past into Dad's room. He was still sleeping.

No Rachel.

I walked out, stretching, feigning nonchalance for the sake of my wife. "Seen Rachel?"

She saw through my mask and flipped off the vacuum. In a moment she was out in the yard, calling Rachel's name. "Rachel Elizabeth Conners!"

Joanne circled left. I circled right. We met in the backyard with the same thought. *The water.*

We ran together toward the pier with our anxieties colliding and expanding with unseen momentum.

"Rachel."

Joanne's eyes were fixed on the creek. "Oh God, oh God."

"She wouldn't have come here," I said. "I'm going to check with the neighbors."

In the next hour we asked every resident of the street if they'd seen our little girl. Everyone we questioned returned the same concerned stare, as if we were bad parents. They never said it, but I felt it at every doorstep. *You let your little girl go out by the water alone?*

We called the county sheriff's office.

My wife began to cry.

It seemed that in a moment of time, with the swiftness of a weather change on the Chesapeake, my life had forever changed. I'd gone from helping my father to searching for my precious Rachel. In only a few minutes everything in my perfect life had fractured.

Perhaps my wonderful life had been only illusion, a teasing of security while all the while I walked on a high wire, oblivious to the trouble beneath. Unaware of the precarious balance that takes only a brisk breeze to send everything crashing.

I pushed aside the phone and stared helplessly at Joanne.

Slumping on the couch, I took a deep breath, unable to calm my racing heart. This was not the first time my world had been upended. The shore, once my refuge, had again become my enemy, snatching precious life. I saw the wave lifting above me about to crest, carrying with it the turbulent white foam of horrible memories that I'd run from the shore to forget.

I followed Joanne out of the house and to the marsh at the creek's edge. We were lost, buoys escaped from their anchor and tossed upon turbulent seas. Without restraint, we waded at the water's edge, not caring that the mud saturated our clothes and slicked our skin black.

I knew how Jo would react. With the swiftness that only life-catastrophe could bring, I watched her change. Numbly, she cried her baby's name until hoarseness slowly stole her voice away.

She waded into the marsh, a soggy soup thick with sharp grasses and a tangle of cattails. When her voice faded, we found each other and limped to the shore.

There, we huddled together, unspeaking.

And then the rain began again, and my perfect life dissolved in heaven's tears.

FOR JOANNE, THE days passed in a collage of images, the dreadful stuff destined to embed forever in her mind.

A volunteer squad of local fishermen in yellow rubber hip boots sloshing through the marsh.

Rescue divers in their scuba gear.

David staring toward the Chesapeake, wondering if it had reached out and swept his daughter away.

Interviews with county deputies, dedicated if not simple men who insisted that a strong tide was responsible for her daughter's disappearance.

An overheard conversation of two watermen. *"Remember Tom's boy? Tide took the body all the way from the creek to Virginia Beach. Washed up by the Ramada Inn.*

A rescue boat dragging the creek, dredging up unhappy crabs, an old truck tire, and a mangled grocery cart, but no Rachel.

Such were the images welded into her very being.

She sat on the dock, clutching her cell phone, trying to remember feeling normal. It seemed that feeling was gone, drowned with her daughter.

She looked toward the house, prompted by the sound of crunching gravel. *Must be David, back from the sheriff's office.* Instead, she was startled to see her father's Mercedes followed by a news van.

As her parents, Gary and Tricia Morgan, stepped from their car, they were immediately flanked by a woman in a business suit and a cameraman. The cameraman held up his instrument and began recording as the senator walked toward his daughter.

Joanne stiffened. *How dare they invade—*

Her thoughts were stifled as her mother called her name and quickly enveloped her with a hug.

"Mom! You invited the media?"

Tricia finished the hug by patting Joanne's back. She pulled away and brushed aside a tear. She conveyed a look at the cameraman who understood, lowering his camera. "Don't mind them," she said quietly to Joanne. "You know your father has an obligation to the public. They will want to know what he's going through."

What he's *going through? What about me?*

Joanne fought the urge to go to battle with her mother over this in front of the cameraman. *Of all the nerve! My mother traipses in here like the Queen of Sheba . . .* Instead, she turned to hug her father.

Her father's voice was soft. "How are you, darling?"

She took a deep breath. "How do you think?"

"I know this is just horrible for you," he said. "But look at it this way. The media attention may actually help. Someone may know something and come forward."

Tricia turned around, taking in her surroundings. "So this is 'the shore.'" She framed the last two words in quotation marks with her fingers, her voice gilded with judgment.

The woman in the business suit stepped forward. "Gina Thompson," she said, holding out her hand. "Channel Three, *The News at Noon.*"

Joanne shook her hand.

"We won't interfere. We would like to take some footage around the house and waterfront." She paused as if she didn't know what to say. "I'm so sorry."

Joanne's mother eyed the cameraman carefully. "You know

our agreement. No pictures of David's father or the front of the house." She pointed to the dock. "Interview the senator over there."

Tricia Morgan had silver hair and a tongue to match. Her husband, the senator, had chosen wisely. If anyone had the polish to balance the life of a politician, it was Tricia. She'd always been the one to handle the media, spinning everything to her husband's advantage—including canceling her daughter's elaborate state wedding when she eloped instead with the son of a Chesapeake Bay crabber.

This was the first in-person interaction Joanne had had with her parents since Rachel's disappearance. She should have known it would turn out like this. Tragedy was worth nothing if you couldn't exploit the public's sympathy—especially during campaign season.

The irony struck. *They should be comforting me, not using this for political gain.* She looked around, wanting to be anywhere but there. She desperately wanted David to return and save her from her parents.

"We can't stay the night," Tricia said. "The senator has a breakfast meeting in the morning in Norfolk. We'll be staying at the Omni there." Her mother brightened. "Can you join us for supper? We'll take you and David to that inn he talks about over in Oyster."

"Sure," Jo muttered. She looked at the news anchorwoman, then motioned for the cameraman to move toward the dock. Jo smiled curtly at her mother. "That is if you think you have time. You may need to do an interview for Channel Three."

Her father sighed. "Jo, this is the price we pay for being public servants. The public has a right to know."

"Do they? Do they really want to know how horrible this has been for me? My only child has disappeared! I feel as if someone has ripped my heart from my chest! I can't sleep. My whole world has been swallowed in darkness." Her voice choked to a halt.

Gina Thompson asked her cameraman, "Did you get any of that?"

Joanne stomped toward the cameraman, thinking of how it would feel to shove him off the end of the dock. She pointed at his blue-checked shirt. "You stay away from me!"

He backed up, staying one step in front of Joanne all the way to the water's edge. "Of course!"

That night Jo and I endured dinner with her parents. Everyone carefully avoided the minefield of subjects that would upset Joanne. In essence, we had a quiet evening punctuated by talk of the weather and the food. The senator and his wife left by eight so that they could reach the Omni in Norfolk by a reasonable hour.

Joanne and I were left to contend with the loss on our own. I watched as Joanne teetered near a precipice of depression. I felt helpless to pull her back. Day by day, she was continuing to withdraw beyond my grasp.

After four nearly intolerable nights spent sleeping in my childhood bedroom, we headed for home.

Without Rachel.

The next morning I woke and stared at the ceiling. At least, I thought I was awake. It seemed that everything was normal. My first thought wasn't of agonizing loss, but of breakfast. Rachel was sleeping down the hall, I was sure. Nothing catastrophic had happened to us. Rachel's disappearance was a nightmare, nothing more. My life, my career, my marriage were all on track.

It was in that foggy state that I remembered the revving of a car engine outside my father's house. And I knew. The sheriff's department was all wrong. The Chesapeake hadn't stolen my baby.

I sat up, wiping sweat from my forehead. Instead of heading for the coffeepot, I went straight to my study and picked up a business card for the sheriff who had jurisdiction over Rachel's disappearance. He was an oysterman turned lawman, with a wiry build and thick white hair buzzed to military specs. Denton Reynolds picked up the phone after one ring.

"Sheriff Reynolds."

"Sheriff, this is Dr. Conners, uh, David Conners calling."

The sheriff sighed. "Yes, Mr. Conners." He paused. "You're calling for an update. The Coast Guard has been—"

"I'm not calling for an update, sir. I remembered something I feel is significant. Right before I went outside to look for my daughter, I heard a vehicle accelerating down the street. It meant nothing to me then, but now I'm concerned there might be a connection to my daughter's case."

Another sigh. "Listen, you told me all about your experience being followed by the red convertible."

"I'm not suggesting that it was them. It could have been, sure, but the timing of the noise is unmistakable. It must have been a few minutes before I went outside to look for Rachel. Someone's taken her, Sheriff."

"Did you see a car? Can you give me a description?"

I felt small. No. I hadn't seen anything. But it had seemed so significant that I remembered the noise of the car. I hesitated. "No, sir," I said. How could I convince him of something based on such an unsteady platform?

"Why would someone take your daughter? You haven't received any threats or a request for ransom?"

I lowered my voice. "No. But she *is* the granddaughter of a state senator."

"I'm aware of that. I met the senator and his wife," he said. "And I had to endure that reporter from Richmond's Channel Three *News at Noon*." His voice was laced with sarcasm. "This isn't the kind of media attention Tippins needs right now, especially with the Crab Festival coming up."

I huffed. I couldn't care less about Tippins' image.

He softened. "This is terrible for you, I know."

I wanted to rage at him, to tell him that he couldn't know how terrible it was, that every moment since her disappearance I felt an unseen horror, that I had trouble taking the next breath, that my wife's despondency frightened me, and that if he had a shred of decency, he'd exhaust every law enforcement official in the state to find my life again. Instead, I choked on my own sorrow. "Sure."

"I'll look into whether anyone saw or heard anything, and update you as soon as I have any information."

I couldn't speak. My own hometown had betrayed me. They were so small-town and naïve that they couldn't seem to imagine something sinister in their midst. I hung up the phone and padded on zombie feet toward the coffeemaker.

I took out my frustrations on Kenya AA coffee beans, grinding them to fine dust in my electric grinder.

Joanne appeared as I poured my first cup. She set her favorite mug, a souvenir of Topsail Island, beside mine. I poured coffee without speaking. When I leaned down to kiss her cheek, she turned away and sipped her coffee as if she hadn't seen my attempt.

I took a deep breath. "Jo, I don't think Rachel fell in the water. I think she was taken from us. Abducted."

She sat at the kitchen counter on a high oak stool and cradled her coffee to her chin with both hands. She spoke through the steam. "Don't do this to me, David."

"Do what? Are you afraid to hope?"

"I'm afraid of false hope."

"Why do you think they haven't found her in the water?"

Joanne slammed her mug against the counter, sloshing coffee

onto the phone book. "And the sheriff and all the investigators are wrong?"

"Yes." I added gently, "Because they've been dealing with drowning victims for years, that's their first thought. In the quiet town of Tippins, no one would ever believe that evil could be lurking behind the happy, white-clapboard façade."

Joanne looked drained, unable to find light in the darkness. Her accusation, when it came, wasn't unexpected. "This is all your fault." Her voice was emotionless—as though she were accusing me of forgetting to buy milk, not blaming me for our daughter's disappearance. "If you hadn't insisted that we go to the shore, if you hadn't have insisted that we take Rachel, if you had only listened to me when I wanted to go home . . ." She got up and carried her coffee into the den. Evidently, she was done.

I walked to the refrigerator and plucked Rachel's school photo from underneath a magnet. I took it into the den and began scanning it onto my desktop computer.

"What are you doing?" I looked up to see Jo, hands on hips, silhouetted in the doorway.

"I'm going to make a poster."

"How is that going to help?"

"Our daughter may be alive."

"And this idea is supposed to make it easier for me to accept her disappearance?" She rolled her hand in the air. "Some crazy idea that Rachel was stolen from us and may be somewhere, held against her will, perhaps being molested by a madman?" She paced the small, paneled study. "For her sake, I'd rather the Chesapeake claimed her."

"Listen, Jo. Right before I went looking for her, I heard a car engine accelerating away." I sat at my desk and stared into the computer screen. "I can't get that sound out of my head."

Joanne started to cry. Again.

I left my post to take her in my arms and felt her resist momentarily before she laid her head against my chest. I knew she wasn't heartless. She was heartbroken. Afraid of the truth—no matter what the truth was. How does a mother's mind begin to accept the unthinkable?

I could almost palpate her agony. I sensed her slipping into a protective cocoon. I hated to leave her, but I *had* to go, even at the expense of the pain I would experience in leaving Jo. "I'm going back to the shore."

Her silence was all the reply I needed. She wouldn't go. Perhaps she couldn't go. I understood. She was coping the only way she knew how. Half self-pity and self-preservation, and the rest, a mixture of blaming me and denial.

"I'll call Jim from the car. They'll just have to understand." I had to pursue this possibility. I didn't want to just *cope*. I wanted *action*.

I had to find my daughter.

I went to the clinic before office hours. I wasn't in the mood for concerned people, hugs, or tears. I picked up some medications for my father from our sample closet, stopped at a print shop, refueled at Starbucks, and headed for the shore.

On the way, I called the senior partner at Richmond Family Medicine Associates. "Jim, this is David."

"David, I'm glad you called. How can we help you?"

"I'm going to need some time off."

"Sure. I told the clinic manager to clear your appointments for the time being."

"Thanks. I'll keep you in the loop. I'll be back in Richmond in a few days."

I folded my cell phone and cracked the window for a little

fresh air. Unlike on my last trip, the day was sunny, with a fore-cast of temperatures in the nineties. Perfect beach weather.

I sipped Starbucks and attempted to form a strategy.

Only one small problem.

I had no idea how to start investigating an abduction.

Four hours later, I was with my father again. When I arrived, he was sitting in the den eating a crustless peanut butter sandwich.

I handed him a small bottle of pills. "If you start these, there's a good chance we can get your catheter out."

"I can't live like this."

"You have options. Go see a urologist in Norfolk."

"You're a doctor. You help me."

I sighed. We'd been through this before. He'd watched my mother die of breast cancer in spite of surgery, chemotherapy, and radiation. "You know what I think."

"I have prostate cancer," he recited mechanically. "It has spread to my back. It's blocked off my urine flow."

"Exactly."

"It's too late for remission. I'm not going through what your mother did."

"I've got one more option. An injection. A medicine called Lupron. Prostate cancer grows in response to testosterone, the male hormone. Lupron blocks testosterone. If I give it to you, there's a good chance you'll find relief from some of your symptoms."

"But . . ." he said, trailing the sentence out for me to finish.

"But what?"

"There's always a 'but' with treatment of cancer."

"You'll lose your sex drive." I paused. "No more manly hormone pulsing through your body."

He laughed. "Nothing like beating a man when he's down." He sobered quickly and looked up. "You think it will help me?"

I nodded. I didn't know what else I could do. My options were limited. What else could I do? "I'll have to bring it from a pharmacy." I pointed to the bottle in his hand. "For now, take one of those. In a few hours we'll see if your body works properly without the catheter."

"I need a favor."

I looked back at him without speaking.

"I've got three hundred crab pots that I haven't emptied since Friday."

"You want me to work your line?" I shook my head. "Dad, I'm here to find Rachel."

He scuffed his foot against the floor.

"Can't you call Ned's boy? He's always looking for extra cash."

He waved his hand at me. "Sure, sure," he said, "I can call any number of people. I was just hoping that you'd want to help."

I sighed. I couldn't deal with this. "Look, Dad—"

He held up his hands. "Find Rachel. You really think she's alive, don't you?"

I tried hard not to choke as I felt my voice thicken. "I have to believe it."

Dad's face was stern. "Follow your heart, son."

By five p.m. I'd plastered posters all over the small town of Tippins and visited about a third of its residents. When I knocked on the door of Dad's neighbor's house, it opened an inch, revealing a quick flash of a light brown face and dark eyes. The door closed.

"One moment," a woman said. When it opened again, I was face-to-veil with a Somali female. She wore a long dress and some sort of upper body covering. The only thing visible for my inspection were her eyes—dark and hinting of mystery. Or was the sense of mystery caused by the black veil that covered everything except for a slit across her eyes? I held out my hand. "I'm David Conners. Gus, your next-door neighbor, is my father."

The woman looked at my hand and seemed to hesitate. In a moment she lifted her arm toward me, tenting up the large black veil, with her arm and hand completely concealed. I didn't know how to respond. I shook her wrist through the cloth and wondered what cultural taboos I had broken.

"I'm sorry—"

"I'm Amina," she said. "Don't be sorry, David."

Her use of my first name disarmed me.

"Your father, I've helped him with the house a few times."

"You called to let us know he was ill."

"Your father is a proud man." Amina's eyes smiled. "Too proud to ask for the help he needs." She quickly looked away. "My father told me you stopped in the other day."

"The day my daughter disappeared. Here's her picture," I said, lifting a poster.

A hand appeared from beneath her long veil. The back of her hand was decorated with ornate black lines, some sort of tattoo design of flowers starting at her wrist, across her hand, and twisting around each slender finger. She took the paper from my hand. "She has not been found?"

"Not yet." I cleared my throat. "Amina, I don't think Rachel fell in the water and was swept away by the tide. I think she was abducted."

I waited for a reaction. I heard a faint gasp, but nothing more.

"Any chance you saw a vehicle of any kind on the street Saturday afternoon?"

She shook her head in response, then said, "Your father is very proud of you."

I could have refuted her statement on the basis of my personal experience, but I wasn't ready to tell this stranger my problems.

"You need to take care of him."

I cleared my throat and felt my defenses riding up an express elevator. "Sure," I said. "I'm trying."

"You're his only son."

I looked at this woman, wondering where she got off giving me family advice. We were obviously from different worlds. She was Muslim. I used to identify myself as Christian, but the last few days I had been wondering where God was. I was American. She was from an ocean away, the horn of Africa. Besides all that, I'd only just met her. "Listen, A . . ."

"Amina."

"Amina. I'm not sure what my father tells you, but he's turned down plenty of offers for my help."

She looked up at me for a moment and let her eyes rest upon mine. It was quick, but in that instant, I felt she stared right through me. This was unfair. She could see who I was. I suddenly wanted another glimpse of her light brown face and I wanted to be the one covered.

"Wh-why do you—" I stopped.

"Wear this veil?"

I felt heat in my cheeks. "Yes."

"In my religion, women are protected from the hungry eyes of men." She said it smoothly and with a hint of accusation.

Immediately I realized that I'd been staring, trying to imagine her face and form. If anything, her covering, designed to make me see less, notched up the mystery, and made me want to see more. I looked away, coughing to cover my discomfort. "If you hear or see anything that might help in my search, please let me know." I stepped off the porch.

I was walking across the yard when she called after me. "David, is it true that Gus is dying?"

"He told you that?"

She nodded.

My throat tightened. I turned toward my father's house. "Yes," I said. "He's dying."

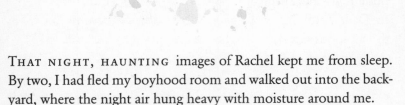

THAT NIGHT, HAUNTING images of Rachel kept me from sleep. By two, I had fled my boyhood room and walked out into the back-yard, where the night air hung heavy with moisture around me.

I looked at the sky and thought of the nights that Rachel and I had named as many constellations as we could. Now the heavens mocked me with their majesty and silence.

I felt so helpless. I was spent, empty of ideas, and weary of knocking on doors. The sheriff's department frustrated me.

I'm not sure how I got there, but the next thing I knew, I was kneeling, face to the grass, weeping, convinced the ache in my soul would tear me apart. Moments later I felt a hand on my shoulder. My hand gripped my father's. I stood to lean into his embrace.

If I'd ever cried in his arms before, I didn't remember it.

"Shhh, Davy," he said. "We're going to get through this."

I couldn't speak. My father, even in his weakened state, remained my emotional rock. I buried my face in his neck and wept like a child. All the while he kept stroking my head and whispering the name he used for me as a child. "Davy, Davy."

When I looked up, his face was wet with tears of his own.

I stayed for three more days. I think I met everyone in Tippins. Not one had seen a little girl with a stuffed Pound Puppy named Bobo.

So sorry. They didn't have to speak. Their eyes bearing pity said all I needed to hear. *An abduction here in Tippins? More likely the child was swept into the Chesapeake.*

I came back to Dad's place knowing that I'd come to the shore to find my daughter, but sensing that something else important was occurring at the same time. I needed to say good-bye to Dad. And that was made more difficult because so many things about our past pain had gone unsaid between us.

I knocked softly at the door before pushing it open, and I saw him, lying on his old couch in the den. I studied his pale complexion, almost waxy, a sheen of sweat on his face highlighted by the afternoon sun. He was still. Too still. Immediately my heart was in my throat. "Dad!" I whispered, fearing the worst.

Suddenly I was a lost child, a desperate orphan without guidance. I dropped to my knees, sick that I hadn't told him how I felt, angry that I'd let every moment pass between us without saying the things I needed to say.

But surprising to me, I felt angry. I'd wanted his *forgiveness*. And now he had slipped away without telling me that I was going to be okay.

I touched his forehead. Cool. Clammy. I placed my lips against his face, his two-day-old stubble abrading my skin.

And then I felt his breath. It sucked through a dry, cracked mouth that collected thick mucus in the corner. Life. Ebbing like the tide.

Yet he stirred, and his stale breath smacked me with reality.

"Davy? I was dreaming of your mother."

I refrained from gasping and didn't tell him of my fear.

"You need to drink."

I brought him sweet tea from the refrigerator.

He sat up and rubbed his eyes.

I began to cry. "I don't want you to go."

When everyone else on the shore thought I was crazy for running off to pursue my dreams of medicine, my father had stood beside me. In doing so, I'd forced him to labor on with his crab business alone and to abandon his dream of passing the mantle to me.

"I want to see your mother." He paused, his eyes fixed on mine as if he wanted to see how I would respond to his next words. "And your sister."

I nodded. I wanted to speak about her, but the subject had been closed for so long. *Forgive me.*

He reached for my hand, cradling it in his. Calluses stroked my palm.

We were different, my dad and me. The contrast was evident in our hands. His were rough, cracked with exposure to sun and salt, and spoke to me of years of labor, the only language of love that he knew. Mine were soft, pampered, and protected by my chosen work.

He squeezed my hand with remarkable strength. Even in his weakened state, the grip of a crabber had been preserved. In that moment, his hands talked to me as clearly as if he'd spoken with his tongue. In his own way, he communicated what I needed to hear. We were okay.

"Dad." I choked on the words. "Ra-rachel," I sobbed.

"It wasn't your fault."

Anyone else would have thought we spoke of my daughter, but we knew different. He knew I'd carried a load of guilt surrounding my sister Rachel's death. For too many years it had hung unspoken during my visits to the shore.

I'd always loved the shore. But coming back always threatened to drown me with pain.

I nodded. *Not my fault.* I let his words bathe my soul, but like ground hardened by the lack of rain, the first drops of relief often run away, unabsorbed.

I watched as he sipped the tea and set the sweaty glass on the coffee table. "There's a trap off the end of the dock. I want to eat crab cakes tonight."

I smiled. He'd worked the bay his entire life, and yet he never tired of its fruit. I suspected some would think his tastes were simple. But I knew he'd merely been brought up on some of the sweetest delicacies known to man. "Sure," I said. I had Mom's recipe memorized. Soon I would combine bread crumbs, the best back-fin selection of meat, a sprinkling of Old Bay seasoning, egg, and a few tablespoons of fresh cream.

We sat together, the meal a savoring of home, bringing with it the memory of a thousand gatherings around the round oak kitchen table.

I watched Dad eat, and for a moment his illness was erased, his tired taste buds revived once more.

But after only one crab cake, eaten slowly and pulled through a red streak of Tabasco sauce, he pushed his plate away.

I understood.

He burped happily.

I couldn't say the words, but we both knew I'd said it in the preparation of the crabs. *"Good-bye, Dad."*

Monday evening I arrived back in Richmond to find an extra car in the driveway. The only one I knew with a red Porsche 911 was Blake Swenson, my former friend and business associate, and more important, the former fiancé of my wife. If anyone had the ability to complicate our lives, it was *him*. I parked in the garage but decided to walk around to the front porch to enter.

Just the thought of him brought added turbulence to my troubled mind. Blake, Joanne, and I had a *history*. It was dark, and throbbed with betrayal, lost friendship, and a broken engagement. We'd both pursued Joanne, and I'd emerged as the victor. I always suspected that Joanne was conflicted about her choice. Blake and I had slipped into an unspoken agreement that he was to stay away from my wife.

It was all the more difficult because Blake and I had once been the best of friends. Medical school can do that. Relationships are forged in the foxholes of life, and we'd been through everything that MCV could dish out and survived. We'd fallen for the same woman, ensnared by the same alluring smile and the gentleness of her kisses.

Every time I saw him, a tangle of emotions threatened me with insanity. Suspicion and skepticism compounded with my own guilt, because I was the one who had betrayed my friend.

I opened the door to find Blake standing in the entryway hugging my wife. It may have been innocent, but I was in no mood to give him any slack.

My sanity disappeared in a volcano of emotion. He looked up. "D-david."

I grabbed his collar with my left hand, pushing him backward and off balance. Then, I wound up and delivered my best right hook to Blake's nose. He fell backward onto the floor.

Joanne screamed and stepped between us. "What are you doing?"

Blake stood up slowly, touching his sleeve to his nose.

Joanne touched his face. "You're bleeding!"

He pulled out a handkerchief and held it to his nose, cursing me and my mother. "For God's sake, David, I was just giving my condolences."

My sorrow found vent in anger. "Stay away from us!" I yelled, pointing toward the open door.

"Blake," Joanne said, "I'm so sorry."

Blake stumbled toward the door. "Don't apologize for him."

I followed him onto the porch. "Joanne is vulnerable," I said. "But I guess you knew that."

He turned toward me, fists clenched. "She invited me."

I felt sure he was bluffing. I stepped toward him, ready to strike.

I must have looked as wild as I felt, because he threw up his hands and backed into the yard. "You're crazy, man!"

I stood on the porch until he got into his Porsche and drove away.

I walked back into the house and straight into Joanne's verbal assault. "That was completely uncalled for. You're acting like a child."

"He shouldn't have come here. He knows he's way out of line."

"At least *he* was here for me! Where have you been?"

I felt suddenly deflated. "Joanne, you know——"

Tears started flowing and her voice quivered as she yelled. "I've had the worst week of my life, and you were at your father's."

"I was looking for our child!"

She turned away from me.

"And caring for my dying father." I touched her shoulder, but she pulled away. "Joanne," I said softly. "We're going to get through this. Don't pull away from me. Together we can make it."

She turned to me, her eyes moist. Then, she fled down the hall to our bedroom and shut the door.

The following week I stayed at our home in Richmond at Joanne's request, but we bumped around in our empty house like strangers. I tried to engage her, but she wrapped herself in a cocoon of silence.

Mealtime was torturous. Before, Rachel had kept us entertained with a daily rundown of school adventures. For the longest time she had insisted that we set a place for Bobo, her Pound Puppy. One evening she insisted he was hungry, so she continuously dipped his nose in her tomato soup, making obnoxious slurping sounds until Joanne intervened.

"That's enough slurping, Rachel," Joanne said, restraining the laughter I knew was at the surface.

"It's Bobo. He loves tomato soup."

"Well, tell Bobo to be quiet. He needs to use appropriate manners if he's going to eat at my table."

Rachel slurped once more, then set Bobo aside. His normally white nose was now stained red with soup. For weeks after that I caught Rachel sucking on his nose. I suspected it tasted a little like tomatoes.

Without Rachel's delightful presence, Joanne and I talked about the weather or lobbed pleasantries over the table about the food, but sooner or later, one of us would say something that connected to Rachel and our conversation halted, ground to a stop by our grief.

One evening I looked at her, both of us teary after remembering how Rachel used to make a thousand crazy excuses not to go to bed. I sighed. "I need to go to work."

Joanne nodded. "Go," she said. "Someone has to act normal."

I GROUND MY way through the morning's office visits, dealing with obesity, low back pain, a diabetic foot ulcer, and three preseason physicals for high school football team hopefuls. I was filling out a disability form when Tyce Andrews poked his head in my doorway. "Hey, David, got a minute?"

I pushed the form away. "Sure."

"Since you've been back a week, I was hoping you're caught up with your patients. Is there any way I can get you to see a couple of these? I'm really backed up here." He handed me two charts.

I looked at them. Sarah Jacobs, age seven. Brittany Bransford, age six. I took a deep breath. I didn't feel ready to see little girls. "Look—"

"You've got to help me out here."

I nodded. "Sure."

"Sarah's in exam room B."

I walked down the hall, reading the chart. Sarah had an earache. *Should be simple.*

I pushed open the door to see a little girl sitting on my exam table. She wore a pink shirt and blue jeans. She had ribbons in her hair. *Just like Rachel liked to wear.* "Hi, Sarah," I said. I looked at her mother. "Good afternoon. How can I help you today?"

I examined Sarah while her mother chatted on about her busy schedule. Soccer practice. Ballet. Playdates with friends. *All the things we did with Rachel.*

At the end of the visit I scribbled a prescription for Amoxil and nearly ran from the room. Everything reminded me of my missing daughter.

I escaped to my office, willing myself to breathe. I shut my eyes for a moment and leaned against my desk.

"Conners? You okay?"

I looked up to see Jim Ashton, my senior associate. "Uh, yeah, I'm fine. Thirty-second vacation," I said. "I was at the beach." I forced a chuckle.

His face soured. "Well, I need you here. The waiting room is backing up."

I pushed past him into the hallway. "On my way."

I picked up the next chart. Brittany Bransford. Sore throat. I pushed open the door to the exam room. The patient was sitting on the exam table. I'd seen her mother a month ago for a breast problem. She stood as I entered.

"Dr. Conners, I wanted to say how sorry I am about your daughter. I heard about it from the Pattersons. Brittany here was on the same soccer team with Rachel back in kindergarten."

I remembered. Amoeba ball, I'd called it. The kids were too young to stay in position, and everyone clumped around the ball like one big roving unit. I was about to open my mouth to thank her for her concern, but she continued.

"Rachel was such a special girl. Brittany always liked her, didn't you, Brittany? It must be horrible not knowing. Have they found the body yet?"

"I, uh," I said, stunned at her insensitivity. "No." I tried to concentrate on the chart while Mommy droned on. I cleared my throat. "Now," I said, looking at Brittany. "What seems to be the problem?"

She opened her mouth and pointed. "My throat hurts."

"Hmmm, any fever?" I looked at Mom, who, for the moment, sat with her mouth closed.

"No."

Before she could elaborate, I pounced again. "Runny nose? Cough?"

Brittany answered with a demonstration, sniffing loudly. "A little."

"When did it start?"

"Two days ago," Mother volunteered.

"I'm going to need to examine you." I picked up a wooden tongue depressor. "Open up and say, 'ahhh.'"

I looked into the back of the throat. Her tonsils nearly touched in the middle. "Hmmm," I said, not wanting to sound too alarmed. "Does she snore?"

"Yes. How'd you know?"

"Just a hunch. From the size of those tonsils, I would think her breathing might get noisy."

"My brother says I sound like a train."

The mother nodded. "He's right."

"I'm going to need to do a strep test. In addition, I'd like to see her back in a week. If those tonsils haven't improved, I'm going to refer her to Dr. Neal. He's an ear, nose, and throat specialist."

"Yes, I know him," she said. "His little Stephanie was on the soccer team, too." She looked up at me and covered her mouth with her hand.

I didn't want to hear any more about little girls playing soccer. I reached for the door. "I'll ask the nurse to do a strep test. If it's positive, I'll write a prescription."

I escaped before she could say any more.

A minute later my receptionist buzzed the intercom in my office. "Dr. Conners? A woman is on line three insisting on speaking to you. Her name is Amina Mohamed or something like that. I tried to take a message, but she's persistent."

Dad's mysterious veiled neighbor. "I'll take it." I punched the blinking light on my phone and picked up. "Hello, Dr. Conners speaking."

"David, it's Amina."

"Yes."

"I'm afraid I have some bad news."

I felt my gut tighten. "How's Gus?"

I listened to her sigh into the phone, then a tapping sound, as if she was drumming her fingers against the mouthpiece.

"Is my father okay?"

"He's not okay." Another sigh. "He's dead."

Three days later I sat in a small, waterside, white clapboard church to listen to the watermen eulogize my father. Joanne and I were in the front row. Jo fanned away the moist heat and shifted to see which woman kept crying. Sam Crenshaw wore a three-piece suit, something few of us knew he owned, but kept his fishing hat firmly in place as he approached the podium. After his wife cleared her throat, he slowly removed his hat and gripped it in his hand.

"If anyone ever had salt in his blood," Sam began, "it was Gus Conners. I've known him since we were kids. When we were teenagers, we started a crab business together. When I was sick, Gus never hesitated to lend a hand. When his Naomi was sick, he was always there for her." He hesitated, and touched the end of his nose with his coat sleeve. "God knows I'll miss him."

At the graveside service a small group gathered and listened to Reverend Ben Brown talk of heaven. As Gus's only child, I was expected to say a few words.

Reverend Brown gave me a look that said *your turn.*

I cleared my throat. "My father was a stubborn man." I looked up, watching the small crowd of Dad's best friends. "I can see by your faces that you understand. In the end, he was dead set on steering clear of therapy he thought was futile." I glanced at Joanne. "My wife helped me see that the best way to love him in return was to let him make his own decisions and set my own judgment aside.

"Most of you know Gus bucked every one of you who thought I should stay on the shore and work the saltwater like he did. He supported me when others doubted." I paused, my voice cracking. "Just last week was one last example of how Dad continued to be a strength for me up until his end. I was overcome by grief over our little Rachel's disappearance. He gathered me in his arms and promised me that we'd make it." The crowd disappeared in a blur of tears. My voice closed completely. I couldn't bear to say good-bye. I reached down and picked up one handful of dirt and let it slip through my fingers onto the top of his casket.

Behind me, Reverend Brown's voice intoned, "Ashes to ashes, dust to dust . . ."

The wind began picking up, and the sky darkened as the small group of mourners prepared to leave the cemetery. I was getting in the Explorer when I heard my name. "Mr. Conners?"

I looked up to see a young couple. I'd noticed them before, standing apart from our group, visiting a small grave. He appeared to be no older than twenty-five, wore a two-day scruff on his chin and a Baltimore Orioles baseball cap. The woman wore a faded blue dress and gripped his arm as if he might escape. In his hand he held a crinkled paper. He lifted it to me. "This your daughter?" he asked.

I recognized the flyer immediately. "Yes," I said, and closed the Explorer door. I reached my hand out. "David Conners," I said. "That's my daughter."

The man exchanged looks with his wife. "Earl Whitson," he said, extending his hand. "We need to talk."

We followed Earl and Tammy Whitson's red pickup from the cemetery to their home two streets over from Dad's.

Joanne stared through the side window. "Why are you doing this?"

"They said they lost a little girl, too. A daughter a lot like Rachel."

"This isn't going to bring our daughter back."

"What if there's a connection? What if the same person that took their daughter, took our Rachel?"

Joanne sighed. "The Whitsons said they thought their daughter had fallen into the bay."

"But they never recovered her body. And after looking at Rachel's flyer, they're starting to wonder."

"Is this fair to them, David? To give them false hope?"

"What if it isn't false hope?" I glanced at my wife. She was coping the only way she knew how, trying to accept Rachel's death and move forward. "I can't be like you."

"How?"

"Accepting the conclusion of the sheriff." I shook my head. "She might still be alive." I pulled into the Whitsons' lane. "Coming in?"

She kept her face toward her window. "I can't."

I understood. Her grief was too raw and personal to share with others. And she feared her life would turn into the hell it once was. But I needed to see what Earl Whitson wanted me to see. If there was any connection to Rachel's disappearance, I needed to know.

I followed Tammy and Earl up three brick steps to their front porch and into their house. Their front room was furnished with a green sofa and matching recliner chair with worn patches expanding from beneath white doilies. A coffee table sat at knee level in front of the couch, groaning under the weight of pictures and other memorabilia that enshrined the life of a little girl.

Earl sat on the edge of the couch and touched the top of a picture. His daughter, missing her two front teeth. "The sheriff's department convinced us that Brooke had drowned. But your poster made me wonder." He picked up the picture and handed it to me.

The similarity was obvious. Gripped tightly in her hands was a gray stuffed puppy. I nodded and held the picture up against the poster I'd made. "They must have sold a million of those silly puppies. Rachel took hers everywhere." I paused. "I heard your daughter—" I said, hesitating, "I heard they never recovered a body."

Tammy gripped her husband's arm. "They said the currents would have taken her far away."

Earl shook his head. "If you ask me, I'd say the mayor is more concerned about a bad reputation spoiling our Blue Crab Summer Festival than anything else."

"When did your daughter disappear?"

"Six weeks ago."

"Where was she seen last? Next to the water?"

Earl pushed up the brim of his Orioles cap. "Not even close. She was playing in the front yard."

"I'll talk to the sheriff again."

Earl dropped into his recliner and sighed. "Good luck with that."

"Do you have a picture of your daughter that I can circulate?"

Tammy sniffed. "Take this one," she said, handing me the photo of Brooke with her stuffed puppy.

I studied them for a moment. "Who knows of your suspicions?"

Tammy held a Kleenex to her nose. "Only you."

Earl leaned forward. "How well do you know those Arabs that live next to your father's place?"

"I, well, they're not Arabs. They're from Somalia."

"Whatever. They're from over there," he said rolling his hand in the air. "Violent people, that's all I know."

"My father spoke fondly of them."

Earl rolled his eyes and went quiet.

I paused. "If the sheriff's department won't take this seriously, would you mind if I mentioned this to a reporter?"

Tammy squinted. "Newspaper?"

I shrugged. "Perhaps. It may help if someone else is snooping for a story. If anything, it might pressure the sheriff's department into looking into this a bit closer."

Earl shook his head. "I don't know. I don't want to be the focus of attention. Pretty soon people will think they should pity us, or—"

"Earl," Tammy interrupted, "what if she's alive? Shouldn't we do whatever we can?"

He considered. "Okay," he said after a moment. "Do what you think is best."

In Richmond, Blake Swenson picked up the phone after three rings and silenced the baseball game on TV.

"Blake, this is Tricia Morgan."

"Tricia, I didn't expect to hear from you."

"I need a favor."

Blake was curious. Why would Joanne's mother be calling him? He tried to hide his excitement. "What could I possibly do for you?"

"It's Joanne." She hesitated. "She needs you."

"She needs me?" He lifted his hand to his face. "The last time I tried to get close to her, David punched me in the nose."

"So leave David out of it. I've encouraged her to get away from him."

"You have?"

"Joanne needs space. Time away from David." She sighed. "He's dragging her down."

"How can I help?"

"I know she broke your heart, Blake. To tell you a little secret, mine, too. I'd always dreamed of Joanne marrying well." Another sigh. "You know as well as I that David Conners isn't worthy."

"And what am I to do? She's a married woman."

"Married, but unhappy. She'll be vulnerable without David. Help her remember the good times she had with you."

"An affair would look bad if the media got wind of the senator's daughter playing around."

"The public is very forgiving about this sort of thing. And in the long run, we both know she'll be happier. The Conners are so . . . blue collar."

He looked at the TV and closed his fist in celebration as Chipper Jones pounded a three-run homer against his former teammate, Greg Maddox. "Earthy," he added.

"Exactly. What Joanne needs is a little more sophistication."

Blake stood up and started to pace. He walked to the refrigerator and retrieved a cold Heineken. "You want me to break up your daughter's marriage?"

"It's already broken, Blake. I'm only trying to influence who might fill the void. Listen, if you're not interested—"

"It's not that. It's just, well—" He halted. "You know I've always been very fond of your daughter. But she's pretty distraught about Rachel's disappearance. I'm not sure I should—"

"Take advantage of her misfortune?"

He popped the cap from his beer and turned up the bottle. He wiped his mouth with the back of his hand. "Right."

"If I've learned one thing in this big world, Blake, it's that you can't control the things that happen to you, but you can take advantage of the unexpected and difficult situations, turning them into your benefit if you stop to think a little."

Political spin. Your specialty. "I've always hated what David Conners did to me."

"Harness that feeling. Here's your chance to get even."

Blake shrugged and took a long draw from the cold, green bottle. "Thanks for the tip."

That night we were lying together on a pullout couch at my father's, without covers because of the heat and closeness of the moist air. Joanne snuggled up to me and spoke softly, "The memorial service was nice."

I stared at the ceiling. "Yes." I looked at Joanne in the dim light. She wore only a loose nightshirt, something she would consider less than sexy, but to me, amorous. I reached for her. We hadn't lost ourselves in passion since Rachel's disappearance.

Joanne pulled away. "It's too hot."

Apparently, our surroundings weren't conducive to arouse the female species. For me, and most males, I suspected, any surroundings would do in a pinch. A lumpy pullout couch on a languid night in the midst of packing boxes. *What could be better?*

Alas, Joanne was feminine and needed more. And that drove me even madder for her.

My arousal was short-lived. It was as if sorrow had taken up permanent residence in the den of our lives, and any attempt to dethrone the grief monster was quickly countered by his over-powering presence. I looked at Jo's face and touched her cheek, fresh with quiet tears. Soon, silence was broken by the rhythmic gasps of her crying. That, of course, uncapped my grief again, and I wondered if I we could ever find the bottom of the well of nightly tears.

After an hour her breathing became regular, and I thought she'd fallen asleep until she spoke again. "I need to do something, David. I want to have a memorial service for Rachel."

My first thought was an urgent *no!* but I held my tongue and took a deep breath. "Joanne, I—"

"Please, David. We need to do this."

You *need this. I need to find my daughter.*

I sighed and rolled toward her. "Having a memorial service feels like giving up."

She put her index finger against my lips. "It's not a funeral. It would be a celebration of her life."

"But—"

"Da-vid," she said, drawing out the syllables of my name the way she did when she was warning me to go no further. "Listen to me. How many times did we teach Rachel not to go anywhere with a stranger? How many times did we teach her to scream and run?"

She didn't give me a chance to answer.

"Dozens of times. You of all people, Doctor Compulsive, should know."

I thought about it. I had gone over and over kidnapping scenarios with her, playing little role-playing games and never being able to trick her. "Maybe she didn't have a chance to run. Maybe someone snatched her before she could scream."

"She knew better. She wouldn't have approached a strange car."

I felt annoyed. "Your point?"

"The sheriff might know what he's talking about. If you insist on trudging forward with your ideas, it will freshen our hope every time you imagine another lead, and our pain when the lead doesn't pan out."

"And if I'm right?"

"What if you're wrong?" Joanne started to cry. "What about what I need?" she said, rolling away to face the wall. "Can't you see I need this to grieve?"

I didn't want to argue. I touched her shoulder and felt her stiffen. "Joanne," I whispered, "let's have a memorial service." I hesitated. "But I can't throw away my hope."

She sniffed. After a minute of silence she spoke again. "I want to go home."

I groaned. "You go. I'll come in a few days after I pull Dad's crab pots. I'll drive Dad's pickup."

Another sigh. Joanne didn't need to talk to tell me how much she disapproved of me being away from her while she was grieving.

"Why don't you start planning a memorial?"

Her silence tortured me.

From the day we'd met I'd been forced to understand this woman—perhaps more than I wanted to. Far from heartless, Jo was a sensitive and sensual woman. It was probably from these depths that she pulled away from me now. The effects of her postpartum depression had lingered at the edges of our lives for years, unspoken but not forgotten. Jo remembered the place of stillness and sorrow that threatened not just her, but our marriage. A wise physician-counselor, the right combination of psychopharmaceuticals, and precious months of time finally caused light to break into our lives after she was sure the sun wouldn't shine again. So agree with her that Rachel was gone and close the chapter, I couldn't. But understand her need, I did.

"This place needs work before we can put it on the market. If I don't work on it now, it won't be easy to take off work later to do it."

"Fine."

I winced at her tone.

It's best this way, I thought. *I need a chance to look into Rachel's disappearance without upsetting Joanne.*

BACK IN RICHMOND on the following day, Joanne pulled out of a parking lot with her Volvo filled with groceries. As she accelerated, she felt the steering wheel tremble. Something wasn't right. She pulled into a 7-Eleven store to investigate. Stepping outside the car, she stared at her right front tire and sighed. The last time she'd changed a flat was in college.

At that moment she looked up to see a familiar red Porsche pulling in beside her. Blake Swenson lowered his window. "Bummer," he said, looking at the tire. "Got a spare?"

Joanne nodded and watched as he parked his car. "Perfect timing," she said.

He flashed a white smile. "I was on my way to a credentials meeting at the hospital. I couldn't be happier to be here instead." He laughed.

Joanne felt her gut tighten. The one man in the world who could make her feel so many conflicting emotions had to be this knight who showed up to help the damsel in distress. She pointed him to the spare tire and stood back to watch.

He made quick work of changing the tire. "Look here," he said, rolling the flat to the rear of the car. "Here's a nail."

They stood for a moment, facing each other behind the Volvo. He tilted his head to point to the store. "Care for a cappuccino? They have a wonderful little machine inside."

She forced a smile. "You remembered my refined taste. 7-Eleven cappuccino."

"French vanilla," he said.

"I should be going."

He shook his head. "You're not getting away that easy. I rescued you, so the least you can do is let me buy you a cup of cheap coffee."

She looked down, feeling a twinge of guilt. "Okay."

"Besides, I need to hear about how you are doing. And this strikes me as a safe place—free of raging jealousy."

"I'm so sorry," she said, cringing. "How's your nose?" She reached for his face.

"Careful," he said, intercepting her hand. He held it for a second, then released it. "I'm good. Really."

He disappeared into the store and returned carrying two tall cups. "Your car or mine?"

"Yours."

She sank into the leather seat and held the cup beneath her nose, letting the aroma carry her to a memory of a similar rendezvous.

Blake leaned forward, capturing Joanne's attention. "Tell me," he said in a soft, serious tone. "How are you doing? Really."

She shifted in her seat. Guilty for sitting in the car of a man she swore she'd never see again. Tempted by his compassion and the gaze of his wonderful eyes. "I shouldn't be here."

He sighed. "Joanne, I'm your friend. David does let you have friends?"

She sipped her coffee. "Sarcasm doesn't suit you."

He shrugged. "Friends talk. They support each other through tough times." He seemed to hesitate. "You didn't answer my question."

She took in a deep breath, afraid if she started to unload, the tears would follow. "I'm hanging in there."

"And David? How's he doing?"

It was the conversation of two strangers. Polite. Remote, without the intimacy they once knew.

"How does David always do? He's an eternal optimist. He's convinced that because the Chesapeake hasn't delivered up a body, that he's going to find his daughter someday."

Blake tapped the steering wheel. "His daughter?" He turned toward her. "You didn't tell him?"

"Tell him?" She shook her head. "We don't really know, do we?"

"No!" he spoke forcefully. Halted. Then continued in a quiet, controlled manner. "You know this," he whispered. "I know I do. I knew it the first time I laid eyes on her."

Joanne didn't want to go down that trail. The forest was too thick and the memories too painful. She shook her head and whispered, "We don't know." It was a self-reassurance of an unknown, the only way she'd been able to carry on beneath the weight of a secret.

"Where's David?"

"The shore."

He nodded his head knowingly. "Of course." He paused. "You stayed with him because of Rachel."

"He adored her."

"And that qualifies him for fatherhood?"

Joanne reached for the door handle.

"Jo, don't go. I'm sorry. It was a cheap shot. But you have to know I'm a bit out of sorts here myself. When I heard that Rachel was gone—" His voice cracked. "It brought everything back for me."

She looked at him. "You're grieving for a girl you couldn't love."

"You put me in an impossible position, Jo. I loved her, but I couldn't show it."

She studied his face for a moment. "I'm sorry for you." She

took a deep breath, willing the tears to remain unshed. "Rachel is gone. So there's really nothing between us to talk about."

"Hold onto the good memories," he said. "Remember when we camped down at Pocahontas State Park?"

She gave him a weak smile. "Our tent leaked."

He laughed. "We didn't care." He touched her thigh. "That was before David."

"I should go." She looked away from his searching face. Like it or not, she couldn't deny that Blake had always had the ability to touch a soft place in her soul. It was a gift of his, something she hadn't thought of for a long time.

He tapped her arm. "Eat dinner with me."

"I don't think it's a good idea."

"Old friends," he said, "that's all." He set his coffee in between his legs and held up his hands. "You need a chance to lighten up."

You complicate my life. She looked at him and understood. His life and their past relationship was like the Nile River. Broad, deep, and smooth, but with the threatening sound of turbulent rapids just beyond the calm. She opened the door. "Thanks for changing my tire."

"There's a quaint microbrew pub just down the street from the Tobacco Company. I'll be there at eight."

"Good-bye, Blake."

As soon as I entered the sheriff's department on the Eastern Shore, I sensed a Southern hospitality that overwhelmed professionalism. I was greeted by a receptionist, a pert girl who looked no older than high school age, who ushered me toward a couch below a sailfish mounted on the wall.

"Sheriff Reynolds will be with you in a few minutes." She

lowered her voice as if telling me a juicy secret. By the animation in her voice, I could tell that the department had little in the way of exciting challenges. "He's in a meeting with the mayor, finalizing security plans for the Blue Crab Festival next weekend. The sheriff says we might see twenty-thousand visitors this year."

I smiled. "And I'll bet you're running for Miss Crustacean."

She giggled and put her hand over her mouth. "Oh no, I'll be selling funnel cakes to raise money for the firehouse."

She disappeared, and I sat beneath the sailfish. I leafed through an old *Field & Stream* magazine, half expecting to see Barney Fife or Andy Taylor walk in.

Ten minutes later my smiley receptionist returned and escorted me into the inner sanctum. The work area had three desks, with a backdrop of a large whiteboard upon which someone had written what looked to be a schedule of officer coverage for the upcoming festival.

Sheriff Reynolds came out of his office talking with a man in a gray suit, the mayor, I presumed. "As long as this weather holds out, we'll be fine. Coolie's field should be dry enough to handle the parking overflow." The two shook hands and the gray suit swished past without a Mayberry greeting.

Denton Reynolds looked at me, becoming serious. "Dr. Conners, I'm afraid I have no news to report."

"I'd like to show you something," I said, laying my poster and a picture of Brooke Whitson on the desk. "This is my daughter, missing since July seventh. This is Brooke Whitson. She lives two streets over from my father's place. She disappeared May twenty-third." I paused and watched the sheriff exchange glances with another man seated at the closest desk.

"Neither body has been found," I said. "Don't you think it's time to consider that something other than drowning happened to these girls?"

The sheriff touched the top of his silver flattop and cleared his throat. "We're considering other possibilities, of course."

"Where's the media been in all of this? I spent the morning in the county library and found only a one-paragraph funeral announcement for Brooke Whitson. Isn't anyone concerned?"

"Dr. Conners, we are all concerned. The disappearance of a child is a horrible thing. But it's premature to alert the public."

Inside, my frustration over their naïveté began to boil over. I pointed at his chest. "If I'd have known that a little girl disappeared from my father's neighborhood, I'd have never let my Rachel out of my sight."

His right eye twitched. "Your father's neighborhood is surrounded by water."

"That's true. But then where are the bodies?"

He shook his head slowly. A man wearing a name tag bearing the name of "Deputy Wilson" stood up and extended his hand. Reluctantly, I took it. "Steve Wilson," he said.

I nodded.

"We've done recent studies in the fingers of the Chesapeake, Dr. Conners. Blue crabs from your father's neighborhood river can be in the Atlantic Ocean in forty-eight hours."

I didn't feel like arguing. "What are you doing to prevent further abductions?"

The sheriff raised his hands in surrender or to calm me down. Either way, it wasn't effective in soothing the anger in my soul. "We don't know that these girls were abducted. Nonetheless, we've added a patrol and tripled the passes through your father's neighborhood."

"So you are concerned. But what about actually looking for the missing girls? Don't you think the public needs to be alerted?"

I followed his eyes to a stack of trifolded pamphlets advertising the Blue Crab Festival. *Of course. Earl pegged it—we wouldn't want to upset the chances for a successful festival, would we?* I picked up one of the flyers. "How much is the festival worth to the shore?"

The sheriff coughed.

I continued, "It sure would be bad press if another little girl disappeared from the festival grounds."

"Dr. Conners, we are planning extra security for the festival." He kept his voice even. "I'm sure this must be horrible for you."

I didn't want his pity, just the knowledge that he was doing the right thing. I handed him a new poster I'd made with the assistance of a library copier. It had Rachel's and Brooke's pictures with the dates of their disappearance and a plea for information. "I'll be distributing these at the festival," I said.

"I'm sorry, Dr. Conners. No one is allowed to pass out literature on the fairgrounds. Last year we had to chase off the Jehovah's Witnesses and some Hare Krishna fanatics." He pinched his lips closed and raised his eyebrows as if to say, *My hands are tied.*

I was sorry I had told him of my plans. "I'll leave you these," I said, handing him a few of my new posters. "For your deputies."

As I turned to leave, my eyes fell on those of the young receptionist. Hers were moist. *At least someone in this office has compassion for my plight.* "Keep in touch," I said, casting a final glance at the sheriff. "You have my number."

That afternoon I headed out in Dad's crab boat, the *Beautiful Swimmer,* to empty his pots and remove the vestiges of any baitfish he'd used. I needed to either sell everything quickly and let someone else run the line, or pull out all the pots, a daunting task that would take me multiple trips and time I didn't have. Instead, I opted for leaving the pots in for now, freeing his catch, and removing the bait to keep the pots empty.

As I headed out with the salt air in my face, my mood lifted in response. The solitude, the low rumble of the diesel engine, the slap of the waves against the hull, and the cry of the gulls overhead combined to create resonance in my soul. Dozens of times during summer vacations away from the University of Virginia, I'd sought similar respite from outside pressures to clear my head and sharpen my resolve. Every significant decision I'd ever made, I'd sealed from this deck. To leave home. To pursue a career in medicine. To ask Joanne to marry me. I'd made them all with a sheen of salt drying on the hairs of my arms and the smell of baitfish in the air.

I reached the first pot marked with Dad's signature blue-and-white striped buoy, shoved my hands into his gloves, preparing to hoist the pot from its resting place. The simple act struck me as profound. My father, at times my only advocate, was gone, his work gloves empty.

I halted with the freshness of his voice in my mind. *"Shhh, Davy. We're going to get through this."*

I steadied myself and grasped the side of the boat. I could draw on the strength of my father's blood that pumped within me. I looked at the horizon, taking in the magnitude of the Chesapeake and let it whisper to my soul. *I will do anything it takes to find my daughter. If she is dead, I'll see that whoever is responsible will pay.*

I brought up pot after pot, shaking a valuable catch of crabs into the bay. As the sky began to color, I shook two dozen crabs into a basket and turned the *Beautiful Swimmer* toward home.

Night nestled in around the Conners house with an eerie isolation for Joanne. She walked from room to room, pausing for the third time to straighten Rachel's dresser. Comb, brush, and mirror were adjusted, perfecting their positions in relation to the dresser's front edge. A stuffed bear was tilted to the left, a pillow fluffed, and a row of Barbie dolls inspected on a wooden bookcase beside the bed. In all, the room was exactly like the day Rachel had disappeared.

Joanne twisted a music box, and listened to the lullaby she'd played to Rachel a thousand times. Then, with fresh tears to salt her cheeks, she turned down the bed, just as she had when Rachel was alive. With a trembling hand, she stroked the sheet where her daughter slept.

Can I dare allow my heart to hope like David's?

She pulled her daughter's pillow to her face, searching for a fading scent, tangible evidence to keep Rachel from disappearing from her mind.

Alone, she cried, sobbing deeply until she couldn't get her breath and threw the pillow across the room.

Joanne stared at a crayon masterpiece—three stick figures and a house. The perfect little family. A small figure in the center held the hands of the other two. *Rachel. The glue that held us together.*

From the moment of conception, Rachel had turned Joanne's world upside down. It seemed each day since her troubled arrival had been marked by the unexpected. It was as if she carried the quality of surprise as a constant companion. Sure, it was fun, but Joanne too often felt unprepared and unsure, as if another unmarked turn was just beyond the rise.

But love her, she had. Slowly but surely, Rachel had come into their lives and cemented a bond between them that Joanne was confident would never crack. Rachel's smile helped heal the loss of David's mother. Rachel's laugh brought the brightest of joy to her family. Best of all, Rachel had matured her, bringing her to a place where giving to another slowly replaced her self-centered instinct. It was in giving to her daughter that she found the satisfaction of charity in a way that her relationship with David had never been able to do.

Tears spilled over and were brushed away. *Without Rachel,* she thought, touching the picture frame, *where's our glue?*

After a moment she heard the Westminster chimes from the grandfather clock in the hall. Eight o'clock. She laid aside the pillow. *Why should I wallow in my sorrow alone?*

She stood and inspected her face in the mirror, wiping the tears. She took a deep breath, aware of a change in her thinking. Her husband had to cope in his own way. And so did she. Aware of the warmth from an old flame, she toyed with the idea of meeting her former fiancé. The thought scared her. But intrigued her. Threatened her. But held out the chance to smile again, if only for a few minutes. *He has a gift of laughter. Blake is a good friend, a shoulder for support. That's all.*

She walked toward the garage, lifting her car keys from a hook next to the door.

That evening, I dropped a six-pack of Samuel Adams beer into an ice bucket, covered the picnic table on Dad's back patio with newspaper, and put a dozen crabs in a large steamer pot with a little water seasoned with Old Bay. I turned the burner to high and called Joanne.

Six rings. *Maybe she's in the shower.* Eight rings. *Why isn't the answering machine picking up?* I tried her cell phone. Left a brief message—*call me.*

I returned to the stove, listening as the crabs began to sense the heat. Frantically, they flailed to escape. The scratching of claws and legs against metal was unforgettable. I remembered a time when I was in the first grade and cried for my mother to release them.

"Stop!" I screamed, covering my ears.

She smiled, large dimples forming at the corners of her generous mouth. "It's just the water boiling," she said. "It scratches the crabs against the side." She bent over me and kissed the top of my head. "Go outside and play, Davy. We'll have a feast in no time."

In my current bitterness I enjoyed the punishment I dealt to the crustaceans. If the Chesapeake took my baby, I was going to torture hers.

Life for life.

In fifteen minutes I drained the water, dumped the reddened crabs onto the picnic table, and opened my first Samuel Adams.

I was three crabs and two beers into my feast when I looked up to see Amina, my veiled neighbor. She was carrying a bowl of steaming rice. "You are struggling," she said.

She sat next to me and took off her veil, laying it on the bench beside her. With nimble fingers, she selected a crab and made short work of picking it clean. She set the small mound of crabmeat on the newsprint in front of me.

I watched her, trying not to stare. I had no idea that such beauty was hidden behind the veil—dark eyes, a rounded nose with a slight upturn, high cheekbones, and a long slender neck cradled by tight black ringlets of hair. The skin of her face and hands was a light brown, almost almond, but darker. Her figure was full and alluring. She deftly cracked and extracted succulent backfin, lump, and clawmeat with fingers ornamented with black winding tattoos.

"How'd you—"

"I work at Johnson's seafood processing. They won't keep you unless you are fast." She pushed more crab in my direction. "Eat," she said, gesturing toward the rice.

When she saw me hesitate, she smiled. "Americans," she said. "Like this." She demonstrated by lifting a clump of rice to her mouth with her fingers.

I imitated her, and dribbled some rice off of my chin in the process. "Mmm. What's in this?"

"A Somali secret," she said.

I took another bite. Raisins and a seasoning I couldn't quite place accented the rice dish. I clumped a bit of the rice against the growing mound of crabmeat in front of me and dropped it in my mouth. "This is amazing."

She nodded, a smile teased at the corner of her mouth.

"Eat," I said. "You're doing most of the work."

She obeyed, sampling the rice and crab. "You are a good cook, David."

"For some things." I glanced back at her house.

"My father's away. He drives a seafood truck on a nightly route to serve the crab house restaurants in Baltimore."

"I wasn't wondering about him," I lied. I sipped my beer. "Would you like something to drink?"

"A soda?"

"I take it Somalis don't drink beer?"

"Faithful Muslims of any nationality avoid alcohol."

"And you are a faithful Muslim?"

"You question?"

I lifted my hands palm up in surrender. "Of course not. It's just, well, you—"

"I can't pick crabs and wear this veil."

I went to the kitchen and returned with a Coke.

I opened another beer and touched the edge of her soda can with it. "Here's to good neighbors."

She took a sip and continued working on the crabs.

I tried to think of anything I might know about her country. Other than having seen the movie *Black Hawk Down*, I was coming up blank. "Tell me about Somalia."

"Somalia," she said with a dreamy inflection, "used to be a garden spot." She made a clicking noise with her tongue. "Now, clan wars have turned the streets into battlegrounds." She shook her head. "Somalia is its own worst enemy." She paused. "Where is your wife?"

"Richmond." I left it at that, preferring not to explain.

I detected a subtle lift of her head.

I waited to gaze at her face again until she turned her attention to a new crab. As I ate, I found myself nearly mesmerized.

"Don't stare," she warned. "I'll put back on the veil."

I felt heat in my cheeks and inwardly cursed the beer that had lowered my inhibitions. I cleared my throat. "Tell me about yourself."

She looked at me from the corners of her dark eyes. "My name is Amina Mohamed Osman." She pointed to her index finger. "Amina is my name." She touched her middle finger. "Mohamed is my father's name and," shifting to touch her ring finger, she added, "Osman is my grandfather's name." She paused. "Every Somali I know can name at least twenty generations."

I started thinking. I imitated her actions. I pointed to my index finger. "My name is David." Next finger. "My father is Gus." Next finger. "His father was Clyde, and his father . . ." I struggled to remember. "Samuel, I think."

"I find Americans difficult to understand." She paused to lift the rice and crab to her mouth. After a moment, she continued. "How can you know who you are if you do not know the blood that brought you here?"

She'd made her point. I couldn't reply. I shrugged.

She watched as I dribbled another clump of rice down my chin. Embarrassed, I quickly picked it off my shirt and popped it into my mouth.

"You are like your father," she said. "He loved my rice, but he needed a fork."

"You cooked for my father?"

"He was my neighbor." She offered no further explanation. Obviously, to Amina, that's what neighbors did.

She turned on the bench and faced me. "When we first moved here, the community was suspicious, closed." She tilted her head and smiled. "But your father reached out to us. He helped my father and me get jobs."

"How about your mother?"

She turned away, suddenly sober. "She died in the war, killed by a stray bullet." She seemed to be staring toward the water, seeing a distant horror.

"I'm sorry," I said, touching her arm with my hand.

Her eyes glistened. "Perhaps one problem with knowing twenty generations is our inability to forget old hurts. Somalis are first faithful to their clan and second to Allah." She looked at me. "It's painful to lose a parent. You know it."

I nodded, probing my soul for an emptiness left by my father. Already, perhaps after my experience on the *Beautiful Swimmer,* the void seemed smaller.

We talked on until the crabs were picked clean and my head buzzed from my fourth Samuel Adams. She told me about her mother, the family's experience in a refugee camp, of emigrating to Minnesota, and finally her move to the shore. Three other siblings remained behind, trying to eke out a living in Mogadishu.

We laughed about the upcoming festival and she joked about running for Miss Crustacean while wearing her veil.

I chuckled, imagining. "Even so, I'd vote for you."

She began rolling up the shell fragments in the newsprint while I brought over a large trash can. She glanced toward her house. Maybe she worried that her father would be home soon and wouldn't be too happy to see her sharing food with me.

"You don't worry about eating with a married man?"

"You are my neighbor. And you are sad."

I nodded, disarmed again. I took a deep breath. "Thank you."

A smile toyed with the corner of her mouth. "Good night, David."

I CRASHED ON the couch at eleven-thirty, fatigued by the beer and the events of the day. I stared at the ceiling, letting the images blur in my tears. Finally, after what must have been an hour, sleep relieved me of torture. At two I woke, my bladder screaming for attention. I headed to the bathroom with a fog of a dream still floating around my head—Amina feeding me cake with her fingers.

Before heading back to the couch, feeling guilty for my dream of another woman, I called Joanne.

After the message machine picked up, I rechecked the time and hung up. I couldn't imagine her being out this late. So either she had turned down the ringer so she could sleep, or she was torturing me for staying away from her in her time of sorrow.

I took four ibuprofen tablets to head off a hangover and collapsed on the couch. There, I quickly resumed a sleepy state of obsessions about Amina. This time she didn't stop with just feeding me cake.

I awoke at three, dreams fresh, and disappointed in my headache medication. At six I crawled from beneath a thin sheet and dripped coffee straight into a mug emblazoned with a blue crab.

By early morning light I'd photographed the *Beautiful Swimmer* and downloaded the images to my laptop to make a For Sale flyer.

By ten I had posted the flyers at the docks, the community center, and the local Exxon station. At the Waterman's store, I bought caulk, a new caulking gun, four gallons of beige paint, and a new roller.

By noon I was in the middle of giving Dad's place a once-over when the phone rang. It was Joanne.

"Hi, babe," she said. "How's the fight?"

"I'm painting. Once I boxed up all the stuff on the bookshelves, the walls looked pretty bad."

She sighed. "When will you come home?"

"I want to stay for the crab festival this weekend. There will be so many people there, I'd like to circulate a few posters."

Another sigh. "Jim called. He says things are tight at the office. He needs to know something from you soon."

"I think I can finish up around here in a couple days. I've sorted through most of Dad's stuff. I threw away his mattress. I'm going to take a load of clothes to the Salvation Army on my way home."

"Okay." She didn't sound enthusiastic.

"I love you, Jo," I said, upset that immediately an image of Amina danced through my brain.

She stayed quiet.

"See you soon," I added.

"Bye."

Frustrated, I set the phone down. When Joanne was angry, this was her MO. She just clammed up.

By evening I was hungry but didn't want to eat anything around the paint fumes that had collected in a cloud within the house in spite of every window being open, so I showered and headed south to Oyster. At Captain Billy's I ate stuffed flounder, slaw, and hush puppies, washing them all down with sweet tea. As I left, I handed the hostess a flyer about the missing girls.

She covered her mouth with her hand. "I've seen this one before," she said, pointing at Brooke. "She went to preschool with my granddaughter. I thought she drowned."

"That's one theory."

She looked at me with wrinkled distress. "You really think someone abducted her? This is terrible."

"Yes. We need to get the word out."

"I'll put this in the window."

I thanked her and left. At Dad's house I was greeted by the smell of fresh paint, so I retreated with two beers to the dock to wait for sunset.

I was on my second Samuel Adams and feeling guilty for wishing Amina would join me when I saw her father drive up in a seafood delivery truck. I finished my beer and went back inside the house.

There, I called three newspapers—one in Dover, Delaware, one in Virginia Beach, and one in Norfolk—advising them of the two missing girls and the upcoming Blue Crab Festival. Then I called Norfolk's TV Channel 3 and gave the same report.

The news reporter at Channel 3 asked me to fax him a poster of the two girls.

I took down the fax number, gave him my cell phone number, and wondered if I'd ever hear from him.

I caulked around the tub in the only bathroom before heading back outside. There, using the porch lights, I trimmed the bushes back to a lower level so they wouldn't cover the windows.

I spent Friday painting and doing yard work. By Friday at midnight, I actually believed that the house could be shown with a hope of finding a buyer. When I finally hit the hay, I was bone weary, but as had become my routine, sleep didn't come before tears. As I stared at the ceiling, my soul sagged toward despair. *Could the wound in my soul ever heal?*

I set the alarm for six thirty. I didn't want to miss a minute of the Blue Crab Festival—an event I was sure would bring the creeps out of hiding.

Saturday morning dawned with moist heat and a promise of a temperature near ninety. The Crab Festival was held at the county fairgrounds. Although the sheriff had warned me not to pass out literature on the grounds, he hadn't said anything about posting them. So I taped flyers to the poles supporting the tents. When I was done, I headed to the highway where the traffic was stalled, bumper to bumper, trying to make a turn into the fairgrounds. I handed flyers to anyone who would take them. To my surprise a man in a white car with a *Virginian Pilot* newspaper emblem on the side asked me if he could get an interview.

I hopped in his car. "David Conners," I said, extending my hand.

"Paul Andrews," he said. "I think we spoke on the phone." He paused. "So you really believe someone is targeting young girls?"

I studied him for a moment. He was young, perhaps just out of college. He could have been the quarterback on a football team. "It sure looks that way. Two girls have disappeared from this community in the last seven weeks."

"Why isn't anyone saying anything?"

"A good question for the sheriff." I shrugged. "And maybe the mayor. Everyone seems to be convinced that the girls drowned and were swept toward the ocean."

"But you think otherwise."

"I'm a father. My girl is missing. Her body was never found. She knew better than to play by the water alone." I held up my hands. "What else can I believe?"

"Did she know better than to get into a car with a stranger?"

I didn't like his tone of voice, but I guessed it was typical of his profession. "Of course. But maybe she was forced."

He seemed to be studying the two pictures. "Weird. Both blondes. Both holding the same type of stuffed animal."

I nodded. "Weird."

"I'll need to know details. When and where your girl disappeared, and under what circumstance." He paused. Any chance you can hook me up with Brooke's parents?"

"I can try."

He pulled into a gravel parking lot next to a huge tent that covered dozens of picnic tables. Beside the tent people from the Methodist church were making fresh donuts in huge vats of oil.

"Did you say you were a doctor?"

"I practice with Richmond Family Medicine Associates," I said, fishing a business card from my wallet. "My cell phone number is here."

He took the card, and I filled him in on every detail I could remember about Rachel's disappearance.

He listened carefully. "I need to talk with the sheriff. I'll run a story. Maybe someone somewhere saw something that could help." He opened a camera bag. "Can I print a picture of the poster?"

"Sure."

"Here," he said, getting out of the car. "Let's get a shot of you holding up the poster."

I hung out, talking to anyone who would listen, and in general keeping my eyes open for men who seemed to be alone. I walked back and forth among rows of picnic tables filled with feasting mainlanders, who were attacking fresh steamed crabs with nutcrackers and small metal picks. By one o'clock I was in need of refreshment, so I ate a half dozen crabs and drank the Miller Lite served from iced kegs.

That's when the man in a clown costume caught my eye. He was standing at the edge of the tent, observing the young women ready to take the stage in the Miss Crustacean contest. Actually, it was more like leering, but the big red smile painted on his face certainly softened his appearance. He was a harmless, happy clown.

But that's why he caught my attention.

Children would trust him. He was alone. He wasn't doing anything. Not entertaining the crowd. Not juggling. Just observing. Scanning. And his eyes seemed to be resting on the young women.

I sipped my beer and pretended to watch the contest. The clown bought a Coke and walked behind the stage. A minute later I saw him stop and stare at one of my flyers, one I had taped to a light pole at the edge of the tent. His expression changed. Even his clown makeup couldn't disguise his anger. He ripped down the flyer and crumpled it in his hand. I looked around. *Where are the deputies?*

I wanted to punch his big bulbous red nose, but held back, deciding to watch and learn. Obviously, he didn't want people reading my flyer. Then he seemed to be scanning the crowd inside the tent. Back and forth he walked between the rows of tables, pulling down four of my flyers in the process.

When he walked toward a row of carnival games, I followed at a distance. He stood aloof, waving or smiling when someone looked his way. Then he seemed to brighten. I followed his gaze to a little girl eating a candied apple under a tree at the edge of the lot. Behind her was a row of green portable outhouses.

She was alone.

The clown was off, pushing his way through a crowd, with

me trailing from a few feet back. When he broke free of the crowd, I hung back to watch.

The clown bent over the young girl and held out his hand.

She took it.

In a moment he was hurrying her away, practically lifting her with his giant clown steps.

I looked around for help.

Everyone was oblivious. There were no deputies in sight.

I couldn't just let him whisk her away. I screamed, "Police!" and sprinted after the clown.

When I reached them, I grabbed the girl by the wrist. "Not so fast," I said, trying to sound authoritative.

The little girl screamed.

The clown punched me in the nose and pulled the girl away.

By this time either my cry for police or the commotion in general attracted a crowd, and a deputy sprinted to my rescue as I flailed to grab the girl again. I recognized him as Steve, the one from the office the other day.

Instead of grabbing the clown, he tackled me.

One moment I was upright. The next, I was facedown on a sawdust path leading to the Porta-John. "What are you doing?" I cried. "Stop the clown. He's taking that little girl!"

"He grabbed my granddaughter!" The clown pointed at me. "Creep!"

The deputy assisted me to my feet. I wiped blood from my nose with the back of my hand.

The deputy shook his head. "Dr. Conners, I'm sorry. I didn't recognize you." He cleared his throat and pointed at the clown. "This is Amos Whitson." He emphasized the last name.

My head felt sluggish. I fought back a wave of nausea and rubbed my left side. I suspected the moose deputy had fractured my ribs, maybe even my spleen. *Whitson, Whitson. How do I know that name?*

It came to me as I was leaning over with my hands braced against my knees. "Brooke Whitson?"

The clown nodded. "Brooke is another one of my grand-kids."

I grunted through the pain in my side. "Why did you take down my flyers?"

He sneered at me through his clown makeup. "You're the one stirring up my son, raising false hopes?"

The girl tugged the clown's sleeve. "Grandpa! I have to go!"

The clown snorted his disgust and opened the door to the Porta-John.

I couldn't speak. *Of course, he was rushing her off to the bathroom!*

Deputy Steve Wilson looked at the crowd. "That's all, folks. There's no trouble here."

A man walked up carrying a paper plate laden with a large funnel cake. "Steve, have you seen Crystal?"

Steve nodded and tilted his head toward the Porta-John. "Your father took her to the bathroom."

I didn't want to look at anyone. I coughed. Rib fragments stabbed the tender flesh just left of my heart. Apparently, Daddy Funnelcake hadn't seen me try to rescue his daughter. Satisfied that he wasn't interested in attacking me, I limped off, wanting to lose myself in the crowd.

Back at my father's place, I raided the medicine cabinet, finding most of the codeine tablets that I'd prescribed for his backache. I took a cocktail of two codeine and four ibuprofen and crashed on the couch. I slept until seven and felt worse when I got up.

I hadn't been doing much in the way of grocery shopping, but found a few eggs and cheese, so I made an omelet to stave off my hunger.

I didn't feel like calling Joanne. I didn't want to explain how crazy my day had been. Instead, I pulled two beers from the refrigerator and limped out to the dock to let the day fade away with the sunset.

The sun was half submerged into the marsh when I heard footsteps.

Amina's voice. "Why did he call his boat the *Beautiful Swimmer*?"

I looked up. She was in a dress, her usual billowy fare, but not wearing a veil. Perhaps my gaze was no longer a threat. I wondered about the change but decided that since it worked for me, I wasn't going to ask questions. "*Callinectes sapidus,*" I said.

She sat beside me, swinging her feet off the end of the dock. "Callinec—"

"Callinectes," I repeated. "It was my father's gesture toward science," I said. "*Callinectes sapidus* is the scientific word for the blue crab. It's Greek, I think. It means 'beautiful swimmer that tastes good.'"

"A blue crab is the *beautiful swimmer*?"

"You think Gus would have named his boat after something else?"

She laughed. A giggle like the water ripples chopping against the side of the pier—a splash of happiness.

She made me smile.

After a moment she spoke again. "No, I guess not."

We sat in silence for a minute, the night moist and warm around us. The air was a blanket, typical for summer at the shore.

Her eyes were mysterious—dark and full of wonder. I found myself drawn by them. And scared. Perhaps it was the mystery of the different culture, but I wanted to stare and run at the same time.

I glanced at her, hoping my investigations were unseen.

She was smiling.

I think she knew exactly what she did to me. I was a school-boy, peering into the unknown of a woman's unmentionables' drawer.

I risked one more look.

The last of the sun's rays danced off the water and onto her eyes. Flickering. Teasing.

I had to know what was behind her eyes.

THE NEXT MORNING music from my cell phone jarred me from sleep. I reached for the phone and gasped, having forgotten about my ribs. "Hello."

"David, Jim Ashton here. Have you seen this morning's paper?"

I looked at my watch. Seven a.m. I yawned. "Jim, I'm down at the shore, I don't even get the paper."

"I think you'll be interested in an article that the *Virginian-Pilot* shared with *The Richmond Times-Dispatch*."

I tried to sit upright, but my side objected. "I'm listening."

Jim's voice slid into a newscaster cadence while he read, "Tempers flared at the Blue Crab Festival when a fight broke out between a clown and Richmond local physician, Dr. David Conners. Conners apparently mistook the man in a clown costume for someone who may have abducted his daughter, who had disappeared from her grandfather's home on the Eastern Shore July seventh. Conners, who practices with Richmond Family Medicine Associates, carpeted the festival with flyers picturing his missing daughter, and apparently took it upon himself to prevent other possible child abductions at the festival. Sheriff Reynolds declined comment on the investigation other than saying that they have no evidence that Conners' daughter was abducted. 'More likely,' he said, 'she was swept into the Chesapeake and was a victim of drowning.'"

Jim sighed.

I groaned. "Is that the whole story?"

"They printed a picture of you being held by a deputy. You have a bloody nose."

I hung my head. I hadn't realized anyone snapped a picture.

"Listen David, I'm going to recommend that you stay on indefinite leave."

The blow wasn't entirely unexpected. Jim was a friend, sure, but he was my boss first. At the office business was business, and money was the bottom line. He was on a rescue mission to salvage his practice from taking on water. I was an anchor he didn't need. He needed to cut and run.

"Jim," I protested, "I only need a little time." I'd been his golden boy, a recruit from among my peers. Best of all, I'd made him more money than anyone else in the last year. "I'll be back in Richmond in a day or two. I can be back on the job by—"

"You're not listening, David. You're obviously too distracted to put yourself into medicine right now. Mistakes would be a nightmare."

Sarcasm threatened to erupt. *Easy come, easy go.* "I can focus. I need a diversion. I only need a little time to get my father's place in order. I'll—"

"David, stay away. We've got things covered here for now. Get your act together, and we'll talk about your future in a few months."

"A few months? You can't—"

"A few months, David. You're a good doctor. But you're no good to the practice the way things are."

"I just lost my daughter, Jim. My dad just died. Give a guy a break."

"I know, I know. But I have a business to run. I'll keep you on my short list. Get your act back together. Then come back and we'll talk."

I sighed. Jim and I had a good history together. I knew he'd take me back. Eventually. He'd recruited *me*. He ran one of the tightest, most efficient practices in the state and had the respect of every resident that rotated through his practice. He could have had his pick of the multitude of doctors that came through, yet he had taken me. We'd fallen into a close mentoring relationship, one that had even survived me taking a bold shot at his drinking. And now he was shutting me out. I felt one more pillar in my support structure giving way. Rachel. Dad. My job.

"But—"

"David, I've watched you carefully since Rachel, uh, disappeared. You have been understandably distracted." His breath whistled into the phone. I thought I heard the clink of ice being swirled in a glass. "Come by the house sometime. We'll have a drink. We're still friends." He lowered his voice as if his partners were looking on. They were, for all I knew. "My hands are tied here, David. I'm giving you all the slack I can. I feel terrible, but I have to treat you like I treat everyone else."

I felt heat rising in my cheeks and knew what he was thinking.

I could feel the swell of the wave before it lifted my feet from the bottom. In a moment I'd be swimming alone. "Look at the figures. I brought in more than—"

"Call me in a month, then." A crack. A concession. *Dare I push him one more time?*

"But—"

I stared into the phone. He'd hung up. I muttered a curse. I'd gone from partner shoo-in golden boy to unemployed in a few short weeks. It was a quick fall.

The first thing I thought was how angry Joanne was going to be.

I didn't have to wait long. My phone sounded again in thirty minutes. It was Jo. Embarrassed and steamed.

"I thought you were fixing up your father's place."

"I was. I told you I was going to the festival. You knew—"

"And now, so does all of Richmond."

"Jo, I'm sorry, I—"

"Sorry doesn't cut it, David. I want to figure out how to live life without our baby. But you're making that nearly impossible, aren't you?"

"Two girls have disappeared from one small town. Why doesn't that concern you?"

"Two summertime drownings in the Chesapeake. Why can't you believe what the sheriff is telling you?"

I didn't feel like arguing. But Jo didn't seem in the mood to let me off the hook. "I'm dressed for church," she said.

I rubbed the back of my neck. *It is Sunday, isn't it?* Since I'd taken the job with Richmond Family Medicine Associates, we hadn't been attending. I stayed quiet, unsure of where she was going with this.

"I've been talking to the preacher about a memorial service for Rachel."

I sighed. "Fine."

"He agreed it's a good idea," she said as though discussing the weather. "I told him I'd give him the song selections this morning."

"I can help." I paused, trying to remember any song that Rachel liked that would be an appropriate choice. "How about asking the children's choir to perform?"

"They will be at a music festival in Raleigh."

"When is the service?"

"Next weekend." Her speech was clipped. Short. The way she talked when she was irritated.

"I'm coming home soon, Jo. I need to show the house to a Realtor."

I listened as she sighed again. Then, just before she ended the conversation, she said, "Don't hurry."

The conversation with Jo spurred me to action. The longer I stayed in Tippins, the more Jo pulled away. I called six Realtors before finding one who could come out on short notice on a Sunday afternoon to see Dad's place. I signed an agreement, left a set of keys with the Realtor, packed Dad's truck, and headed for home.

Dad's pickup, I quickly realized, was marginal transportation. I changed the flat tire, but the spare looked marginal. It took me five minutes to locate and retrieve the seat belt from its buried position in the crease of the seat. In the meantime I found stale french fries, fifty cents in change, an overdue parking ticket, and a large black button. Going south toward the bay bridge-tunnel, I discovered an annoying tendency of the vehicle to pull toward the right. The steering wheel rattled when I traveled more than fifty miles per hour. It was going to be a long trip home.

I arrived at nine-thirty and turned off the ignition. The rebellious pickup continued running for a few moments before finally dying with a loud backfire and the smell of exhaust.

I found Jo in the kitchen with a bottle of 2003 French Chablis half empty on the table in front of her. She looked up. "Do you know how many kooks have called me today, saying they might have seen a little girl of Rachel's description?" She looked down into her glass. "Why'd you put our home phone number on your poster?"

She pushed a pad of paper toward me. Six phone numbers were listed.

"Call 'em if you like." She pointed to the top number. "This woman was convinced she saw Rachel pushing a shopping cart full of aluminum cans in downtown Baltimore."

I sighed. I hadn't anticipated that kind of response. "Sorry, Jo." I kissed her forehead and poured wine into a second glass from the table. "Expecting company?"

"If you drink alone, drink from two glasses. Never admit to being lonely." Her eyes were heavy and her speech slow.

I pulled one of the flyers I'd made from my shirt pocket and unfolded it in front of her. "You have to admit, Jo. The similarity between the two girls is amazing."

She shrugged. "Don't you think thousands of parents purchased Pound Puppies for their kids?"

"It's not just the stuffed animals. It's their age. How they look. Everything," I said, gesturing in wide circles with my hands. "It's the way they disappeared. Without a trace. It's spooky." I paused. "Why can't you entertain abduction as an option?"

"I can't do it, okay?" She drained her glass in two gulps and wiped a drop from her chin. She imitated my wild gestures with her hands. "Children disappear. Without a trace. That's what the Chesapeake does." She shook her head slowly. "Dragging this out is killing me." She stood and walked back the hall toward our bedroom. A minute later she reappeared, heading for the couch with her pillow and a blanket.

"Joanne, what are you doing?"

"Pretty obvious, I'd say. I'm sleeping on the couch."

"Honey, I—"

The sharp look she flashed my way interrupted my attempt to warm up to her. I didn't understand. She'd wrapped herself in a protective cocoon that kept her from hope.

"My mother called," she said.

I raised my eyebrows in question.

"Your antics are hurting my father's campaign."

"Is that what this is about? Since when have you cared about politics?" I put my hands on my hips. "And since when do you defend Tricia?" I said her name with a scowl.

"I'm not defending her." She seemed to hesitate. "But he is my father. Perhaps that should concern you."

She walked away, blanket trailing.

I withdrew to my study and tried to read, but I couldn't concentrate. At least in pulling away, Joanne hadn't thrown me out of our bed. When I tiptoed past the couch in the den thirty minutes later, her breathing was regular—either she was sleeping or pretending.

When I went to the master bathroom, I saw the medicine cabinet ajar. Investigating, I found two small prescription bottles. I lifted the bottles to inspect the labels. One was a mild tranquilizer and the other a common sleep aid. *Joanne Conners.*

I felt my gut tighten as I read the prescribing doctor's name. *Blake Swenson.*

THAT NIGHT I lay staring at the ceiling, feeling hopeless, wanting to help Joanne escape from her depression but not knowing how to penetrate her shell. By two I was still awake. Every few minutes my mind ran a different direction. If it wasn't Joanne, it was Rachel. If it wasn't Rachel, it was Dad. If it wasn't Dad, beautiful Amina would tease from the corners of my mind and rob me of slumber.

By seven I was awake again. I crept to the kitchen with a plan. I fixed Joanne's favorite breakfast—blueberry waffles topped with whipped cream, served with fresh coffee. I put them on a tray and headed for the den.

Jo protested waking as she uncurled from the couch. She plodded to the bathroom. When she returned, she sat on the couch and feigned interest in breakfast. I sat opposite her and sipped black coffee.

She ate without speaking, but I could see her mind was busy. I knew when she was ready, she'd tell me what was on her mind. When she finished, she took her tray to the kitchen and returned with a second cup of java. "I need space, David."

I wasn't sure what to say. Was it time to protest? Did she want me to assure her how much I needed her? "Joanne, we can make it through this."

"We're on different roads," she said flatly. "Perhaps we have been for a long time. With Rachel around, it was difficult to see."

I rubbed the back of my neck. "We need to pull together."

"That's just it. We can't. I can't pull with you on this one. I need space to grieve the loss of my daughter and see if I can move on." She stood up and walked to the windows, her face hardened. "I can't be around you anymore."

"Jo, I love you. Let me help. Leaving isn't the answer."

She kept her chin pointed toward the windows, not daring to look at me. Then she walked away, stopping at the kitchen desk to retrieve a small paper bag. She returned and handed me a small card. On the cover was printed, RACHEL ELIZABETH CONNERS, AUGUST 15, 2000–JULY 7, 2007. "Maybe you'd want to attend your daughter's memorial service."

She watched as I read the order of the service. "My doctor says I need to do this," she said.

"Who," I said, unable to hide the sarcasm from my voice, "Dr. Swenson?" It was a cheap shot, one that was precipitated over my annoyance that she was taking medicines that her former lover had prescribed.

Her eyes bore in on me. "Dr. Jacobs," she said. "I saw him last week."

Dr. Jeff Jacobs was a great psychiatrist, the one who'd helped Joanne through her severe postpartum depression. "Good," I responded. I moved to the couch and sat down, dropping my hands between my knees. This wasn't the way the morning was supposed to unfold. I wanted to redo it, starting with breakfast. I sighed. "Look, Jo, I'm sorry. I'm okay with the memorial service."

"But you're going to keep hoping she's alive."

I couldn't say no. I held up my hands. "Is that okay?"

She looked down. "Just do it away from me."

I started to protest, but she raised her voice. "Dr. Jacobs says I need closure."

"I respect that." I paused. *But I need to hope. I can't give up. Not yet.*

She nodded quickly, as if trying to convince herself that it was true. I studied her for a moment. She'd folded herself over her hands, gripping her stomach and rocking like someone trying to hug away a pain. She was pale, fragile. A harsh word would send her adrift on the wind like a dry leaf of winter. She closed her eyes and made a statement. It sounded stiff and practiced, like a line delivered in an amateur play. "I need you to move away. I need space to grieve. Space to recover from the loss of my child."

I studied her for a minute. She was vulnerable, and we both felt it. Darkness had shattered our world, and she didn't want to face it. "I know you're scared."

She stayed quiet for a few moments. When she spoke, there were tears in her eyes. She said what we were both thinking but afraid to voice. "What if Rachel was the only reason our relationship worked?" She wasn't just grieving the loss of Rachel. She was also grieving the loss of *me*.

It wasn't true that Rachel was all we had in common. I'd wondered, too, but I wouldn't give it my full consent. "It's not true. Sure, Rachel held us together, but what about love?"

"If it's not Rachel, then time apart won't destroy us."

"But—"

"We got married because she was on the way. Don't deny it."

"We got married because she was on the way, but we were in love. She's simply the reason we got married when we did."

My logic was lost in her stare. I wanted to argue, but the hollowness that met me in her gaze was one that made me stop short. It was the abject fear of someone on the brink of sanity. It was a look I had seen only once before—on a snowy winter morning as I delivered my wife to the door of a psychiatric hospital. So now, as irrational as it seemed, I nodded my consent.

I felt my throat closing. My eyes blurred with tears. "Where am I to go?"

She took a deep breath and held my hands in hers. With tears, she said, "The shore. You can stay at your father's place." She raised her eyebrows. "You've lost your job, haven't you? When were you going to tell me that gem?"

"How'd you find—"

"A secretary called. She wanted to know if she should mail your last check."

"I was planning to tell you."

"Was that why you made me waffles?"

I opted for humor to soften my response. "Some news is better received with favorite food."

She walked away from me toward the bedroom. "You're ruining your life with this obsession. I won't have you ruining mine."

"Jo."

She didn't stop until she reached our bedroom door. "The memorial service is Saturday at ten. It would be best for my parents if we could sit together."

I packed a suitcase and left Dad's truck in the driveway, opting for my Ford SUV. I thought about my rooming options. I could show up late at the hospital, sleep in a call room and shower in the men's operating room locker room, crash in the home of a colleague, or find a hotel. I opted for number three, not wanting to attract unwanted attention in the hospital and not feeling like explaining my problems to anyone else.

I checked into the Marriott downtown and called Kim, the receptionist at my old workplace.

She answered with her normal sunshiny sweetness. "Richmond Family Medicine Associates. May I help you?"

"Kim. It's Dr. Conners."

"Dr. Conners, we've been so concerned about you. Everyone is asking how you are. Mrs. Buckwalter has called three times to find out when you're coming back."

Bless her heart. She'll have to manage her diabetes without me. "I'm calling about my last check. Can you hold it for me at the office? I'll just come by."

"Oh my," she said. "I already gave it to Dr. Swenson. He said he was going to swing by your place to check on you."

"Dr. Swenson?"

"Yes, isn't he the greatest? He volunteered to help fill in while you were on leave."

On leave? Is that what we're calling this? I tried to control my voice. "Dr. Blake Swenson is filling in for me?"

"Just started. His true test happens this afternoon. I scheduled Mrs. Buckwalter to see him."

I took a deep breath. "Thanks, Kim. He's a real peach."

I hung up before I could say what I really thought.

By Saturday morning I was stir-crazy, sick of knocking around my old med school haunts and unsuccessful in raising any interest in getting hired by any of the other family practice groups in town. Everyone had too much respect for Jim Ashton. It seemed that if Dr. Ashton thought I needed a rest, so did everyone else.

I looked online and downloaded an application for a locum tenens outfit. Maybe I could find temporary work out of town. Honestly, the idea left me cold. It was hardly the career path I'd chosen. I should be on my way to full partner in a respected firm, not toying with temporary jobs that no one else wanted.

So for now, I was jobless. Daughterless. Wifeless. Fatherless. I was starting to feel like an arrow without a bow. I needed to fly toward some target but lacked the launch that would carry me there. And that's when I started feeling the first stirrings of rage. What would happen if I could channel the anger I felt growing like a watered garden within me?

I got up the morning of Rachel's memorial service, vowing to find whoever was responsible for taking her away from me. I stared at the poster I'd made and promised that someone was going to pay. I smiled. I understood the currency. It was going to be pain.

I showered, put on my black suit, and nodded at myself in the mirror. I looked good in black. But the suit that needed adjusting was the one no one could see. It was the invisible suit I'd tried on just that morning. Revenge. It wasn't part of my regular attire. I shifted around, rolling my shoulders beneath the weight of bitterness, trying to see if it suited me.

I'd always been the kid on the playground pacifying the bully. This felt as though it needed a different approach. Rachel was gone. Joanne was slipping away. My career was on the fast track to nowhere. Maybe it was time I stopped being the passive recipient of pain. Losing Rachel seemed to have changed that already. In fact, losing her had changed *everything*. I'd gone from swallowing my suspicions to punching Blake Swenson in the nose.

I had no plan. But there, staring at my reflection in the hotel mirror, I could sense my attitude changing. Outside, I could be the same, but inside, I felt a subtle shifting away from niceness. I felt raw. Invigorated.

I arrived at the memorial service twenty minutes early and hoped no one would notice that Joanne and I drove separately.

We sat in the second row, two statues, silent and unmoving. When Joanne finally gave vent to her tears, I put my arm around her, but felt her stiffen beneath my touch.

The preacher, a balding man with the build and disposition of the Pillsbury Doughboy, seemed to be staring at the ceiling.

"We know that all things work together for good for those that love the Lord," he quoted.

I shifted in my seat. *But what about me? I'm not sure I can love a God that thinks it's good to let my Rachel be taken away.*

In the parking lot after the service, I leaned toward Joanne's ear. "Can we get coffee?"

She stayed quiet, scanning the parking lot. I followed her eyes to the lot's exit. There, I saw a familiar car approach. *Blake.*

"Jo, you're not—"

"He knew today was going to be hard for me. He offered to take me to lunch." She looked away. "A friend. That's all," she said.

"Blake has never pretended to want to be your friend. You know that."

Joanne looked toward several of our neighbors standing in the doorway of the church. I caught her silent message—quiet down and don't make a scene. I lowered my voice and gripped her elbow. "Don't do this, Jo. Don't pull away. We need to work through this. Together."

A moment later I watched Jo's expression change. I looked over my shoulder.

Blake. Smiling. Mr. Plastic.

I wanted to punch him.

I tightened my grip on Joanne's arm. "Leave us, Blake."

"Let her go, Dave."

I turned to face him, still holding on to my wife. I kept my voice low. "Do me a favor and walk away. We need some time alone."

"Hey, I'm just here to support an old friend."

I dropped Joanne's elbow and tightened my fist. "We don't want your friendship."

"David." Joanne's voice in my ear. Pleading. Her hand against my arm. "Don't."

I was only slightly aware of a gathering crowd. Everything seemed to blur except for my focus on Blake.

He took a step back. "Joanne, let's go."

"Not with my wife!" I shouted. I grabbed the front of his shirt and shoved him backward onto the hood of a Cadillac.

"Maniac!" He jumped back up, brushing his clothes and looking at the crowd. "Did you see that? He's crazy!"

Two strong hands gripped me from behind, and Tom Hendrick, a church elder who coached a high school football team, stepped in front of me. I turned to see Nathan Prevast with a strong hand on my elbow. "Be cool," Tom said. "No one needs to—"

I twirled and pulled away from Nathan, lifting my hands in surrender. "Easy," I said. "Step aside, Tom. This doesn't concern you."

"Whatever happens on church property concerns me."

"Then you should be concerned that my wife is leaving with another man!"

I looked around, suddenly aware that Joanne had slipped away. I put my hand on Tom's linebacker shoulders and strained to see around him. I threw my hands up in despair. Exiting the parking lot was the red Porsche 911. A caramel blonde in the passenger seat.

My cell phone sounded at seven the next morning. I groaned and looked at the incoming number. It was another cell, a number I didn't recognize. "Hello."

"Dr. Conners?"

The voice sounded vaguely familiar. "Yes."

"Paul Andrews here. We met at the Blue Crab Festival over in Tippins."

"Your story got me fired."

He chuckled. High pitched. More of a nervous laugh. "I certainly meant no harm. I had no idea my boss would include that picture of you with the deputy."

Right! "So you're calling to apologize? Save it for the next guy you humiliate."

I was about to terminate the call when he rushed to speak again. "Don't hang up. I called to give you some information. Something you might be interested in."

"I'm listening."

"A deputy over in Tippins picked up an exhibitionist in Chincoteague yesterday. Seems a little girl strayed away from her family while they were viewing the wild horses. Some dude exposed himself and tried to get her into his car."

"Any connection to my daughter's case?"

"Don't know. Sheriff Reynolds is tight-lipped. He's not saying anything about this."

"So how do you know so much?"

"I've got a source over at the Oyster Point Correctional Facility. The guy is being held there."

"So why are you telling me this?"

"You gave me a good story. I owed you one."

What I wanted to hear was how sorry he was for depicting me as crazy in his newspaper, but maybe this was as close to an apology as I could expect from someone in the media. "Okay. Thanks." *So what am I to do? Go over there and interrogate him myself?* "What's his name?"

"Riley Johnson."

"Does he have a history?"

"Don't know that, either. But when I questioned the sheriff directly, he seemed quite smug. My take on it is that he thinks his department is on to something."

"He doesn't have room for smug. It's amazing that he's open to thinking of anything but drowning."

"Give him some space. You need him on your side."

I sighed. He was right. "Riley Johnson," I muttered.

"Right. Gotta run."

I snapped my phone shut. *Okay, so now perhaps I have a direction.* I looked around my hotel room. Without an income, I certainly couldn't stay at the Marriott forever. I decided to head back to the shore and stay at my father's place while I sorted through my options. In the meantime, I'd try to find out what I could about Riley Johnson.

An hour later I entered my west-end home to find Joanne up and wearing her nursing whites. She addressed me without a greeting. "You can't just show up here anymore. You need to call first."

"We're married, Jo. I live here, remember?"

"Married," she mumbled.

"I'm here to collect some things. What are you doing?"

"I've been working again. I'm in the day-float pool at MCV."

I nodded. She hadn't wasted any time in reentering the workforce. It had always been a source of contention between us. I stood on one side, wanting her to stay at home with Rachel; Joanne, on the other, wanting to further her career. "Good," I said. "Getting out will be good."

She waved at me. "Lock up when you're done."

"When can we talk?" I hesitated. "Maybe we should see a marriage counselor before we make too many decisions alone."

She shook her head. "I need space."

Space, her new mantra.

She paused, and I could see moisture in her eyes. "I need this, David." She paused and reached for my hand. "*We* need this." She touched the edge of her face, something she did often when she was in a contemplative mood. "I'd forgotten how much I loved work. I love giving back something."

She disappeared through the door to the garage, leaving me standing in the kitchen, remembering how healthy it had been for her when she went back to work after Rachel's birth. Work had given her one more reason to get up and get going. And she had seemed happier. That was a huge plus in my book. Anything to ward off another season of darkness.

In truth, it had taken months of calls from a hospital supervisor to convince Joanne. The nursing coordinator had even tried to get me to intervene. *"Your wife is the best we ever had on the medical-surgical floor. So competent, and she really cares."* I knew it was more than words.

Joanne was an excellent nurse but had no idea because she had poor self-confidence. For that, I blamed Tricia. She'd told Joanne how many times to chew her food, how to walk in a manner worthy of her heritage, and how to appear respectfully happy in all social situations. She'd practically convinced Jo that she was incapable of anything but being a garnish or window dressing.

It wasn't until the early years of our marriage, when Tricia practically disowned Joanne for marrying me, that I saw the true strength that Joanne possessed. It was during those years that I saw her claw her way through depression darkness, fighting for the right to breathe without sorrow. On her own, she was formidable. But losing Rachel had proven to be a matching formidable blow to her world.

And so I watched Joanne withdraw and resort to dysfunctional ways of coping, somewhat of a Morgan family trait. I wanted to help her. *Longed* to help, but Jo was nothing if not fiercely independent. I'd have to hope that she'd come through this tunnel glad to be hand in hand with me on the other side.

I looked around, preparing my mental list of items to take to the shore. I groaned, pushing down a threat of fury. On the table sat a racquetball racquet and a can of balls. We'd not played in years. Joanne hated racquetball—or so I understood. Blake, however, was a fanatic.

We used to play together when we were friends back in medical school. During a fiercely competitive game of racquetball early one afternoon before a party at a mutual friend's, Blake couldn't stop talking about his new girl and how he thought she was "the one." I'd told him to get real, that I'd heard it a dozen times before.

That evening after a grabbing an ice-cold beer, I stepped onto a balcony overlooking a small backyard to escape the clamor of the party.

Blake's girl was alone, standing at a white railing, staring down at a small group gathered around a gas grill where Blake entertained. "Oh, hello," I said.

Joanne turned her head, and I could appreciate her fine features in the dim light that was spilling from the glass door behind me. Blake always dated gorgeous women, and this one was no different. She held a wine glass in her hand. She quickly turned away, but not before I saw the moisture in her eyes.

"You must be Joanne."

She dabbed at her eyes with the back of her hand and turned again to face me. "Yes, I'm Jo Morgan." She paused. "And you're David Conners."

I smiled. "You know me?"

"All the nursing students know who you are."

My smile broadened, and I felt heat in my cheeks. This was certainly news to me—the nerd. Popularity among the females wasn't known to be my strong suit. I didn't know what to say, so I lifted my bottle of Amstel to my lips to hide my embarrassment. I nearly choked. Coughing, I responded, "Me?"

"Don't act so surprised. If you'd ever emerge from the library, you might understand."

I shuffled my feet and followed her gaze down to the partyers in the yard. "Blake's a great guy," I said.

We stood at the railing, stealing glances at each other from the corners of our eyes. "Do you always do that?"

I cleared my throat. "What?"

"Call attention to someone else when someone gives you a compliment?"

"Are you always so direct?"

I could see a smile bringing up the corner of her mouth. She had blond curls. A perm perhaps, but I wasn't knowledgeable about such things. All I knew was that she was disarmingly beautiful.

She didn't answer and kept her gaze downward toward Blake.

"Are you in love?" I asked.

She kept looking at Blake, but again, I saw a smile tease the corner of her mouth. "Why, Mr. Conners, we've only just met."

I covered with a laugh. "With him." I gestured toward the grill with the beer. "I'm a friend of Blake's. Don't want to see him hurt, you know."

"Or are you just dipping your toe in the water to see if the swimming would be nice?"

She turned toward me, taking one step. I was completely defenseless. I had no experience with this kind of dance. Physiology, not psychology, was my forte. I steadied myself with my right hand, knuckles whitening against the railing. I looked away toward the yard below, observing Blake laugh with another young lady, wine glass in one hand, the other on her neck. "I-uh, n-no," I stuttered. "You're dating my friend."

She glanced down at Blake one more time before brushing past me, kissing my cheek as I pressed myself against the railing. She paused, her breath dancing on my skin. "Loyalty is an admirable quality," she whispered.

She stepped away, leaving me alone and breathless. That feeling was something I never quite got over. Every time I was around her from that moment forward, my soul was always alight and slightly off balance in a delightful tingle of unexpected passion.

I lifted the racquet, weighing it in my hand, and tried to think of anything or anyone besides Joanne, to move past the ache in my gut. I shook my head. How had I let her get away?

Was Rachel really all that held us together?

I closed my fist in resolve. Whoever stole Rachel away had

swept Joanne along in the current and left me drifting alone. *Pity the man responsible for this.*

I walked with a soul-limp back to the master bedroom and began gathering a few things to take with me to the shore.

Obvious questions were my only companions. How to pack? How long would I be gone? Could I hope that Joanne would break free of her sorrow? Would I get another chance at her love?

I carried out a second suitcase of clothes before stopping in the kitchen for a bag of Kenya AA coffee beans, my coffee grinder, a box of strawberry Pop-Tarts, and an economy-size box of Wheaties—which was about as close to Joanne's fiber cereal addiction as I ever got. Into the backseat I threw my memory-foam pillow, a blue-and-orange UVA fleece blanket, my laptop, and a stack of medical journals I had never had time to read with Rachel around. After that, I wandered through the house and garage, selecting two pictures of Rachel, a family portrait, and a picture of me and Joanne huddled at the top of a ski lift in Snow-shoe, West Virginia. I turned a small, framed photo of Joanne and me on the table beneath the hall mirror to face the front door—so any visitors would be certain to see it. Next, I grabbed my favorite fishing pole, the *Band of Brothers* DVD series and, last of all, a Bible. It couldn't hurt to keep God on my side.

At the last minute I added a cooler of ice and stopped at Bill's Barbeque on my way through town. I bought two pork bar-beque sandwiches, a cup of coffee, and two pints of minced bar-beque for the coming week at Dad's place.

With that, I was back on I-64, heading east to the shore and contemplating the next step in tracking down my daughter.

I glanced at the Bible on the seat beside me. *Maybe I should pray.*

I sighed. I doubted God would want to hear from me. It had been so long since I'd darkened the doorway of a church, asking

Him for help now seemed like a college student never calling home except for money.

Couldn't hurt to try.

I didn't know what to say. Instead, I cried and let my tears knock on heaven's door. Through the blur, I kept heading east toward the bay.

After I'd met Joanne on the balcony during the party, the next real contact I'd had with her was the Friday before med-school graduation. Blake and I were trading off call in the emergency room—he was coming in, and I, tail dragging, was heading home to sleep. It was eight in the morning, and I pointed at the patients I'd been assigned to check out to the next student. "Jones," I said, pointing to the far stretcher, "is a frequent flier."

Blake nodded. "Don't tell me. Found down."

"Yep," I said, laughing at the history we'd all heard a hundred times.

With a yellow IV bag hanging above the stretcher, it was a picture all too familiar to anyone who spent time in an inner city emergency room. "Rally pack?" Blake referred to the yellow B vitamin IV supplement that we administered to alcoholics.

"Yep again. CT head is normal. Alcohol level is 2.4."

Blake shook his head. "Amazing."

I pointed to stretcher number three. "Beatrice Thompson is an out-of-control diabetic, in with diabetic ketoacidosis. I've called medicine. The intern made me do finger-stick glucoses every hour all night while we waited for him. She should be going up to the ICU within the hour."

"Sweet."

"Her blood, or the fact that she's out of here?"

Blake smiled. "Both."

"Next stretcher, Anna Svenson. Ninety-two-year-old with

three days of diarrhea, progressing to lethargy and near coma. Serum sodium 158."

"Salty."

"Like blood." I paused. "Too salty. Better remember all the symptoms. Dr. Fleet's here, and I guarantee he'll ask you."

As we spoke, the attending walked in. Blake shot me a panicked look. "Lethargic state," I whispered, uncurling each finger, one at a time, adding, "weakness, irritability, coma, seizures, and death."

He whispered back. "Thanks."

I headed toward the automatic doors.

"David."

I turned.

"I left my guitar at your place. Can you drop it by my new house? Joanne should be there decorating."

"Sure."

I plodded toward the parking lot, thinking about Joanne. Since I'd met her on the balcony, every thought of her intoxicated me. I'd seen her only a time or two after that. Brief encounters. Polite exchanges with Blake around. Once in the library. Another time when I dropped by their table in the Skull and Bones, the infamous diner across the street from Sanger Hall at the Medical College of Virginia. But each time, I'd met her gaze, held it for a moment, and walked away, cradling it in my heart. Weird for me, but maddening as I watched her and Blake walk forward in their relationship. A magical whirlwind courtship. Engagement. The medical school dean's son and the daughter of a Virginia state senator.

I was the nerd son of a crab fisherman.

All of this made her unreachable. And made me want her all the more.

I reviewed the symptoms of hypernatremia—too much salt in the blood. Lethargy. Weakness. Irritability. *Me without Joanne.*

I crashed in my apartment and set my alarm for four. When I woke, I showered, donned a clean black T-shirt and blue jeans, and headed out the door with Blake's guitar. On the porch I was struck with an idea, so I returned to my small kitchen table and retrieved a woven basket, part of a centerpiece filled with Red Delicious apples. I paused, taking out all but two of the apples, and left.

I stopped at a Kroger to stock my basket. I added a wedge of Edam cheese, a small box of table water crackers, a Toblerone bar and a fourteen-dollar bottle of red wine. Equipped with my housewarming gift and Blake's guitar, I ascended the outside wooden stairs to his second-floor apartment in the Fan district of downtown Richmond.

She answered the door, wearing a pair of cutoff blue-jean shorts and a too-large white shirt with a button-down collar. A Blake signature. She had light blue paint on her left cheek and hadn't buttoned up the shirt far enough.

I lifted the guitar. "Blake left this at my place." Then I lifted the basket. "A little housewarming gift."

She smiled, completely disarming me.

Suddenly my throat was parched. I didn't know how to proceed.

She took the basket and placed it on the table. "Ooh," she said, lifting the bottle of wine. "This is nice."

"Does Blake know you're wearing his shirt?" Silently, I cringed. Could I have chosen a lamer question?

She giggled through her answer. "I didn't want to get paint on mine." She squinted at me. "I couldn't talk you into helping me a minute, could I?"

I shrugged and followed her down the hall to a bathroom, once beige, now mostly light blue. The smell of fresh paint was strong in the air. She pointed at the top of the wall. "I can't reach to trim it out next to the ceiling."

The house was circa 1950s with high ceilings and a Williams-burg feel. I looked around, moved a small step stool toward the corner, and picked up a brush. "At your service," I said.

For the next hour I crawled from the top of the bathroom vanity counter to the step stool and back, carefully painting up to the wooden trim at the top of the wall. Joanne sat on the commode, leaning forward, her generous cleavage not quite covered by Blake's loose-fitting shirt. Distracted, I stole looks as often as I could.

She chatted on about music and movies, the stresses of nursing school, and the pressure from her mother to plan the perfect wedding. I laughed at her imitation of her nursing professors. She listened, really listened, to my adventures from my last month in the emergency room.

I was washing out the brush and roller at an outside faucet when she asked me to stay for supper. She leaned out a back window over my head. "Let's order a pizza. Can you stay?"

Duh. I thought about it for less than a second. "Sure."

"My treat," she said. "Call it payment for the painting."

I'd have paid to do it, just to talk to you. I smiled.

"What do you like? Pepperoni? Mushrooms? Veggies?"

"Everything."

She disappeared from the window. When I rejoined her a few minutes later, she'd washed the paint from her cheek, applied fresh lipstick, and changed into a yellow top that exposed her belly button.

We listened to the Red Hot Chili Peppers and drank the wine while waiting for the pizza. We talked about parental expectations and the pitfalls of modern relationships. She asked me about my dreams and pressed me to tell her my most embarrassing moment, laughing when I told her I wrecked my father's truck picking up my date for the senior prom.

After her first glass, Joanne sat sideways at one end of the leather couch, dropping her bare feet onto my lap. "What about you? Have you ever been in love?"

I raised my eyebrows. "Sure," I said, feigning confidence, and hoping to hide how smitten I was by everything about her. "First grade. Miss Stevenson. Fresh out of college." I beamed. "I was the teacher's pet."

A knock at the door signaled the arrival of our pizza. We transitioned to the floor to eat out of the cardboard box she'd placed on the coffee table in front of the couch.

I'd had two glasses of wine and was feeling a pleasant buzzing behind my forehead when Joanne steered the conversation back to my first love.

My defenses were down. I should have stopped with one glass.

"So tell me about Miss Stevenson. Just why were you so smitten?"

"She was a blonde," I said, smiling. "And she had . . ." I gestured with my hands, cupping them to my chest.

She laughed. "Big breasts?"

I nodded, and my words stumbled forward before I could stop. "Like you."

She covered her mouth. Evidently, she didn't expect such behavior from the nerd.

I was hopelessly wondering how to get beyond the issue when she rescued me by changing the subject. "I'm afraid of getting married."

I paused and looked intently into her eyes. "Tell me."

"Blake's parents," she said, waving her glass of wine around, "are all about the image of the perfect couple." She shook her head and looked away. "Mrs. Swenson bashes all his old girlfriends in front of me, making disparaging comments about their social status or lack of proper graces." Jo raised her eyebrows. "She thinks I'm perfect. The daughter of a senator."

"Fortunately, you're not marrying Blake's parents. Blake seems to have his head on straight."

"You're wrong. I *am* marrying his parents. It's a package deal, you know."

"You don't have to invite the in-laws over every day."

She sighed. "My parents are no better. For my mom, it's all about the ceremony. For Daddy, it's another social contact. He's already schmoozing with Blake's father—they're golfing."

I leaned against the couch. "I want a simple wedding. Maybe even outside. If I get married, that is."

"I'd love that. Something simple, I mean."

She swirled the wine in her glass and fell silent. I quietly ate another slice of ham-and-mushroom pizza. When she spoke, her voice cracked with tension. "Have you ever felt you were being swept along by what everyone else wants?" She sniffed. "I don't even know if I love him. But everyone says we're the perfect couple."

I looked at her. Everything in me wanted to scream that she shouldn't marry Blake if she didn't love him. That she should fall for me as hard as I'd fallen for her. "Joanne."

She returned my gaze.

"Think about what attracted you to Blake in the first place. Maybe you can recapture it."

Jo looked beyond me, staring at the wall. "Blake is funny. Caring, in a Blake sort of way. I thought he was interested in a great relationship," she added, looking back in my direction. "I was wrong. Blake is interested in a trophy." She held up her arms and let her hands flop outward. "Me."

"What are you interested in? What are your dreams?"

"Love. A family."

I smiled. *My kind of girl.* "Blake could give you those things."

She put her index finger against my lips. "Don't talk about him."

"I—" my voice closed.

She leaned in and kissed my lips. I was so stunned; I didn't have the sense to close my mouth. And that made it warm and all the better. Her lips were salty.

She pulled away and looked at me. "Don't look so surprised. You've done nothing but worship me with your eyes from the moment we met."

I tried to swallow the lump in my throat. I was a puppy willing to follow her anywhere.

"That's what I'm looking for. Love from a man who adores me."

I kissed her again, and she leaned against me and cried.

I stayed, ignoring my studies, and watching the sunset from the back deck. She told me of growing up as a senator's daughter and asked me all about the simple life on the Chesapeake Bay.

Later, we were lying on a second-floor deck looking at the stars, talking softly as she stroked my hair. My hands were folded behind my head. I was in heaven, Romeo basking in the love of forbidden Juliet.

She lifted my T-shirt and placed her hand against my abdomen, just below my navel. My skin was alight with her touch.

My breath was short. "Your hand is cold."

She whispered in my ear, with her breath warm against me. "I'm nervous."

"Me too." I hesitated. "I should go."

"Blake won't be back until morning."

Now a light rain began to fall. With my memory interrupted, I flipped on my headlights and windshield wipers. I drove on with sadness on the seat beside me, a stark contrast to Joanne, who'd been a near constant companion since that fateful day when I painted the bathroom of a friend.

A light drizzle was falling when I arrived at my father's home—something I felt in my soul as well. It was only my second trip to the Eastern Shore since Dad had died, and I felt his absence like a cancer.

There were two cars in the driveway, one a green Volvo with a Shore Realty bumper sticker, and the other a generic sedan, a Ford, I thought. Nothing special, but in desperate need of a car wash.

I knocked and entered. Sally Protheroe, my chosen Realtor, shook my hand, and rolled her eyes in a way the couple behind her couldn't see. "Dr. Conners, what a pleasant surprise." She turned and gestured toward a couple standing in the den. "I was just showing the Reynolds your father's place."

The man, a burly fireplug, wore blue jeans and a flannel shirt that was unable to hide a tuft of white chest hair. In fact, hair was the first thing I saw: bristles of white prickling through the slick of a tanned scalp, small tufts growing from his ears, and more sprouting from bulbous nostrils in the center of a face wrinkled by the sun. His wife lurked behind him, picking up the few items remaining on the bookshelves one by one. A book about water birds. A photograph of the *Beautiful Swimmer.* She turned and inspected each one as if the accessories might be for sale as well. Or perhaps to let the trinkets of a life speak about the owner.

I watched as the man shook his head and mumbled something about Arab terrorists.

The man stepped forward, squinting at me. I extended my hand. "You Gus's boy?"

I nodded. "David Conners."

His grip was blue-crab strong. "Bob Reynolds. Known your father for years. Good man. Remember seeing you on the docks. Must have been this high." He held his hand at the level of his generous waist.

I smiled and wondered if he knew how to speak in complete sentences.

He glanced over his shoulder. "Lillie!"

She stomped forward and past me, but not before inspecting me up and down as if I might be part of the deal as well. After her scrutiny, she gave a nod. I must have passed.

Bob grunted. "Too bad. Arabs are taking over."

Sally cleared her throat. "We have four Somali families living in Tippins," she said, her voice a cheery contrast to Bob's. "They are hardworking people."

Bob took Lillie's arm, directing her toward the door. "Stealing jobs at the seafood processing plant."

Sally extended her hand to Mr. Reynolds, the hairy crab. "If you'd like to take another look, just give me a call."

The couple disappeared, leaving me alone with Sally. She held up her hands. "I've shown the place three times. Every time, your neighbor comes out with her scary uniform." She shook her head and handed me a stack of flyers highlighting the features of my father's house. "Try asking your neighbors to stay indoors," she said curtly. "Or you may never sell."

THAT EVENING AMINA showed up on my doorstep with a plate covered with aluminum foil. "I thought you might be hungry."

The truth was that I had been planning a personal encounter with Bill's pork barbeque and a generous amount of Texas Pete hot sauce. I peeked under the edge of the foil, intrigued. "What is this?"

She motioned toward the table inside the house. "Sit. Try it."

I smiled. "You don't have to do this."

"You are a man. My neighbor. And you are alone." She paused. She waved her hand in the air. "Besides, I have to cook for my father. To add another is no problem." She looked at me intently. "And you are Gus's blood."

I shrugged. "Come in. Will you have some, too?" I smiled. "You're not wearing your burka." I gave her a skeptical look. "Is that okay?"

"I'll risk it." She laughed. "The burka is not traditional Somali dress. The head and face covering is the result of fundamentalist Islam." She pointed at the plate in front of me. "Try it."

I recognized spaghetti pasta with some sort of seasoning. Piled high beside it appeared to be strips of beef mixed with peppers, onions, zucchini squash, and tomatoes. I sampled the beef first. "Mmm." It was lightly seasoned, a flavor I wasn't able to identify. "This is good."

"Camel," she replied.

I took another bite. "This is camel?"

She nodded. "To the Somali, this is a delicacy." She smiled. "It reminds me of home."

"Where do you buy camel meat?"

"My father gets it from a Somali butcher in Baltimore."

I ate quietly. Amina busied herself in the kitchen, steeping water and milk on the stove. She retrieved tea and spices from the cupboard. In a few minutes she poured two cups of steaming tea. "Somali tea," she explained. "Ginger, masala, and lots of sugar, just the way your father liked it."

I sipped the sweet mixture and nodded. "You made this for my father?"

"He was a man. He was my neighbor. He was alone."

I understood. It was as simple as understanding the role of a Somali woman in her society.

We shared tea quietly. I looked across the table at her and grieved the loss of my Joanne. "My wife asked me to leave," I said.

"For good?"

I shook my head. "Just to allow her time to sort out her feelings about our daughter."

She looked down. "In Somalia, the loss of a child is a stressful time. Many men leave their wives in the wake of such a tragedy." She spoke with a quiet confidence that made me wonder about her past.

"Is divorce common in your country?"

She laughed as if this should have been obvious. "Allah allows men to have four wives at one time. When a wife does not please a man, it is easy for the man to divorce her."

I set my cup on the table. "Thank you." I paused. "In Somalia, were you—" I hesitated.

"Married?" She nodded. "Of course. Somali women frequently marry young." She sipped her tea and didn't offer more information. "You are angry."

The surprise must have registered on my face.

"Ever since you mentioned your wife, your face has hardened."

I thought for a moment. She was right. I was angry. Angry at the beast who had stolen my baby and threatened my marriage. I held up my hands. Busted. "Yes." I waited for a moment. "I have a right to be."

"Anger rarely hurts the one whom you are angry toward."

"You are a philosopher now."

She shook her head. "I am experienced."

Across the cultural divide we sat, me unsure if I should probe, wondering if she was truly a friend or only behaving in a way that any young lady in Somalia would consider proper.

"My father will be home soon," she said. "I should leave."

"Would he disapprove of your visit?"

"Too much time alone with a man is dangerous." She stared at me for a moment and spoke again, but not before a smile teased at the corner of her mouth. "My father is fundamentalist. You don't want Mohamed to catch you with me alone."

I smiled back. "Or maybe you don't want your father to catch *you*."

She picked up the empty plate in front of me. My volley had evidently scored a point. "Good-bye, David."

That night, thoughts of the haunting beauty of my Somali neighbor seemed to hang over me like fog over the Chesapeake. I watched the clock, unable to sleep, and wondered about her warning. *What would her father do if he found me alone with his daughter?*

I rolled around beneath a thin sheet. Without air conditioning, it was the only cover tolerable.

Was she playing games with my head? Or was the threat real?

Amina's warning about being caught reminded me of the night when I thought Joanne and I were beyond capture. The night when my betrayal of my friend was nearly discovered.

I didn't leave her that night we'd had pizza and wine, watching the stars from the deck. I'd held her in my arms since midnight, basking in the freshness of discovery of her desire for me.

The night was pure magic for me. We had a connection I'd only dreamed of. She trusted me with her pain. Transparent, she cried over her desire not to hurt Blake or their families. We talked softly for hours and slept in each other's arms with her head against my heartbeat.

We were from different worlds, but we shared a similar journey. We both sought to escape the stereotypes that those around us assumed we'd take. I escaped the shore community where it was assumed I'd become a crab fisherman. Jo wanted to eschew the role of a wealthy woman living to throw parties for her uppity friends. We'd both overcome the opinions of others and charted our own courses. It was a commonality that bonded us securely in the beginning.

I awoke to the softness of her lips against mine. "I'll talk to him this morning. I'll gather the strength you've given me to call the wedding off."

I was about to respond, when we heard a key in the door.

Joanne uttered a hushed curse. "It's Blake."

I whispered. "He's not supposed to be off until eight."

"You've got to get out of here!"

The door opened against a chain lock. "Joanne!" Blake called. He knocked. And knocked.

I panicked. I was all for Jo telling Blake about us, but this wasn't the way it should go down. I stood, unsure of a plan. Hide?

Joanne pointed to the sliding door leading out to the second floor deck. "Go!" she whispered.

I stumbled into the Richmond night. I stared over the balcony. I only remember thinking it was too high. But that didn't matter. I had to get out of there. I climbed over the wooden railing, hung for a moment, and dropped.

The pain in my left ankle was scalpel sharp. Excruciating. I fell to the ground and explored the skin with my hand. Relieved that I didn't feel protruding bone, I struggled to my feet. *Bare feet. I've left my shoes inside!*

What else could I do? I hobbled to my car. I had time to sleep for two hours before heading back to the emergency room.

I drank black coffee and ate a pork barbeque sandwich for breakfast before calling Sheriff Reynolds.

"David Conners here, Sheriff. I'm calling to see if there is any progress in the investigation of my daughter's disappearance."

"No news, Dr. Conners. I'll let you know when we have something of substance."

"What about Riley Johnson?"

"Where did you hear that name?"

I wasn't about to give away my source. "Is he a suspect in my daughter's disappearance?"

The sheriff exhaled loudly into the phone. "I don't have a confession."

"Is he a suspect?"

"Everyone's a suspect."

"Has he been charged?"

"Not with kidnapping." I listened to a tapping noise, as if he was drumming his fingers on the back of the phone. "This is an official police matter. I really need you to let us handle this."

I understood. *Butt out!*

I didn't respond.

"Do you really understand the situation, Dr. Conners? The likelihood of finding a child alive after being gone this long is near zero."

Thanks for your encouragement.

I took a deep breath and tried to keep my voice steady. I needed this man on my side. "Please don't give up on finding my daughter."

"No one is giving up. I just want you to be realistic."

I wanted to scream. If it were his daughter, would he be arguing for realistic? A parent is designed to hope against hopelessness for their lost children.

"I'd like to talk to Riley Johnson," I blurted. "See what he might know."

"Absolutely not. I will not have you interrogating him. His case is a police matter."

I nodded and realized he couldn't see me. "Of course." I paused. "Keep in touch."

I hung up the phone. I wasn't sure what I had thought I could accomplish by talking with the suspect. I just felt compelled to do something. *Anything.* I wasn't ready to give up. It didn't help that the lack of a job to occupy my mind was either going to drive me crazy or spur me into action of another sort: retaliation. What I really wanted to do was torture whoever was responsible for taking my daughter away. That person must be made to pay, to suffer as I had.

I drove down the long lane leading to the Oyster Point Correctional Facility, thinking that it could have been the road to any upscale country club. A tree-lined drive, well-trimmed shrubs, azalea beds, and an expansive lawn that was golf-course green spoke a clear message: cheap prisoner labor.

Once inside, the upscale feel quickly disappeared. Everything was painted institution green or beige. I approached a glass that was reinforced with wire mesh. I cleared my throat and looked at the uniformed woman on the other side. "I'm here to visit a prisoner."

"Sunday is visiting day," she said pointing to a bulletin board on the wall to my right. "Regulations and requirements are listed."

"Thank you." I read the visitors policy. Bummer. No visitors except those on the personal list submitted by the prisoner the Friday preceding the intended visit.

I knew that wasn't going to happen. I started to walk away when an EMPLOYMENT OPPORTUNITIES notice caught my eye. The second job on the available list was clinic medical director. I stood reading for a moment and smiled. *Perfect*.

I walked back to the window. "I'd like an employment application, please."

She didn't look up. "Personnel office is the third door on your right down the hallway."

She pointed to the left.

"Thanks."

I threw back my shoulders and pressed the front of my shirt with my hands. Already a plan was forming. A perfectly wonderful plan of revenge.

Back at Dad's place, it didn't take long to find what I was looking for. There, sitting in the butter storage area in the door of the refrigerator, was a small vial of clear medicine that I'd bought for Dad but never used. Lupron, a powerful drug that blocked testosterone production—the chemical way to emasculate a man. Neat. Precise. Long-lasting. No blood.

I rolled the cool container in my hand for a moment, fighting back a surge of guilt. *Could I actually bring myself to a betrayal of professional ethics?*

I put the vial away and took out ingredients for tea. As I attempted to re-create Amina's beverage, I allowed myself to return again to the weekend Joanne and I betrayed Blake.

Saturday, the day after our pizza picnic and the day before my medical school graduation, I was pulling my last shift in the MCV ER and trying to do anything to avoid prolonged standing on my sore ankle. I'd wrapped it in an ace as soon as I arrived, but because of swelling, I had to loosen it twice in the previous three hours.

At two p.m. I was sitting at the nurses' station with my feet propped up, filling out the chart of a kid with an earache, when Blake walked in carrying my shoes.

"You left these at my house," he said, dropping my Nikes on the counter.

I felt a stab of guilt and kept staring at the chart in my hand. "Thanks. I took them off to paint." Inside, I winced. What a lame excuse. "Where were you this morning? Did you cut out on your shift last night?"

"Things were slow. The intern sent me home."

I looked at Blake, wondering if Joanne had broken the news that his best friend had stolen her heart away. His face was neutral. His voice, casual. No judgment. Eyes normal. No squinting. No look of suspicion.

I took a deep breath. *So far, he doesn't have a clue. But I still feel guilty.*

"So," Blake said, "Joanne's folks are throwing a party for me. Kind of a graduation deal. You're invited. Bring your folks."

I shook my head. "They can't. My father called. Mom isn't doing well. He's going to stay at the shore and take care of her."

Blake nodded. "That's tough." He knew all about my mother's battle with cancer. "Anyway, Joanne's dad is throwing a party for me over at their place. There's sure to be plenty to drink, and pretty young ladies for the eligible bachelors like yourself." He paused. I couldn't look up to meet his eyes. "Joanne's cousin will be there. I hear she's a firecracker. I could introduce you."

"I don't know, Blake, I—"

" 'Course, I'm sure she's no Joanne." I watched as he stared into space. "Joanne," he whispered. He shook his head as if bringing the world back into focus. "Maybe we could sneak away as a foursome and get some drinks."

"You're the guest of honor."

"I know, but Joanne's dad only does this to entertain his political friends. I'll make an appearance, then they'll all drink so much they won't care if I sneak off."

"Maybe," I said. "I'll be out of here by five." I interlaced my fingers behind my head. "My last shift before they have to call me 'doctor.'"

He walked away. "The party's at seven. I'll call you with directions."

Great, I thought, watching him disappear through the double doors leading into the Richmond heat. *All I need is a double date with Joanne and Blake.*

My next thought bothered me, but I shoved it back, trusting that Jo would come through in the right time. *She didn't tell him about us.*

When her senator husband walked into his study, Tricia turned her back and continued her conversation on her cell phone, walking toward the windows overlooking the James River.

"I didn't expect it to take this long," she said in a hushed voice.

The male voice on the other end of the phone was confident. "Hey, there's movement in the polls. Another few percentage points and he'll have McGinnis against the ropes."

She sighed. "I guess. I just want this to be over."

"There is one more thing I need you to do."

"What now? Gary's already getting the vote from every sympathetic parent with young children."

"Call more attention to it. Offer a reward."

"But—"

"It will make you appear more concerned. Just do it."

"Oh, so now you're stealing a Nike slogan?"

He laughed. "Anything to put the senator where we need him."

She closed the phone and turned to her husband.

"Who was that?" he said.

"Another fan who wants you to stay in office a little longer."

She walked to the window. "What would you think about offering a reward for information about Rachel?"

"Hmm. I guess that would be all right."

"It would make you look concerned."

"I *am* concerned."

She read the defensiveness in his voice.

"Now, now, *I* know you're concerned. We need the public to know it, too." She paused. "A little sympathy wouldn't hurt, either."

"I want to be in office because I stand for the right policies, not because my granddaughter has gone missing."

"Perception is everything."

"So you've told me." He began straightening the items on his desk. The senator always did that when he was nervous. And he always seemed nervous when she started talking about working political spin in his favor.

"We make a good team. You stand for the right thing, Gary. I make sure that everyone else finds out about it." *But you're too much of an idealist. People don't vote for the one with the best ideas. They need someone they can trust. Someone who has been involved in real life.*

"I'd like to offer a reward if it will help bring Rachel back."

And it will sway the on-the-fence voters in your favor.

She smiled and put her arms around his waist.

He patted her back absently. "You're good at this."

She lifted her head. "At what?"

"Being my support. Whatever success I've had, you've been there all the way. And you get no credit."

"My rewards are different."

"Like what?"

"I'm the wife of one of the most powerful men in America."

She rested her head against his chest. *Someday you'll learn just how much you owe me.*

⊷⊶

Three days later I again drove the long, well-manicured lane to Oyster Point Correctional Facility. Within a few minutes I was sitting across from Dr. Martin Saunders, an aged clinician who had spent more than forty years taking care of the state's prisoners. "Think you can do this?" he asked. "The patients are manipulative. They want out of work. They lie. They rape. They fake illness. They can't be trusted to do what you ask."

I nodded. "I've dealt with prisoners before," I responded with more bravado than I felt. "Back at MCV, I took care of the locked unit."

"Experience will help." He threw a film onto a lighted X-ray view box. "What do you make of this?"

I studied the film for a moment, thinking that he must want me to see something other than the obvious—a razor blade in the middle of the abdomen. Nothing else stood out. I shrugged. "Better tell the X-ray technician to do the film again, but this time check first to see if the patient has the razor blade taped to his skin."

"Oh, the tech did that the first time. There is no doubt. Nope. This jerk swallowed a razor blade. Wanted to go to the hospital. Claimed he wanted to die."

I sat quietly.

He prodded again. "You haven't told me what you would do."

"Send him to the hospital. Consult a surgeon. Can't let that razor leave the stomach; it will slice the bowel all the way to the other end."

Dr. Saunders chuckled. "That's what I did the first few times I saw this. But not anymore. This guy has undoubtedly taped the edges of the blade, so it protects his insides from being cut to pieces. He just wants out of prison for a few days. He wants a vacation in the hospital." He shook his head. "But he won't get it from me." He paused. "It will take a few months to get used to their tricks."

The doctor leaned forward, staring so intently that I had the urge to check the corners of my mouth or my front teeth to see if there was something embarrassing caught there. "How are you dealing with your daughter's disappearance?"

I sighed. "You know about that."

"Of course. I called Jim Ashton, your former boss. He told me about you. Said you were distracted at work."

"That's true." I hesitated. "But I need to do something with my time. I can't sit at home waiting for the phone to ring."

"He also said you were the best doctor he's worked with in a long time." He leaned back again. "He wants you back when you're able."

Nice to know he meant what he'd told me. I stayed quiet.

"Look, I'll be honest with you. I don't have doctors knocking themselves out to take this job. The pay is reasonable. We only open the clinic three afternoons a week, but you need to be on call for emergencies when the clinic is closed."

"Fair enough."

"You start tomorrow. Stop at personnel to get an ID badge. It will give you access to the clinic area."

That evening, I received an unexpected phone call. Joanne's mother.

"David," she said, "we need to talk."

Immediately, my defenses were on alert. Tricia never talked to me unless it furthered her own agenda. "Hi, Tricia," I responded. "I wasn't expecting to hear from you."

"I need to talk to you about Rachel. Do you really think she may be alive?"

"You're calling because you have your doubts as well?"

"I want to offer a reward. The senator would like to put up a hundred thousand dollars to any person giving information leading to her rescue."

"Wow." I hadn't anticipated that. But perhaps, given that an election was coming up, the media attention and sympathy surrounding a missing grandchild could be huge. I hesitated. "I don't want this turning into a media circus. Joanne isn't up for the attention."

"I'd like to call a news conference to announce the reward."

Of course. I wasn't sure how to respond. I was grateful for any help, but suspicious of her motives. "Why now?"

"For a time, we believed the information as we were given it through Joanne. After reading the newspaper, we've started to wonder."

I nodded. "A reward might help. Should the donor be anonymous?"

"I think not. The senator has an obligation to be transparent before his public."

Transparent? Sounds like political spin. "I'd like you to explain this to Joanne. Make sure she knows that I'm not initiating this."

"What, so I need to handle your wife?"

Your daughter.

She went on. "Perhaps we should keep this between us. Let her find out like everyone else."

Tricia was the queen of family secrets. *We mustn't have anyone reflecting badly on the senator.*

"I'm going to tell her," I said. "I don't want her in the dark on this."

"She'll try to ignore it. It's Joanne's way. A huge problem is looming in her face, and she wants to pretend it's not there."

I knew Tricia was right. But still Joanne had a right to know.

Tricia tapped her fingernails against the phone. They were her pride and joy. Long, lacquered, and brilliant red. "I'll set it all up. You needn't worry about a thing."

I was about to mumble my consent when she ended the call. Evidently, Tricia had communicated all she needed.

She'd called unexpectedly before—during my internship, before Joanne and I were married. I was finishing a patient workup in the ICU when my pager alerted me to call the operator. I picked up the phone and dialed zero.

"Dr. Conners, I have an outside call."

I listened as the connection was made. "Dr. Conners, this is Tricia Morgan calling. We met a few months ago at a party that we threw for a friend of yours, Blake Swenson. I believe you know my daughter, Joanne Morgan."

I held back a sigh. Just the mention of Joanne's name pitched my soul into torment. Since we'd begun our clandestine relationship, Jo had assured me that she was only discerning the proper timing to end her engagement to Blake. Yet as the weeks passed, I sensed a paralysis in her—an inability to slip from her family's expectations. I took a step away from the nursing station and faced the wall, my attempt at privacy. "Of course I remember you."

"I'll get straight to the point. Joanne's in a bit of trouble, and I know she trusts you. Of course, you, as a physician, understand the necessity of complete confidentiality, especially in matters concerning the senator's family."

I was puzzled and intrigued. "Of course."

"I need you to talk to her. Talk some sense into her stubborn head."

"What's the problem?"

"You know my daughter's engaged."

"Sure."

"But she's gotten into trouble."

I stayed quiet. Had Joanne told her mother about me?

"Joanne's pregnant. The wedding isn't for another two months. I know you have medical connections to take care of these things. I need someone out of town who I can trust."

I was stunned. *Pregnant? Is this why Joanne has been so reluctant to break away from Blake?* "I, uh—"

"I need for you to arrange an abortion."

I NEEDED TO tell Joanne of her mother's plans to announce a reward for Rachel's rescue. I held the phone and waited for her to answer, but I suspected she may not have wanted to talk to me. When the machine clicked on, I said, "Jo, pick up. We need to talk." I waited for another moment and then continued. "Look, call me. Your mother is planning some sort of media event to announce a reward for information about Rachel's disappearance. I thought you should know."

I hesitated a few more seconds before hanging up. *Better to let her call me on her own time.*

Joanne had barely parked the car in the garage and made it to the kitchen when the doorbell sounded. She looked through the peephole. Blake was grinning at the little circle like a schoolboy posing for a picture.

"Cute, very cute," she said, opening the door.

He shrugged. "I knew you'd be watching." He held up a plastic bag. "I brought Chinese."

She smiled. "Who invited you for dinner?"

"I did." He hesitated. "Aren't you going to ask me in?"

"Only because you have food and I'm starved."

He followed her into the kitchen where she set the table. "Beer?" she asked.

He picked up a photo of Rachel. "Sure."

He held the picture next to his face. "She has dimples." He smiled large. "Like me."

"Don't even go there, Blake."

"Maybe I think we should go there." He took the cool green bottle from her hand and tipped up his beer. "Ever wonder what it would have been like to be a family . . . you, me, and Rachel?"

"You weren't ready for kids, remember?"

"And you were?"

"I didn't have a choice." She paused. "At least, not a good one."

He sat at the counter on a tall oak barstool. He slumped over his beer, defeated. "I made mistakes, Joanne. I shouldn't have pushed you away."

"It's too late for regrets," she said, opening the lid to a plastic container. "Spicy shrimp." She pushed a second container toward Blake. "What's in here?"

"General Tso's chicken."

She loaded her plate and sat at the bar beside him. "You didn't exactly push me away."

He stared across the room, avoiding her eyes. "I didn't know what she would be like. Not having Rachel would have been such a loss."

Joanne sighed. "You didn't come to cheer me up."

"Sorry."

They ate without speaking, the clink of silverware punctuating the silence.

Finally, he spoke again. "You didn't answer my question. Do you ever wonder what it would have been like to be a family?"

"David wanted to be a father," she said. "You wanted to play."

"I wanted to be a father. In time." He finished his beer. "Rachel was our daughter."

"You don't know that." She levered the cap off a Heineken.

"It's time for you to move on, Blake. David raised her. Love made him her father."

"Love."

"Yes. You had your chance."

"What if we could start over? I'd do things differently, Jo. I could be a good father." He leaned forward. "What if Rachel is alive?"

"What if? What if?" She shook her head. "I can't live like that. I'm trying to move forward."

He turned toward her, touching her arm. "So let's move forward. Together."

She slid away from him. "We had our chance. There is too much between us that I need to escape." She took his hand. "Although we did have some great times."

"We could find happiness again."

"I'm married, Blake."

"I never stopped loving you."

She opened her hand and stood. "You should go."

"So where is your supportive husband?"

"Doing exactly what I've asked. Giving me space."

"We can start over. Recapture what we had. Before David."

She walked to the front door and opened it. "Thanks for the Chinese."

I lay staring at the ceiling, feeling a bit like an elementary school kid before the first day of class. Transitions were hard for me. I liked routine. Put me in a predictable situation and I'd shine. Rock me on waves of uncertainty and I started feeling seasick. Since Rachel's disappearance, it had been just like that. Everything felt sloshy. Unsteady. On unsure footing, I was afraid that I'd fall.

Tomorrow I'd have to face another change. A new job. Alone. All because someone stole my Rachel away.

Not that life with Rachel was ever really predictable. She had a delightful way of keeping me off guard. Not far enough that I feared that we'd capsize, but just enough left of center balance to keep things interesting and fresh. It had been that way from the beginning. And when I say the beginning, I mean the very beginning. Right from conception, Rachel added a topsy-turvy element to my life.

When I first learned of Joanne's pregnancy, I rushed to her side. I got off the phone with Tricia, swapped call nights with a fellow intern, and headed back to Richmond to see Joanne.

She opened the door as I knocked. She carried herself as if an invisible ball and chain weighed her down. Her normally perfect posture was bent with soul pain. Her eyes met mine. She didn't speak. Even then she was pulling into a protective cocoon, reluctant to communicate.

"Can I come in?"

She opened the door wider, and I stepped inside.

She sat down on a large pillow on the floor and leaned against an easy chair. I sat on the couch opposite her. "Your mother called. She told me about the pregnancy."

She stared at the floor.

"Is this why you've been avoiding telling Blake about us?"

"No."

I leaned forward, hoping to catch her eyes. I'd thought of what I'd say a hundred times on my way up from Newport News. "The baby doesn't change the way I feel about you."

She stared at me with hollow eyes.

"We can elope. We wanted to have a family someday. We'll just start a little sooner than planned."

She shook her head.

"Jo, I get this. The baby is Blake's?" I paused. "It doesn't matter. I love you."

"You still want me?"

"Of course."

She smiled as if she knew a secret. "You so don't get this."

"Jo, I understand you thought you were going to be with Blake forever. I wasn't even in the picture. I won't hold this against you."

"Blake doesn't know."

She didn't wait for my response.

"My mother wants me to get an abortion."

"She told me."

"She doesn't want Blake to find out. And of course, there's *the senator.*"

"You need to tell Blake. He has a right to know."

She sighed. "I thought you'd agree with my mom."

"So, you're still learning about me."

A smile tickled the corner of her lips. "So what is this, a marriage proposal?"

I swallowed hard. In my concern over the situation I hadn't even processed the fact that I hadn't ever really asked. "Oh, I messed this up, didn't I? I didn't even bring a ring."

"A ring doesn't buy love." She looked down at her hand. "I've already got a diamond. But not love." She lifted her eyes to mine. "Until now."

I dropped to one knee. "Joanne, will you marry me?"

She nodded and brushed back a tear. "Of course." She sniffled. And then she smiled a beautiful, face-transforming smile. "Oh, you so don't get this."

"What's to get?"

"The baby is yours."

JOANNE WAS SURPRISED when her mother picked up the phone.
When conflict was inevitable, Tricia's MO was avoidance. While
never close, her marriage to David had strained her relationship
with her mother to the point where they rarely spoke. Even a situation as large as Rachel's disappearance hadn't worked to bring
them together.

"Hello, Jo. I expected I'd hear from you."

"Mom, you can't offer a reward for a child who drowned in
the Chesapeake."

"If that's true, I'll save money, won't I?"

"This is about Dad's reelection bid, isn't it?"

Only the naïve would have believed her response as genuine.
"Oh, no! This is about finding my granddaughter."

"You're acting like a fool."

"What can it harm?"

"This will make me look like a fool."

"I'm willing to take that risk if it means finding Rachel."

"You're serious."

"David seems convinced."

"David is hopelessly optimistic." She sighed. "Like his
mother. She claimed she was going to beat her breast cancer right
up until the day it killed her."

"The senator is nearly lost in his grief over Rachel's disappearance. He needs to do something."

Joanne closed her fist and tried to keep her anger in check.

When she spoke, her voice was laced with sarcasm. "Convenient time for you to find an interest in your granddaughter."

Tricia gasped.

"Yes, mother, it seems odd that the granddaughter you rarely saw has now become precious." Jo raised her voice. "Since you can twist this tragedy to your advantage, you want to pay attention to her."

"Joanne," Tricia cooed, "you know we're disappointed that you didn't bring Rachel around more. I never had anything against little Rachel."

Only her father, is that it? "So why don't you do this little thing quietly?"

"Honey, we have to do this big. The media attention may help us get the word to someone who may know something."

The cap on her long-held bitterness blew off. "You've never hidden your feelings, Mother. You didn't think I was ready for motherhood."

"I didn't think you were ready to be roped into a marriage you'd regret."

"So why didn't you leave Rachel out of it? She did nothing to warrant being ignored."

Tricia sighed in the uppity gesture of someone too bored to be bothered.

Joanne's knuckles whitened against the phone. "Pardon me if I don't show up. I want nothing to do with this." She knew Tricia wouldn't be dissuaded, but still she felt compelled to voice her distaste for making Rachel's disappearance political.

"On the contrary, dear. If Rachel is found, your sorrow will be banished."

"And if she's not, Daddy will get the sympathy vote."

"A side benefit."

Joanne felt consumed by disgust. "Tell the senator I send my love." She ended the call with the push of a button.

First David. Then Blake. Now her mother. Why did everyone want to force her to hope for the impossible?

I spent the following morning getting familiar with the clinic within the walls of the Oyster Point Correctional Facility. At first glance the infirmary looked much like any other emergency room. But at closer inspection, the difference stood out. Other than an eye chart and a poster about sexually transmitted diseases, the walls were bare, off-white, and uninspired. The floor was concrete covered by a thin layer of vinyl that was laid out in a pattern of gray and white squares, except for two black stripes that seemed to correspond with the traffic flow. Glass windows with wire reinforcement separated the nursing station from the patient stretchers. A steel door leading from the hall was locked. A second, which led to the nursing station, was also locked.

Supplies in the patient area were minimal. No glass or sharp objects were allowed unless they were being used by the staff. Needles, syringes, and other items of routine use were in locked cabinets. Surveillance cameras were mounted here, in the hallway, and the nursing station. The final evidence that this was a different place was that the patients were generally cuffed to the stretchers.

I saw four walk-ins, prisoners not on the schedule but suffering from acute illnesses. Two from the same cellblock had strep throat, another suffered from diarrhea, and the last from an acute migraine. Six others were on the scheduled follow-up list, mostly patients finishing up antibiotics for minor infections.

The clinic functioned much like any other I'd been in, except that each prisoner came in with shackles around his ankles and was escorted by a guard.

The clinic was divided into three basic rooms: a waiting room, a business area that contained the patient files, and my clinical room, a large tiled area with two stretchers that could be curtained off for privacy. In the corner of the exam room sat a desk. That morning I'd made it mine by placing two pictures on the left side facing my chair: Rachel with her Pound Puppy, and one of Joanne, a photo she hated but I'd treasured since I'd snapped it when she was greatly and beautifully pregnant.

I had two employees. A crabby receptionist named Dorothy sat behind another wire-embedded glass window, scowling orders to each patient. She chewed cinnamon gum noisily and seemed permanently fixed to a chair that she rolled around the business office to complete her duties. The chair had a padded red vinyl seat too small to control the spillover of Dorothy's generous backside. It immediately gained my sympathy and admiration for standing up under that kind of abuse.

My nurse, a recent graduate, liked to talk and punctuated most of her sentences with a giggle that bubbled out every few lines like a period after a sentence. After our first conversation, I was sure she couldn't write an e-mail without adding those annoying little smiley symbols. She said her name was Jen, tee-hee.

By one o'clock I was sitting at my desk, finishing my chart work and thinking about lunch, when shouting from the waiting room disturbed my muse about hush puppies and oyster fritters. I looked up as the electronic lock snapped and the door opened, revealing two prisoners in front of a guard.

The first, a thin man, stumbled forward, straining against his ankle restraints. Blood trickled from a laceration above his eyebrow. Below the cut, his eye was swollen and purple, a grape bulging above sallow cheeks. His one good eye darted around the room, as if he expected another attack. His eyes lighted on my desktop and froze for a moment on my pictures.

The second man was muscled, something to appreciate even in the bulky orange jumpsuit. He appeared well, except for the fact that he held a handful of bloody toilet paper against his nostrils. He swore viciously at the first man.

The guard pointed at the stretchers. "Lie down, both of you!" He gestured with a meaty finger at the second patient. "Shut up." The guard looked at me. "Sorry to barge in. These clowns decided to liven up your day."

"What happened?"

"Fight in the lunch line," the guard said. "Newbie orientation. Johnson here hasn't learned that T-bone always sits in the chair closest to the line."

I studied the inmate whom the guard identified as a newbie. *Johnson? Riley? Can't be.* I tried to keep my heart from pounding. *Johnson is a common-enough name.*

Jen moved to set up a suture tray for me to repair the laceration.

I put on a pair of gloves and frowned as I leaned over the first patient. The cut was jagged, extending irregularly in three directions right along the ridge above the eye. I probed the wound, sliding my finger gently through the parted skin.

"Ow!" he said, pulling his head away.

"Sorry," I responded. "I need to check for a fracture." I looked at Jen. "Bone feels intact. Why don't you add a scalpel to the tray so I can debride back the rough edge for a smooth closure? I'll need some 6-0 nylon and some lidocaine."

Jen nodded and dropped a sterile scalpel onto the suture tray. The guard took a step closer, eyes bouncing between the prisoners and the tray.

I turned my attention back to my patient with the laceration, picking up a syringe and filling it with saline for irrigation. "When was your last tetanus shot?" I asked as I flushed the wound.

As I turned to refill my syringe, I was jerked backward by my collar. Suddenly I was cheek to cheek with inmate number two. He pressed the scalpel to my neck.

Although the guard had jumped to his feet and lifted a gun from the holster, he wasn't fast enough to stop T-bone from grasping the scalpel. The gun waved in our direction. "All right, T-bone, don't do anything crazy. There's no way you'll get away with this!"

T-bone tightened the grip he had around my neck, lifting me from the floor. I struggled for air. I felt a pinch of pain, then the sensation of warm fluid on my throat. I gasped.

The pressure on my neck lightened, but the scalpel remained cold against my skin, dancing just below my Adam's apple.

"Lay the gun down!" T-bone demanded.

The guard responded.

"Johnson!" T-bone shouted. "Get the gun! We're getting out of here."

Johnson picked up the gun.

"Give me the keys," T-bone ordered. "Lay down on the floor!"

The guard complied, but said, "Don't be an idiot, Johnson. You haven't even gone to trial."

Jen cowered on the floor. My eyes rested on hers, seeing only fear.

T-bone shoved me to my hands and knees on the floor. "Kill the men. The girl comes with us."

I saw the gun make a sweep in my direction. Time froze, and my thoughts rocketed with light speed. Random thoughts assumed control. This wasn't happening. I wish I hadn't been so annoyed by Jen's giggle. I would have tried to be more tolerant if I'd known it was to be my last day. I needed to make peace with my wife. I hadn't found my daughter.

Rachel! I need to find Rachel.

For a moment my eyes met with the one good eye behind

the gun. The look he gave me was one of pity. Perhaps he was sorry to have to kill me.

What does it mean to have your life pass before your eyes?

I'd heard it quoted a hundred times with the same doubt generated in my mind. But just then, with a gun in my face, I found the cliché to be absolutely true. Instead of joy over having lived and loved, my stomach bloated with regret. I looked into the barrel of the gun, shiny black metal bobbing just in front of my head. I closed my eyes.

I heard the sharp report of a gunshot and marveled at how painless it all was.

I didn't feel a thing.

I HEARD THE clatter of a metal tray and instruments striking the floor, followed by a dull thud. Jen screamed.

I opened my eyes to see T-bone lying face down on the clinic floor. Johnson knelt and slid the pistol toward the guard, then covered his face in his hands.

It began to register. Call me slow.

I hadn't been shot.

I lifted my hand to my neck. Blood. T-bone had cut me. But I wasn't dead. Johnson had turned the gun on his fellow inmate.

I scurried to the downed prisoner. I rolled him over to see a wet, red circle over his upper abdomen. I felt for his carotid pulse. It was whisper weak, the normal pulse now more of a suggestion than a demand. He gasped and stopped breathing, his face paralyzed in waxy white, his lips parted in a gaping O.

"Grab an IV," I said. "Do we have an emergency cart?"

"Get away from him." A hand clamped firmly on my shoulder.

I looked up to see the deputy guard. "He's dying."

"And he just tried to kill you. Let him go."

I shook my head. Letting death win wasn't part of the deal. Somewhere, I'd taken an oath that dictated that I preserve life. But in the confusion of the moment, I couldn't articulate it. "Get me some gauze. We need pressure on the wound."

"It's too late, Doc. He ain't going to make it, even if I'd let you try." He touched my shoulder again. "Now step away from the body."

I felt again for the pulse. This time, nothing. "We need to start CPR." I scowled at the guard. "It's my job to try to save him."

The deputy trained his gun on the kneeling prisoner. He spoke without making eye contact. "And it's my job to be sure every threat is neutralized."

Neutralized? Don't you mean dead?

I looked at my nurse assistant. With her hand lifted to her mouth, she shook her head rapidly.

Something wet touched my knee. I inspected my leg. Warm, sticky, and red. There was blood everywhere. The patient. His clothes. And on the floor, a widening circle of exsanguination and death.

The guard sounded an emergency code on his radio.

I went through the motions. An IV. CPR. After two minutes uniformed men arrived, and I slumped over the body, finding myself a bit breathless. I backed away. My hands and my clothes were red.

I looked at the prisoner, still kneeling on the floor under the watchful eye of the deputy guard. "You killed him."

He looked at me, his eyes wide. "I saved your life."

Three hours later, after giving my eyewitness account of the clinic slaying to four separate officers, I finally had a chance to repair inmate Johnson's laceration. When I set up the new tray and lifted a scalpel to straighten the wound edge, the guard touched his hand to his gun holster.

"Never, ever take your eyes off a sharp instrument, Doc," the guard said.

I was tempted to roll my eyes but knew better. Three other interviewing officials had given me the same reprimand. I looked at him, acknowledging my error. "First day," I muttered.

"Not mine," he said. "But it might be my last."

Jen gave Riley a tetanus booster. When I finished, a guard escorted the prisoner away.

I sat down with the patient record, opened the file—a thin one—noting that the inmate had some entry data from a recent admission physical, but otherwise no clinic visits. That's when my eyes came to rest on the patient's name. Riley Johnson.

Just as I suspected. My heart quickened. Perhaps fate might finally be working in my favor. I thought back to my conversation with the reporter. He said that Riley had been picked up for exposing himself to a child and attempting to lure her into his car.

I scribbled a note about the laceration repair and closed the file. The medical files had none of the entry data about charges, court appearances, or sentences. The medical record was just that: information about clinical matters only.

I reflected on the situation. *Riley Johnson.* What were the odds? His appearance felt like a gift. I wasn't against accepting a gift of divine providence, although I doubted God had much interest in my problems. Besides, I felt certain He would be unwilling to help me because my quest was justice. And in my eyes, that would be achieved through r-e-v-e-n-g-e. If memory of my Sunday school God served me correctly, He was supposed to prefer mercy.

I'd certainly done my share of praying since Rachel's disappearance in spite of the fact that the faith of my childhood had pretty much been pummeled during my college years. Truth be told, I'd cried more than I'd prayed. My mother always said tears were a prayer of sorts. She'd brush the hair back from my forehead and smile. *It's what happens when our hearts can't say the right word.*

But God hadn't answered my mother's tears, increasing my belief that God wouldn't provide personal help, yet that didn't stop me from hoping.

The simple fact remained: Riley Johnson had been brought to me. I hadn't orchestrated the fight. Sure, I'd thought about pulling his record, asking him to be brought in on any number of concerns. Perhaps his vaccination record might be incomplete. There may have been missing items of concern on his intake exam. But I didn't need to do anything.

And that, I thought, could be dumb luck—something I doubted—or providence, which I doubted even more, or just the randomness of the universe finally exerting itself in my favor. Maybe God had seen my tears and decided to drop a gold nugget in my path. Even if I was plotting revenge, it would have been silly not to imagine there had been some otherworldly influence in my day.

I thought about the murder I'd witnessed and the blood. The huge amount of blood. I'd never witnessed a killing before. *Will it change me? Will I be different because I've seen the purposeful taking of life?* Can anyone be the same after such horror?

I listened to the electronic snapping of the lock and looked up to see Sheriff Denton Reynolds. He took one look at me, and I thought I'd have to close his mouth myself. His jaw was apparently unhinged or paralyzed or maybe both.

He walked around my desk, staring at me as if I were an alien. I'd shed my bloody clothes, trading them for a pair of scrubs I'd found in the clinic's storage area. When he finally spoke, he was leaning across my desk, propped up by stubby, muscular arms. Beads of sweat glistened his forehead below his white flattop. "You!" He wagged his head.

Apparently, it wasn't a question.

It sounded like an accusation.

I wasn't sure what he'd been told, but my first impression

was that he thought I was the one who'd pulled the trigger. He took a small black notepad from his front pocket. "You're D. Gustafson Conners?"

"In the flesh."

Immediately, I felt heat rising in my face. I'd intentionally used my first initial and middle name to avoid calling attention to my application in case it was reviewed by the sheriff's department. Which it apparently was.

"Why are you here?"

"I needed work."

His eyes narrowed. He wasn't buying it. I was a lousy liar. "You expect me to believe—"

"Believe what you want, Sheriff. I needed some part-time work that would allow me the freedom and time to look into my daughter's disappearance."

The sheriff turned away, sighing as he ran his fingers across the top of his hair.

"Now maybe you can answer my question. Is Riley Johnson a suspect in my daughter's disappearance?"

"He doesn't admit to anything."

"I guess after today, that's not going to be an issue." I hesitated. "What of your suspicions? You must think—"

"He's guilty."

"W-what?"

Though we were alone, Denton Reynolds kept his voice low. "After the incident with the little girl, we obtained a search warrant. His place is full of stuff you don't even want to think about. He's into child pornography. He's—"

I held up my hand.

The sheriff stopped talking.

"My daughter," I said. "Did he take her?"

"We caught a fox in the henhouse and a hen is missing. What's your answer?"

My gut tightened. "Why did you continue to insist it was the Chesapeake?"

"Because that's what I really thought. Picking up Johnson has made me rethink everything."

The sheriff lifted a folder in the air. "I've read the deputies' reports of your view of today's events. Do you have anything else to add?"

"No."

He walked toward the door. "You took this job under false pretenses." He turned and faced me. "I should have you fired."

"Not true, sir. Dr. Saunders knew about my daughter because he checked with my former associate."

"You took this job so you could get information about Johnson."

I paused, unable to swallow the lie that would likely allow me to keep my job. "Yes."

He pushed his lips forward and nodded slowly.

"Can you be okay with that?" I asked.

"Maybe I'll have to be. We've been looking for someone to fill Dr. Saunders' shoes for six months."

Not exactly a ringing endorsement, but something I could live with.

"You won't have access to any police records. And any time you see Riley Johnson, you'll need a chaperone."

"I'm okay with that."

"You have to be."

He put his hand on the door, paused, and spoke again. "Why do you think he did it? I mean, why would he kill when there was another option?"

"Maybe he didn't see any other option."

"I'm not buying that. He could have given the gun to the deputy."

"He felt sorry for me."

"What?" The sheriff didn't attempt to hide his disbelief.

"In the moment he held the gun on me, his expression . . . his eyes . . ." I paused, realizing it made little sense. "He just seemed sorry, that's all."

Reynolds shrugged. As he left, he added. "I'll be watching you."

THAT EVENING I moped around Dad's place like a lost mutt dropped at the side of a country road. I recognized things around me, but nothing had the smell of home. Perhaps it was the traumatic day I'd had. Or maybe it was just the natural course of being away from Jo for two weeks—longer than I'd ever been since we married. As I slumped on the couch, I found myself on the verge of tears. I was lonely and out of my element without her. I couldn't describe it beyond the sense that my soul was out of breath. It wasn't physical, like what I'd experience running on the beach, an act that drove my respiratory and heart rate up in compensation. It was emotional air-hunger. I'd shown up in the den of my soul, and no one was home.

I paced, ate a peanut butter and jelly sandwich, and retreated to the pier with a six-pack of Samuel Adams to quiet the ache. Granted, the feeling wasn't entirely new. Ever since Jo had entered my life, I'd never felt completely at ease without her near.

The warmth of the day was melting away, but the humidity still owned the air. Night approached, and the sky had begun a colored transformation toward darkness. The cicadas' symphony grew with the loss of light, and the serenade washed over me, combining with the alcohol to give sound to the buzz behind my eyes.

I stared over the marsh toward the salty Chesapeake and let the peace of the water soothe my heart.

Joanne and I eloped just before a long weekend away from my internship. We spent our honeymoon in a cabin in Pipestem, West Virginia, a far cry from the European extravaganza that Blake had schemed up with Joanne's mother.

I was sitting on a small deck overlooking a small creek, seeking the solace of the trickling water and dreading my return to the real world where I'd have to face Joanne's parents and explain what we'd done. There would be no envious church wedding for the paparazzi seeking a glimpse of the senator's daughter. There would be no happy couple gallivanting around Paris, no linking of the upper-crust families for political or social gain. There would only be me as their son-in-law, the geek son of a waterman who had stolen their daughter away.

I felt her touch on my shoulders. She massaged gently before encircling my chest and kissing the top of my head. "Are you worried about going back?"

I nodded. "How about you? How do you feel?"

"I'm free, David."

I closed my hand over hers, clutching it to my chest. "I'll bet they know. Your mother has her network. Did you see the flash of recognition from the guy at city hall? He gave us the license, but I'll bet he made a phone call after we left."

"They'll know soon enough, anyway." She paused. "Don't worry about them. My mother will be upset for a while, but in time, she'll warm to the idea of us."

I forced a chuckle. "Grandma Tricia."

"*That*, she's not ready for."

"Let's not talk about your mother. We'll deal with her tomorrow."

I turned to drink her in. Joanne the beautiful. "Would you like to walk with me? Let's explore along the creek."

She took my hand, tugging me toward the little cabin. "Later," she said, loving me with her eyes. "Later."

Now, the marsh blurred from the tears of my loneliness. Jo was gone. I needed to find a way into her heart again, but I feared it meant giving up on the only other gift I treasured above this world, our precious Rachel.

And then my wife was there with me, sitting on the pier. I leaned toward her to kiss her. "Joanne," I whispered. "You came back to me." She pulled away, and I felt the sting of her slap against my face.

I touched my cheek as reality emerged. *Amina!* I shook my head. *I had been dreaming.*

Fire burned behind the dark eyes of my neighbor. "You dare call me by her name!" She shoved me away from her, nearly sending me into the water. "You're drunk."

"No, I——"

Amina scrambled to her feet and stomped toward her house, grabbing the material from her shoulders and covering her head as she went.

I listened to the slam of her back door and waited.

My heart sank with the sun. Now, to add to my loneliness, fear tickled the edge of my heart. The night chorus of cicadas could not soothe my soul. *What have I done?*

And what will Mohamed do to me?

The next day I rose early and washed down four ibuprofen and two extra-strength Tylenol with a tall cup of black coffee, and willed my brain to stop throbbing.

I went to work an hour early to debrief with Jen. I'd hoped to gather my whole staff—all three of us—to talk through the violent event, but Dot declined. She'd been a fixture at the prison for years. There was little she hadn't heard or seen, and she wasn't about to let yesterday interrupt her stride. I couldn't say I knew her, but if I had to guess her modus of operandi, I'd say that at the end of the day she escaped work and found her solace in a generous serving of gooey comfort carbs.

I sat across from Jen on a section of orange chairs bolted to the floor in the waiting room. The chair was hideously uncomfortable, the vinyl covering only a ruse of padding, a disguise of sorts, to hide the institutional hardness beneath.

I looked at her, really looked at her, for the first time. She was young. Brunette hair cropped neatly above her ears, accenting a face in want of the sun, pale but pretty in a fragile sort of way. She wore clinical white, definitely not the right thing for her. Petite, with a posture that spoke of timidity. When she spoke, giggles still punctuated her speech. Today I didn't mind. She'd earned the right to exhibit nervous, annoying habits.

"It wasn't until I went to the bathroom that I realized I had blood splatters on my face." She knotted her fingers in her lap and leaned forward. "It was so gross. There was a small spot here," she said, pointing. "To the left of my mouth. Almost unnoticeable, but horrifying, like I'd left a bit of ketchup stain on my face. I leaned closer to the mirror and about freaked. I had small specks of blood dotting my face like small freckles."

"I was covered," I said. "My hands. I must have scrubbed my nails for ten minutes."

"My mom got all weird about it. Started talking about the Passover, telling me how the blood sprinkled on the doorpost saved the sons of the Israelites. She's always talkin' that way, finding something religious behind everyday life. She said that man's blood kind of saved us. It was sprinkled on me and kept me from being taken hostage or something." She seemed to be concentrating on rubbing a spot on the back of her hand.

I nodded, giving her an assurance that I understood. Which I didn't, but I didn't want to let on. I was supposed to be the strong one here. The boss. The leader to help Jen process a taste of hell. Instead, I felt like a poser.

I studied my hands and thought about telling her how pitifully I'd coped with yesterday's horror. I got drunk, almost kissed my neighbor thinking it was my wife, and spent the night sleepless in anticipation of Mohamed's revenge. I thought it best if I held my tongue, but I told her anyway.

I looked up. She held her hand up to her mouth, with her eyes bright with delight. She couldn't contain her laughter. She laughed at me, pouring cold water over my openness. I'd taken a chance to help her see that we were both struggling. I'd bared my soul to a woman without a heart.

And then I laughed, too. Her giggles actually became the trigger that released my dark introspection and let me laugh at myself.

We organized ourselves for work and saw ten patients, three of whom suffered from strep throat. It looked like block D was a veritable streptococcus playground. I thought about putting the whole lot of them on prophylactic penicillin, but didn't, knowing I would be placing them all at risk for significant drug side effects.

As I walked out the door, Jen mumbled something about jihad and warned me to lock my doors.

As the door closed, I could hear her laughter behind me.

That evening, I stayed away from the house, preferring to take a leisurely dinner at Captain Billy's down in Oyster. And for an hour, crab cakes drizzled with red pepper sauce, hush puppies, slaw, and steak fries were the only things that mattered.

But that was before I got back to Dad's place. I glanced at

Amina's. No seafood delivery truck. That may have meant Mohamed was out for late deliveries in Baltimore or beyond. Nonetheless, I felt a notch relieved and was just sitting down with a cold beer when I heard the crunch of gravel and a familiar diesel rattle to a halt.

It was five minutes by my watch from the time Mohamed arrived home, until he knocked on my door. I looked at him through a slit in the curtain. He'd had just enough time to hear Amina's version of my adulterous behavior.

He wasn't smiling.

I was toast.

I thought of leaving through the back door. I looked at the beer bottle in my hand and hid it behind the TV. *Best not to offend him right off.* I answered the knock in spite of my misgiving.

Opening the door, I said his name, immediately aware that I'd added a giggle to follow his name. Just like Jen did. "Mohamed," I said, holding out my hand. "So nice to see you." Another giggle.

He took my hand and shook it.

"Would you like to come in? Why don't I make some tea?"

He smiled. It was really only a half smile. In fact, if I hadn't suspected that he was here to extract my liver for touching his daughter, I'd have thought he seemed happy. He pointed at the couch. "Mind if I sit? It's been a long day. *Safar wanaagsan.*"

"What's that?"

"A good journey."

I put water on the stove and rattled around making tea as close to the way Amina did as I could. From there I could hear him chuckling.

"Dr. Conners," he said from the den. "I believe I have something you want."

"Something I want?" I stifled a giggle just as it attempted to skirt out from behind my lips. Stupid anxiety.

"A deal."

"What sort of deal?"

"After we share tea. We will talk."

Great. He probably wants to sell me his daughter.

I brought him the tea, which he slurped noisily. I thought silently about how to react to such a deal that he might propose. *I'm a married man. Certainly he knows that. Of course, in Somali culture, Amina says I could have four . . .*

"You want something from me," he said, setting his cup down and capturing my gaze.

I squirmed in my seat. "I can explain. You see—"

"No need to explain," he said, waving his hand. "These things happen all the time."

"They do?"

"Sure." He leaned forward. "But there has to be give and take. You get something. You give something. Understand?"

"Of course. But Mohamed—"

"I can tell you that it's true. She's a beauty. Your father certainly thought so."

"Dad? Oh sure, he was a kind man. He sure could recognize quality."

"I'm sure she's expensive."

"Oh yes. She is, she is," I echoed. I pushed back from the table. "I'm not sure we should be talking about—"

"I can pay you. It might be best if you took a little down and then a little more each month until—"

"You want to pay *me*?"

"Of course."

I shook my head. "No."

He stood up. "You are biased against me because I'm Somali."

I held up my hands. "No, it's not that."

He pulled out a flyer, one I recognized as an ad for Dad's

crab boat. He slapped the paper. "My money is good. I'll treat her well."

You want my boat?"

He nodded. "The *Beautiful Swimmer.*"

Relief!

"I'd like the whole operation. Pots, boat, everything." He smiled. "You want something from me," he said, "my money."

"And you want my boat."

"Are you understanding me? Sometimes I struggle with English."

I smiled. "Of course," I responded. "Let's make a deal."

THAT NIGHT I dreamed. I've never been one to put much stock in psychobabble or dream interpretation, but as I awoke, I felt the night might have changed my mind. Or made me aware of something changing in me.

Oh, I've had weird dreams before, but they were nonsensical enough that I didn't wake with the idea that they held any real threat for me. I'd do something really stupid in a dream, wake in a sweat, and then find relief in knowing I could never do anything so horrible or stupid in real life.

But last night was different. I dreamed of shooting Riley Johnson, just like he'd done to T-bone. I held a gun to his chest and listened to him admit he'd taken my daughter away. And then I killed him. In the aftermath euphoria of my dream, I slipped awake, but this time, instead of horror at what I'd done and relief in knowing it wasn't true, the first thing through my mind was disappointment that it wasn't real.

And that scared me more than the dream.

I kept the stupid dream on the back burner throughout the day, letting it simmer as I drove Dad's pickup truck all the way to a landscape nursery in Dover and back, returning with sod for the yard and an assortment of bayberry bushes and azaleas.

I mulled it over while I worked, pulling out old bushes and replanting new ones, and laying sod along the drive where the grass had long since disappeared into the sand.

Each time I went over the dream, I reached the same conclusion. Someone, whoever it was, hadn't just slipped in and stolen my daughter away. That someone had ripped a canyon in my life, extracting my soul at the same time.

I'd never been a vengeful guy before, but as I tamped the dirt around the bushes into place, I considered, *Wasn't "an eye for an eye" biblical?*

Although I understood the reasons, I mourned the change.

That afternoon, from the safety of my kitchen window, I watched Amina hanging wash on the line, aware of the tension she created in my gut. She was beautiful, and I longed for comfort. She'd suffered loss in her life as well.

Sharing our sorrow was only natural and good.

So why did I feel so guilty?

A week later I lowered the truck window on my way to work. The wind swept in, Eastern-Shore salty and heavier than air has a right to be. I lay my arm in the open window, looking at crabbing boats off in the distance. Thoughts of Mohamed purchasing the *Beautiful Swimmer* brought laughter at how confusing our conversation had been. Jo and I had experienced similar confusion the day we broke the news of our marriage to Tricia and the senator.

On that memorable day we drove into the circle drive of the Morgans' riverfront home and parked behind a police cruiser. "What's with the police?" I asked.

"Probably nothing. Daddy always has security around."

I shrugged, taking the keys from the ignition. I looked at Joanne. "Ready?"

"I can do this," she said, sounding unconvinced.

"Sure you can," I said brightly. I kissed her, and we exited the car together.

Joanne rang the bell once and opened the door, leading the

way through an expansive tile foyer into the kitchen. Around an old oak Amish-made table sat her parents, Gary and Tricia, Blake, and a state patrolman in uniform.

Blake and Tricia stood and rushed to embrace Joanne.

"Joanne, we were so worried," Blake said, taking her hands in his and leaning in for a kiss; he was awarded one full on the mouth.

I stared at Jo as reality dawned. *You didn't tell him about us!*

Gary stood, but kept his place behind the table, never the one to make too much of outward displays of affection. "Where were you, dear?"

Joanne stood there, the proverbial deer in the headlights. I froze, unsure what to say in front of Blake.

I cleared my throat. It was my place to speak for her now. I traded glances with Jo and her mother and kept my voice low for Joanne's ears only. "Maybe now's not the time to discuss this." I offered a plastic smile to the men at the table. A little louder, I said to them. "No need to worry, guys. She's not really missing."

The senator chuckled and raised his eyebrows. "Probably just some wedding scheming by the bride and the best man." He nodded toward Blake. "Can't say in front of you, I'll bet."

Tricia looked at me and winked. It was a quiet interchange, something meant only for me. "I'm sure there were good reasons for Joanne to find a little time away before the big day." She gestured toward Blake, pulling Jo away from him. "Come, dear." She waved at the men. "I need a little time with my baby girl." She smiled at Blake. "You won't mind. We'll just be a moment."

I followed them down the hall to the master bedroom suite. When I entered the bedroom with them, Tricia gave me a look. *Who invited you?*

"This concerns me, too," I said.

Tricia sighed. She took Joanne by the shoulders. "How are you holding up?"

Jo's answer was tentative. "I-I'm okay."

"I don't think I need to reiterate how important it is to keep your little secret to yourselves," Tricia said.

"Our secret?" I responded. "You *know*?"

She turned to me. "Of course. And I thank you for rescuing my daughter." Tricia gestured toward the bed. "Sit down, honey. You must be tired."

Joanne sat, and we traded looks. *What's going on?*

"Where did you go?"

"West Virginia," I said. "A quiet little cabin in a state park."

"And no one knew you were there?"

I shook my head.

"And that's the way it will stay." She paused, taking a deep breath. "Now, let's get back out there and reassure the men in our lives that everything is fine."

Tricia turned to leave.

I cleared my throat. "I can't do this."

Tricia whirled. Ready for attack. "You can and you will."

"I can't keep this a secret."

Tricia's eyes darkened. "Haven't you ever heard of patient confidentiality?" She squinted at me. "Or do you have a political agenda of your own? I'll have you know I'll have your medical license so fast that—"

I held up my hands. "Whoa, what are you talking about? I'm not your daughter's doctor." I paused, looking at Joanne. "I'm her husband."

Tricia dropped her head forward and lifted her eyes. A look that questioned my sanity. "You're *what*?"

"You heard him, Mother," Jo said, standing and taking my arm. "David and I are married. We were honeymooning in West Virginia."

Tricia pushed the door shut and backed up against it. She spoke through a forced whisper. "You did an abortion on your own wife?"

Jo shook her head. "No, Mother," she gasped. "We're going to have a baby."

Tricia's jaw slackened. "But—" She coughed. "You, you—" She halted. "You're serious."

I put my hand over Jo's as they encircled my arm. "Completely."

"But you love Blake! The wedding!" She braced her hands on her hips. "I just made a down payment on a caterer and confirmed seven-hundred people on our guest list."

Jo shook her head. "No, Mother, *you* love Blake." She squeezed my arm. "I love David."

I smiled. "Keep the caterer. We can have a big reception."

"I'll do nothing of the sort!" Her eyes narrowed. Blake knows nothing of this." She pointed at me. "You conniving—"

I looked at Jo. "You told me he knew."

She winced. "I tried to tell him. I even got out the words, 'I'm getting married,' but before I could get to the 'to David' part, he swept me in his arms and said, 'I know, I know!'"

That hurt. Bad. But I knew we couldn't work it out in front of Tricia, so I kept it all in.

Tricia, however, didn't hold anything back. She glared at her daughter. "Ruin your life. See if I care."

I DROVE THROUGH the entrance to the Oyster Point Correctional Facility. I was due to see Riley Johnson back in the prison to check on his laceration repair. I knew that without intervention I might not get to see him again after that, so I wanted to make the most of the opportunity. I couldn't just outright ask him if he'd taken my daughter. I was sure he wouldn't admit it. So I'd devised another plan. He needed to be softened first.

A few minutes later, walking into the prison clinic, I slipped my hand inside my white coat pocket and closed my fingers around a small syringe.

I felt my pulse quicken and sensed a knot forming in the top of my gut. *Just what the doctor ordered.*

This time Riley Johnson came in ankle cuffs and handcuffs and sat under guard on the exam table. He appeared older than before. I noticed gray streaks in his otherwise greasy cake of dirty blond hair.

I inspected the suture line. No redness or drainage. Edges clean. Minimal early scar formation. "The wound looks good." I looked at Jen. "I'll need a scissors to remove these sutures."

Jen moved away.

"You're just like me," he whispered.

"Excuse me?"

"I saw the way you watched her," he said, jerking his head toward Jen. "She's young enough to be your daughter."

I wanted to point out we were only about ten years apart. I

knew it wouldn't help. He was just trying to get under my skin, and he was succeeding.

He used crude vernacular to ask me whether I was intimately involved with her.

I looked at the guard. Apparently he hadn't heard a word.

I ignored Riley.

"I'll bet you'd like to be. She's young. Pretty. You're married, experienced. You could teach her."

I didn't attempt to keep my voice low. "You know nothing about me."

I tugged on a suture as I slid the scissors beneath it for removal.

He winced.

I did it again. Because I could.

He whispered a curse.

"The man I killed was going to kill me," he whispered again. "My lawyer thinks he can get me off because it was self-defense. You could be my witness."

"You come in here and insult me, and then expect me to do you a favor?"

"I was just pointin' out how we was the same."

I felt heat in my face. "I am nothing like you." I paused. "What are you in for?"

"I ain't done nothing wrong," he said. "I offered a little girl a ride, that's all."

I didn't reply.

"I need something for sleep."

"We don't give out sleeping medicine, Mr. Johnson."

He cursed my paternity this time.

I glanced at the guard, a young man. His expression hadn't changed. He'd heard it all a thousand times. Another cursing inmate didn't faze him.

I opened Riley's chart and sat at my desk, filling in a progress note for today's visit. When I looked up, Riley's eyes were on me, staring at my space. I shifted the small photographs of my family toward my eyes only. Everything about this man creeped me out. I didn't think I'd looked on anyone with the same disdain before. It wasn't a good feeling. I felt repulsion, rage, and irritation. And as if that wasn't enough, I found myself feeling a bit guilty for my inability to view him as a decent human being. As a physician I had sworn to treat people regardless of their social and ethnic background. *But does that mean I have to treat child molesters well? Especially one who may have taken my daughter?*

I felt my pulse pounding. I had decided that if I ever had the chance to even the score against Rachel's kidnapper, that I would do anything in my power to seize it.

I slipped my hand in my lab-coat pocket and felt the syringe I had taken from Dad's refrigerator back home. *What if he's not responsible for Rachel's disappearance?*

He's still a creep. And a murderer. Don't forget that.

I sat thinking for a moment before coming up with another idea. I reached for my coffee cup and brushed Rachel's picture as my hand passed, knocking it over. This time, I set it upright, but tilted at an angle where I was sure Riley could see it.

Then I sat back and observed his reaction.

His eyes were blue-gray and set too far back in his skull. And when they passed over Rachel's picture, I saw him blink and look again. He stared, brought his cuffed hands to his mouth, and pulled his hand across a bushy mustache.

And I saw something else, mixed with the evil that lurked in blue-gray shadows.

Recognition.

It was only a glimmer, but something flashed before he lowered his eyes to the floor.

And in that moment of recognition, I wanted nothing more

than to hurt him the way he'd hurt me. The way he'd hurt Rachel.

I stood and walked toward him, stopping only when I could smell his breath. I kept my voice barely above a whisper, trembling not from fear, but from anticipation. "Do you know that little girl, Riley?"

"Take me back to my cell." He started to stand.

The guard took one step toward him.

"Hold on a sec," I said with all the casualness I could muster. "My patient needs an antibiotic."

I turned to Riley. "It was a dirty wound, Mr. Johnson," I said. "Just a precaution." I touched his forehead. "The wound edge is a little pink."

I rolled up his sleeve, swabbed his shoulder with an alcohol swab the syringe into his arm up to the hilt of the needle.

I hesitated.

You deserve this.

Another expletive.

I emptied the syringe contents into the muscle—a dose enough to last four months. "There," I said, pulling down his sleeve. "I'll need to see you in a week to do a recheck on the wound."

That evening Joanne left the Emergency Room through the automatic double doors and took a deep breath. The day had not been easy. She'd helped with two codes, one an overdosed teenager whom they'd saved, and another they hadn't: a seven-year-old girl who had drowned in a backyard pool. Jo turned right and padded toward the parking deck on heavy feet. *Why'd she have to be seven?* The memory was still fresh and threatened her with tears. Again. She'd put her arms around the mother and cried. In truth, she'd cried for her own daughter, but the patient's mom was genuinely touched by Joanne's display of emotion. It felt good to be able to identify with someone else's pain. She walked away, having seen the first glimpse of a silver lining in the dark cloud of her pain.

"Beautiful evening."

Joanne turned toward the familiar voice. "Blake, what are you doing here?"

He shrugged. "Waiting to see you."

She turned her back and kept walking.

"What? Is that any way to treat a friend?"

She didn't turn around. "It's been a hard day."

He sped up to walk beside her. "Buy you a drink?"

"Okay." She stopped. "I don't think so."

"*What,* Joanne? What am I supposed to do with an answer like that? Yes-no, yes-no. Mixed messages abound with you, Jo."

"Deal with it."

She stomped across the parking lot, holding out her keychain to use the remote to unlock her car. He followed at her elbow.

"You weren't ever very good at listening to me say 'no,' were you?"

"On the contrary, I'm listening to all the messages, not just the ones you send with your voice. They're very confusing."

"I'm not sending any message except one. I'm going home."

"Jo, what's wrong?"

"Blake, it's been a horrible day. And I don't think we should be hanging out. I'm married."

"And I'm a friend."

She completed his sentence. "Who wants to be more." She got into the car.

"Have a drink with me. What are friends for? You need to unwind from your day. Tell me all about it."

"I need to go home." She reached for the door handle.

He held the door. "Did you lose a kid today?"

She felt a lump swell in her throat. She didn't want to do this here. "I—how did you know?"

"Hunch." He hesitated. "Want to talk?"

She pulled on the door. "I need to go home."

She didn't look back until she got to the exit of the parking lot. Then she glanced in the rearview mirror and saw Blake with his head hanging forward over slumped shoulders, still standing in the same spot.

His image touched a memory of a day of mixed happiness and sorrow. Perhaps it was his eyes or the longing expression, but nonetheless, it was the same unforgettable face he'd worn the day she and David broke the news of their marriage to her family.

On that day Tricia had exited the bedroom after receiving the news, then slammed the door, leaving Joanne and David together. He looked at her. "We've got to tell the rest of them."

She nodded, a lump in her throat. "Let's go."

When they got back to the kitchen, they found Tricia pouring gin into glasses and setting them in front of Gary and Blake. Fortunately, the police officer was gone.

Gary smiled. "What are we toasting?"

"Our marriage," David said.

Joanne watched as the information registered on Blake's face. He'd never been one to disguise his emotion, and she could see hurt, longing, and anger all rising from beneath the surface.

"Here, here," Joanne's father said, lifting his glass.

"You're not listening, Gary," Tricia said. "We're not toasting anything. This is an anesthetic," she said, adding another splash of gin into her glass, "not a celebration!"

He pulled his glass away from his mouth. "I don't understand."

"Our daughter has eloped," Tricia began. She pointed at David's chest. "With him!"

Blake stepped forward, leaving his glass on the table. "What's this all about?"

Joanne wanted to speak, but froze, her eyes fixed on Blake's angry expression.

David moved in front of her. "Blake, I never intended for it to be this way. But the more I saw of her, the more I fell in love." He paused. "And fortunately for me, it soon became a two-way street."

Her mother heaved a too-obvious sigh and sucked noisily on her drink.

"Mom!"

She gestured with her glass. "Your wedding was going to be the highlight of the season. I've got to call the caterer, the minister, the string quartet, the videographer, the florist, and my seamstress," she added, numbering off each item with a finger. "You've decided to ruin your life and drag the good Morgan name down with it."

A large knot formed in Joanne's throat.

Blake's head dropped forward. "Joanne, is this really true?"

"I—I—" She halted, feeling the first hint of tears. Finally, when she spoke, the words accelerated like a car going downhill without brakes. "I tried to tell you. But the plans kept getting bigger and bigger. Our parents seemed so set. You seemed so set." She paused. "I was afraid. I felt so trapped."

Blake's eyes locked on David's face. "You betrayed a friend."

Tricia slammed her glass down on the counter. "And you've betrayed this family," she said to Jo.

David looked down. "I'm sorry, Blake. I did not do this to hurt you."

Blake clenched his fist. Joanne's father moved around the table and put his hand on Blake's shoulder. Blake pulled away, shaking his head. "He's not worth the punch," he said, pointing at David. He looked at Jo. "But I'll fight for you."

Joanne winced and held up her hand. "It's too late. We've eloped," she said, flashing her ring.

Blake's expression hardened. He pushed past Gary, passing between Joanne and her new husband, a hand on each shoulder, giving them a shove apart. With that, he stomped off and out of the house, slamming the door as he left.

David took a deep breath. "That went well."

"So," the senator said, clearing his throat. An awkward silence followed. He shuffled his feet. "What about that toast?" He held up his glass of gin. "To the bride and groom," he said.

No one else responded. The senator shrugged and drained his glass.

Tricia ran from the room.

Joanne couldn't hold back the tears. She couldn't shake the image of Blake's anger and disappointment. *Oh, why did love have to hurt?*

That night loneliness engulfed me like a fog. I walked around the house, touching pictures of Jo and Rachel, hoping to find a spark to rewarm my heart where the coldness had crept in. Instead, all I felt was loss.

Is it possible that I'd let Rachel take over the biggest part of my heart, so that when she disappeared, little was left for Jo and me to hold to?

Can I ever win Jo's love again?

Another thing bothered me. All I'd thought about for weeks was getting revenge. But now that I'd sipped from its well, I felt no fulfillment. I still felt thirsty.

Staring at Joanne's picture, I realized my focus had shifted. Perhaps it was because Denton Reynolds had decided to spill the beans on Riley Johnson. Or perhaps it was the natural course of these kind of disasters. I'd moved from focusing on finding my daughter to revenge. And somewhere in the process, bitterness had moved in front of hope.

It scared the life out of me.

I sat down on Dad's dingy couch and called Joanne. "Hey," I said when I heard her voice. "I just needed to hear your voice."

"How are things?"

I sighed. "I got a job. It's not much. An afternoon clinic at a correctional institution." I stopped. "How are you?"

"Mostly good." I listened as she breathed. "David, what are you doing? You've got so much promise. You're the best family practice doctor Richmond has seen in a long time. Remember the recognition given to you?"

The last year at my program I was given the Hiram Long Award for Excellence. The staff all called it "Resident of the Year." I sniffed. "I remember."

"Then find that guy and bring him back. You're too obsessed with finding your daughter to remember who you are."

"I've been talking to the sheriff. They think they know who took Rachel."

She didn't speak.

"Joanne, I know you don't want to hear it. They've picked up a guy. The sheriff thinks he may have been involved in Rachel's disappearance."

She didn't speak for a moment. When she finally responded, it was tentative. *Hope?* "Really?"

"Did you hear what I said? The sheriff thinks—"

Her voice quickly hardened. "What he thinks is not bringing our daughter back!"

I winced. Her protective shell was back up. "But maybe at least we'll know—"

"Some things are best unknown, David." Joanne began to cry. "I—" she stuttered and halted. "I'm afraid to hope."

My heart broke listening to her sobs. "Jo, I'm sorry." I waited, listening to her breath in my ear. "I can make him suffer, Jo. Suffer like we've had to suffer."

She took a deep breath, slowing the tears. "David, listen to yourself! Revenge won't bring Rachel back. I think I liked you better when you were obsessed with finding Rachel alive. What has happened to you?"

"Someone has stolen my life."

"So don't give up what you have left by doing something stupid. Leave revenge to God."

"Where was God when someone stole our Rachel?" I paused, releasing a secret. "I'm scared, Jo. I'm changing."

"When your mother was sick, you missed the awards banquet. When Randy lost his job and needed to make a car payment, you made it for him, even though you were saving for a car of your own. When your dad was ill, you missed your partnership promotion." Her tone became urgent. "Find that guy again."

She was right about one thing. All my adult life, I'd practiced putting other people's needs in front of my own. So maybe she should understand why I needed to do something for me.

I didn't know what to say. "I want to come home."

"No," she said.

"I'm sorry."

"Me, too," she said.

A click told me that had been her good-bye. Frustrated, I set the phone down and sighed.

<hr />

Saturday evening I placed flowers at my mother's gravesite, a country cemetery next to a Presbyterian church down in Oyster. I knew I'd lost my footing in the wake of Rachel's disappearance, and I hoped that a small act of ceremony might bring some of my mother's wisdom back to me.

My mother had been my biggest supporter, a wall of defense when the town's men thought I was crazy for pursuing a career in medicine. I remember the day when I'd made a decision to forego my dream and stay to help my father instead.

She looked up from where she stood in front of the kitchen sink. "Take those boots off outside, Davy. I live with a crabber. I don't have to live with the crabs."

I obeyed, then walked to the refrigerator. I studied her for a moment. She was dressed and wearing lipstick. "What's up? Are we going out?"

"I am. I took a job waiting tables down at the Wharfside Inn."

I selected an apple from the counter. "Why? You're already working extra shifts at the processing plant."

"Have you seen the price of your tuition?"

I turned a kitchen chair around and straddled it backward. I leaned over and shook my head. "I've decided to stay on with Dad."

"Davy—"

"Mom, Dad has done fine for himself. It's what I want."

"Phooey. I've listened to your dreams."

"Maybe I was too naïve."

She sighed, folded her apron, and pointed at my chest. "Now you listen to me. You've got crabbing in your blood, I know. Always have. Probably always will. But God has given you something else—the brains to do more, and the compassion to help."

"But if I leave, Dad will have to scale back."

"We'll manage, Davy. The good Lord will take care of us."

"I could start saving for medical school now. If I go to college and medical school, it will be years before—" I stopped in mid-sentence when her rolled apron smacked down in a rainbow arc onto my head.

"Stop it! I didn't raise you to take the easy way. Or to do what everyone else does." She threw the apron onto the counter. "There's stew in the refrigerator in the saucepan. Feed it to your father when he comes in."

"Dad will never go for this. He's set on having my help."

"You leave your father to me. He'll come around. He just needs my help to see the way." She paused at the door. "I'm going to work. And you're going to school. I won't have you giving up on your dreams. That's final!"

With that, she bounded down the porch steps and let the screen door slam behind her. I'd give her one thing. She knew how to get her way.

I reached to her grave and plucked a wilted petal from the edge of a red rose. "Thanks, Momma," I whispered. "Thanks for helping me remember."

I was only a bit self-conscious that I was whispering to a gravestone when I heard my name spoken by a voice I recognized.

Blake.

I STOOD QUICKLY, stumbling to my feet without grace. "Blake. What are you doing here?" I squinted at him. "How'd you find me?" The last time I'd seen him I was shoving him across the hood of a Cadillac.

He held up a six-pack of Amstel. "Maybe I know you better than you think." He paused, shuffling his feet. "I came to apologize."

I stood there looking at him, wondering what would have motivated him to travel three hours. "Okay."

"Look, David, long before there was a Blake and Joanne, or a David and Joanne, there were two friends, David and Blake. I started thinking how much I'd messed up in throwing our friendship away."

I eyed him suspiciously. After a moment I nodded. "Let's go back to my place."

Before walking to the car, we paused at the memorial stone next to my mother's.

"Gus?"

I nodded.

"I heard he was sick." He read the inscription and looked up. "I'm sorry, David."

"Sure."

"He could pick a crab faster than anyone I knew."

I thought about Amina's nimble fingers.

We walked in silence toward our vehicles, mine a tan Volvo

sedan, and Blake's the red Porsche 911. That's the way we'd always been. Me, safe—a little geeky—but reliable. Blake, edgy, fast, and fun. I had always wished I were a bit more like Blake.

As he followed me to Dad's place, I tried to understand this turn of events. It wasn't like Blake to apologize. I looked in the rearview mirror and squinted at him, suspicious of his motive.

Once at the house, we walked out to the pier where I pulled up a crab trap I'd set the evening before. Water poured through the wire mesh to reveal a layer of blue crabs. "Something to go with the beer."

I put water in a large pot, added Old Bay seasoning and all the crabs it would hold, took it inside the house, set it on the stove, and clicked the burner on.

"I've been thinking," Blake said, after tipping up his beer. "You and I are a lot alike."

I shook my head. "I'm nothing like you. I'm shy. You're—"

"Not shy," he said.

"I was going to say arrogant." I smiled. "I'm a geek. You're a playboy."

"So? I always wanted to be more studious."

I chuckled. "And I always wanted to be more of a playboy." I paused. "You had so many girls."

"And you had only one. The one I wanted." He paused, then continued to attempt to prove his original point. "We're both doctors."

"True, but we're still not alike. Maybe that's why we got along."

I listened as the crabs started scratching the sides of the pot. Gently at first, then frantic. My emotions clawed as frantically inside me. "You've been seeing her again?" I asked, trying to disguise the anger and hurt, and not certain I really wanted to know the answer.

He shook his head. "She won't see me. I've run into her a

time or two, trying to be a friend, but she refuses." He sat down at the table. "I think I'm the kind of guy women have a hard time being friends with."

"That's sad, Blake."

He shrugged. "Hey, don't look at me that way. I was only trying to offer my friendship."

I wasn't sure I ever wanted to be his friend again. I turned my attention back to the crabs.

"We had a lot of good times before Joanne," he offered.

It had been a long time since I'd thought of any.

"Remember waterskiing behind the *Beautiful Swimmer*?"

I smiled. "The wake behind that boat is a monster."

"Remember picking up girls in Virginia Beach on the board-walk?"

"I remember watching *you* pick up girls in Virginia Beach."

He laughed. "Okay. How about skinny-dippin' in the creek?"

"I remember my mom coming down to the pier to watch the sunset and we had to tread water for twenty minutes until she decided to go back up to the house."

Blake laughed again, and that made me laugh. But inside, a quiet dread crept into my consciousness. Blake had always been a player. Could I trust that he was genuinely interested in being a supportive friend now?

We took the crabs outside and sat at the picnic table to eat after covering it with newspaper.

Blake gave me a long and steady look. "It took me a while, but I finally decided I couldn't be mad at you for being like me."

"Being like you?"

"Falling for Joanne."

"It wouldn't have worked for you."

"Why not?"

"You were never very good at being a one-woman man." I paused. "I know she found you with Delores Thomas after your engagement."

"I'll bet she didn't tell you she spent the night at Ed Beckly's to get even."

I sipped my beer. *That,* she hadn't shared with me. *That,* I had a hard time believing.

He looked across the table at me. "So tell me. How are you doing?"

I took a deep breath and exhaled slowly. It felt good to be sitting with someone who wanted to know, even if it was Blake—and even if he was pretending. "Terrible," I said. "Joanne won't see me, either," I said. "It's killing me. I want us to be together in this madness."

I went on to tell him that losing Rachel was a pain worse than death, that I couldn't imagine the rent in my soul ever healing. I told him about weeks of thinking of nothing but Rachel, of hearing her voice when I went about my work, of thinking I caught a glimpse of her when I was out in a crowd, of holding on to the belief that I could find her, and of finally watching my grief turn into anger. I told him about Riley Johnson, and how fate had brought me into his path and how the sheriff made it plain that they suspected he was involved in Rachel's disappearance.

I wasn't sure why I shared my soul with him. Maybe I wanted him to see that I was hurting and hoped he'd lay off trying to hang around Joanne if he saw that it would cause me more pain.

"I've thought of nothing but revenge for days. The thought of getting even really gets my blood going."

"Maybe that's why the sheriff allowed you to stay there."

I emptied my Amstel, set it aside, and opened a second. "What do you mean?"

"Think about it. What lawman isn't frustrated by our court

system, seeing guilty men walk with minimal or no sentences? Maybe he thinks this Riley dude is guilty, but believes he doesn't have the evidence to get a conviction. So he leaves you with him, hoping you'll take care of the problem."

"I don't think so."

"Think about it."

Things fell quiet except for our busyness cracking crab legs and claws. Then he said, "Do you think he took Rachel?"

I told him about letting him see Rachel's picture and watching his reaction. "Yes, I do."

He stared at me from across the table until my eyes met his. "Then I think you should kill the man." He nodded matter-of-factly, as if he talked of selling a boat or mowing the grass. "For you. For me."

"For you?"

"Yes," he said. "She was my daughter."

I dropped the crab in my hand to the table and wiped my hands on a napkin. "You're out of your mind."

Blake raised smug eyebrows and stared at me. He really believed his paternity theory. "Am I?"

I didn't feel like arguing with him over the paternity of my daughter. I'd known Blake suspected this. Jo had told me as much. But she'd also assured me that Rachel was mine and that was answer enough for me. I stared at him. "A simple blood test would tell the truth." I felt my blood beginning to heat up. How dare he come here and try to provoke me with something so outrageous!

"If they don't find her, you'll never know."

"No, Blake, I *know*. She's my daughter. You're the one with the fantasy about me raising your child." I rolled my eyes. "You need to go."

"Easy, bro. We were getting along so well." He held up his beer. "Besides, I can't drive like this."

Blake sipped his beer and fell silent. In silence we ate succulent crab, although after his comments, I didn't have much of an appetite anymore. In silence we watched the sun set over the bay. When he broke the silence, there was longing in his voice, a window to deep pain. "Why do you think I showed up again after leaving you and Joanne alone for so long?"

You're an opportunist, that's why. Take advantage when and where you can. I held my thoughts to myself. "You tell me."

"Because Rachel disappeared. I knew how it ripped me apart to hear about it. I couldn't imagine what you two were going through."

"But you can understand why I wasn't happy to see you."

"You mistrust my motives, bro. I'm not after Joanne. I wanted a chance to share some of the pain."

I looked away and counted under my breath. I'd thought of him as a home wrecker for so long that I couldn't quickly change my way of thinking. I stayed quiet and stared into the western sky.

"Who is that?" Blake asked, pointing with his bottle.

I looked over to see Amina gathering laundry from the wash line in the fading light. She was working quickly, mostly paying attention to the wash, but I made eye contact with her and lifted my head in a quiet greeting. "Her name is Amina."

Blake leaned forward and with a hushed voice, but still embarrassingly loud said, "Wow. She's beautiful." He chuckled. "Does Joanne know there are such temptations so close by?"

"I'm already committed."

Blake returned to staring at Amina until she returned to her house. And for a moment I was her father, wishing she had worn her head covering to protect her from the gaze of lustful eyes.

As if reading Blake's mind, Amina quickly came out of the house again, retrieved a burka cloth from the line and wrapped it around her head.

"Maybe you should let your neighbor comfort you."

I stayed quiet. The comment was all too Blake. And another reason for me to be cautious about soaking up his friendship.

We retreated from the mosquitoes at dusk and stayed up 'til past midnight talking about old times. Actually, I listened more than I talked. I couldn't stop thinking about Blake's claim to fatherhood. Maybe he'd just dropped that bomb to get under my skin. Regardless, I wasn't much into our conversation after that. I thought about how I'd punched Blake in the nose when I'd found him in my home. A second image of Blake sprawling over the front of a Cadillac flashed through my memory. It was late, and I started feeling guilt. "Blake," I said, "losing Rachel has turned me into someone else. I—"

"Forget it, Davy. Forget it."

"I wasn't apologizing. I was explaining." I stared at him. "I'm not sorry."

He shrugged and walked down the hall to the bathroom.

By twelve thirty, we'd soaked our sorrows in the tradition of our college days, and I knew I would pay the price in the morning. I took two Tylenol and four ibuprofen to head off the pain and left Blake to crash on my couch.

IN THE CLINIC Monday afternoon, I treated three cases of pink eye—or conjunctivitis—from cellblock C and two cases of what the prisoners called, "Oyster Point bowel." From what I could tell, it seemed to be a mild case of food poisoning. I decided to do a record review and maybe have a look around the kitchen.

When Riley Johnson came in, he was talkative, as if probing around my brain while I examined him. I wanted to see if I could detect any early effects of the Lupron injection.

"I heard about your father, Dr. Conners." He halted when I looked at him. "Before I was in. I read his obituary."

"He was a good man," I said. "A good father."

"My old man died when I was three. Then my mother's brother moved in."

"Did he help raise you?"

He snorted. "Abused me and my sister." He kept his head down and continued. "Made us do all kinds of stuff to each other. He made movies of it."

I didn't exactly want to hear about his abusive childhood. "Take a deep breath," I said, laying my stethoscope on his chest.

"My last attorney talked a judge into going light on me because of my bad upbringing."

"Last attorney? You were in before? What for?"

"I agreed to meet a young lady over the Internet. Turned out I was talkin' to a thirty-five-year-old detective."

"I'm going to need to examine you for hernias."

He complied and lowered his jumpsuit.

I inserted a finger and positioned it correctly. "Cough." Casually, I examined his anatomy. I hadn't examined him before, but I would have laid money on the fact that his testes were shrinking.

All because of the wonders of the medical castration I'd given him.

I looked at him. *You're getting what you deserve.*

"My lawyer thinks the judge will get the murder charge dropped. Self-defense."

"That's nice." I paused. "Do you have headaches since the assault?"

"Some."

"Maybe we should touch base in a few weeks."

AFTER WORK I took Dad's pickup to buy mulch for the new shrubs. I enjoyed driving with the window down until the rain started. When I arrived home, I wasn't even in the house before Amina came hustling across the lawn, concern etched on her face. "David," she called.

"What's wrong?"

"They've found a body."

I froze. "What kind of a body? Who? Where?"

"My father was making a pickup at the docks, when he heard. Nate Samuels found a body tangled in one of his crab pots."

My face must have paled, as Amina put her hand out and grabbed my elbow as if I needed support.

I did.

"A girl?"

"I don't know. The police put up yellow tape separating Nate's boat from the rest. They're investigating."

"At Tippins Pier?"

She nodded.

"I need to go."

"May I come with you?"

"Sure. Let me get my car keys." I dashed into the house and returned with the keys to my Volvo. "Let's go."

We drove in silence. *Please God, don't let this be Rachel.*

We pushed as far as we could into a crowd standing at the entrance to the pier. The mass stood, umbrella to umbrella, eyes fixed toward a collection of uniformed men farther down the dock.

A black sedan sat next to the pier's entrance. The chatter of the crowd said it belonged to the medical examiner from Virginia Beach.

I saw Earl Whitson and began moving toward him. Fathers with the same agendas: find out if the body had been identified. Could it be Rachel or Brooke?

"Hi," I said, approaching. "Does anyone know anything?"

"I talked to Nate," he said. "All he could say was the body was small, a child. And that there was a tangle of blond hair."

"Sounds like it could be—"

Tammy Whitson snuggled closely to Earl's arm. "I know it sounds horrible, but I almost hope it's Brooke. At least then I'll know she drowned and didn't suffer at the hands of some sicko."

I nodded numbly. I figured now wasn't the time to point out that some sicko could have dumped the body into the bay.

We watched the proceedings from a distance, not daring to step past the yellow police tape, anxious for information.

The rain slowed to a drizzle, a haphazard dripping that dared us to lower our umbrellas and punished us when we dared to do so. The rain made us stick together beneath them. I noticed several of the townspeople sizing up my neighbor who had pushed in tight beneath my umbrella.

After an hour of small talk and speculation, my patience thinned. I looked over my shoulder in response to my name.

It was Sam Crenshaw. The last I had seen him was at my father's funeral. He took off his green John Deere hat and asked, "Can we talk?"

"Hey, Sam, of course."

The look on his face told me he wanted privacy. I left the umbrella with Amina and walked with him to a small covered gas-pump island next to the pier.

I looked at his wrinkled face. He seemed older than when I'd last seen him.

"I've heard rumors. You're selling the *Beautiful Swimmer*?"

"Already have. I need to liquidate some of Dad's things."

He glanced over his shoulder before continuing. "What you do on your own time is your business, but I heard tell that you were selling to one of the Somalis."

"That's right."

"Ever stop to wonder what your dad would think?" He laid his hand on my shoulder. "I mean, your dad was the biggest supporter of the local fishermen that I've ever known. He wouldn't look too kindly on outsiders comin' in and takin' over our livelihood."

I didn't expect this type of comment out of Sam.

"Look, I'm selling to a neighbor. They were good to Dad. When he got sick, their family cooked for him. They looked after him since I was away."

"Maybe you shouldn't have left him so high and dry, huh?"

"Sam, that's not fair. He supported—"

"Supported, my hat! It broke his heart to see you decide not to crab." He hesitated. "And he sure wouldn't approve of you giving these Muslim people our business."

I took a deep breath and tried to control my voice. "I'm certain Dad would be glad I've found a willing buyer. Money's tight for so many, Sam."

"You've forgotten all about September eleventh?"

I grimaced in frustration. "This isn't about September eleventh, Sam. My neighbors had nothing to do with that."

"No one will buy crabs from a Muslim Arab. Why don't you save them the misery?"

"They're not Arabs. They're African. Somali. And people will buy crabs from anyone who sells them at the right price. Always have." I strained my eyes toward the pier.

The sheriff walked toward the crowd. "Excuse me, Sam," I said as I pulled away.

Denton Reynolds lifted his arms toward the crowd. "I want you all to go home. A body was found. Badly decomposed. It's a little body, that's about all we know. Now the medical examiner is going to be removing the remains for further testing, so I'd appreciate it if you would all go home."

Several murmurs rose from the crowd as they began to move away.

I was thinking about what to do next when the sheriff called for us. "Dr. Conners, Mr. Whitson," he said, waving us toward him.

When we were standing face-to-face, he spoke again. "I understand your anxiety. Bear with us, we'll try to find out the information you want. I do have a favor to ask you. We're going to need dental X-rays of your daughters. Blood samples from both parents would be good as well. I can send a lab person by your house to draw the samples if that's okay. It will be helpful for the forensic pathologist to determine whether this body could be one of your daughters."

He looked at me and continued. "Your wife can go by the police lab in Richmond if she doesn't want to come to the shore. The body will be taken to Virginia Beach for the exam." He handed me a business card. "Tell your wife to have her blood forwarded to the medical examiner there. Hopefully, we'll know something in a few days."

There was little else to say.

I headed home with Amina, aware that the dispersing townspeople were watching. I didn't care. She was a good neighbor. Let 'em gawk. I wanted to get home to call Joanne.

Joanne had just stepped into the shower when she heard the phone ring. She let the answering machine pick up. After toweling off, she checked the messages and realized her caller had phoned twice, both times while she was in the bathroom. There were no messages. At least not spoken ones. The first was someone breathing as if in agony or ecstasy. The second, the caller, a male, continued the heavy breathing, and then concluded by whispering her name. She wished David had invested in a phone with caller ID. He had told her that their old phone worked just fine.

At times David was too frugal. And this was one of them.

She wrapped her robe tightly around her body and moved through the house, shutting curtains and checking the locks on all the doors. The house, once a dream home filled with Rachel's giggles, felt too large for a woman alone.

A minute later the phone rang again. "Hello?"

A whisper. "You picked up. Talk to me." More breathing. A gasp. A grunt. "Joanne, I'm watching you."

She slammed the phone down and walked away from the kitchen counter only to turn back and stare at the phone.

She paced the house, feeling uneasy, watching the street through a slit in the drapes in the darkened front room. After ten minutes the phone rang again. This time, she wouldn't pick up, but waited for the answering machine.

"Joanne, it's me, Blake. I called to see how you were doing."

She grabbed the phone. "Hi."

"Hey, what's up? You sound a little out of breath."

"I've been getting prank phone calls. I thought he was calling back."

"Creepy."

"Tell me about it."

"Say, you need an ear? Want to grab something to eat, get out of the house?"

Getting out of the house sounded perfect. Even if it was with Blake. "Can you meet me at O'Brenstein's in the mall?"

"Sure. How about eight?"

"I'll be there."

Amina remained quiet as we drove away from the pier. She gazed out the window with her burka shielding her face.

"About the other night," I said. "I owe you an apology."

"No," she said. "I was stupid."

"You're not stupid."

"You're in love with your wife. It's obvious."

"I was drunk." I glanced at her.

She frowned at me. "You don't get drunk often, do you?"

"Of course not."

She looked away again. "When you drink, maybe you do things that you really want to do, but your mind won't let you."

I thought about it. "Maybe."

"I'm sorry about your daughter. I don't know whether to hope that the body is hers or not. What do you want?"

"Of course I want my daughter back. But—" I halted, unwilling to admit that I'd lost hope and wanted to make someone pay.

She nodded. When I pulled into Dad's driveway, she spoke again. "Your friend told me that your wife doesn't want you back."

The revelation surprised me. I didn't know Blake had talked to her. Momentarily speechless, I couldn't reply.

Amina touched my arm. "I know what it is like to suffer rejection."

I didn't know what to say. I started to protest. I wanted to tell her it wasn't true, but she stopped me.

"Shh," she said. "You've lost your daughter. Now your wife. Believe me, I understand."

Somehow, looking into her dark eyes, I believed her. She'd seen her share of pain, deep areas of loss I wasn't quite ready to explore.

She opened the door. "You need to eat."

"I'll manage."

"It's late. I've already prepared food for Mohamed. He would want me to share."

"Amina, I—"

"I'll be a few minutes," she said. "Call your wife."

I tried Jo but got only the answering machine. I left her a message. "I have something urgent to talk with you about. Please call me." I called her cell—the message system picked up right away, indicating she had turned the phone off or was using it—and repeated the message.

Amina returned with steaming dishes of Somali rice and a stew of carrots, potatoes, and shredded goat meat. The meat was a bit chewy, but tasty, and overall worth the effort.

As I ate, Amina shared more details of her life in a refugee camp in eastern Kenya, where she had lived for six months prior to coming to the U.S. "There is no work to do and only a small allotment of the staples for our diet. No trees, only desert sand and lots of heat."

"If they have a choice, why would anyone choose to live that way?"

"It's not a matter of choice. It is safer than the streets of Mogadishu during the fighting. Many women seek refuge in the camps so that they can work on having the babies that the war stole from us."

It was ten o'clock when Joanne finally called back. I was just pushing back from the table and Amina had begun singing some lilting Somali melody.

I picked up the phone. "Hello."

"David, it's Joanne. I just got your message."

"I have some, uh, news."

"What?"

"One of the crabbers pulled a body out of the bay."

Joanne gasped. "Is it our baby?" Her voice grew urgent. "Do they think——"

"It's too early to tell. All they know is that it's a small body with blond hair."

"Where? When?"

As I spoke the words, I had to fight to keep my voice steady. "Early afternoon. The body was somehow entangled in the crab pot line. The ME has taken the remains to Virginia Beach to conduct forensic studies," I told her. "We need to help by giving them Rachel's most recent dental X-rays."

Joanne's voice sounded stoic, ready to tackle the business at hand. "I can go to Dr. Rich's office and get them tomorrow."

"Good. They want a sample of our blood as well to help determine whether the remains could be a close enough match to be our offspring."

Joanne tapped a fingernail against the phone. "Fine. How do we do that? Do I need to come to the shore?"

"No. You can go to the local police station and give it. Or, if you're going to take Rachel's X-rays to the ME's office in Virginia Beach, you could give the sample there."

"David, do you think this is it? Is our waiting over?" I could hear the change in her breathing—she was trying to hold back deep emotion. "Rachel must have slipped into the water like the sheriff said."

"This doesn't prove that, Jo. It only proves that *this* body ended up in the water. It could be Brooke Whitson. Some weirdo could have thrown the remains in the bay."

A sharp intake of air.

"It's the truth, Jo. Maybe I'm the one with a realistic outlook here. Maybe it's time for you to take a hard look at reality."

I regretted being harsh with her as soon as the words were out.

Jo spoke softly, the voice of reason. "Maybe neither of us can take a hard look at reality until we know what that reality is."

"Jo, the sheriff told me he thinks they may have picked up the suspect."

"You told me. Has something changed since then? Did he give a confession?"

"No, but you'd hardly expect—"

Joanne protested. "What proof do they have to link him to the crime?"

"Nothing directly. He was picked up in the act of a crime against a little girl."

"That doesn't mean he had anything to do with Rachel's disappearance. That's really a long shot, isn't it, David?" She halted suddenly, then said, "Who is making noise in the background?"

I cleared my throat. "Amina. The neighbor. She's washing dishes."

"What is she doing there? It's past ten."

I cringed. "She brought me dinner." I hesitated. "She's just being a good neighbor. She used to feed Dad."

"Blake told me about her. I think he called her a caramel beauty."

"Blake would say that. When did you run into Blake?"

"He's a friend, okay? He told me he was reaching out to you."

Some friend. He shouldn't have told Joanne about Amina.

"Amina is my friend," I countered. I looked at Amina. She diverted her eyes. I felt bad trading barbs with Jo in front of her, but Dad's phone wouldn't let me move any farther away. I lowered my voice. "I'm sorry."

"For what? Have you done something you should be sorry for?"

"Jo, I've done nothing—" I halted. "I meant I was sorry for sounding so accusatory when I asked about Blake."

She sighed again. "It's getting late. I'm on at seven in the morning. I'll get off early to get the X-rays."

"Thanks." I didn't know what else to say. It seemed I couldn't have a reasonable conversation with Joanne since Rachel's disappearance.

The line clicked off, and I set the phone down. Amina approached, carrying the dishes. "She doesn't understand you," she said, touching my hand.

I let my eyes linger on her face. "No," I said softly. "She understands me too well."

I AWOKE SOMETIME in the night to the sound of a car accelerating. Not fully awake, I appreciated only the vague discomfort of an old memory of a car moving away on the day Rachel disappeared. I groaned and looked at the clock: 1:34 a.m.

I spoke her name into the night. "Rachel, Rachel," I whispered, but found no comfort in my recitation, only the profound loss of a father for a child. I began to weep as if the scab had been freshened again, picked away from some random memory. I rolled over, tucking the pillow into my heaving chest.

KABOOM! BOOM! BOOM!

The percussion of an explosion rattled the windows, jolted my heart into my throat, and adrenaline into my system.

I jumped from bed, scrambled into a pair of jeans, and headed outside, pulling a T-shirt over my head as I went. I yanked open the back door to flames licking the sky as high as the lower branches of a pine tree next to the pier. A swirl of yellow-orange heat surrounded the *Beautiful Swimmer*. A black plume curled upward into the infinity of the moonlit sky. I spun around, darted to the phone, and dialed 9-1-1.

"Nine-one-one. Could you state the nature of your emergency?"

"A boat is on fire at Nimble Creek at a pier behind the house at sixteen Shore Drive."

"Is there anyone on it?"

"There shouldn't be."

"I'm dispatching fire and rescue units now."

I dropped the receiver into the cradle and ran to the back-yard, stopping to scoop up a coil of old water hose that Dad had used to clean crabs behind the shed. I spun the knob on the faucet and ran toward the *Beautiful Swimmer* with my thumb pressed over the nozzle.

The whole boat was engulfed in orange, with a thick over-hanging canopy of billowing black smoke. I could barely make out the outline of the roof over the captain's chair. I marveled at how quickly the flames swallowed the boat. There was no doubt the *Beautiful Swimmer* was already a total loss.

A bigger concern was that the ropes had burned free, allow-ing the tide to bring the floating blaze under the edge of the pier. Fire had crept halfway across the cross boards like a locust plague on tender leaves. I heard shouting from Amina's, and in a flash Mohamed and Amina were at my side.

"What happened?" Mohamed asked.

"I don't know." I said, concentrating on spraying down the pier, hoping to at least save the first two sets of piling. The heat kept me from getting close enough to be efficient. The smoke was thick and black, and the smell of diesel mixed with the acrid odor of burning creosote from the pilings.

Amina had grabbed a bucket and was wading into the water on the far side of the pier. Swiftly, she worked to slosh water from the creek onto the pier.

"Here," I said, handing the hose to Mohamed. "I'll try to push the boat out from under the pier." I grabbed a long oar lying next to the shed and waded into the water beside Amina. From below the pier opposite the boat, I attempted to place the oar against the boat at the waterline, the only section of the boat not raging with fire. I couldn't get close enough to do any good, the blast of heat searing my face. I ducked fully into the water. From underneath water level, I gave it a shove. Fortunately, it moved. I popped up to get a breath, then dove under to give it a second and third shove until it was coasting into the middle of the creek.

Amina worked tirelessly in waist-deep water, dousing the flames on the pier and soaking down the untouched section next to the shore.

After a few minutes we retreated to Mohamed's side to watch the flaming boat begin to sink in the center of Nimble Creek. The hiss of steam joined the snapping of the fire in an odd percussion out of place in the silence of night.

Mohamed turned off the water hose. "This was no accident."

"I heard a car racing away before the explosion. I think that's what woke me."

In the distance I could hear the warble of an approaching siren.

Mohamed started walking toward his house. "I am going to put on dry clothes," Amina said and began to cry. She was dripping wet from her efforts, and for the first time I realized she was wearing something other than a flowing Somali dress. She turned to me, clad only in a nightshirt and pair of blue jeans and began to shiver. Her face was slick with salt water.

I looked at her, seeing the reflection of the flames dancing in the darkness of her eyes.

She reached for me, and there on the grass I held her as she wept, not separating until a fire truck pulled in a few moments later.

By three in the morning I'd changed out of my wet clothes and Amina was serving hot tea steeped in sweetened milk to the firefighters and other officers who had gathered. Denton

Reynolds ran his fingers through his short cropping of white hair and sighed. "Any idea who might have done this?"

I'd already been reviewing my day, combing it for possibilities. "Listen, Sheriff, I've known Sam Crenshaw all my life. He doesn't seem like the type, but . . ."

"But what?"

"I talked to him this afternoon, down at Tippins Pier. He said some of the crabbers were upset that I'd sold the boat to Mohamed. He said my father would roll over in his grave."

Sam nodded. "The watermen have had a rough go lately." He paused, sipping his tea. "But I agree, Sam's as gentle as they come. A bit hardheaded when it comes to the way crabbing ought to be done, but harmless in my read of him."

"It could be that he speaks the sentiment of the group. But who would dare?"

"Hard times prompt the sane to do the insane sometimes."

I looked up at the sky, with large clouds backlit by a full moon. The effect was Halloween-spooky. "Say," I said, clearing my throat. "Anything on Riley Johnson?"

"Not much. I need a confession."

I studied him in the moonlight. Denton was a crusty chap, hardworking and determined. Perhaps I'd misjudged him as a too-gentle Mayberry officer. In his eyes, I could see a message of tiredness. He seemed a man beaten down by the misdeeds of men.

"Hang in there," I responded. "I think something is going to break this case yet."

SHERIFF REYNOLDS STOOD on the Crenshaw front stoop in the morning sun, knocking persistently until Sam opened the door.

"Mornin', Denton, what brings you 'round?"

Denton tipped his hat. "Morning, Sam. Mind if I come in?"

"Not at all. Mildred was just fixin' a little breakfast. Coffee?"

"Don't mind if I do." They sat at a small kitchen table with a Formica top. Denton had learned long ago that friendships couldn't be taken for granted in police work. And talking to the watermen of Tippins had to start with local life before honing in on the problem at hand. "How's business?"

"Aw, you know. Up and down. Sometimes I think I ought to take the crabs over to Baltimore myself. The processing plant just dropped a nickel off the pound price again."

"Harvest okay?"

"I'm ahead of last year. The festival for us was huge." He sipped from a mug emblazoned with a blue crab. "Sugar?"

Denton reached for the mug. "Black." They sipped coffee while Mildred fried bacon. The smell was heavenly. He stretched out, arching over the back of the chair and groaned. "I'm too old for late nights anymore."

Sam nodded and laughed. "I've gone from the Rolling Stones to kidney stones."

"From going out with our wives to our backs going out."

"I hear ya."

The two chuckled for a moment before Denton asked, "Did you hear about the fire?"

"I heard sirens in the night. Nothing in the morning paper," he said.

"Gus Conners' boat burned last night." The sheriff watched for a reaction.

Sam was cool. Not even a twitch.

Mildred wagged her head and made a clicking sound with her tongue, something Denton suspected she used to do in the classroom when an elementary student misbehaved.

Denton sighed. "Sure looks like arson. The boat's a total loss, burnt half the pier, too."

"That's awful."

They sipped coffee and stared at the tabletop.

"Won't you have breakfast, Sheriff?" Mildred offered.

"Kind of you, Millie. It's been a long night."

"Scrambled or sunny-side up?"

"Scrambled," Denton said. "You wouldn't have heard any talk about stopping the Somalis from getting into the crabbing business, would you?"

Sam shifted in his seat.

"Dr. Conners tells me that you were upset that he sold Gus's boat to Mohamed."

"What are you sayin,' Sheriff? That I had something to do with this? Denton, you know me—"

Denton held up his hands. "Listen, Sam, I'm just following leads. I knew you'd have the best handle on the current scuttle-butt around the docks. I thought maybe you'd know if someone was bragging, or threatening to do something."

"Sure, there are some guys that are upset. Me included. That David Conners should have respected Gus's opinion and sold to a local." He stopped when Mildred put a steaming plate of eggs and bacon in front of him. "But we're not fools,

Denton. No one would go torchin' a fine boat like the *Beautiful Swimmer*."

The sheriff lifted a forkful of scrambled eggs under his nose and inhaled, aware that the fatigue of the night and too many cups of coffee were catching up to him.

They ate quietly, as a tension hung between them. The sheriff liked it that way. The guilty often respond to silence by filling the gap with confession.

After he finished, Denton pushed back from the table. "Thanks, Millie. Finest breakfast in Tippins." As he walked toward the door, he added. "Sam, keep your ears open for me, would ya? You can find me in the office."

At the curb, while opening the door to the cruiser, he looked to see the curtains in the upstairs window suddenly move as though someone had been watching him.

Joanne learned the art of using a secret to her advantage from her mother. To her, a secret concealed could be leverage for gain; a secret revealed was a loose fox in a house of hens.

She reported for work early and made calls to the next shift until she found someone willing to substitute so she could leave early. By noon, she was out into the Richmond heat. By one, she was on her way to the ME in Virginia Beach, armed with Rachel's dental X-rays.

Today, as she traveled, the blue sky mocked the clouds of her inner turmoil. Since Rachel's disappearance, old secrets had haunted her. At first she had thought that she could finally let it all go. With Rachel gone, what could be gained by a confession now?

But David had become obsessed with finding his daughter, suffocating Joanne with the guilt she so wanted to shed. And so she'd asked him to leave. She'd picked up an old ball and chain, one that she'd worn for too many days after Rachel's conception. And shedding it was more difficult than she'd imagined.

She dropped the X-rays at the ME's office, resenting the secretary's smiling face, and headed to the shore.

As she crossed the bay bridge-tunnel, she found herself checking and rechecking the rearview mirror, but her vigilance and a strong antacid couldn't quiet the burning in her upper abdomen. She lowered the window, taking in the scent of the sea. It was something David always insisted on as they reached this point in their destination. He would take in huge breaths, filling his lungs and acting as if it was a lifeline to a drowning sailor. "Ah," he'd say, "take me home."

At the sheriff's office, a chatty, young receptionist ushered her in to Denton Reynolds' office. *Why did everyone have to be so cheerful?*

"Mrs. Conners, nice to see you." He pointed to a chair and sat in his, behind a desk weighed down with stacks of paper.

She shook his hand, pleased by the firmness of his response. Reynolds was no limp fish.

I told your husband that you didn't need to come down. Did you come to inspect the fire?"

"Fire?"

He sighed. "The *Beautiful Swimmer* burned and sank last night. Half the dock was torched."

She gasped.

"Mrs. Conners, does your husband communicate with you?"

"I—well, he told me that a body was found."

"So you've come to give a blood sample then? I told the doctor that you could give a sample to any police lab and—"

I understood that, but I wanted to have it done here because"—she shifted in her chair—"there is something I need to tell you."

He pointed to a coffeepot on the counter behind him. "Coffee?" he asked, pouring himself a large mug.

"No thanks."

He sipped his coffee, and his eyes bore in on hers. She felt exposed, here in the presence of this lawman. "Just what is your concern, Mrs. Conners?"

"My husband isn't to know any of this."

His eyebrow twitched.

"I'm not sure David is Rachel's father."

It took me all morning to find a salvage outfit available to lift what was left of the *Beautiful Swimmer* from the bottom of Nimble Creek. They would try to come the following day. It would take time to float the barge with a crane down from Oyster. I hoped that at least the engine could be restored.

At four I walked next door to talk to Mohamed.

"Come in," he said.

I walked into the front room, noting the presence of what appeared to be a couch without legs in an L-shape around two corners of the room. Large pillows decorated a carpeted floor and a low table sat in front of the couch. "Here," I said, holding out a check. "I hadn't even put it in the bank."

"You do not wish to finalize the sale?"

"Of course not. I couldn't sell a neighbor a burned and sunken boat."

"You are thanked," he said. "May Allah bless you."

I shrugged. "The boat was insured." I put out my hand. "Besides, it's what neighbors do."

I found it impossible to leave, as Amina immediately began making tea when she heard my voice.

I stayed for tea and asked Mohamed about his plans.

"We are not wanted here." He hung his head. "Perhaps I will find another boat. Maybe we will move on. *Inshallah.*"

When I wrinkled my face in question, he translated, "If God wills."

I nodded and wished I felt anywhere close to God's plan.

A minute turned into twenty and then into one hour. I politely refused an offer for dinner and escaped only to see a familiar SUV in the driveway.

I opened the door, my heart not believing my eyes.

"I WAS IN Virginia Beach dropping off Rachel's X-rays." Joanne shrugged. "What's another hour?"

I smiled. As usual, she looked great, but I could sense the understandable cloud of melancholy continuing to engulf her. "You holding up?"

"Doing my best. You?"

I held my tongue, not knowing what to share. I wanted to talk about Rachel. The body. But didn't know if I dared. I decided to keep the conversation on safer ground. "Did you see the pier?"

"It's a mess. The *Beautiful Swimmer*?"

"Gone. It had to be arson, Jo. I'd sold the boat to Mohamed. I'll bet some good ol' boys from the docks came down and torched it so Mohamed couldn't get into the business."

"They would do that?" She sat with her arms across her chest.

"I'm afraid it's a closed group. To be a waterman pretty much means you have to have been born into it." I hesitated, looking at the clock. "Can you stay in town for supper? I was planning a trip down to Captain Billy's." I paused, evaluating her responsiveness. Her hand running through her hair meant she was uncomfortable. If she opened her arms, she would say yes. "Tuesday night is crab-cake night."

She opened her arms.

I grinned like a schoolboy.

I changed my clothes and let Joanne drive.

We ordered the crab cakes, slaw, and fries. I started with a beer and hush puppies slathered with butter. I wanted to talk about Rachel, but tiptoed through our conversation lightly for Joanne's sake. Instead, I told her about my conversation with Sam Crenshaw.

She stole one of my hush puppies. "He speaks his mind, but I don't think he'd do something like that," I said. She popped it into her mouth. "I still bet it was motivated by not wanting the Muslims in the business."

She raised her eyebrows. "That's serious, David. That would be a racially motivated hate crime."

I didn't know too much about the law but suspected she was right.

"I talked to Sheriff Reynolds," she said. "Seems like a competent enough guy."

I nodded, my mouth too full of hush puppy to talk.

"He says Nate found the body just down from the mouth of Nimble Creek—exactly where an outgoing tide would have dumped it."

"They dragged the creek," I pressed. "They didn't find a body."

We'd hit our first uncomfortable bump. We were both seeking what we considered reality: She believed nature had stolen our daughter. I was into sinister theories.

We sat quietly, not willing to let the conversation degenerate as a result of our stubborn positions.

When the meal came, eating was safer than talking. When Joanne did speak, she seemed to be staring straight through me. "How did two people like us end up together?"

"My handsome chiseled features?"

She smiled. "That helped." She paused as her smile faded. "I'm serious."

I kept my voice low and leaned forward. "You were pregnant with my child, remember?"

Joanne stiffened. If I hadn't known her well, I wouldn't have noticed. But having been the recipient of her moods over the years, I knew how to read her. The corner of her mouth tightened. She didn't like something I had said.

"So that's it, huh? We wouldn't be together without her? Well, now she's gone." Jo put down her fork. "So where does that leave you and me? Do we still share anything?"

Fortunately, I'd spent weeks of soul-searching looking for an answer to that very question. I wanted to take her hand, but our little table was crowded and I couldn't reach straight across. "How about love, Jo? How about our love for art, the outdoors, and cinnamon gum? How about shared dreams of travel and exploration? How about our disdain for plastic materialism in search of the joys of relationship and family?" I took a deep breath, every bit of my heart behind my words. "Don't you know that every time I see a sunset over the bay, I think of you and wish I could stand behind you, my arms wrapped around your waist, so you could see it, too? Don't you know that when something funny happens at work, the first thing I think about is how fun it's going to be to share it with you?"

The edge of her mouth relaxed a little. I even detected a glimmer of moisture in her eyes. "So can we be a couple in spite of losing our daughter? Can we find some other glue?"

I wanted to say yes. But what she didn't know was that she was asking me to give up the bitterness that had a lock on my soul.

Evidently, my hesitation was all the answer she needed. She stopped talking and picked up a dessert menu. "Is the key lime pie any good here?"

I felt a touch on my shoulder. It was Leroy Baker. "Heard about your boat," he said, shaking his head. "I sure hope they're wrong about the arson thing. Tippins is too nice a place for such nonsense."

I nodded. "I agree, Leroy. How's Alice?"

"She's fine. Working the second shift at the processing plant." He smiled. "So Tuesdays I eat at the Captain's."

I overheard another couple, two tables away, sitting beneath a large mounted blue marlin. "Did you hear that someone burned a crab boat up in Tippins?"

My eyelids started rebelling, threatening to close in spite of my desire to spend time with Joanne.

She ordered pie and I drank coffee, something I could do right up until crawling into bed.

She ate slowly, sucking sweet lime filling off her fork. This was a luxury to Jo. I knew she rarely gave way to the temptation of dessert.

"I think I have you figured out," she said suddenly.

I looked up, curious.

"You feel guilty."

Now she had my interest.

"That's why you can't give up your quest for revenge," she said. "You'd feel guilty if you let someone off the hook."

"That sounds funny coming from you." My voice was sarcastic. I let my gaze fall to the table. "I'm sorry."

"No, you're right. I've carried my share of guilt around. Maybe I'm the queen of it, you know? So maybe, just maybe, I can speak with a little authority on the subject."

"All right, I'll give you this. Guilt is a great motivator. Back when I went to church, I'd say half the members sat in those benches every week, 'cause they'd feel guilty if they didn't."

"Pretty sad, I'd say. Aren't you supposed to be getting rid of guilt by going to church?"

I sipped my coffee. "What's wrong with revenge?" I asked.

"Nothing. But maybe it's not our job."

I nodded and let the sarcasm slip into my voice again. "Vengeance is mine, saith the Lord."

"Exactly."

"Aren't we the pair?" I said. "Two of the backslidden, quoting the Bible."

"Just because I don't regularly attend church doesn't mean I don't think that the Bible doesn't have a few good things to say."

"Okay," I hesitated, then plunged ahead with my standby objections to faith. "If God loves me, like my mom used to teach, why did he allow Rachel to be taken from us?" I stared her down. "If that's love, maybe I don't want it."

"I don't know. But all through the ages, Christians have debated that question, and it seems sooner or later, suffering touches everyone."

I looked at her. "You deal with it your way. I deal with it mine."

She pushed her pie toward me. "I'm stuffed."

I welcomed the chance to stop talking. I took a bite of the pie and let the cool, sweet filling dance on my tongue. But the sweet was in contrast to my mood, so I continued. "You want to pretend nothing has happened? I'm sorry, but I can't do that."

"And you want to dwell on this thing and plotting ways to get even? Is that going to help?"

"Maybe it's better than doing nothing."

"Revenge will poison you, David. It will drain the joy right out of your abundant little cup."

I thought about my life. Nothing about it seemed abundant. Particularly not abundantly joyful. "My cup isn't exactly full."

"Right now, neither is mine. And may never be again." She leaned forward, her eyes intent on me. "What has gotten hold of you is far more than the loss of Rachel and being a grieving parent. Something ugly has taken over." She paused. "Be careful."

I sulked. She was right. But I was helpless to understand it. I was reacting to life, not acting. I finished the pie, unappreciative of its taste. "Okay, Jo. You've figured me out, have you? If I'm motivated by guilt, what is it I feel guilty for?"

She took a deep breath and looked full into my face, watching, I was sure, for a sign that what she was going to say, was true. "You've opened an old wound. Rachel's disappearance brought it all back, didn't it?"

"Brought it all—what?"

"You can't forgive someone else for taking your daughter away, whether it was God through the water, or some sinister creep, because you've never forgiven yourself after all these years."

The expression on her face was serious. But more than that, I could see that she felt sorry for me.

"You've picked it all back up again, haven't you?" she said, her voice full of compassion. "That load of responsibility and guilt that sat beside you all these years—that you've tried to ignore, hoping it would go away."

Before the next words came, I knew exactly what she was going to say. It was a dark place of my past that I preferred to keep behind steel doors, locked tight. The place of pain I'd shoved aside, didn't want to visit again, refused to think about. I'd been trying to avoid it these past few weeks even though I was right back where the pain had first ripped my heart in two: Tippins. I'd been wandering around my home feeling out of sorts, with that low-grade dread that ate away at the corners of my mind as my constant companion. I'd blamed it all on losing my daughter, but I knew Joanne was intuitive and it was likely I was pushing her away as sure as I'd pushed away my own pain.

She looked across the table with tears cresting the edges of her eyes, speaking the words I did not want to hear. "You think you killed your sister."

"You don't think you've punished yourself enough?" Joanne asked.

I blinked back tears and fought to speak above the knot in my throat. "Let's go home." I plodded to the car on heavy feet. I pitched her the keys. "You drive."

We were quiet on the twenty-minute drive back to Tippins. I think we both had enough to chew on, and I knew we were both lost in silent conversations of our own. I didn't know what was motivating her, perhaps secrets of her own pressing in around her heart. All I knew was that a melancholy had settled over us, squeezing us until we were soul-breathless and in need of a taste of escape.

So I've turned guilt into anger? Salt in an old wound has turned into bloodlust?

Her accusation was an arrow, swift and true, striking a tender bull's-eye in my soul. I stared out the window, watching the white line on the edge of the highway. I wanted to think of anything but my old pain. It was unfair for Jo to bring it up. *What right does she have to judge me?*

I pressed my fingers against my forehead, a vain attempt to keep back my hurt. I tried to focus on anything outside. A seagull flying west. *What would it be like to escape like that? Fly out toward the third island on the bridge-tunnel, letting the air currents lift you.* The seagull soon escaped my vision, and I fixated on the mailboxes at the end of long, sandy lanes. They were drably the same, metal-colored, uniform shape with black numbers and red flags. Why didn't anyone on the shore break out of the mold and get one of those fancy designer ones? I'd seen a crazy one once, a mailbox that looked normal in the back, but the front was the face of former President Clinton and the opening lid swung down so you could slide mail into his mouth. It was a disgusting idea. *Who would want to read mail coming from there?*

I glanced at Joanne, feeling an old connection in spite of her pointed accusation. She seemed more of the old Jo. Caring. And I was comforted that she seemed to have taken the first steps in a healing process of her own, finally able to look out with some insight into what was going on around her. No husband wants his wife to be consumed by the misery that I'd seen suffocating my wife.

It was like that when she pulled out of her postpartum depression, too. Finally when she started caring about the things around the house that I was doing, even if I was bugging her, it seemed to reflect a lightening of her mood.

She looked at me. "What?"

I shrugged. "You're beautiful."

She made a face, snarling her lips like an angry dog. I smiled. *So like Jo,* I thought. She'd often made the same face as a child when her mother wanted to take a nice family photograph.

She followed me inside, touching my shoulder as soon as the door was closed behind us and we were alone in the unlit house.

I turned to her, and in the fashion of seasoned lovers we tarried, eyes locked in an understanding of what we wanted, what we needed to happen.

Our love was at first frantic, a race toward some emotional mountain. I did not know if she'd found a heart for me again, or if she used me as a slave. Truthfully, I did not care. All I knew was that we were both hurting and the best solace we could find would be together.

When she slept beside me, I thought of our first night together and slowly drifted off. Later, I awoke to her tears and gathered her in my arms. This time love came gently, but again without speech, even whispers. I was left to read her eyes and her hands, as she had no voice to tell me her heart.

In the morning she dressed quickly and left, stopping to kiss my cheek. A promise, or a good-bye, I couldn't discern.

Mildred Crenshaw looked at the mess in the bathroom. There was a small smear of blood on the white Formica and soiled gauze in the trash. "Sam," she called. "Are you hurt?" The resulting silence reminded her he'd gone down to the boat.

An hour later, while cleaning the kitchen, she eyed her seventeen-year-old grandson, Jimmy, as he slid past her on the way to the coffeepot. "You okay?"

He sniffed. "A little cold is all."

"Is that why you're wearing long sleeves? And what about the mess I found in the bathroom. Was that yours?"

"I spun my bike out on the gravel. I got a road rash on my arm." He tugged on his sleeve. "But last night my fingers went numb."

She touched his forehead. "You're burning up. Are you sure that thing isn't infected?" She lifted her nose to catch the stench. "Something smells awful."

"It's probably that cream I put on it. Sorry for makin' a mess, Grandma. I thought I cleaned up."

"You sound like your grandfather. 'Thought I'd cleaned up' means Grandma is going to have to go over it again." She touched his arm. "Let me look at this."

He sat on a kitchen chair and dropped the shirt off his arm. He'd covered the burn wound as best he could with ointment, a gauze, and an ace wrap. The skin above the burn was pink and tender. "Ouch," he said. He began to slowly unwind the bandage but suddenly moaned and laid his head on the table. "Whoa. My head's spinning."

"Let me help," Mildred said and picked up the bandage to finish the job and gasped as each unwind revealed more of his arm.

Jimmy snuck a peek.

His arm was greatly swollen, at least twice the size of his other arm. Tomato-size blisters had busted, leaving the skin rolled back in a wrinkled shore around a lake of yellow pus. He stared at his arm as though it belonged to someone else.

"We need to get you to a doctor."

Jimmy appeared suddenly agitated. "Let's just wash it here. It will be okay. It doesn't hurt, really. We don't need any more bills." He moved his arm away.

"You need an antibiotic. This is infected."

"Doc Larimore won't take walk-ins anymore. And I sure ain't goin' to the Emergency Room over in Nassawadox. It would be too expensive."

Mildred tapped her fingers on the table. "Maybe we could get Dr. Conners to look at it. He lives just a few streets over and I'm sure he wouldn't mind. His father and Sam were good friends."

"No!" Jimmy said sharply.

She looked at him, trying to figure out what had gotten into him.

"I mean, no," he said, a little softer. "I'm not about to take advantage of the man to get some free advice. I've got a little savings. I'd rather go up to Nassawadox."

He stood up and paled.

"Jimmy, what's wrong?"

He clutched at his chest. "Pain," he said. "I can't get my

breath." He collapsed, striking the edge of the table on the way to the floor.

Mildred felt for a pulse. "Jimmy!"

She lifted the phone on the counter and called 9-1-1.

I wasn't expecting to see Riley Johnson during my Wednesday clinic, but there he was, penciled in at the end of the schedule. "Stomach pain," was written by his name.

He came in with an escort, legs and arms in shackles. "Can I see my doctor in private?"

The guard looked at me in question.

I sized Riley up. "As long as you leave him in those," I said, "I'm okay with it."

The guard stepped into the waiting room, obviously unaware of Sheriff Reynolds' mandate.

"Let's see," I said. "The intake sheet says, 'stomachache.'"

"I had to tell 'em something so they'd let me come down here."

I squinted as he sat on the exam table. "Something's happening to me, Doc. Something bad."

"What? Pain?"

"I'm losing my drive," he said softly. "I think God is punishing me."

"What makes you say that? Do you need to be punished, Riley?"

He stared at me with hollow eyes. "We all need to be punished, I guess," he answered slowly.

Apparently, he was scared, but not ready to confess.

"My manhood's shrinkin'."

"What do you mean?"

"Help me get this down," he said, pointing to his orange

jumpsuit. He lifted his sac into view. "I'm serious, Doc. Something's not right."

"Maybe you've had an infection. Were they swollen and painful? Ever had the mumps?"

"When I was a kid. But they don't hurt. They're just shrinking!"

"How do you feel?" I studied him for a moment. "How is this affecting the way you think?"

"I told you. My drive is down."

Perfect.

"Can you help me, Doc?"

"Nothing to do for now. Maybe it's temporary. We'll wait and watch before we take any further action." I paused to let him stew. "Or maybe you're right."

"Right?"

"Maybe God *is* punishing you."

Riley gulped. "You're freaking me out. Don't say that."

"Maybe you should ask to talk to the chaplain. Come and see me next week. I want to know how you're doing. And I want to know what the chaplain thinks."

"Why?"

"Maybe you're dying, and God is giving you one last chance to get right."

21

JOANNE DROVE TO Richmond in time for her nine-to-nine shift in the ER. By quitting time, she was beat and in quest of some solitude.

She arrived home after sunset and approached the front door. Immediately, her guard was up. Wood fragments were scattered across the front porch and the doorframe was splintered. It appeared that someone had tried to break in, perhaps using a crowbar on the doorframe. Regardless, the door was intact and the dead bolt still secure.

She let herself in and called the police. She walked through the house checking windows and doors, and only when she was satisfied that everything was intact did she return to the kitchen. A red light flashed on her answering machine. Six messages.

She pressed play and listened. Each one was the same disgusting breathing and a whisper of her name.

A young Richmond police officer named Bradley Quince took her report.

"Apparently, something scared the perp away. I'll ask the neighbors whether they heard or saw anything. That's about all we can do at this point." He paused. "You don't have a phone with caller ID features?"

She shrugged. It was David who'd insisted on a phone with only the basics. Not only was he frugal, he also hadn't wanted the obligation to return calls to patients if he knew they were having trouble and trying to reach him. In her mind, it was head-in-the-sand thinking. Instead of trying to explain, she simply said, "No." She and David were certainly behind the times, and she regretted it. She put a new phone on a mental list to do the next day.

After he left, Joanne walked room to room, turning on lights, turning on music. Anything to make the house look occupied.

The phone rang.

She picked it up after the first ring. "Listen, you creep. If you think you can scare me with—"

"Jo, it's me."

Blake. She sighed with relief. "Sorry. Someone has been leaving prank phone calls again."

"I called to check on you. I tried you last night."

"I went down to the shore. They found a body."

"Oh, Joanne. Rachel?"

"They don't know. They need to do some tests. I took them Rachel's dental X-rays. They even took my blood." She hesitated. "It was late so I stayed the night."

She listened as he sighed, apparently not happy that she'd gone to the shore again.

"Listen, Blake, I had to go. I needed to talk to the police about David's blood sample. I didn't want them to assume it wasn't Rachel in case the remains they found didn't have a DNA match consistent with David being the father."

"So you're admitting that Rachel is mine." He sounded smug.

"I'm not saying that."

"So you spent the night in Tippins." He paused. Took a breath. "With David?"

"With my husband."

Another sigh. "I thought you said that you needed some space away from him so that you could move forward. He's dragging you down right now. You don't need that kind of negativity around you."

"He's still my husband, Blake. We're trying our best to find our way through the pain."

"And for you, that means looking ahead. Look for the good on the horizon." He paused. "Need some company? Have the phone calls freaked you out?"

"I'm okay. I want to get some sleep."

"Call me if anyone tries to creep you out. I'm glad to come. I'll sleep on the couch."

"Maybe it's best if we didn't see each other so much."

"No!" He halted. "It's just, I mean, why should you pull away from your friends when you're going through so much right now? That's when friends are needed most."

She didn't want to argue with him. "Thanks, Blake. Good night."

She set the phone down and trudged to the bedroom, leaving the rest of the house bright and music playing on the sound system.

Joanne prepared for sleep, putting in a pair of foam earplugs to seal out the noise.

Then she lay down and tried to sleep.

Mildred Crenshaw had spent an agonizing day at Nassawadox Community Hospital. The rescue squad had whisked Jimmy off, who apparently was barely holding on to life. She arrived at the hospital feeling out of sorts. He had been a healthy seventeen-year-old. Vigorous boys weren't supposed to be at death's door without warning.

Sam joined her in the afternoon, after cleaning up from the day's work. As they sat in the ICU waiting room, Darrel Mason loped in. Darrel was twenty-one, a crabber with a penchant for beer and trouble. Mildred didn't like the fact that Darrel had seemingly taken Jimmy under his wing.

Sam flipped through an outdated boating magazine. Darrel pushed three green padded chairs together and stretched out. Mildred tried to work on a cross-stitch, but had forgotten a thimble, so the work was slow. She didn't feel like doing it anyway.

She worried about Jimmy. They'd had him since he was one, when their son was killed in Iraq. His mother was dysfunctional, unable to stay off drugs in the wake of her husband's death. Sam and Mildred had taken Jimmy in to keep him out of foster care. Last year, against their wishes, he'd dropped out of school to help on his grandfather's crab boat. It was hard work, but he liked the money. And after work, he liked to hang out on the docks with some of the older guys who'd chosen crabbing over college.

Sam had done the best he could, but the years had been tough for him. He grew to resent the Iraqis in particular and the Muslim world in general.

At ten Dr. Harrison Evans, an internal medicine specialist, joined them in a quiet corner of the waiting room. "How's Jimmy?" Mildred asked.

"He's alive." He spoke slowly and loud enough for Sam to hear. "We've had to put him on a ventilator to help him breathe. He wasn't getting enough oxygen."

Darrel yawned noisily, stretched, and wandered over to join them in their conversation.

Mildred made the introductions. "Dr. Evans, this is my husband, Sam. And this is one of Jimmy's friends, Darrel Mason."

The doctor nodded. "Jimmy's had a rough go of it. Let me see if I can take you through what has happened, step by step."

Sam nodded. Mildred moved closer and gripped his arm.

"Jimmy injured his arm. Although you said he injured it by scraping it on the gravel, it looks like something else. A burn."

Sam and Millie exchanged looks. *A burn?*

The doctor continued, "Unfortunately, the wound traveled all the way around his arm, and so, when the scab formed, it was tight like a band around his forearm, limiting the blood flow to his hand. That was why he complained about his fingers. They weren't getting enough blood. Then the wound became infected, causing his arm to become extremely swollen. Because of the sluggish blood flow, the main vein leading out of his arm clotted off. Because of the infection in the arm, I believe the clot in the vein got infected, too."

Dr. Evans paused, looking each person in the eyes to see if they were understanding. Millie and Sam nodded, but Darrel kept his eyes riveted to a spot on the floor in front of his chair.

"Anyway," Dr. Evans said, "It appears from our studies that he's had a pulmonary embolism."

Mildred leaned forward. "Embolism?"

"It's when a clot breaks loose and travels toward the heart, passing through the heart, then into the lungs. I believe this must have happened after he unwrapped the arm this morning. The clot must have dislodged and traveled to his lung. That's why he collapsed with chest pain."

Mildred covered her mouth. "Is he going to be okay?"

"We're doing all we can. A surgeon had to cut through the burn scar on both sides of his forearm to allow blood to flow to his hand again. If he survives, he will probably require an amputation of several fingertips that have turned gangrenous in the wake of starving for blood for so long. In addition, he'll have to have skin grafts to cover the wound on the arm. For now, I'm worried about the spread of the infection to his lungs. Remember, I think the clot in his arm was infected, and when it broke loose, it carried all of that foul infection into the lungs. His body is trying to fight the infection. For now, his blood pressure is very low without the support of medications."

Sam touched the sleeve of the doctor's white coat. "Do everything you can for him, Doc."

"Is there any reason to believe Jimmy could have been burned, but have been too embarrassed to talk about it?"

Sam shifted in his chair. "Maybe when he wrecked his motorcycle, his arm laid against the muffler."

"It is unlikely to cause a burn like this. This one circles all the way around his arm."

Millie looked at Darrel, whose eyes were still fixed on the floor. "He was with you on Monday night, wasn't he?"

Darrel chewed his gum loudly. "Yep, but he was fine, then. Bob and Jimmy and I had a few beers, Mrs. Crenshaw. I know you don't like him to drink, but no one forces him."

The doctor sat up straight and seemed to hesitate. "I know there was a fire that night, a boat that burned. Any chance that Jimmy could have been around that fire and was reluctant to talk about it?"

Darrel stood up. "Listen, Doc, I'm telling you he was with me. I don't know nothing about no fire. If Jimmy was involved, you'll have to ask him."

"Right now that's impossible. He's got a breathing tube passing down his throat, so even if he was alert enough to talk, which he's not, he'd be unable to because of the tube." He paused, his eyes boring in on Darrel. "If he lives, maybe we can question him."

Darrel huffed. "Well then, I guess you'll have to believe me, then. Jimmy was with me, and we weren't anywhere close to a fire."

The doctor stood up and faced Darrel. "For now, we're going to treat his arm as if he has an infected burn. Any information that you find that might help Jimmy would be appreciated."

With that, the doctor left. Mildred and Sam looked at Darrel.

Darrel snorted. "That guy has some nerve. He acts like I'm holding something out on him."

Sam stepped forward. "Are you?"

Darrel cursed him. "I can't believe you, old man!" he snarled and disappeared from the waiting room into the hospital corridor.

Denton Reynolds liked his job as county sheriff.

Denton Reynolds hated his job as county sheriff.

It depended on the day. On Thursday morning his office assistant, Carol Peterson, buzzed the intercom. "Sam Crenshaw on the phone. He says he needs to speak to you."

The sheriff lifted his head from his desk and moaned. This week he hated his job. Arson, dead bodies, and missing children all swirled around in his consciousness, robbing his sleep and filling his days with Maalox moments. He picked up the phone. "Sheriff Reynolds."

"Denton, it's Sam. I thought I'd better tell you what's going on with Jimmy."

"Your grandson?"

"Right. He's awful sick, in the hospital. May not even survive. He had some sort of infection in his left arm that spread to his lungs."

"That's awful, Sam. How's Millie holdin' up?"

"Not so well. On top of it all, she's layin' in bed this morning, moaning about her back." He paused a moment. "Listen, Denton, I thought you ought to know. The doctor thinks Jimmy's problem all started because of a burn on the arm. A burn he would have gotten on the night Gus Conners's boat burned."

"What did Jimmy say?"

"He said he scraped his arm on the gravel when he dumped his motorcycle."

"Hmmm."

"All I know is that he, Bob Smith, and Darrel Mason were out at the docks drinking that night. Darrel got all bent out of shape when the doc asked him if he knew if Jimmy had been around the fire."

"Why don't you ask Jimmy?"

"We can't talk to him. He's on life support."

"Maybe I'll have a little chat with Darrel. Was anyone else with them?"

"Not that I know of." Sam cleared his throat. "I don't trust Darrel. A thought crossed my mind that he might not like to see Jimmy recover if he's going to implicate him in a crime."

"Come on, Sam, this is Tippins. You can't believe that Darrel would—" He halted when he thought about the craziness the town had slid into over the past month. Maybe he should expect the worst. "Tell you what, Sam. I'll put a tail on Darrel. I'll make sure he doesn't interfere."

THAT NIGHT I rose at midnight, unable to sleep. I'd put off dealing with my old pain well enough during the day when I had distractions, but at night, I couldn't escape. Without something to do, I was doomed to deal with haunting memories that oozed like pus from an infected wound. It was as if I'd built up a tough scab covering over the years, and with one directed cut of Joanne's scalpel, she'd debrided away the crust holding back the sleeping pain.

I knew I needed to think about it, maybe even tell someone about it to help get it out in the open. But who?

Pray. Tell God.

I wasn't sure that was a good idea. I was still pretty sure He wouldn't be too happy with my plans for revenge. I pulled on a pair of jeans and an old black T-shirt emblazoned with the logo from Boston—the old rock band, not the city. I poured myself some sweet tea and went out in the backyard to remember. Something was driving me, and I thought maybe I could unearth some old memory that might get me off the hook. Maybe, just maybe, in the wake of a tragedy, I'd screwed up the memory and gotten it wrong.

I sat down at the picnic table and took a sip of sweet tea. The taste helped transport me back to the hot days of childhood summer vacation. Summer days in Tippins meant time spent with my dad on the *Beautiful Swimmer*, riding bikes with Tommy Schroder, and swimming in Nimble Creek. But that fateful Thursday, Dad had left early, promising to take me up to Dover later to see a movie, so I was left playing with Rachel, my toddler sister, and trying to stay out of my mother's hair, a not-so-easy task when you're ten years old. I'd bugged her all morning to play a game of Monopoly or The Game of Life, but Mom had to clean house.

She made me pick up my clothes and straighten the collection of comic books I had spread all over the floor from the first issue to the last.

When I appeared in the kitchen a few minutes later, she was making cupcakes, a surprise for Dad when he got home.

"Go outside and play. Will you watch Rachel for a little while? She's so fussy when she's cooped up indoors."

I looked at my baby sister and moaned. "Okay. Come on, Rachie, let's go play. Want to play ball?"

I led my sister outside into the backyard. It was a typical day. The air was thick with moisture and the smell of marsh grass was in the air. I pushed Rachel around on a Big Wheel until little beads of sweat gathered above my upper lip.

"Look, Rachie," I said before licking the salt from my lip. "I've got a mustache."

We splashed each other in a little round baby pool that Dad had bought at Sears and Roebuck. We played hide and seek.

I set my sweet tea on the old picnic table, unsure whether I wanted to go further. I didn't want to tread on that load of guilt.

I paced the yard, aware that I was sweating. I'd ventured close to the point of deep, emotional pain, and the caution lights were flashing. *We were playing hide and seek.* I looked into the night sky. *Come on, think. Maybe it wasn't my fault. I was only a boy. I was trying to help my mom. I was trying to entertain Rachel.*

I remembered lifting little Rachel out of the baby pool. "Come find me, Rachie."

That's when I got the idea to hide by the shed. I kept sticking my head around the corner and singing out, "Oh, Rachie, come and find me."

As soon as she'd look my way, I'd act surprised and jerk my head around the side of the old shed.

I slid down and sat on the ground with my back against the wall, listening to her giggle. My hand rested against an old crab trap. I kept calling her name, but stopped looking back. With all the noise I was making, even a two-year-old could find me without looking at my face.

I ran my hand over the wire cage. I picked up a stick and started poking through the wire mesh at some strands of dried fish remains in the center of the pot. *What did I do next?*

I teased off a stinky lump of fish guts and used the stick to draw in the sand and thought about going to the theater with my dad. I loved summer! Fishing. Swimming. Shooting at squirrels with my dad's old .22 rifle.

Soon enough, I got distracted by the pier, and then I remembered the crab pot that Dad let me place off the end of the pier into Nimble Creek. I pulled it up. A crab or two could be sacrificed to use for catfish bait, and I could fish away the afternoon until heading to Dover. Water streamed through the wire mesh to reveal my catch. I had four crabs and a large snapping turtle. That, of course, excited me even more, because Dad told me if I ever caught that big snapper, that Mom could cook up some turtle soup.

I dropped the trap onto the pier and ran toward the house. "Rachel," I called. "Look what I caught!"

She didn't answer. She must have gone inside.

I headed for the house calling for my mom to come and see.

"Mom!" I let the screen door slam behind me. "We caught a turtle in the crab pot."

She sighed and as she pulled a tray of fresh cupcakes out of the oven. "I don't have time to deal with a turtle just now."

"I'll do it."

Her expression said *Don't you dare,* and *Not in this lifetime!*

I winced. "I can wait for Dad. He'll show me."

Another sigh. "Okay, leave him in the trap for now." She lifted a mixing bowl and put it in the sink. "Where's your sister?"

"I think she came inside. Maybe in her room. Hey, Rachel!"

"Do you have to scream?"

My mother was drying her hands on her apron as she walked out on the back patio.

That's when I heard her scream, and my world turned crazy.

I felt my stomach churn.

I felt that way even now—a bit like I wanted to throw up and make the pain go away.

But I couldn't, and it wouldn't.

Images were burned into my memory without a delete key. A little blue foot sticking over the edge of the baby pool. My mother hugging a wet, limp child to her breast. My mother screaming at me to call an ambulance.

Is this why I'm so reluctant to admit that my Rachel might have drowned? I can't face that the same thing happened to my little daughter. I felt the lump in my throat growing. I cried, not caring to wipe the tears from my face.

I paced around the yard in the moonlight, tempted to berate myself over my compulsion to go over old memories I'd left undisturbed below the surface.

Instead, I began to pray.

THURSDAY AFTERNOON I sat on my scorched pier and watched as the boys from Simmons' Salvage raised what was left of the *Beautiful Swimmer* and set her remains in the backyard. Charlie Dodd from Tippins' Boat Works had promised to bring a truck over the weekend to take the engine in for an overhaul.

While I sat there, it occurred to me that I'd dropped a crab pot off the end of the pier, something that had probably disappeared into ash.

After the salvage guys left, I put on my bathing suit and waded out into the water. The problem was, Nimble Creek was so muddy, you couldn't see beyond a foot or two in front of your face. For that reason, I took a deep breath and swam in the direction of the end of the pier, waving my hands out in front of my face to guide the way. Sure enough, my hand closed around a wall of the wire pot. I hauled it toward shallow water, kicking my way toward shore.

Once in the shallows I lifted the pot to drain the water through the wire cage. Excited to see my catch, I lowered my head to the edge and gasped. There, sitting in the middle of an island of crabs, was a big snapping turtle.

"Well, I'll be," I whispered, feeling suddenly weak in the legs. It seemed almost surreal. I hadn't remembered catching a turtle since the day my sister died. I walked toward shore, letting the pot drop onto the sand and falling to my knees. *What is this? An answer to my prayers, a chance to complete something I'd wanted to do years ago?*

I glanced again at the turtle and then slowly lifted my eyes toward the house. In my mind, I could see the little wading pool, and above one edge, a pale little foot hanging over the side.

"No!" I ran toward the house, falling down at the edge of the pool, reaching forward to rescue the child. As my hands struck the grass, the image disappeared. I covered my face and began to cry. Old tears of loss and pain. *If only I'd been faster. If only I would have been watching. If only . . .*

I stood, as another thought challenged my sorrow. *Could it be that God had sent another turtle to give me some sort of closure?* I paced, sniffing back tears, and formulated a plan. I searched the garage for the right tool, and marched out to the pot, armed with Dad's old hatchet. I opened the trap and shook the turtle out onto the ground where he landed on his back. He squirmed, four legs flailing through the air, swimming against the wind. I picked him up, pointing his head away from me. I placed him carefully on the center of a large tree stump at the water's edge. *I'll give you closure,* I thought.

Slowly, I raised my hatchet in the air. I stopped at the top of a high arc, wondering if I could really follow through. But, in a moment, I realized I *had* to do this. I had to complete what I'd wanted to do on a very different day a long time before on a day that ended in tragedy and without turtle soup. It all seemed rather silly to make something of a little thing, yet, at the same time, a part of me *had* to do this. With determination and a sudden belief in second chances, I brought the blade down on the turtle's back.

Crunching madly through the thick shell, I sought my revenge against my own sin.

After a few minutes I sat sweating on the ground.

It was muggy and hot and the water slid happily from my nose to the ground. I laughed at myself. I had no idea how to cook a turtle.

I called Captain Billy's and talked to the chef, who gladly doled out advice about the delicacies of turtle soup. I tried to lay my memories to rest in the kitchen, slicing potato and onion into a large pot of turtle meat I'd cubed and salted. I thickened it with flour and milk and let it simmer to the right texture.

Then I sprinkled it with a slick of white cheddar cheese and extra large garlic croutons and sat down for a feast.

Tomorrow, I promised myself, I'd go talk to my mother.

Sheriff Denton caught up with Darrel Mason at a waterside bar called Pirate's Brew. Mason was throwing darts with Pete Maggins and flirting with Pete's little sister, Kerri.

"Darrel, could I speak with you?"

"Sheriff, can't you see I'm entertaining a young lady?" He winked at Kerri.

"Outside."

Darrel took a sip of his beer, set it on a nearby table, swaggered toward the door with the sheriff. "What's this all about?"

"I need to know what you and Jimmy Crenshaw were up to on Monday night."

"I was down at the Tippins Pier, cleaning my boat. I got done early, so I celebrated with a little beer."

"Was Jimmy drinking?"

"He's underage, Sheriff, you know that." He paused and wrinkled his nose. "But he's got a mind of his own. I think he snitched one or two when I wasn't looking."

"Have any idea how he might have burned his arm?"

"No idea. What's your take on it?"

"I think you guys might have decided to keep the Somalis out of the crabbing business."

"What makes you say that?"

Darrel was too smooth. Too easy.

"Because Monday night, someone torched Gus Conners' boat."

"I wouldn't know."

"Sam Crenshaw says Jimmy didn't get in until after two that night. That was after Dr. Conners called nine-one-one."

"We were down at the pier. I heard the sirens myself."

"The docs say that Jimmy Crenshaw may die. If they knew exactly what happened to him, it might help save his life."

"You're makin' that up. Those doctors can treat him even if they don't know what happened."

The sheriff cleared his throat. "How'd you like to go into a fight with one hand tied behind your back?" He paused. "If you change your mind, I'm sure a judge would look kindly on your help."

That night I awoke sometime early in the morning with a fresh memory pushing up like a dandelion through soft soil after a rain.

I was ten, lying on top of my Star Wars sheets, listening to my parents in the room next door to mine.

Mom was crying. Long, gut-wrenching sobs that my father couldn't comfort, and left my ears feeling raw.

I listened to her cries and Dad's whispers of "Now, now" until I couldn't stand it. I pulled my pillow over my head, only daring to lift it up again when I thought I would suffocate. And then, as on so many other nights before, I tiptoed down the hall and out into the moonlight to sit on the pier.

So now, just like when I was a little boy alone with my fears and sorrow, I padded down the hall to the back door.

The moon was up, one day past full, and I could hear the song of frogs seeking love on the edge of the soggy marsh. I walked to the end of the pier, sat on a charred board, and stared off into the summer sky. Maybe Joanne was right.

But I had a problem. I'd always been a justice type of guy. It seems my bread was always buttered with fairness. I'd always wanted the bad guy to get his due.

And I'd never gotten mine.

I lay down, looking at the stars, thinking of how often I'd done the same thing with my daughter. Eventually, even in my sorrow, I was able to lift my thoughts and take a small step forward. Life *now* was demanding my attention. I stood and paced off a small area to the left of the pier, envisioning a way to rebuild after the fire.

There, I'd build a gazebo, connected to the pier by that neat decking that lasts forever and is made out of sawdust and recycled plastic bags. The pier would be rebuilt, but twice as wide, with a covered boathouse where I could house a new boat, maybe a multipurpose-type boat for water-skiing and fishing. I dreamed of replanting the backyard, leveling it off with a new expanded back deck instead of the patio. I'd landscape the yard into three levels with azaleas and flowers bordering the step-downs leading to the water. At the water's edge, a bulkhead retaining wall would create a sharp border with the creek, eliminating the irregular marshy-lawn interface. There would be a slate path—large fitted stepping-stones creating a natural flow from the back deck to gazebo to pier and boathouse.

Excited by my dreams, I returned to the house and began sketching. Before long, I thought of ways to turn the house into a wonderful escape from city life. I'd knock down the wall between the kitchen and dining room, planting two columns in its place.

That would create one large working kitchen-dining area. I'd like to replace the old floor with tile, update the kitchen cabinets, and rebuild the old chimney with a new stone one that opened on two sides—one facing the kitchen and one the den.

I walked down the hall. The master bedroom could be twice as big if I eliminated the third bedroom, which would require knocking out another wall. A master bath could be added, plumbing the fixtures into the present hall bathroom.

I paced around the outside of the house. The old siding could be removed, perhaps utilizing stucco. The front stoop could be discarded, and the roof expanded to overhang a wrap-around porch. Tippins weather was perfect for life under the shade of a large porch with ceiling fans.

Too excited now to return to bed, I dripped fresh Kenyan AA coffee and took a shower, thankful for any project that would help me divert my sorrow.

By nine that morning I was on my way to the small gravesite next to the clapboard Presbyterian church in Oyster. I wanted to say "I'm sorry," and I supposed this was the best place of ceremony to do it.

I thought about my mother's tears in the wake of my sister's death. For years, I'd thought that I'd make up for the loss of my sister by being a great dad for my Rachel. But now even that had fallen through my hands.

I was lost in my remorse, not hearing the approach of another when I felt a hand on my shoulder.

"Hello, David."

I turned to see an older man I recognized as Reverend Brown.

"How've you been?" he asked.

"Okay." *Boy, I'm sure he can see through that lame answer.*

He had a faraway look in his eyes. "I baptized you here," he said.

I'd been baptized according to the teachings of the Presbyterian church. I forced a smile. "I'm afraid it might not have stuck."

He chuckled. "It's not a matter of sticking. It's just a symbol. Your mother thought it was important."

We were quiet for a moment before he added. "I heard about your daughter. We've been praying."

I felt like telling him that I'd prayed more in the last few weeks than ever in my life, and yet I felt the heavens were silent. My prayers had taken me nowhere. Instead, I only said a weak, "Thanks."

I followed his gaze to my mother's grave. "You're angry about your daughter's disappearance."

I nodded again, aware that my head was bobbing like one of those stupid dolls.

"Your mother struggled with anger, too. She was angry at God for taking away her baby girl."

"That was my fault." The words were out before I could stop them.

He shook his head. "God didn't turn his head away that day, David. You were only ten years old. It wasn't your fault."

I couldn't speak. A knot of dry grass had replaced my voice.

"Your mother finally understood that. She had to let God's plan be God's plan."

"And why would a God of love allow such pain?"

"There are no simple answers to that one. We only know that His love is trustworthy, even when it comes disguised as suffering."

"Sounds to me like you're letting God off the hook for misbehavior."

He smiled. "In a sense, we are letting God off, forgiving Him, so to speak, although it's not for misbehavior, or for His *needing* forgiveness by any means."

I wrinkled my nose in a question.

"Forgiveness isn't so much for the one getting it. It's for the one giving it. A decision to let God be God is letting Him off the hook."

He turned and looked toward the little church building. "Don't make yourself so scarce, Doc. Sharing your pain with others might do you a world of good."

I swallowed at the grass in my throat.

He walked away on the path that led toward the church. I stood there, watching him go, in a bit of wonder over a prayer answered with a turtle and a minister who was as close to a messenger from God as I'd ever seen. I'd heard my Christian barber use a phrase once: "a God thing," and I wondered what kind of crazy talk it was. But just then, I found myself looking after Reverend Brown and thinking that I'd seen it for myself.

I turned and looked at the tombstone. I brushed back a tear and whispered, "I'm sorry, Mom."

32

LATER FRIDAY MORNING I got a call from Sheriff Reynolds.

"Dr. Conners, I've got some news. Good or bad, you decide."

I waited, so he continued.

"The guys at forensics say the little body wasn't your daughter. The dental X-rays match a little girl missing from a playground in Dover, Delaware."

"How long ago did she disappear?"

"The week after Rachel."

"When did you find out about this other disappearance?"

"Just now, when I got a call from forensics."

I felt like cursing. Undoubtedly, it was the work of the same freak.

"The good news is, it doesn't seem there have been any disappearances since we've had Riley Johnson incarcerated."

"And the courts are going to let you keep him that way without evidence?"

"We're got enough for now."

"Have you interrogated him over the Delaware case?"

"I will. This afternoon."

I took a deep breath. So much for closure. Instead, all I had was more anger toward a beast who dared wreck so many lives. "Thanks, Sheriff. I'll tell my wife."

Friday afternoon Mildred Crenshaw was convinced a miracle had taken place. Dr. Evans felt sure Jimmy was strong enough to be taken off the ventilator. He'd responded to the blood thinners and antibiotics, and his blood pressure had stabilized off the medication. It was time to see if he could make it without mechanical support.

Thirty minutes later a nurse came to the waiting room and looked at Sam and Mildred. "You can visit with him if you like."

Mildred gasped when she saw him lying there surrounded by so much machinery. A breathing machine sat at the ready. A heart monitor recorded his cardiac rhythm, and a second monitor displayed a dazzling array of numbers. Several plastic IV bags of fluid hung overhead, his arm suspended by a sling attached to what looked to be some sort of pulley, and below him was a bag collecting urine.

Jimmy offered a weak smile. "Hi."

"Oh, Jimmy, we thought we'd lost you." Mildred started to cry.

Sam clutched his John Deere cap in his hands. "Lots of people have been praying for you."

"The doc explained to me what happened," Jimmy said. After only a moment he appeared to be blinking back tears of his own. "I'm so sorry. I didn't mean to cause such trouble."

Mildred leaned in so she could hear. "Hush. You're no trouble."

He shook his head. "No," he said. "The doctor was right. I burned my arm."

Sam twisted his hat, saying nothing.

"Do you want the whole story, or just part of it?" Jimmy asked, looking ashamed.

"Tell us what we need to know, son," Sam said.

Jimmy took a deep breath, looked toward his arm, and began. "Me and the boys went to the pier to hang out. Darrel brought beer." Jimmy's head jerked up, looking between his grandparents.

"Continue," Sam said in his no-nonsense way.

"We were celebratin' a good catch. We talked about stuff. You know, guy stuff."

"Girls, crabs, and boats," Sam offered.

Jimmy gave a hint of a smile. "Yeah." He looked at his grandmother and sobered.

Mildred looked at him, then down at her hands that gripped the railing around his bed until her knuckles had turned white. "Tell us the story," she managed to say, although she knew it would be hard to hear.

Jimmy cracked the tab on a beer and slurped cold foam overflow from the side of the can. "My grandpa says the Somalis are gonna take over our crab business."

Bob Smith sat on the pier's edge and stretched his bare feet out toward the water. "That just ain't right. We can't have no Muslims takin' over."

Jimmy pushed his baseball cap up on his forehead. "Some Mohamed guy just bought Gus Conners' boat. Gramps says Gus will roll over in his grave."

Darrel Mason took a long drag on a cigarette and tossed the butt into the water. "That doctor-son of Gus don't care. As long as he gets his money."

Jimmy gulped his beer, feeling the start of a great buzz. He wobbled over to the cooler to swipe another. "I think we should just tell the buyers to overlook 'em. Send 'em back to the Middle East where they belong."

"The buyers won't care as long as the crabs are good and the price right," Bob said.

"The Lightner boys wanted another boat. But the doctor's price was too high." Darrel grumbled. "It's unpatriotic."

Jimmy opened another beer. "How you figure?"

Darrel cursed the Muslims. "They freakin' terrorize our nation on nine-eleven, right? So we just turn around and invite 'em into our country and let 'em freakin' take over our businesses."

"What can you do?"

"We don't have to sit around and let 'em take over the bay. Crabbing's all we got."

Jimmy nodded his head and cussed his own sentiments. "It's our heritage."

Jimmy and the boys continued drinking and talking. They talked about dream girls who loved watermen, cooking, and making more watermen. They smoked. They cursed the topsy-turvy market that kept them on the boats for long hours and made their fathers worry. They talked of war heroes, and Johnny Blakemore, the only boy from Tippins to go to the U.S. Naval Academy. If you weren't on the water catching crabs, you might as well be on an aircraft carrier. At least then you would be protecting your country from the freakin' terrorists.

But what could they do?

They drank until their bravado was up and their judgment was down.

Darrel started to smile. Bob and Jimmy had a pissing contest off the end of the pier.

Sometime after midnight Darrel picked up a can of diesel fuel. "Let's go have some fun."

Thirty minutes later, the trio pulled up into the cul-de-sac beyond the Conners' house in Jimmy's old Ford Taurus with the lights off. Both Gus's house and the house with the Muslims were dark.

It took five minutes for Darrel to slosh five gallons of diesel fuel all over the *Beautiful Swimmer,* splashing the sleeve of Jimmy's sweatshirt in the process. "Careful, Darrel," Jimmy said, swearing. "You're gettin' me wet."

After drenching the boat, they retreated to the pier where Bob was stuffing a rag into the open top of an empty Coke bottle. "I've seen this on TV," he whispered. "Pour the last of the fuel in here."

Darrel poured the fuel in the bottle and saturated the old rag wick. Then he pulled out a small propane lighter, his favorite, the one with the picture of an American flag wrapped around a woman wearing nothing but high heels. As he tried to light the wick, Bob's hand weaved with excitement. Jimmy reached down to steady Bob's hand. Suddenly, flame leapt up Jimmy's arm. His sleeve was on fire. He swatted it with his free hand to no avail. As his flesh began to steam, he swore and jumped off the pier.

Darrel and Bob laughed hysterically.

Jimmy pulled himself up a barnacle-laden ladder and spat. "Fools."

Just then Bob held up his torch and threw it onto the deck of the *Beautiful Swimmer.* Flames engulfed the boat, reaching into the night sky.

Darrel and Bob started running. Jimmy ran behind, cursing his decision to go along with the plan. He looked at his left arm where the sweatshirt seemed to have melted to his skin.

Jimmy dug his keys out of his pocket. "You drive," he said to Darrel. "I've got to get this off my arm."

"Let's get out of here."

The room was silent when he finished. Mildred had handed him a hankie she kept in her pocket, and Jimmy swiped at his wet face, obviously embarrassed by his tears. "Man, I messed up bad this time."

His grandfather stepped forward. "I don't want you to talk to the sheriff if he comes by. I'm going to hire a lawyer. You'll talk to the law only in front of him."

"Okay."

"Listen to me, Jimmy," Sam said. "The sheriff told me that the prosecutor will want this to go down under a hate crime. That's going to mean some serious charges, but if you make a deal with them and agree to testify against Darrel, I think a judge will go easy on you."

Jimmy nodded.

Mildred smiled and brushed back her tears. "After you talk to the lawyer, I'm going to want you to talk to Dr. Conners."

"Yes, ma'am."

The next time I saw Riley Johnson was the following Wednesday afternoon. Again, "stomach pain" was written beside the appointment registry.

With the guard outside the exam room door, I began my interview. "How are you feeling?"

"Low, Doc."

"Low tired, or low in some other way?"

"My equipment's failing, Doc."

"And you know this how?"

"Come on, Doc. A man knows when his manhood is failin.' "

"They found a little girl in the bay, Riley. A girl that went missing from a park in Dover. Did you ever visit Dover?"

"The sheriff already asked me about her."

"What'd you tell him?"

"I don't know anything about little girls in Dover."

I listened to his chest and heart and went through the motions of checking his pulse and blood pressure. Last of all, I did another scrotal check. His testes were shrinking. Right on schedule.

"What's going on with me, Doc?"

I kept my voice low and steady. "You're losing your manhood because your testicles are shrinking."

"What can you do about it?"

"Me? Nothing." I paused. "Maybe you can do something."

"What do you mean?"

"Remember your theory? That God was punishing you?" I sat on a chair beside the stretcher he was sitting on, wishing that Riley could just spill the beans and validate my theory. Instead, I felt my conversations with him were repetitive, leading to my frustration and arousing his suspicion. I pressed on. "Why would God punish you by shrinking your manhood?"

"I've done my share of bad things, Doc."

"Did you see the chaplain? What did he say?"

"He said God could forgive any sin. Even mine."

"What about payment for sin, Riley? Did he say anything about that?"

"Yeah, he did."

"That's right, isn't it? God demands a payment."

"You feeling guilty, Doc? Is that it? What did you do?"

I stayed quiet and fumbled with my pen. "This isn't about me."

Riley grunted. "My attorney hopes to get me out of here soon. He's getting a hearing set up. He may even want you to testify how bad the prison's been on my health." He hesitated. "Maybe you'll even have to testify how my manhood's going away."

I sighed. I definitely didn't want to tell anyone about that.

"Say, Doc, what if a man did all those horrible things that the sheriff keeps talking about? Do you think Jesus could forgive a man for that?"

I sighed. I wanted to tell him that child molesters should burn in hell, but I thought about my own struggle not to lust for my neighbor and stayed quiet. When I finally spoke, it was what I thought in my head, but not in my heart. "Sure, Riley. God can forgive a man for anything." I paused, stood up, and let my hand rest on the picture of my daughter. I turned it so that Riley could see. "The question is, can a man?"

Two days later I found myself at the bedside of Jimmy Crenshaw. He was flanked by his grandparents, and in the corner sat another man, whom Sam had introduced as Mike Dodson, Jimmy's attorney.

Jimmy was pale, and looked worse lying against the light green hospital sheets. "I wanted to tell you myself."

"Okay, tell me what?"

"I was there the night your boat was burned. It wasn't right, but I went along with it."

"Because I'd sold the boat to my neighbors?"

He looked at his attorney, who prompted him ahead. "Yes."

I took a deep breath.

"I'm sorry," he said.

I sat on the edge of his bed. "Why'd you do it?"

"A lot of reasons. None good."

"Explain it to me."

"When I was a little boy, my father was killed by a car bomb while serving in Iraq." He looked away. "And then there's nine-eleven. Everyone knows what the Muslims did to our country." He paused. "That night, my buddies and I were drinkin' and talking about the Muslims comin' in and taking over our businesses. We got riled up and said it wasn't going to happen here. I decided it was time for me to help do something to them instead of the other way around."

"Payback time, huh?"

"Yeah."

"But instead . . ."

"I ended up here."

I sighed. "You've learned an important lesson. It isn't your place to avenge your father's death."

"No, sir." He paused. "I'm willing to work to help pay off your debt."

"Gus insured the boat. I'll be paid for it." I pointed at his arm. "I think you're paying your debt right now."

"So you forgive me?"

Suddenly, I felt like such a poser, and I wasn't willing to spout platitudes to make him feel better. "Tell you what, Jimmy. I'm at a place in my life when I'm trying to figure this all out. I'm not willing to say words that I don't mean." I paused. "I know you didn't do this to hurt me. If anyone needs to forgive, it's Mohamed."

Jimmy pressed his lips together. I don't think it was what he wanted to hear, but he nodded his assent.

I walked down the hall and shoved two quarters into a machine promising fresh-brewed coffee. I listened to a clunk followed by a whirling noise of grinding beans, and finally watched a stream of coffee fall into a Styrofoam cup. It passed the sniff test.

I hated myself for being such a fraud. I was amazed how easily I could deal out advice, but not be ready to listen to it myself. I walked outside and sat in my car, thinking of my mother.

I was nine when my mother tried to teach me how to forgive. Billie Martin had borrowed my new three-speed bike with a banana seat, but he left it out after promising me he would store it in his garage. The bike disappeared before the next day.

"You need to forgive him, Davy."

I shook my head. "He's not getting off that easy. He needs to suffer."

"Forgiving him isn't for him. It's for you."

How I could dig up old advice like my mother's and let it slide off my tongue like it was heartfelt unnerved me. But my case was different, wasn't it? I wasn't dealing with a stolen bike. I was dealing with someone who stole my daughter away. Surely an eye for an eye was the justifiable response, wasn't it?

My conscience stung me. I felt like an imposter, trapped in the shell of a nice family doctor.

Tricia smiled when she read the headlines. She called to her husband, who sat staring at a computer screen. "The little body they found belonged to a family up in Dover."

"Horrible," he grunted. "Just horrible."

"But this will do wonders for your bill. I think any house member that votes against you is going to face a barrage of media criticism."

He grunted and tapped the screen with his index finger.

His bill, a comprehensive reform of the sexual offenders law, stiffened penalties, made prison time automatic, and made offense records public knowledge for any offender moving out of prison. Around Richmond, they were calling it Rachel's Bill. Capturing a win for his bill would look great on his résumé and would provide excellent PR in his bid for a national Senate seat.

Tricia crossed her legs and lowered the paper. "I know what happened to Rachel was a horrible thing, but maybe through this bill, something good can come out of it." *And so convenient.*

"The *Richmond Times-Dispatch* poll shows me fourteen points ahead of McGinnis."

"Thanks to our little granddaughter. You were two points down before Rachel disappeared." She paused. "You've got a news conference in twenty minutes. Are you ready to practice that speech?"

33

THAT EVENING I didn't feel like cooking. I made a ham and cheese sandwich and covered the cheese with green olives—the kind with the little pimentos stuffed into their hollow middles. I called Roy Dyerle and asked if he'd be willing to do some construction work around the home place. He indicated his willingness, so I called my Realtor. She answered as she always did, with her plastic smile shining through her voice.

"Helllllloooo, this is Sally."

"Sally, David Conners here."

"Oh, Dr. Conners, I'm glad you called. You don't know how hard I've tried to get someone interested in your father's place. But honestly, your neighbors aren't doing you any favors. Right now, with all the buzz around Tippins about the fire, I'm afraid I'm not getting any nibbles."

"But—"

"If you want this thing sold, you're going to have to come down on your price. There's no wiggle room in the market. I know you were hoping some rich Baltimorean would want it for a second home, but honestly, Doctor, they're looking for charming little places that—"

I interrupted to get a word in. "Sally, I called to tell you that I'm taking it off the market. I've decided to work on it a bit."

"Oh, I see. You'll list it again once you've done a bit of fix-up. The market will likely be up again next spring, and I can list it in Washington, Baltimore, and northern Virginia so—"

"Just call it therapy. I need to do this."

"Oh, well, okay. I'll remove it from my listings. Honestly, the way it was, I didn't see much hope in getting any fish to bite."

"Thanks, Sally."

After hanging up, I paced around the house, dreaming of changes while eating my ham, cheese, and olive special. My thoughts inevitably turned to the significant events that happened inside the walls of our little place on Shore Drive. I thought about my mother's struggle against breast cancer. Specifically, I remembered the day I had to face the idea Mom was likely to die.

Blake and I had escaped Richmond at the end of our second year, seeking a quiet place to cram for part one of our National Board exam. We'd turned Mom's dining table into a king-size desk of sorts, with books, papers, and scattered coffee mugs replacing the normal floral centerpiece. I'd barely noticed how tired Mom seemed to be. It wasn't until she sat down at the table that it hit me.

She moaned as she sat.

I looked up from my biochemistry notes. "Are you okay?"

She shook her head. "Just so blasted tired lately. And the rheumatism in my back is worse than last year."

The look on her face told me she was holding out. Something else was eating her. "Okay, what else?"

She lowered her voice so that Dad couldn't hear from the other room. "I've got a lump," she said, cupping her hand to her chest. She shook her head. "Your father doesn't know."

"A lump?" I traded a look with Blake. "Have you shown your doctor?"

"Oh, he'll just create a fuss." She pursed her lips like she did when she was thinking hard. "Could you check it?"

I held up my hands. There were a lot of things I would do for my mother, but I drew the line somewhere to the left of doing a breast exam. "I don't think so, Mom. You need to see your family doc. Or better yet, a surgeon. Up at Nassawadox there's—"

"I could check for you, Mrs. Conners."

I looked up to see Blake was serious.

She looked at me, searching my face for approval. "I guess that's okay," I conceded, "but you're still going to have to see a real doctor to find out what it is."

"Maybe Blake will say it's nothing."

I raised my eyebrows. "Why haven't you told Dad?"

"No need to worry him. He's always fretting about his business, you know that. Why worry him if it's nothing?"

"Because you're worrying. It's supposed to be a shared thing. You're married."

She waved her hand at me and tsk-tsked. "Phooey," she said. "When you've been married as long as we have, you learn that sharing some things aren't worth the misery."

She glanced toward the other room and asked Blake to follow her. They disappeared down the hall together into the master bedroom.

I returned to my memorization of the Krebs cycle, marveling over its efficiency in extracting energy from carbon substrates, and trying not to think of what was happening in the back room.

The next thing I knew, my dad was screaming. I realized he had tromped back the hall to the bedroom and must have interrupted the exam. I jumped up to try to smooth over the misunderstanding.

"What in heaven's name are you doing?" he screamed.

I hurried in to see my mother pulling a sheet up over her breasts and Blake backing up against the wall.

"Naomi, how could you?"

Gus reached for Blake and had him by the collar.

"It's not what you think, sir," he said, holding his hands in front of his face.

"For goodness' sake, Gus. Let the boy go! He was just giving me an exam."

"I could see that." He dropped Blake's collar. "In our bedroom, too!"

"A clinical exam, Dad. Mom said she found something and wanted some advice."

Dad looked at Mom. Then at Blake. Then at me. "I just reacted . . . I didn't think, well, I shouldn't have thought that—"

"That's okay," Blake said. "But I had barely gotten started. Why don't you stay, and I'll complete the exam and tell you what I think."

My father shrugged. That was my cue to exit stage left.

As I walked down the hall, the craziness got to me. I had to run to the kitchen so they wouldn't hear my snickers. And at that moment I knew I would never forget the look on Blake's face when my father had him around the throat and thought he was taking liberties with his bride.

My laughter was short-lived. A few minutes later Blake came out shaking his head. He sat down, straddling a dining chair backward, and kept his voice barely above a whisper. "She's been ignoring something for a long time."

"What did you find?"

"A rock-hard mass in her left breast, near the axilla. The overlying skin is dimpled and red. She has lymph nodes under the arm with metastasis for sure."

I wasn't very far along in my training, but even a medical student knew the implications of skin involvement and lymph node spread. His words were indigestible, oil incompatible with my water way of thinking. I set my notes aside. This couldn't be happening. My mother had been a rock of support to me. If anyone's encouragement had lifted me above the local criticism, it had been hers.

That moment became unforgettable. The exact time when my mother became mortal to me. Before then I'd always taken comfort in the fact that she would always be there to care for me. But just then the pendulum swung back toward the center, and I knew our roles would reverse as the weight picked up speed.

I now stood in that very room, on the other side of Mom's illness and the slow dance with death she'd stepped, always looking to me to take the lead. It was only in looking back that I realized how selfish my decisions had been. I couldn't separate the fact that I needed her and made her suffer through so much just so I could have her a little longer.

There was only one time in her saga of sorrow that I was glad I'd pushed her to fight so hard. It was the happiest and saddest day of my life. But as soon as my mind lit upon it, I pushed it away. And even as I shoved it down, I was aware of the dangerous game I played.

Some things are too painful to be regurgitated.

People push them away unconsciously. But I had been all too aware of the misery that rehashing that pain would bring me. Maybe Jo was right and it had something to do with my unwillingness to let myself off the hook for my sister's death.

And for now, without Rachel or Joanne, I knew I couldn't do it.

Joanne found the damage when she made a compulsive check of every window and door before bed. It appeared that someone had broken out a small windowpane adjacent to the back door. It was close enough for someone to reach in and unlock the door.

She shuddered and called the police. And for the second

time in a week, an officer responded, but had no reassurances that the perpetrator could be apprehended.

"My house isn't secure," she said, her voice trembling.

"Is there somewhere else you can stay tonight?"

"Not that I know of." She hesitated. "Can you have someone watch the house?"

"Tell you what, I'll circle the neighborhood during my patrol tonight." He paused. "You're alone?"

She nodded, trying to quell a rising panic. "I can't stay here. I'd never sleep, wondering when this creep was coming back."

"Knock, knock."

Joanne looked up to the sound of Blake's voice. "How'd you get in here?"

He pointed with his thumb. "The front door's open." He nodded at the officer. "Trouble?"

"Broken window." The officer stated. "Maybe the house is being targeted. There was some damage around the front doorframe a few days ago."

I looked at Blake. "What are you doing here?"

"You're not returning my calls."

She didn't want to have a conversation in front of the officer. She'd been wanting to tell Blake that she needed space, but he wasn't taking any hints. In light of the broken window, it did feel nice for him to be checking on her. She shrugged. "Things have been crazy."

The officer took a step toward the door. "Let us know if you find anything else."

"Sure."

After seeing the officer out, she turned, entertaining her options. It was getting late. She needed to rest but knew it wasn't going to happen in her home alone.

She either needed to go to a hotel or ask Blake to sleep on the couch. She looked at him and sighed. "I'm going to see if the

Marriott downtown has any rooms. I can stay there until my window gets fixed."

"Don't do that. I'll stay here with you. Save your money."

"Won't you find that a bit too tempting?"

He smiled. "Maybe you'll find it too tempting."

"Keep dreaming, Doc."

"Jo, I'll stay right on this couch," he said, pointing to the den. "I won't budge unless you beg me."

She pointed at his nose. "You stay put. And it's only for one night." She turned to go. "And only because I'm too tired to find a hotel."

She was aware of his eyes on her back as she walked to the master bedroom. At the door she paused. "Oh, thanks."

THAT NIGHT BLAKE woke at two and scrounged in the hall
closet for an extra blanket. He found a fleece emblazoned with
a University of Virginia Cavalier, draped it around his shoulders,
and tiptoed softly to the door to Joanne's bedroom. He leaned his
head against the door and listened. All was quiet except for the
sound of her breathing.

For Blake, wooing her had become an obsession. He'd had
all the women he wanted in medical school, young nursing students desirous of the social status a life with him could offer. He
had turned so many away, tossing some aside like used clothing,
discarded after only wearing the item a time or two. But Joanne
was different. From the beginning she'd played the game of hard
to get. Even when she wore his engagement ring, her eyes told
him a different story: pursue or lose.

When she'd told him it was over, he sensed her desire to be
pursued and vowed to fight to get her back.

In the days following Jo and David's return from their honeymoon, Blake grew sullen. He performed his intern tasks without enthusiasm and found the days passing at a grinding pace.
On a Saturday a few weeks later, he'd traveled to Newport News
to find her. He waited outside their apartment, slinking low in a
parked car until David left for the hospital.

He slipped through the unlocked front door moments after
David had sped away. The apartment was quiet. He moved down

the hall to the doorway of her bedroom and paused with his forehead against the door, listening to her breathing.

Regular and deep, sonorous in their quality, her breaths convinced him of slumber. He slipped in silently and sat in a chair by her bed, watching her sleep.

Her shoulder was exposed. He imagined the rest of her body to be equally unclothed, and he was nearly mad to slip in beside her.

Instead, he lifted his feet to rest upon the bed and waited, watching the rhythmic rise and fall of her chest.

When she woke, eyes blurry from sleep, she screamed and gathered the sheet up around her neck. "What are you doing here?"

"Sorry to startle you. I was only waiting."

"Get out of here! You can't come in here uninvited."

"We need to talk."

"I can't believe you."

He held up his hands. "I want an explanation."

"It's easy, Blake. I don't love you."

"I can change."

"You don't get it. There's nothing to change."

"So you like me the way I am."

She sighed. "It's not that. It's—" She halted, still wadding the sheet in a knot under her chin. "I'm pregnant, Blake."

"Pregnant!" He was stunned. "But how? We were careful."

"Not us, Blake. The baby is David's."

He sat up, dropping his feet to the floor in front of him with a thud. He studied her for a moment while understanding dawned. She cowered in the corner of her bed. He jabbed his finger toward her. "You made this up, didn't you?"

"What?"

"That this pregnancy, this . . . *thing* . . . is *his*. You knew I didn't want children."

"This isn't a *thing*. It's a *child*." She glared at him. "And you're not involved."

"How can you be sure it's not mine?"

"Trust me. I know. Besides, what would you have said if I'd told you about the pregnancy a month ago?"

He glared back. "Get an abortion. We're not ready for this."

"Well, *I'm* ready."

"And David is the mature, fatherly type?"

"He's reliable, Blake. He's faithful."

"Touché." He stood up and began to pace the small bedroom. "I know a clinic. You could put this chapter behind you. We can get your marriage annulled." He softened. "Jo, I want to be with you. I'm willing to fight for a chance."

"It's too late for that," she said. "I've made my choice."

He pulled his arms up beside his head, elbows forward. "No."

"I'm sorry, Blake. I wish it hadn't happened this way. But it wouldn't have worked for us."

"You'll be sorry."

"Now, will you leave?"

He continued to walk the small room, his energy escalating, shaking his head. "I can't stand the thought that someone else might be raising my child."

"Put that out of your mind. That's not happening."

"You don't know that."

"Believe me, I know," she said, picking up the phone. "Do I have to call the police or are you going to leave?"

"Jo," he pleaded. "Don't treat me like a criminal. We were engaged, remember? I love you."

"Don't make this hard. Walk away. You've always had plenty of women."

"Yes, but I chose you, remember?"

"Blake, it's over."

"This baby changes that." He looked at her for a moment, vulnerable and wide-eyed, cowering under a sheet in the bed he was supposed to share with her. He had nothing more to say.

Tears welled up in her eyes. "Don't do this."

Blake wanted so much to take her in his arms, for her to respond to him as she once had. *One day you'll be mine again.* He whispered her name and turned to go. As he went, it seemed her name lingered on his tongue, so that when he opened his mouth again, out it came with a sob. "Joanne!"

The intervening years hadn't changed a thing. Standing in the hall outside her bedroom, listening to her breathing, he was transported to that moment and again, he whispered her name. "Joanne." He closed his fist. He felt like screaming.

Instead, he turned and walked back to the couch, trailing the fleece blanket behind him.

The following day I met with Roy Dyerle and listened to his estimates for each of the projects I had in mind. Renovations, it seemed, were expensive, almost as expensive as starting over.

But I was intent on doing something. Dad's place wouldn't sell the way it was, and I saw giving it a new face as a part of my own therapy to exorcize the ghosts from my past that appeared in every corner.

I thumbed through the plans I had to remodel the house and started to prioritize, numbering the projects from one to ten, agonizing over which ones I could afford. I couldn't decide. I liked all of them. Roy suggested that as long as we were modifying the roofline to accommodate the new covered porch, I should include a large central dormer. Inside, a nice touch would be to add a small loft overlooking the den. I liked his idea. I imagined the loft as an escape; a study with built-in oak shelves for all my favorite reads. I couldn't decide which changes to postpone until I had the funds. I liked them all.

My trip to the mailbox changed all that. In the mail was a letter from an insurance company. It seems Dad had purchased a life-insurance policy after Mom's death, payable should he die of cancer. Since he had died of prostate cancer, they were ready to pay one-hundred grand. That plus the insurance payout from the *Beautiful Swimmer* should be plenty for the renovations.

I returned to the house and called Roy.

"I've got news, Roy. I want to do it all."

Sheriff Reynolds took a new deputy with him to arrest Darrel Mason. They had Bob Smith in custody as of the evening before. It was a beautiful morning. The sun had risen over the Atlantic Ocean, reddening the sky with a spectacular display. The sheriff watched the sunrise from his second-level deck, and couldn't help but remember the old adage with a bit of anxiety in his gut. *Red sky in the morning, sailors take warning.*

As he approached the front stoop of the Crenshaw home, he motioned for Andy Somers, his new deputy, to head around back. A few moments later the sheriff's radio squawked. It was Andy. "He's on the run, out back."

The sheriff sprinted around the house toward the back fence, and hoisted his bulky frame over the top with more than a little effort. He landed and rolled on the sandy soil a few yards from an old pickup truck, abandoned and sitting without wheels, on cinder block supports. He looked left. No Darrel and no Andy. Right. The tops of some cattails were waving next to a path leading into the marsh.

He started down the path, sinking his new shiny shoes into the mud. To call it mud was kind. It was more of a thick, black goo, smelling of old fish and marsh grass. The path disappeared completely at the edge of Nimble Creek. Because of the twisty course of the creek, he could only see about sixty feet of the shoreline. A blue heron lifted gracefully from a spot deep in the marsh ahead of him. A red-winged blackbird took flight a few seconds later.

The sheriff surveyed the creeled shoreline. Andy stood at the water's edge studying a groove in the muddy sand. *From a canoe or rowboat, perhaps?* He watched the tops of the marsh grass, as birds lifted off farther and farther from his position. He looked at his new shoes and sighed.

The sheriff felt winded. "Where'd he go?"

The deputy pointed down the creek. "I think he's off on the water."

The sheriff grunted. "Let's get back to the docks. We'll use the boat to catch him where the creek meets the bay."

Ten minutes later the sheriff stood over the severed gas line on the department's only watercraft and muttered a curse. "Darrel must have anticipated this," he said.

The next time I saw Riley Johnson was on Wednesday afternoon. His stomachaches hadn't responded to the acid suppression medication I'd prescribed.

He sat on the exam table and I on a rolling stool in front of him. "It's time you and I stopped playing this game," I said.

"I'm not gaming you, Doc. My stomach really hurts. Maybe it's appendicitis."

"I'm not talking about that game." I stood up and handed him the picture of my daughter. "What can you tell me about my little girl? She's been missing for weeks. I think you know something about her."

"She's pretty."

"What can you tell me?"

"She must take after her mother."

I sighed and pulled the picture from his hands. "What'd you do to her? Did you kill her? Did you make her suffer?"

He stared at me, silent in the face of my accusations.

"Talk to me, Riley. You want my help? You'd better help me."

"I don't like the sound of this."

"She was my life."

"I'm sorry, Doc."

"You're sorry?" I was aware that my voice was too loud, that I'd soon alert the guard outside. Quieter, I continued, "What are you sorry for?"

Again he sat still, staring at the floor in silence.

"I can make your life miserable, Riley. No pain meds. No medicine for your stomach."

He rubbed a short growth of stubble on his chin, considering. "I grew up down in Oyster," he began. "I watched you play football." He paused. "Your father went to every game."

He was right. I was second string, but Dad was always there in case I went in.

"I was too small to play, but my uncle made me go out for the team. I was cut the first week."

"So you couldn't run with the boys, so now you prey on little girls?"

"My uncle took me to a whore in Baltimore when I was thirteen. He thought it would turn me into a man." His eyes turned glassy as if he was seeing something far away. "She made fun of me." He brushed away a tear. "David," he said. "I've always wished I were you."

"Tell me about my daughter."

He shook his head. "I can't help you, Doc."

"Can't or won't?"

He cursed me. "Guard!" he screamed.

"What about the pains, Riley?"

The door opened.

"Take me back to my cell." He glared at me. "We're done here."

I watched him go and inwardly cringed. I wasn't supposed to be harassing Riley to find out information about Rachel, but I'd had about enough of sitting and talking with him and pretending she wasn't on my mind. And now I was starting to fear Riley might bail out soon. In addition, I supposed if they had concrete evidence that he had murdered little girls, that he wouldn't stay long at the correctional facility on the shore. He'd be taken to a maximum-security unit on the mainland, and I'd lose contact with him.

And loss of contact meant no payback.

Is that what I really wanted?

I thought about revenge. It tasted bittersweet on my tongue. It wouldn't bring my daughter back, but at least there would be the satisfaction of knowing that Riley had gotten his due.

But how?

I tapped my fingers on my desk, scheming.

ALEX PRATT HAD served as chaplain at Oyster Point Correctional Facility for sixteen years. In that time he'd heard all manner of sins confessed. He had seen remorse—real and contrived. He'd seen thieves cry over their wrongdoing, shedding tears of repentance; leave; and return after repeating the same crime. All manner of sins committed again and again.

Words without action mean nothing.

But Riley Johnson seemed different. Was it fear or guilt that motivated him? Or was there something deeper working within him, motivating a change for real?

He'd met with him for the last three weeks, and each week more of his sad story unfolded. Fatherless. Abused. Convicted on possession and distribution of child pornography.

Riley sat on his prison bunk and stared at the floor. The air was stale with the smell of sweat.

The chaplain spoke softly. "Maybe if you cooperate with the law, they will go easier on you." He hesitated. "If you've got stuff on your chest, maybe it would help to confess."

"There will be no mercy if I cooperate." He shook his head. "No one could forgive me."

"And will there be mercy if they convict you without your cooperation?"

"There will be no mercy for me." He leaned back against the wall. "If they find out what I've done."

"God has mercy for you, Riley."

He shook his head. "If He's that merciful, then He's weak."

"Weak is having mercy without a cost. That's what makes his mercy so special."

When I arrived home after work, I found the house under full assault, with four different crews at work. It seemed that Roy Dyerle didn't believe in wasting time.

One team was digging footers for a retaining wall next to the creek. Another worked to terrace the backyard into three levels leading down to the water—a task that would require two short stone walls. A third outside group was stripping off the aluminum siding to prepare the walls for a stucco application.

I walked into the house to see an inside team had already opened a large hole in the wall between the kitchen and dining room. The kitchen had been completely gutted—the cupboards already gone.

I drew my index finger across an end table covered with fine dust from the drywall. Sawdust tickled my nose. Roy looked up, probably noticing that my eyes widened at the sight of my house being demolished. "We saved the old cabinets. Why don't we put them to use in the refurbished garage?"

"Sounds great." I continued to look around. "You guys don't waste any time."

The contractor grinned. "Time is money." He pointed to the den floor. "Your kitchen utensils are in those boxes. You should rent a storage unit for the next month."

"All right." So much for being able to use the kitchen anytime soon. I shrugged and made plans to eat out. *I'll go pick up a sandwich down by the docks at the Seaside Inn. Perhaps someone down there has heard something new about Darrel Mason.*

Just after Jo and I married, we drove to the shore because Mom was ill, losing her battle against breast cancer. The house looked different—odd. Dad had constructed a ramp covering the front steps to get Mom's wheelchair in and out of the house to her radiation and chemo treatments.

We arrived on a muggy summer afternoon, Jo's first visit to my home, and my first visit as a married man. Mom looked pale and winced in pain as she moved, but she still smiled when she saw Joanne. "So this is the lady I've heard so much about." She beamed and hugged Joanne. Dad added a hug and slapped me on the back.

"Sit, sit," Mom said, pointing at a worn couch. "Are you thirsty from your trip?"

We sat, drank sweet tea, and shared stories from our brief courtship and honeymoon.

"We'd like to have a reception for you. Something for your old friends and family on the shore. But . . ." her voice trailed off in a fit of coughing.

Dad spoke up. "She's been so weak. Her blood's low again. I'm sure of it."

"I've had eight transfusions so far. It seems my bone marrow has about given up."

I looked at her, studying her sallow complexion and the thinness of her stature. Once robust, she now looked deflated, as if her skin had fallen to reveal every bone.

Her fight had been a valiant one. Surgery, radiation, pre- and post-op chemotherapy had taxed her limits. With a recent report of metastasis throughout her vertebral column, she lived in constant pain.

She looked as if tomorrow might be her last.

Dad cleared his throat. "The doctor says that more radiation might help with the pain in her back."

Mom took a deep, slow breath. "I'm getting tired, David. Most days I want to give up."

It hurt to hear her speak of the end.

Dad came alongside me a few minutes later, when I wandered down to the dock. "She doesn't let on how bad things are. She's lost control of her bladder," he said. "The doctor says her spine is collapsing on the nerves because of the cancer. She gets so constipated from the pain medicine that when she does finally go, it's so painful, she can hardly do it."

I grimaced, thinking of the misery my beloved mother was going through.

Inside again, I was anxious to share our news, hoping to cheer her. "Mom," I said. "We have a surprise. Joanne and I, uh, we, uh, we're going to have a baby."

Mom brightened. "That's wonderful."

Joanne and I helped Dad make dinner while Mom rested in a recliner chair. At least she was supposed to be resting. For the most part she peppered Jo with questions about her family and her childhood.

At dinner we feasted on fried oysters, baked potato, salad, and biscuits. Mom seemed to become exhausted just feeding herself.

I took my mother's frail hand in mine. "I'd so love for you to see our baby."

She gave a weak but sincere smile. "How long?"

"Six months." She didn't look like she could last six weeks.

"It would mean more treatments," she said.

Dad leaned forward. "And more misery."

She coughed, a skeleton rattling loosely around inside her skin. "I'll give it some thought."

I encouraged my mother to fight for six additional, painful, albeit miraculous, months. I should have let her go, allowing her to pursue her personal agenda, not mine.

But as it turned out, Rachel's arrival day turned out to be one of the best and worst of my life.

Joanne's gut tightened when she heard the phone. She'd purchased a caller ID phone and since then, she hadn't had any more prank calls.

She looked at the number. *Blake.*

"Hello."

"Hi, Joanne. How's your evening?"

"Just wonderful." She couldn't keep the sarcasm out of her voice.

"Afraid?"

"Sometimes."

"Look," he said. "Why don't you spend some time at my place? You'll be safe here."

"Blake, that wouldn't be a good idea. Besides, I've had all the locks rekeyed. My window's repaired, and I had an alarm system installed. No one can get in here without my blessing."

"Okay, so you're safe. You could still come over. I'll order a pizza. We'd watch an old movie. You still a Bogart fan?"

"At least you're finally being honest."

"Honest?"

"Yes. You can cut all the bull about needing to protect me. You're just trying to get close to me."

"Busted." He paused. "So how does it feel to be wanted?"

She thought about it for a moment. She was flattered. "Okay."

"Okay? Is that it?"

"Blake, I told you I was separating from David so I could process the loss of my little girl. I didn't say I was ready to launch into a new relationship."

"An old relationship, baby."

"An old, complicated relationship."

"Sometimes complicated is good."

"Blake, maybe another time, huh?"

"You're softening."

"You're persistent."

"Better than annoying."

"Okay, you're annoying. Will that make you stop?"

"Nothing will make me stop."

She tried to laugh it off and not sound nervous, but even to her own ears, her laughter sounded canned.

"When can I see you?"

"Okay, now you *are* being annoying." She spun her diamond around on her finger.

"When was the last time you were happy?"

She thought for a moment. "Before Rachel disappeared."

"So let me help make you happy again."

"How are you going to do that? Bring back my daughter?"

"Jo, I'm sorry." He exhaled loudly into the phone. "I'm going a bit crazy here thinking of you. Thinking of you alone."

"Stop thinking about me, Blake. Or think, 'Jo is off limits.'"

"Honestly, I think you're not going to be happy unless you leave your old life behind."

"And that means starting over with you."

"Something like that. A new family."

"I've got a husband." She closed her fist and her eyes. "Now leave me alone."

"Jo, don't—"

She hung up the phone. There was never an easy way to end a conversation with Blake.

On Thursday Roy's crew dug new footers for the expanded garage and front porch. They had created an open walk-through flanked by two columns to connect the dining room and kitchen. The small fireplace that had opened into the dining room had been dismantled, leaving only the flue. A stonemason was scheduled to begin the following day to construct a new fireplace and mantel. The mason would also build a new skirt around the entire house and assist with the construction of the low walls that would separate terraces in the backyard.

I was pleased and amazed with their speed, but also growing weary of eating out. Roy promised me quick work on the kitchen and sent me over to Virginia Beach in his truck to pick up a new stove and refrigerator.

That evening I walked around inspecting the work. I stopped in the backyard where small stakes had been placed to outline an elaborate deck that would be linked by a walkway to the gazebo, pier, and boathouse. Standing there, I realized I was standing in the place of our old baby pool.

Images of my sister's body flashed like yellowing slides, documenting her appearance from every angle. Her blue lips. Her pale little foot. Her limp form dangling from my mother's arms. My mother's face, contorted with agony, screaming at me. "Where were you? Weren't you watching her?" She, turning to the lifeless form in her arms and laying her in the grass, pumping on her chest, and crying to God to save her little girl. "Breathe, Rachel, breathe!"

It was no use. Rachel was gone, her blue eyes unfocused and staring into the summer sky. All while God was looking the other way.

I stood there shaking, angry at the intensity of my shame after all these years. I finally brought the present into focus again, wiped away my tears, and walked toward the pier to assess the progress of rebuilding.

THREE DAYS LATER Riley Johnson lay back on the examining table. He'd been vomiting. And not from the stomach flu. He reported seeing bright red blood the last time, and from his pale complexion and fast heart rate, I believed him.

"Does this hurt?" I asked, palpating gently in his upper abdomen. I watched his face. He winced. "You're probably bleeding from an ulcer. I want to put you in the infirmary. You'll need an IV, and we'll have to check your hemoglobin."

"Whatever you say, Doc," he replied softly.

I picked up his chart and started writing orders.

"I know why you asked me those questions about your daughter," he said.

I stopped writing and looked up.

"You're going to tell the officials, aren't you? It's your way of getting even."

"I won't tell them anything, Riley. You've heard of doctor-patient confidentiality?" I paused. "I want to know for me."

His face tensed with a spasm of pain.

I looked away. "I'll write you for some pain medication, and medicine to block the acid production in your stomach. If you lose too much blood, I'll have to refer you to the surgeons for a scope."

Riley grunted and lay back on the stretcher. "I came to your reception, Doc. The one your parents threw for you over at the Tippins Community Center."

I took a step toward him. "You were there?"

"Everyone was invited." He took a deep breath and exhaled slowly. "We didn't talk. I stood in the back and ate those little meatballs with toothpicks."

I obviously hadn't remembered him.

"Your wife was pregnant, wasn't she?"

I stared at him.

He shrugged, and I noted the hint of a smile at the corner of his mouth. "I could just tell."

He was yanking my chain. How could he have known? Had I mentioned my daughter's age and he knew when the reception was and figured it out? "How'd you know?"

"You were a bad boy, eh, Doc? You weren't even married." He grunted rhythmically through his pain. "A . . . bad . . . boy . . . like . . . me."

Later that afternoon I smiled as I looked at my new kitchen. I'd purchased hickory cabinets that were premade, and Roy's crew had installed them. Even better than the new cabinets was the new stone fireplace with openings into the kitchen and den, soon to be the great room. "It's awesome, Roy."

"Wait until we open this area up," he said, pointing toward the ceiling. "The new ceiling height will be eighteen feet in this area, giving you enough room for the small study-loft." He unrolled a blueprint on the coffee table. "What do you think of a small winding staircase here to get to the loft? We don't have room for a full staircase."

I nodded. "Looks good."

"I think you should find a new place to sleep for a few nights, well, maybe a week," he said. "We'll be starting on the new master bedroom suite, and it's going to get pretty dusty when we bust down that wall."

"No problem. I'll check down at the bed and breakfast."

I was crossing the parking lot at the correctional facility the next day when I saw the chaplain, Alex Pratt.

"Chaplain," I called. "Can we talk?"

He nodded and extended his hand. "Alex Pratt," he said. "You're the new doctor."

"David Conners." We sat on a bench outside the front entrance. "I've been taking care of Riley Johnson." I searched his face for a reaction.

"I know Riley well." He clasped his hands, letting them drop between his knees. "He's had a pretty rough life."

I didn't really want to think about Riley's rough life. I had other things on my agenda. "Has he ever confessed his crimes to you?"

I watched as his eyes narrowed. "I really couldn't comment on that, Doc. Everything he shares with me is pretty much confidential."

I shifted on the bench. "It's, well, he seems ill at ease around me, like something's bugging him. What with the complex connection with a person's emotional heath and physical health, I was just wondering."

"I can't help you with specifics, David," he said. "But suffice it to say that Riley is struggling with forgiveness issues."

"He's mentioned that to me as well."

"I suppose it's an area we all struggle with."

I looked away and cleared my throat. "Yeah, sure. I guess so."

"I've been telling him about God's wonderful forgiveness, but I'm not sure he gets it." He paused, and I felt his eyes on my face. "He's worried. There are things he needs to get off his chest so that he can forgive himself."

"Maybe he needs to confess so that God will forgive him."

Alex's voice was a deep bass, tender and strong at the same time. "That's a common misconception about God's grace, Doc. God forgives his children simply because of the cross. Confession helps restore fellowship, but if anything is added to the cross, even confession, in order to purchase our forgiveness, then confession becomes penance."

My voice felt suddenly dry. "Maybe he needs to confess his sins to those he's hurt," I said, trying to keep my voice from cracking.

"It could be, but his coming to personal peace shouldn't rely on that, either. The people he has hurt need to forgive Riley, not for Riley's sake, but for their own sake, to protect their souls from the cancer of bitterness."

I stared at this man. It was as if he could see inside my soul. It seemed that this same message assaulted me over and over.

He touched my arm. "Are you okay, Doc?"

I clenched my teeth and nodded. "You sound like my mother."

He smiled. "Smart woman." He squeezed my arm, then stood and walked away.

I collected myself, gathering my emotions into a semblance of control, and followed him into the building.

I knew one thing. I wanted Riley to pay for what I was convinced he'd done to my daughter and for the wreck he'd made of my life. I didn't want to forgive. My anger toward him was all I had.

Perhaps, in some twisted sort of way, I thought that if I let that go, I would be denying my Rachel.

Another thought struck me as I plodded forward. *If I can find it in my heart to forgive Riley, maybe I can forgive myself.*

I walked to the infirmary. I had only two inmates there. One had terminal esophageal cancer and needed an IV for hydration. The other was Riley.

I looked at Jen, my nurse. "How's Higgins?" I asked.

"What, no 'hello, Jen'? What am I, just another nurse to you?"

I chuckled. "Okay. Hello, Jen." I paused. "Now, how's Higgins?"

"He wants to stop the IV. He's miserable. He can't even swallow his own spit."

"So pull the IV. I'll write him for PRN morphine to keep him comfortable."

I paused at his stretcher. "You understand what this means? If we stop the IV, you will dehydrate, your kidneys will fail, and you will die."

"I understand. How long will it take?"

"Days. You're not likely to last a week."

"Okay. Can I get all the morphine I need?"

"Sure."

I walked to the next stretcher and pulled the curtain between the two units.

I picked up the chart at the end of Riley's bed. His hemoglobin last night was 9.7. This morning's value was 9.3, relatively stable. "It looks like your bleeding has stopped, or at least slowed down. How do you feel?"

"The pain's better. I feel weak, is all." He squinted at me. "You look tired, Doc."

"My house is being renovated. My builder told me to get out of the house for a while, but it got late last night, so I tried sleeping on the couch." I shook my head. "Not a good idea."

Riley smiled. It was the first time I remembered seeing any real expression remotely close to happiness.

"What?"

"I was thinking of an old *Far Side* cartoon. A man is standing with the Devil in hell. There are two doors in front of him, and he is being forced to choose. One says something like, 'Burn forever,' and the other says, 'Live in your house while it's being renovated.' So the guy is standing there thinking, 'It's pretty much a toss-up.'"

I chuckled in spite of not wanting to get friendly with him.

His laugh ended with a coughing spasm. He stayed quiet while I was doing paperwork.

"Say, Doc," he said under his breath. "I've been thinking about something." His eyes darted around the room. Evidently satisfied that we were alone, he continued. "If you get me out of here, I'll take you to your daughter."

I stood up, towering over him, and seized his throat. "Rachel? Is she alive?"

He gasped and grabbed my wrist.

I lessened my grip.

"I'm sorry, Doc."

I squeezed again, watching his eyes bulge. It was closer to a confession than Riley had ever come. I thought about what he was saying. Even if all he showed me was a body, it would serve as evidence to put him away for a long, long time.

I released my grip, leaving him red in the face and heaving for oxygen.

"Easy, Doc," he gasped. "You want to know where she is, don't you?"

I leaned toward him until my face was inches from his and I could smell his fetid breath. "Tell me what you did," I whispered.

"Not until I'm outside."

JOANNE LOOKED INTO the hall mirror as she straightened the collar of her nursing uniform. As she reached down to pick up her car keys from the table, she noticed something odd about the small, framed photograph that always resided there. She lifted the photograph and sighed. The frame usually held a photo of her and David, arms around each other, the dusk of a beautiful evening surrounding them. Currently it held an engagement photograph of her and Blake.

She turned the frame around and slid off the back cover, removing Blake's photo to reveal the one of her and David.

Oh, Blake.

Could he have chosen a photo with worse memories?

The day the photograph had been taken began as most others had when she was a nursing student living in the dorms.

She'd left the dorm early, at six thirty, wanting to get settled on the hospital ward early before her nursing instructor arrived. As she rounded the end of the building, she paused and made a quick assessment. Stethoscope. Pen. A small pocket nursing manual. She ran her hand over her left shirt pocket. *I forgot my hospital ID badge.* She pivoted to go back to her room when something caught her eye. Someone was crawling out the window of one of the nursing dorm rooms.

She paused, amused at the sight. Two hairy legs wiggled out in front of a pair of tan shorts that proceeded in front of a red

T-shirt. Someone was escaping after a very late night. She was about to proceed when the man turned and caught her eye.

"Blake!" She stomped toward him.

"Hi, Joanne," he said sheepishly. "Surprise."

She studied the room for a moment and counted the windows between that one and her own. "Whose room is that?" She ran through a mental list. Three doors down. "Wendy? Delores?"

"Look, Jo, Delores wanted some help studying for her endocrinology test."

"So you just thought you'd help her? In her room? All night?"

A window on the third floor opened. "Could you hold it down? People are still sleeping up here."

She hushed her voice, but kept up the barrage. "We're engaged, remember? Or doesn't that mean anything to you?"

"Joanne, of course—"

At that moment, Delores popped her head through the window, gasped, and withdrew it quickly again.

"It's not what it seems," he pleaded.

"I've got to go. I'm supposed to be on the med-surg floor in ten minutes."

She turned and walked away, her head spinning. After taking a few steps, she looked back. "We've got a sitting at the photographer's at four. That is, if you still want to get married."

Joanne's fury and hurt simmered all day. At three, when she was finishing up her last chart, Ed Beckly, a third-year medical student, stopped at the nursing station.

"Hi."

"Hey, Ed." She kept her eyes away from his.

"There's a gang heading down to happy hour at the Tobacco Company at five. Would you like to join us?"

She thought about her schedule. Pictures at four. Patient write-up due at six thirty in the morning. "You're certain you'll be there?" she said, letting her eyes rest on his for a moment, before she turned away.

"I'll be there."

She smiled. *Perfect.* "Then I'll be there."

Joanne shook her head, as if she could dispel the memory. She set the frame back on the table, and her hand trembled slightly as she looked at the picture of her and Blake one more time.

Then, slowly at first, and then with decisiveness driven by guilt, she ripped the picture into pieces.

I searched the shed next to the pier and then the garage before I found what I was looking for: Dad's .22 caliber pistol. It was in a locked box in the bottom drawer of a tool chest next to a full box of shells. The keys were hanging on the wall above the workbench.

Dad had purchased the handgun fifteen years before and carried it with him on those rare occasions when he took the *Beautiful Swimmer* out in the bay or ocean inlet to troll for bluefish, to use in case he snagged a shark. At least that's what he said. The only time I remembered ever firing it was when we were out in the middle of the bay when boredom from a day of unsuccessful fishing set in.

We would stand in the back of the boat and plink, plink away, shooting the whitecaps or an occasional spare crab-pot buoy that had seen the last of service on the line. We'd throw the blue-and-white stripped buoy out and blast away until there were hundreds of little floaters dancing on the water's surface.

And Dad would laugh. He laughed in a scary way that gave me the willies. When he saw me worried, he would laugh again, this time a belly laugh that got me going.

Boom. "Ha-ha." *Boom.* "Ha-ha!" He'd laugh and look at me with an evil eye. Then, grinning, he'd shoot again and again and howl with laughter like he'd stored up everything funny for a month and let it all out on those rare occasions when we were out in the middle of the bay together.

I cleaned the gun and returned it to the locked box, packed myself into the car, and drove to the infirmary. Once there, I unlocked the door and walked in. The clinical aroma was such that with closed eyes, I could have told you exactly where I was. It wasn't unpleasant, but more of the smell of a particular antiseptic that the night crew used with liberality. I greeted the day nurse. "Morning, Jen."

"Morning, Dr. Conners." She picked up a clipboard and smiled at me. Her unrelenting giggles had lessened after the incident. "Census is down to one. Higgins was sent back to gen pop last night per your instructions." She used the jailhouse lingo for general population. "I'll stop and see him a few times a day for the pain meds you ordered."

"Good. How's Riley?"

"He's tolerating soft food. No vomiting last night."

"Vital signs?"

"Heart rate has stayed below one hundred all night. BP's stable."

"Thanks."

I approached his bed. "Morning, Riley."

He grunted his greeting.

"How do you feel?"

"Okay."

I pressed on his abdomen with my hand. "Any pain here?"

"A little."

"I'm sending you back into gen pop. I'm going to put you on iron and vitamin C supplements for a few weeks to help build up your hemoglobin levels again."

"Have you thought about what I said?"

I nodded and looked at his forehead. "You see this little mole? I think it needs to come off."

He wrinkled his forehead and touched the small mole.

"If I take this off, I'll have to use a scalpel, Riley." I touched my neck. "The last time I used a scalpel in my office, I was taken hostage."

He stared at me. "I wouldn't get far, even if they'd let me out the front gate."

"So you won't go out the front."

"What are you talking about?"

I leaned over him and whispered. "Higgins is going to die any day. When he gets close, I'll keep him in the infirmary. When he dies, he goes out on a covered gurney to the back entrance where a hearse will be waiting."

His eyes brightened.

"I'll send for you when Higgins dies. The death gurney will be here."

"I always have a guard escort outside the door."

I nodded. "The last escort surrendered his gun when I had a knife to my neck."

He smiled.

"Unless they think I'm forced, I'll lose my job and face charges of aiding a prisoner in escape."

I stopped at home and inspected the day's work. The pile-driving crew had reset the pilings for the new pier and boathouse. The remodeling crew had framed in a huge opening between the two end bedrooms to create the larger master bedroom. The plumbers had ripped out the fixtures in the bathroom. I snuck a peek in a large cardboard box in the new great room and saw the corner of my new Jacuzzi tub.

In the yard, I saw that the rafters had arrived, reflecting the new rooflines with the large central dormer.

Roy was still there picking up a few stray tools when I arrived. "Come here," he said. We stood in the front yard. He pointed at the roofline. "Look at these sketches. I think we should add two fake dormers, one on either side of the larger central one."

I looked at his sketches and agreed.

"I think we should ask the stonemason to finish out this whole area around the front door. Stone around the base of the porch pillars, the skirt of the house, and around the front door will tie the whole thing together."

"Great," I said. I liked how this was shaping up. So far I'd managed to keep the whole project a secret from Joanne and planned on keeping it that way as long as I could.

I waited until Roy left, then took Dad's old pistol and shoved it and two full clips of ammo under the driver's seat of my Volvo.

I had no idea when Higgins would die, but I had a feeling it was going to be soon.

I sat in the driver's seat and practiced putting my hand beneath the seat and retrieving the pistol. I repeated the motion a dozen times until I could pull out the gun, flip off the safety, and have the gun pointed at the passenger seat in one smooth motion.

Satisfied with my progress, I headed down to Captain Billy's for a late supper.

RILEY JOHNSON'S PROMISE to take me to my daughter was the final hammer blow to my hopes of finding Rachel alive. Now my only hope was to avenge her death and allow her remains to be given a decent burial.

I wasn't sure what was driving Riley, unless he had some clue from his attorney that things weren't turning out as he'd once hoped. Maybe he was looking at some serious time behind bars and he'd decided to do anything he could to make a break for freedom.

I didn't care what motivated him. All I wanted was to have closure. And to have Riley in the open where I could take my revenge.

And it would all look like self-defense.

Thinking of closure brought Rachel to mind almost constantly. As I drove, I thought about how she'd sing while she was strapped in her car seat. I remembered how she told me that I didn't need to come in with her to preschool. "I can walk in myself," she said.

I hadn't been so convinced. She was only four.

When I rose from sleep, I remembered how early she got up and crawled into bed with Joanne and me, snuggling in between us like a little mouse squeezing under a door where there didn't seem to be enough room.

When I went to bed, I remembered her million excuses to stay up.

When I ate, I thought of her favorite foods. Macaroni and cheese, pepperoni pizza, applesauce, and chocolate pudding.

I sat on my bed at the Seaside Bed and Breakfast and thought about Joanne. She certainly might not be into communicating with me, but if her last visit to the shore was any indication, she hadn't given up on us completely. It frustrated me, however, for her to act as if she needed to be away from me so she could get over Rachel. This was something we should grieve together.

I called her on my cell.

"Hello."

"Jo, it's me. I have some news about Rachel. Remember the inmate I told you about?"

She grunted. "Sure."

"He told me he'd take me to Rachel."

"He said she's alive?"

"No. But he knows something. I think he's ready to come clean. He said he'll show me where she is."

"He killed her." Joanne sounded monotone, as if she'd rebuilt a shell around her.

"I think so."

She sighed. "I would rather she'd drowned."

I couldn't think of an appropriate response.

"So what's next? Will he lead the police to her body?"

"He'll give the information to me."

"So you'll have to give the information to the authorities."

"Jo, it's not that simple. This guy, Riley, he won't give out any information unless I help him get out."

"David, you can't—"

"Jo, I have to find out. I have to know."

Another sigh. "Sure."

I waited a moment. "I just wanted you to understand. Because soon this is going to be behind me. Once I know, I'll let it rest."

She stayed quiet. I think she wanted to believe me.

I cleared my throat. "Then we can work on us."

"Things are complicated, David."

I closed my eyes. *Blake.* "We can work things out." I hesitated. "I love you."

I waited for her response.

"Good night, David."

Joanne hung up the phone and held back the horror burning in her throat. She hadn't wanted to believe that Rachel was abducted and mistreated. She opened a bottle of 2001 Bordeaux and sat on the couch. After two glasses, she began to cry.

Her marriage was rocky. She felt responsible for that.

Her little girl was gone. While she wasn't responsible for that, she could hardly blame David.

He'd be better off without me.

She rose and looked in the medicine cabinet. In the back, behind a large bottle of ibuprofen, she found an old prescription bottle of Valium. She took ten milligrams and padded back to the living room, wine bottle in hand.

By the time a knock came on the front door, she was a soggy, depressed drunk.

She opened the door to find Blake. She threw up her hands. "What a surprise."

She turned and walked back toward the living room, leaving the door open for him to follow.

"Jo, what's wrong?"

Life felt joyless without the end-of-tunnel light, just like it had during her postpartum depression. "The question is, what's right?" She slumped on the couch and swirled a glass of wine under her nose. "I don't want to live."

Blake sat opposite her and lifted the glass from her hand. "You've had enough."

"Don't take that. I wasn't finished."

He frowned at her. "Jo, you have so much to live for. You're beautiful. Smart. You've got a great job."

"I've ruined my marriage. My daughter's dead."

"Don't say that. You don't know for sure."

She leaned forward, elbows sloppy on her knees. "David called. He's been talking to an inmate who knows what happened. He's met Rachel's killer."

He sat quietly for a moment while she sobbed.

"Look. You need a change of scenery. Do you have to work tomorrow?"

"I've got the next two days off." She stared at him. He seemed blurry, and her own voice sounded far away.

She stumbled behind him as he strode into her bedroom. "What are you doing?"

"Packing you a bag. You need to get out of here."

It felt as if there wasn't enough room in her mouth for her tongue and the words, too. She pushed the words forward through uncooperative thick lips. "I can't go anywhere with you."

"I'm not leaving you by yourself. You'll drink yourself to death."

That made her cry. Everything seemed so sad. "I don't deserve to live," she said, falling on her bed. "Leave me alone."

Joanne sobbed for a few minutes before Blake gently encouraged her to sit, raising her by supporting her with his arm behind her back. "Here, sweetheart," he said, dropping two white tablets in her hand and holding up a glass of water. "Take these. You'll feel better in a little while."

After swallowing the pills, Blake helped her lie back on the bed. Joanne's head swam. She felt as if she were floating on a busy sea.

She was aware only that he spoke soothingly to her, stroking her forehead. She struggled to keep her eyes open. The room was losing definition. The edges were blurry, and everything seemed to have a purple hue. She felt his lips against hers. She lay quietly, unable to resist. His mouth opened, and she felt exactly . . . nothing.

The last phrase she remembered as everything went black was something Blake repeated over and over. "It's the way it was always intended to be."

I got the call at six in the morning that inmate Higgins had slipped into a coma. The deputy had cleared his throat. "The time is near."

"Take him to the infirmary," I said. "And bring up the death trolley. I'll be there soon," I said. "I'll need to examine him so I can fill out the certificate of death."

I threw my clothes on and jumped into the car.

Maybe it was my obsession with Rachel, or maybe it was just the curious way that the end of life always seemed to make me want to dwell on life's other extreme, but regardless of the reason, something about the way the deputy said, "the time is near," brought the final hours of Joanne's pregnancy back to my mind.

Joanne's obstetrician had smiled and slipped off his examination gloves. "The time is near," he said. "You're six centimeters dilated."

My phone sounded. I traded a worried glance with Joanne. It was Dad.

"Hello."

"David. It's your mother. She's trying so hard, but she can't get her breath. Her breathing sounds like gurgling."

"Call an ambulance. Have them take her to the hospice unit

at Nassawadox Community Hospital. We'll be there in a few hours."

Joanne's eyes widened. "David, I can't travel like this!"

"How long will her labor last?"

The doctor shrugged. "First baby. Could be another twenty-four hours."

"My mother is dying. She doesn't have twenty-four hours."

The obstetrician gave me a stern look. "I can't recommend traveling now."

"We'll only be on the road a few hours. I know every hospital between here and the shore. We'll stop if we have to." I looked at Jo. "You can go straight to the labor and delivery unit at Nassawadox."

"David!" Jo's voice was urgent.

I took both of her hands in mine, looking straight into her eyes. "Mom needs to see this baby. She's been through so much just to make it until the baby—"

Joanne took her hands from mine and silenced me with a look. I guess she could see my determination. "Let's leave now," she said. "If we're going to go, I don't want to waste time arguing."

Her willingness to make the trip told me that she understood my motives. She of all people realized how powerful a motivator guilt could be. She knew I'd been chasing after my own freedom for so long, that now that it was within reach, she knew she couldn't deny me. Fortunately, Jo had packed an overnight bag a week ago in preparation. As we left the doctor's office, Jo gripped her lower abdomen and winced.

My only fear was the twenty-six miles of water that separated the mainland from the Eastern Shore.

JOANNE MADE THE trip lying down in the backseat of our old Dodge Caravan. I drove, half mad, driven by the singular goal that my mother would get to hold her granddaughter, Rachel, before her death.

The sky to the east over the bay threatened a spring thunderstorm, but I was undeterred. I purchased our ticket to cross the Chesapeake Bay Bridge-Tunnel when Jo's contractions were ten minutes apart. By mile six of twenty-six, she moaned and whispered, "Uh-oh."

"What is it?" I glanced over my shoulder and depressed the accelerator a little more.

"My water." She touched her thigh. "My water just broke."

I thought of turning around at the next island.

"Go faster."

"Breathe, honey." It was one of those ridiculous pieces of advice that husbands give their wives during labor.

She moaned. Louder than the last time.

By mile twenty, the rain had started, and I was past the point of no return. Unless I delivered the baby myself, my only hope was getting Joanne to Nassawadox Community Hospital. Soon, I hoped, I would be able to carry little Rachel to her grandmother.

I drove on, pushing the speed to eighty, eighty-five, until Jo begged me to slow down. I relented because the windshield wipers couldn't keep my vision clear at that speed.

"David, I have to push."

"I'm so sorry, honey. But please don't push. Ten more minutes. Just ten."

I could hear her panting, puffing, trying to do anything but push. She moaned in agony.

"I'm so sorry to do this to you, Jo. But—" I edged the accelerator closer to the floor.

Pine trees passed in a blur as the windshield wipers intermittently gave me a vision of the road. Clear. Rain-streaked. Clear. Rain-streaked. Clear. The wipers beat out a rhythmic song. Move it. Move it. Move it.

I was doing eighty when I passed a patrol car parked at a Quick Mart.

Soon a siren joined the song.

Jo panted and puffed. "What's going on?"

I looked at the flashing lights in the rearview mirror. "We've got company."

"Don't stop."

"I have to stop." I slowed. "This will only take a second."

The police officer pulled in behind us, but seemed reluctant to get out in the pouring rain.

"What's he doing?"

"Must be running our plates. He's just sitting there."

"David, do something! I'm going to have this baby."

I jumped from the car, running like a wild man toward the officer. I watched his eyes widen as he reached for his gun.

I waved my hands. "My wife's in labor. She's going to have this baby right here unless you let us go."

He didn't speak. He only pointed down the road and nodded.

I returned to the car, and pulled out behind the patrol car, who proceeded with lights flashing.

Cool. An official escort.

We arrived at the community hospital five minutes later, where an orderly and two nurses met us under a covered entranceway with a stretcher. Evidently, the deputy had radioed ahead.

I followed the nursing crew trying to stay calm and keep up at the same time. "Her water broke while we were crossing the Chesapeake Bay Bridge-Tunnel. First pregnancy."

Jo gasped. "I have to push!"

"Don't push, honey," a silver-haired nurse coached.

Once in her room, they quickly removed Jo's pants and parted her legs for an exam. The nurse slipped a gloved hand between Jo's legs. "Call Dr. Shank. We've got a cord prolapse." She raised her voice, calling to another nurse. "Flo, set up for an emergency C-section."

"C-section?" I stepped forward. "Shouldn't we wait for the doctor to decide?"

The senior nurse looked at me soberly. "The baby's umbilical cord has slipped out in advance of the baby's head. If we allow normal delivery, blood to the baby will be cut off during delivery because the head will compress the cord."

I knew about cord prolapse. Now I was afraid. And glad I wasn't on the bridge. "Okay," I whispered. I was in no position to argue.

The nurse talked to Joanne in a calm voice. "I need to keep my hand right here to keep the baby's head from pushing on the cord. I'm not going to move my hand until the doctor has opened you up."

Jo's eyes widened. "David!"

"It's okay, honey."

A minute later, a young man with sandy blond hair and a coffee-stained white coat arrived. "What've you got, Sandy?"

"Cord prolapse."

He nodded. "Let's go." He looked at me. "I'm Dr. Shank." He let his hand rest on Jo's swollen abdomen. "You need an emergency C-section."

Jo panted. "I get that." She looked at me. "David."

I took her hand.

They transferred Joanne to a stretcher with the nurse keeping her hand on the baby's head the whole time. Time blurred. Down the hall. Onto an OR table. An anesthesiologist putting in an IV, a mask over her face. Brown Betadine was painted on Jo's abdomen. Two minutes later, Rachel was out and screaming.

I had a daughter.

My fear and anxiety shifted to joy. Promise and hope replaced doubt. Looking back, that moment was pivotal. Never again would I first think of myself. Everything would forever be filtered through the lens of being the father of Rachel Conners.

Ten minutes into Rachel's life, as Jo was still under anesthesia, my daughter was in my arms, and I remembered the whole reason I'd rushed to the shore, everything I'd forgotten in the flurry of the emergency birth.

I needed my mother to see my baby girl. And I wanted to surprise her with the name we'd chosen.

It was to be a closing moment of emotional healing for my mom, whose daughter was plucked from her prematurely. Her reaction was to be the moment of forgiveness for my carelessness that killed my little sister.

With Rachel tightly wrapped in a blanket, I slipped into the hall and followed the signs to the hospice wing. It was unlike the other units. It had a homey feel with paintings on the walls and floor lamps instead of fluorescent lighting.

I paused at a desk and asked a woman sitting there, "Where is Mrs. Conners' room?"

She looked up. "I'm sorry, who are you?"

"Her son."

Her look sobered me. She stood, her face etched with concern. "Come," she said.

I followed her to a room on the right down the hall. When I entered, I found my father sitting on the bed, with his head resting on my mother's chest.

Mom was pale and her chest not rising.

My mother was dead, pronounced only minutes before.

Mom was gone. Rachel was here.

"Dad?"

He looked up at me. "David, she's gone. She's gone."

My emotions were already riding the sea. I was up, holding my daughter. I was down, looking at my dead mother. Tears were the natural response to both circumstances and so, joy or sorrow, I surrendered.

"Dad," I sobbed. "This is Rachel. I wanted Mom to meet her."

He sat in a rocker at the foot of the bed and motioned for me to bring the child to him. I laid Rachel against his chest and went to my mother. "I wanted you to meet her," I cried.

I'd been denied the closure and forgiveness I sought.

Dad stared at Rachel and began to sob.

Happy or sad, I wasn't sure, but a steel bond between granddaughter and grandfather was forged in a moment. I looked over at him and studied him in the dim light of the hospice room. For him, it was an obvious healing of a painful, oft-remembered loss.

"My little Rachel," he said, crying. "Little, precious girl."

I took my mother's hand in my own.

The worst day. The best day.

I should have allowed Rachel's appearance to redeem my loss, but I couldn't get over the fact that my mom hadn't had a chance to see her.

My mom hadn't had a chance to forgive me.

And I hadn't had a chance to forgive myself.

Joanne woke in a strange bed in an unfamiliar room. She sat up and immediately felt dizzy. No, not quite dizzy, more like vertigo. It was the sensation that the room was moving, spinning like a slow top. Nausea nipped at the top of her stomach. She closed her eyes. *Where am I?*

"Well, look who's finally up." The voice was Blake's.

Joanne groaned. She didn't open her eyes. Keeping them shut at least kept the world from spinning. "Where am I?"

"Feeling sick?"

"Maybe just a hangover." Her voice sounded distant. Like there was a disconnect between her brain and her mouth. She'd give the order to speak, but when she obeyed, the words sounded like they belonged to someone else. *What happened to me?*

"Here," he said, taking her hand. "Sit up. Take these. They will help you feel better."

She swallowed two white tablets.

She never even opened her eyes before everything went silent again.

I pulled into Oyster Point, parking in the service entrance at the rear of the facility instead of the normal employee lot. I shut off the ignition and pondered how Rachel had changed everything for me. Nothing was ever the same with her. Nothing would ever be the same without her.

I stepped out of the car and shivered as I thought that today I might have to close the chapter that started on that most wonderful and horrible of days.

After failing to give my mother the gift I had hoped, returning to Joanne's room and laying Rachel in her arms seemed to bring the world into momentary focus.

"Oh, my baby girl." Jo spoke the words as though they were part of her breath. "She's beautiful." Tears came, and she held Rachel close, lost in the aroma of new motherhood.

I let her drink in the moments for a time before I put my hand on her arm. "Joanne. We were too late. Mom died as Rachel was being born."

Jo stared at me, her eyes sharp with judgment. "You risked our child's life, and for what?"

"Jo, I couldn't have known that—"

"Rachel almost died, David! And all because of your stupid quest to have your mother see her grandchild. What were you thinking?" She tucked her nose into Rachel's neck, tears coursing down her face.

I hung my head. A prolapsed cord was a freak, random event. Rachel could have easily died no matter where she was born— even if we'd stayed in Newport News. But I knew Jo wouldn't see it like that. And in a way, she was right. A delivery on the bay bridge-tunnel would have resulted in a dead baby.

I walked into the hallway, my conscience attacking. I paced the hall, thinking of how months of relentless thoughts of Mom holding my baby, bringing healing, had put my wife and child at risk—foolishly and selfishly—in hopes of clearing *my* guilty conscience.

Back in the room, I sat in the rocker and smiled at my girls. I knew we'd dodged a big bullet, but I didn't want to dwell on that. I wanted to focus on my healthy little daughter and becoming the perfect dad.

I walked into the infirmary and watched Higgins's breathing pattern. It was a slow, soon-to-be-terminal rhythm. I touched his hand. "Hope you've made your peace," I said.

Jen joined me at the side of the stretcher. "You're in early."

"I wanted to be here to pronounce him."

During my training and subsequent years in practice, I'd had plenty of opportunity to see people die, but for those occasions death had come suddenly, and I'd been involved in a tug-of-war with the grim reaper trying to keep my patients on this side of the divide. With Higgins, it was different. I wasn't going to fight. He had a terminal disease, and he didn't relish living on within the drab walls of his incarceration. For him, death was a release. *Hopefully, he'll be happier in the next life.*

I sat with him for three hours, watching the rise and fall of his boney chest cage. I wondered about his family and why no one seemed interested in him anymore. Even if he was a convicted criminal, it didn't seem right for him to die alone.

Sitting there, I reflected on the end of the road and wondered what people would have to say about me when I died. More important I wondered if everything my mother taught me about heaven and how to get there was true.

If she was right, it all hinged on there being a forgiving God.

Searching my own heart, I found it hard to believe someone could forgive the cruelty of man. Perhaps that's because I'd created God in my own image.

Higgins gasped, then stopped breathing. I stood, and he picked up breathing again. False alarm. Death was at the door, but turned away at the last moment.

There was a white sheen on his forehead. Dried sweat. Salt. I gripped his wrist, feeling for a pulse. I couldn't find it at the wrist, so I felt again just lateral to his trachea. His carotid pulse beat weak and irregular. Bump. Bump . . . bump-bump . . . nothing.

Higgins took one more breath and stopped. Eleven thirty-one. His eyes were open, glazed with death. I pushed his lids closed.

I looked up. Jen was sitting in the small enclosed nursing station freshening her lipstick and staring into a small compact mirror.

I wrote a note on his chart, then filled out a transfer form for the body to be released to a local funeral home.

"Jen," I said casually. "Send for Riley Johnson and set up a minor tray. I need to biopsy a mole on his forehead."

"Shouldn't we get Higgins out of here first?"

"The death cart is here. We can get Riley's escort to help us move the body."

"Poor guy must have been down to eighty pounds."

I listened as Jen phoned to have Riley moved to the infirmary.

I called Seaside Funeral Home and asked them to pick up a body at the service entrance.

Riley arrived ten minutes later in hand and ankle cuffs.

The guard, a young deputy named Lincoln Rodriguez, took off the ankle cuffs so Riley could get on the table.

I'd opened the contents of the minor surgical tray, positioning the scalpel on the edge of the small table.

When I leaned over to inspect Riley's forehead, he wasted no time initiating the plan. He grabbed the scalpel and threw his cuffed hands over my head, drawing the scalpel just above the skin of my neck. From behind me he commanded, "Cooperate, Lincoln, and the Doc here gets to live."

LINCOLN'S HAND WAS on the butt of his pistol.

"I wouldn't do that if I were you," Riley sneered. He motioned to Jen. "Take his gun. Lay it here on the table." He pointed with his head. "The keys, take his keys. Unlock these cuffs."

She fumbled with the pistol and laid it on the table. Then she took the key ring from Lincoln's belt.

"You'll never get away with this, Riley. You'll never get out of here with a hostage."

He smiled. "I'm not taking a hostage out. The doc here's going to take a dead body down to meet the hearse."

Jen opened Riley's cuffs, her hands shaking.

"Chain him to the pipe under the sink," he said, picking up the gun. He kept the pistol trained on me as he edged over and stood on a chair to point a surveillance camera the other way. "Now take his pair," Riley added. "Chain yourself to his wrist."

I watched as the duo were chained to the sink. "The radio. Toss it over here."

Lincoln slid the radio across the floor.

Riley looked at me. "I'm getting on this stretcher, boss."

The death stretcher looked like a regular stretcher at first glance, but it had a large metal tray instead of a cushion. The body lay on the tray and the tray was then lowered until hidden from view behind a blue drapery material on the sides. A thin false top could be placed at the height of a regular stretcher. I supposed it was designed for hospital use, where a dead body might be seen by the public if allowed to be paraded around on the top of a normal stretcher.

Riley lay on the tray. "Now lower me down. I'll have this baby pointed right at your chest, Doc, so don't try anything funny."

I pulled a sheet over his face and he pointed the end of the pistol out into my gut. "Now," he said, "let's go."

We headed down the hall passing only one guard. "Higgins," I mumbled.

He nodded. We stopped at the elevator.

A second guard entered the elevator.

Again, I mumbled, "Higgins." Nervous, I smiled and touched the top of the sheet. "Want to see?"

The guard recoiled and nearly ran off the elevator at the next floor.

Bolstered by our apparent invisibility, I whistled as I wheeled Riley down to the service entrance on the ground floor. I stopped at a locked door and let myself through with a swipe of my badge. I stopped at the exit door and talked to another young deputy. "Has Seaside Funeral Home brought their hearse yet?"

I handed him a clipboard showing the transfer form for Higgins' body.

"Just arrived." He opened the door and pointed. I wheeled the stretcher through the doors and down a ramp, pausing behind the hearse. "We're behind the hearse," I whispered to Riley.

A hushed voice came from beneath the sheet. "Where's the driver?"

The driver was Dale Campbell. He'd been the funeral director at Seaside Funeral Home for thirty years. In that time he'd done every job from janitor to driver to preacher.

"He's getting out of the car. Other than him, we're alone."

Dale came around. "Well, hey there. If it's not the young Dr. Conners." He touched the railing of the stretcher. He began to fiddle with it and pulled the sheet off the body in the process.

I backed up a step and Riley swung around, bringing the butt of the pistol down on the top of Dale's head. He crumpled like a rag doll. I caught him behind the arms and shoved him into the back compartment of the hearse.

"My car's over here," I said, pointing.

Moments later we were on the move; Riley crouched in the back and covered himself with a blanket. "Turn south," he said. "We're going to Oyster."

I kept watching the rearview mirror. No company. No flashing lights. "They must not have found Lincoln yet," I muttered.

"We need to stop at my house."

"That's not a good idea," I said. "That's the first place they will look for you."

"I need to see my mom. Just for a moment."

I glanced at him in the rearview mirror. He glared at me. "You should understand."

He directed me to a gravel road just beyond the shell dump, an artificial mountain made from years and years of depositing oyster shells after oystering. I used to play there as a child, collecting sand dollars from among the discarded shells.

His mother's lane was off on the right at the end of the road, leading into a pine grove.

I watched in the mirror. When his eyes were directed to his boyhood home, I reached under my seat and retrieved Dad's pistol. I shoved it under a light jacket on the seat beside me.

I got out of the car opposite Riley and quickly donned the jacket. Next, when his attention was on the opening screen door of the house, I slipped the pistol into my jacket pocket.

To my surprise Riley laid the deputy's gun on the backseat. "I won't be needing this."

I didn't recognize his mother. She was maybe five feet tall, with dark, leathery skin, and white hair. She didn't smile when she saw her son. Her hand went to her mouth. "Riley, what have you done?"

"I don't have much time, Momma," he said. "I needed to say how sorry I am. I've never been the man you'd hoped."

She shook her head. "Where are you going? What are you doing here?"

"Me and the doc here have some business." He opened his arms to his mother. Reluctantly, she moved forward.

He hugged her warmly, but I saw no tenderness in her eyes. I suspected this son had made and broken many promises that had hardened her heart. He whispered something in her ear that I didn't catch, but she pulled away, saying "No, Riley. It's not the end."

He wiped a tear from his cheek and motioned for me. "Come on, Doc." He led the way across a yellowing kitchen floor and into the garage. There, he picked up a rusting shovel. "Let's go."

We walked through knee-high grass poking up through the sandy, neglected lawn, down a footpath, and out onto the beach. He pointed to a small boat with a Yamaha engine.

"Where are we going?"

"I made you a promise." He pointed off shore to the south.

"Gull Island?"

He nodded.

The island sat three miles offshore and was deserted except for duck season when hunters used a series of blinds along its marshy shoreline.

We pushed the small boat off the sand. I sat in the bow, and he tilted the outboard into the water. He pumped the black bulb of an orange gas tank and pulled on the starter cord. After four pulls, the engine sputtered to life.

When Riley turned around, I had the pistol pointed at his chest.

Joanne sat up and shielded her eyes from the sun. Blake was sitting at her side on the bed. She touched the sheets beside her and eyed him. Had he slept in the same bed? "Where am I?"

"A family place," he said, smiling. He pushed her hair away from her face. "You're beautiful."

"Blake, what's this all about?"

"A damsel was in need of a rescue."

She rubbed her eyes. "I'm hungry."

"Good sign," he said. "Breakfast is coming up."

"And where *exactly* are we?"

"Smith Mountain Lake. My family has owned this retreat for years. My parents rarely take the time to get out of Richmond anymore, so we've got the place to ourselves."

"So I've been kidnapped."

"Rescued."

"Your word, not mine. Take me back to Richmond." She touched the back of her head. "What did you give me?"

"Give you? You medicated yourself." He held up his fingers, counting off. "Let's see, what did I find? Red wine, Valium. You were drunk of your own doing."

She stretched. She didn't feel as though she had a hangover. In fact, she felt rested. Almost good. In fact, she hadn't felt this rested in a long time. She squinted at him. "You didn't give me something?"

"I took you away from something," he said, reaching for her hand. "I was afraid for you. Afraid that you might—"

"Kill myself?"

He nodded. "How do you feel?"

"Like I didn't ask to be rescued." She gestured with her fingers, making quote marks around the last word. "I don't think this is such a good idea. You need to take me back home."

"Joanne, stay with me. At least today. We'll have fun on the lake. Believe me, you needed to get away from Richmond."

She felt herself softening to the idea. It was weird to her. She thought she should be flaming mad at him for taking her away against her will, but somehow, she couldn't find it within herself to be mad. Instead, she felt pliable. Compliant. Almost uncaring as to what happened next. Something had taken the edge off her emotions. "What have you done? What did you give me?"

"You're recovering from a binge." He leaned forward and planted a kiss on her lips—softer than the one he'd given her at the house earlier.

Again, instead of revulsion or reaction, she felt nothing. She pushed him aside and dressed in front of him, uncaring that he watched.

A few minutes later she eyed her orange juice with suspicion, sipped it cautiously at first, and then surrendered to her thirst. When Blake offered her a breakfast of cheese omelets, bacon and toast, she gave in to her incredible hunger. Together they ate on a deck overlooking the lake. It was good.

She shrugged. Maybe she'd stay the day. It couldn't hurt her attitude to relax on the water.

Riley seemed unimpressed by my bravado. "You don't need that." He paused. "Put that down before someone gets hurt."

"That's the idea. You didn't think I'd let you get away."

"Put that down, or we're going nowhere."

I took a deep breath. I looked at the horizon. Gull Island.

He seemed to read my thoughts. "You'll never find her without me."

I shoved the gun back into my jacket pocket. I'd let him show me my daughter and then I'd give him what he deserved.

The sun overhead shone unfiltered through a cloudless sky. The wind was out of the south, coming in from the ocean. Soon

I was gripping opposite sides of the boat as we pounded our way through the chop.

A half mile offshore, Riley slowed. We were being beaten by the sea, and we were getting soaked by the salt spray.

Gulls hovered overhead as if they thought we were going to start fishing. Two sailboats were visible on the horizon. Riley lifted his head and smiled. He looked satisfied, as if he were finally finding a freedom he'd lacked for a long time. Maybe it was just getting out of Oyster Point, but I thought it was more than that. He looked relaxed. At peace. As if he was finally executing a plan that had freed his soul beyond his physical escape.

He tossed me a plastic scoop, an old Clorox bleach bottle with the top and a portion of one side cut out. "Better start bailing," he said.

I obeyed and scooped the water collecting at our feet. We weren't in trouble, at least not yet, but a little maintenance was in order.

"I used to come out here when I was a boy. I'd camp on the island to get away from my uncle." He tapped his hand on the side of the boat. "Guys in my high school used to bring their girlfriends to the island."

"Did you?"

"No."

He didn't elaborate. I couldn't imagine a girl wanting to go out with Riley. I paused from my bailing job. The bay had been my escape when I'd been a boy, too. But I'd been escaping normal childhood pressures, not the maniacal abuse of a relative. "What happened to your sister?"

His gaze steeled, focused on the horizon. "She committed suicide after leaving for college."

"Your uncle?"

His expression didn't change. "I killed him." He paused. "Right after my sister died."

The surprise must have registered on my face.

"No one ever found him, either."

I didn't question him further, but the cap was off and whatever he'd bottled up for years was coming my way.

Riley kept his face pointed toward the wind. "All I wanted was a little peace."

All I wanted was for him to be quiet. I didn't want to listen to his pain. I looked away toward the distant shoreline of Gull Island and wiped the spray from my face with my jacket sleeve.

I tried to concentrate on Rachel and feeling my loss. I thought if I held my sorrow close, revenge would taste sweeter by the contrast.

From behind a tangle of blackberries, Darrel Mason lifted a pair of binoculars and scanned the little boat approaching the shore. He fiddled with the focus. The guy in the back appeared to be wearing a correctional facility jumpsuit, something with which Darrel was all too familiar.

He weighed this new development. He looked at his supplies. His food was running low again, and he sorely missed hot showers. Maybe this was exactly what he needed to make a deal with the law. If he could promise delivery of an escaped prisoner, his attorney could make an appeal for a lighter sentence.

After all, he couldn't live out here forever. He looked at the sky. Midday was approaching. He nodded to himself. It was a plan.

Slowly, he slid three shells into a 12-gauge shotgun and settled behind a tree to wait.

I HELPED RILEY beach the skiff and took a deep breath. It was time. "Tell me about my daughter."

Riley's countenance was sad. "Follow me," he said, pointing inland across the beach. "There's an old duck blind in the marsh across the way."

When we reached a grove of pines, I heard a man's voice, dripping with sarcasm. "Welcome to Gull Island."

A young man leveled both barrels of a shotgun at us. I studied him for a moment and recognized him as Darrel Mason. I knew the sheriff's department wanted him for burning the *Beautiful Swimmer.*

"Darrel?" I said gently.

"So you know who I am." He grinned at me. "What brings you here, Doc?" Without waiting for my answer, he swung the barrel toward Riley. "What do we have here? A prison break?"

"We have no business with you," I said. "I've got a little project with Mr. Johnson here, and we'll be on our way."

"Oh, no, you'll be right back to the Shore telling Sheriff Reynolds exactly where to find me." He stood his ground. "I don't think so."

"You're no threat to me," I said. "Why should I tell the sheriff anything?"

"I think we both know the answer to that." He tapped his thumb against the wooden gunstock. "It was sad to see such a nice boat go down in flames, Doc."

"Jimmy Crenshaw almost died because of you."

"You're not getting on my good side, Doc. Jimmy was a mistake. He sang like a bird, didn't he?"

"Jimmy's still going to have to pay for what he did."

"Not near as much as I am, from what I hear. Old Jimmy hired a good lawyer from the mainland. Someone who talked him into giving me up so that he could get a sweeter deal." He smiled at us. "But now, maybe I've got a little bargaining tool of my own."

"We can't help you, Darrel. Just let us do our business and we'll be on our way, and no one will be the wiser about you."

He made a clicking noise with his mouth. "This is my island," he said. "And I get to make the rules."

"No!"

Darrel looked at me as if I'd gone mad. He raised the shotgun above my head and fired.

The noise of the gun rang on in my ears as I stumbled backward, half from surprise, and half from fear.

Riley spoke. "Don't, man." He stood steady, unshaken by Darrel's bravado. "If you kill us, you'll be looking at life. Believe me, don't get stupid like I did."

Darrel's eyes widened. "Why are you here?"

Riley looked at me. "It's time I finally did a few things right. I made a deal with the doc here. I've got something he wants to see."

Darrel tilted his head. He was interested. "Money? Did you hide a stash over here?"

"Nothing like that." Riley looked out toward the bay. "He is grieving the loss of his daughter," he said slowly. "I'm here to help him find her."

"Touching. You can help him find her once I've turned you in."

I slipped my hand in my pocket, closing my hand around the handle of Dad's little semiautomatic.

Darrel jabbed the barrel of the shotgun toward my chest. "Take your hand out of your pocket. Slowly!"

He walked around me with the gun pointed at my head. Then, while holding the gun with one hand, he slipped the other inside my pocket, pulling out the pistol. He snickered. "Looks like the doc had plans of his own. What were you going to do?"

I mumbled. "Shut up."

"March," he said, motioning along an overgrown path.

"Let the doc go," Riley said. "He's of no use to you."

Darrel ignored the request.

The path quickly became a soggy walkway into the marsh. It ended at a long-abandoned duck blind. Riley climbed the three steps to enter the stilted structure first, pushing open the door with his foot. Scattered beer cans cluttered the floor. The structure had a thick central pole and large openings in the roof, presumably an access to flying game. An empty shotgun-shell box had been discarded in the corner. An old cooler sat against the wall, once a seat or a cold storage for food or perhaps both.

Darrel handed me a rope. "Tie his hands behind his back."

I obeyed, trying my best to make it look like there was no slack, but leaving a little the same.

Then Darrel tied my hands in the same fashion.

"Why are you keeping him?" Riley asked. "The doc's done nothing."

"Can't be too sure of that. You two came out here together, and no one looked forced to me. Maybe he's in with you."

Darrel positioned us on the floor facing opposite directions and used additional rope to secure us together around the center pole support.

"I'll be back," he said.

Joanne spent the afternoon sunning on the front of the Swensons' twenty-four-foot ski boat by Wellcraft, outwardly calm, but inwardly nursing a rising dread. And other than a bit of sunburn, the day had been somewhat enjoyable, and Blake mysteriously quiet.

But something wasn't right. Though outwardly composed, Jo was sure something about Blake's hero exterior was just that, a covering over a very different heart. She'd known all along that Blake had ulterior motives, but never estimated that he'd ever pull a stunt like this. He hadn't brought her here for a rescue. He wanted more, and she needed to find the courage to oppose him face to face.

Once they were back at the lakeside house, Blake came from the kitchen swirling two glasses of wine.

She took the glass he held toward her and sampled the bouquet with her nose. All she could detect was wine. Instead of drinking, she smiled. "Any fine cheese for an early hors d'oeuvre?"

When he walked back to the kitchen, she poured the wine into a potted plant, noting the presence of a white sediment at the bottom of her glass. With the glass empty on the coffee table in front of her, she feigned sleep on the couch.

Blake returned, and she felt his lips brush her forehead as he placed a blanket across her shoulders. This time, instead of nothing, she felt a growing rage. Whatever he was up to, it wasn't good, and she didn't intend on sticking around to find out.

She felt her heart quicken. But what could she do? She was hours from home and didn't have a clue how to get out of there.

She thought about slipping out the front door when Blake was occupied in the kitchen, but feared his reaction if he saw her.

She lay still for an hour and then quietly approached the kitchen, thankful that Blake was occupied with the grill in the

back. She decided she needed a shock-inducing, face-to-face encounter. She pulled the largest knife from a slot on the side of a
wooden block on the counter, moved quietly to the bedroom,
where she slipped the knife between the mattress and box
springs.

She pulled back a curtain that overlooked the back deck where
he was leaning over the grill. "What do you want, Blake?" Jo whispered. "Whatever it is, you're not going to get it from me."

In the distance we could hear the low sputter of an outboard
engine. "He's taking the boat."

"See if you can reach into my front pocket," Riley said. "I'm
still carrying that scalpel."

I slid as close to him as I could, but that made the angle of
approach into his front pocket impossible with my hands tied
behind my back. "Let's try to stand up."

We leaned our weight against the pole and hoisted ourselves
up. In an awkward dance, we managed to gain our footing. Riley
turned himself toward me as much as possible, and I managed to
get my left hand into his front pocket. After several tries I retrieved the thin, metal scalpel.

"See if you can cut the rope."

I didn't have a good angle to sever the rope binding my own
wrists, but slowly cut through the one holding Riley's. He turned
and grabbed the knife and made quick work of cutting through
our remaining restraints.

"Okay, okay," I said. "We're free. Now take me to my
daughter."

"I don't have to," he said. "Darrel took us to her."

"Where is she?"

"Right below us. Here," he said, sliding aside the cooler.

There, on the floor against the wall was a discarded, old Pound Puppy.

I dropped to my knees, pulled the stuffed toy to my chest, and began to cry.

"Rachel," I whispered with my face buried into the musty stuffed animal. "Rachel."

There was finality in the moment. All the mystery of what had happened to my precious daughter, all the agony, and my quest for revenge found a focus in that stupid little Pound Puppy. With my soul in torment, I wept because finally I knew that she was gone and I'd never again experience the spontaneity of her smile. My joy, and the glue of our little family unit, was dead and with it, my heart.

I laid the little stuffed toy aside with all the gentleness that I would have given to my daughter had I been laying her to sleep for the last time.

I picked up the scalpel. Assured now of Rachel's fate, I had nothing left but revenge. My soul was void of feeling, drained by the evil personified in the prisoner kneeling on the floor in front of me.

I grabbed Riley by the collar and shoved him backward against the wall. "Is she buried here?"

I touched the floor, rubbing away the dust. The wood was discolored. Dark. The stain of blood. I looked at his face and his gaze dropped to the wood blemished with blood.

"Beneath the blind," he gasped. "I swear."

I lifted the knife and traced a line across his neck. Soon, blood would spill to pay for his sin.

Riley did not resist, and for this I gained the slightest of respect for him, in spite of my disdain for the life he'd lived.

I stood over him, executioner, ready to send him into eternity.

But then I looked in his eyes.

Slick and brimming with tears, his body shuddered beneath my grasp. "For-for-forgive me," he whispered.

Forgive?

The idea was preposterous.

"Oh God, have mercy on me, precious Jesus receive me."

No! I didn't want this man to be forgiven.

"David," he whispered, looking up into my eyes. "Forgive."

Images hung suspended like a mobile in my mind, spinning and turning, bringing first one and then another picture into focus as they rotated in suspended time.

My mother looking at me as a little boy. "Forgiveness isn't for him. It's for you."

Me giving advice to a young man whose father was killed in Iraq. "It isn't your place to avenge your father's death."

A white-haired minister who'd baptized me as a child. "God forgives his children simply because of the cross."

I felt the warmth of the little hut, felt the sting of sweat in my eyes, and blinked away the salt. *"Confession helps restore fellowship, but if anything is added to the cross, even confession, in order to purchase our forgiveness, then confession becomes penance."*

I pressed the scalpel against his neck, seeing a trickle of blood in response. I could feel the throb of his carotid artery in the neck, a few centimeters below the skin. I wanted to drown out the minister's words with the anger I'd been feeding. This evil man deserved to die. With my heart pounding, I wanted to submit to my plans for revenge.

I watched the trickle of blood form a ribbon curling by gravity to rest in the notch above his sternum. It collected there, evidence of my complete dominance over Riley's fate.

But I felt only remorse.

Revenge. It was so sweet in my imagination, so complete in its ability to free me from the paralysis of my soul.

But I found it a façade, a covering of deeper remorse. A cancer of unforgiveness remained to tint my vision.

I studied the man in front of me and assessed the state of my soul. I could not kill him.

Because I was also a man of sin.

I thought of Riley's words. *"You're just like me."* I stared into his eyes, frozen by the thought.

I knew it was true. I'd done so much out of my own lust and selfishness.

Joanne, I've hurt you.

Jen, Riley saw me watching you and he knew what was in my heart.

Amina, did I lead you on? And why? To salve the hurt in my own soul for a tragedy long buried?

The scalpel slipped from my hand. I'd reached an unexpected point. My need to forgive was larger than my need for revenge. I needed to forgive this man so that I could forgive myself.

I dropped on my knees in front of the man who'd stripped me of my joy, and wept. "It was my fault. I killed her, Riley." I brought my forehead to rest upon the dirty floor, a floor stained with the blood of my daughter, and wept for my sister. "I didn't mean it. I didn't mean to—"

Riley gathered me into his arms and pulled my head to his chest. "Forgive me," he said.

I wept. I was a sinful man. Lost. Guilty. Unable to cast the first stone.

I pulled away, pushing him to arm's length. He was wearing prison clothes, but I was the real prisoner there. His eyes searched mine. His soul was a soul in torment, and he thought I held the key to his freedom.

I studied him, a man like me, a man damaged by circumstances and sin. I looked at my daughter's little Pound Puppy. *She was my only daughter. Is it possible to lay down my anger for the one who took her from me?*

Riley began to cry, but I resisted his tears. I did not want to soften my heart toward this monster.

But I wanted to be free. I wanted to forgive myself, and it seemed that I finally understood that God was offering me this chance, this hope. If I could bring myself to forgive Riley, I believed I could forgive myself.

"Please," Riley cried.

I stumbled at the words. *What if I don't believe?* I pushed aside my doubts. *God, help me believe. Help me forgive.* Quietly, I let the words go. "I forgive you."

He trembled. Tears streamed from his eyes, and a smile broke the surface of his face.

"I came to kill you," I said.

He picked up the scalpel. "I know."

With the suddenness of a bird flushed from its hiding place, Riley swept his hand upward and plunged the scalpel into his neck.

Blood sprayed from the wound as a pulsatile, red fountain.

"No!" I pressed my fingers against the wound. A moment later Riley collapsed onto the dirty floor, with my hand holding back the blood. "What have you done?"

"I want to die," he gasped. His eyes pleaded with mine.

"No, I can save you." Anguish gripped my heart. We were so far from help.

He whispered to me. "Your wish, not mine."

I searched his face, shaking my head. "I can't."

"I . . . don't . . . want to . . . live." He paused. "Please," he said. "You forgave me."

My fingers trembled against the wound. Certainly the carotid artery had been severed. The only thing standing between life and death for Riley was the fact that my fingers were temporarily sealing off the forceful egress of blood.

I kneeled over him. Again, for the second time in minutes, his life was in my hands, his destiny under my will. "Don't make me do this."

The irony bit. Now I fought to save his life. Just moments ago I'd threatened to take it.

Love. The essence of forgiveness.

Could I actually let him die when it was against my will?

Was it right to demand my own way?

"Please, Doc. They'll kill me when they know what I've done."

His blood oozed out from around my fingers. I shifted the pressure, attempting to close the flow.

"Please, Doc. Please."

"Riley, you'll die if I let go."

He gripped my wrist. "Let me."

He pulled. I allowed my strength to be overcome. Sliding my fingers from the wound, the torrent was unleashed, raining blood in a pulsing arc.

The first one flew the highest and each subsequent arc pranced lower and lower above him until he took one gasping breath and exhaled on the other side of eternity.

I sat back on the floor in the corner of the little duck blind and wept.

For the loss of a man who'd taught me a life lesson.

If I could forgive the man who'd stolen my daughter's life, I understood that I could forgive myself.

I looked at the body in front of me and wondered if it was possible that I'd forgiven him. Perhaps time would be the judge. But at that moment I stared at the first evidence that I really had. Riley was dead, and I'd let him go because that's what forgiveness dictated.

I took a deep breath and tried to inventory my feelings. Anguish over Riley's death. Pain over the loss of my daughter. And a suggestion of something else, perhaps only a sprig of a beginning: hope.

I was soaked with the prisoner's life. My face, hands, and shirt were wet and sticky red. I touched my tongue to my lips and spat. Tears or blood, I wasn't sure. It tasted salty, like blood.

Forgiveness.

I understood. True forgiveness, found and given away, originated at the foot of a Roman cross, evidence of a blood purchase.

I shivered, and felt for Riley's pulse. Nothing. His corpse lay drained of salty life.

I picked up the Pound Puppy and left the blind, plodding to the sandy beach to watch and wait.

I waded waist deep into the water and stripped off my shirt, washing out the blood and watching the crimson stain dissipate into the bay. I washed my face and returned to sit on a log near the water's edge.

I hugged the small stuffed animal to my chest and stared out at the bay and the mainland beyond.

I lowered the Pound Puppy, cradling it in my hands. Something tugged at the corner of my consciousness. *Rachel's Pound Puppy was missing one eye.* My fingers traced both eyes of the little dog.

I touched the nose. *Rachel's little dog's nose was stained with tomato soup.*

I shook my head as a thought solidified. *This isn't Rachel's dog.*

Then Riley was wrong. The little girl he brought to the island wasn't Rachel.

TWO HOURS LATER, a boat approached from the east, crossing the choppy water with the bow bouncing like a galloping horse. In ten more minutes the boat ran aground on the sand and the sheriff, the prison warden, and two deputies got out. I walked toward them, realizing my disheveled state, and feeling a bit like I'd been stranded for days.

The warden, a grizzled man nearing a deserved retirement, lifted his hand. "Doc. How are you?"

"I'm okay."

The sheriff stepped forward. "Darrel said he left you tied up."

"We had a scalpel. We cut ourselves free." I paused. "Riley's in a duck blind a few hundred meters that way." I pointed.

The sheriff looked in that direction, acknowledging the information with a nod.

"Denton," I said. "Riley committed suicide. After we were free, he told me he'd buried a little girl beneath the duck blind. Then he stabbed himself in the neck."

Denton looked at his deputies. "Confirm the doc's story. We'll have to get the ME out here before we touch or move anything."

Joanne eased the curtain aside to look across the deck toward the lake. With Blake apparently snoozing in a hammock, she quickly retrieved her cell phone from her purse and dialed 9-1-1.

"Nine-one-one emergency. Could you state the nature of your emergency?"

"I'm being held at a lakeside cabin at Smith Mountain Lake."

"Have you been kidnapped?"

"Not exactly, but I think I was given drugs and brought here while I was sleeping. I don't even know the address of where—"

A strong hand pulled the cell phone from her hand and covered her mouth. "Jo, what are you doing?"

She whirled around to see Blake press the end button to terminate the call. "We're having a little retreat. You needed to get away. You aren't being kept against your will."

"You drugged me."

He gave her a pitying look. "You're turning paranoid on me. You were the one who medicated yourself. Valium and alcohol, remember?"

Joanne shook her head and backed away. She didn't feel paranoid.

"You want me to take you back home? I thought we were having a great time." He held up his hands in surrender. "I'll take you back to Richmond right now if you want to go."

"Okay."

He looked at the counter. Two thick steaks were thawed and ready for grilling. "Suit yourself," he grunted. "At least stay for dinner. I'm hungry."

She took a deep breath and told herself to relax. "You'll take me home after dinner?"

"Right after." He shoved her cell phone into his pocket. "I'll grill the steaks. Maybe you could work on a salad. Veggies are in the fridge."

He busied himself with the grill while Jo worked in the kitchen. When she joined him on the deck a few minutes later, a wine bottle was open and a glass set at the edge of the table, filled with Bordeaux.

Blake lifted his glass. "To a great escape," he said.

She lifted the wine and allowed it to touch her lips before casually walking off toward a boathouse next to the lake. There, she intentionally kept lifting the glass to her lips, glancing back and smiling at Blake.

She sat on the edge of a pier, keeping her back to Blake and swirling the purple liquid. Again, she could detect a white residue circling the bottom of the glass. She poured it into the lake and walked to the house, feigning a need to hold onto the railing.

She passed him, letting her hand drag across his shoulder. "I need to lie down," she said. "I'll be in the bedroom."

Joanne walked back to the bedroom and pretended to sleep. As she predicted, Blake soon joined her, lying down next to her.

She felt his lips on her neck. Soon his hand slipped beneath her blouse.

Joanne reacted suddenly, rolling over the top of him. She kissed his lips to keep him off balance, while slipping her hand beneath the mattress.

She kissed him again while shoving the point of the knife up under his chin. She pulled up to a crouched position. His eyes widened in fear.

"Wh-what?"

"Don't you touch me!"

"Jo, I thought you wanted—"

"You drugged me. I want you to take me home. Now!" Joanne pushed the point of the knife to indent his skin.

"Jo, wait," he said, pleading. "I don't want it to be this way. Please, lower the knife."

She slid off the bed, keeping the knife tightly gripped in her hand.

"I was only giving you a mild tranquilizer since you were so upset. I was afraid for you."

She didn't buy it. "You seem to forget that we're not a couple."

He sat up, his expression one of vulnerability and fear. "We could be, Jo. We could be a family."

Sarcastically, she repeated, "A family." She picked up her overnight bag. "Take me home."

"But our dinner—"

She pointed the knife toward his chest. "Now."

I parked in front of the Whitsons' red-brick rancher and carried the small stuffed animal with me to the front door. Tammy answered after I knocked.

Our eyes met. I wasn't sure what to say. I held up the little Pound Puppy.

"Did they find Brooke?" Her hand went to her mouth.

"The police have found another body." I paused. "Over on Gull Island. The forensics team will have to do an analysis."

"Where did you get this?" She stroked the little stuffed dog.

"Gull Island. Where they found the body. Is it Brooke's?"

She sniffed. "I think so."

Earl joined his wife and stood on the little stoop on the step above me. "Hi, Doc." His wife handed him the Pound Puppy. He took it, turning it over in his hands. "It's hers." He looked at me. "Any word on Rachel?"

"No."

They nodded, appreciating my pain.

After a moment of awkward silence, I shuffled on.

At home, I called Jo. I wanted to tell her about my day with

Riley. When she didn't pick up, I opened an Amstel and began my daily inspection of the renovation. I acted out of habit, a desire to dull my pain. Before I tipped the bottle, I took inventory of my soul. The old weight of guilt was gone. I'd traveled from forgiving the man I thought killed my daughter, to forgiving myself. And that gave me hope that God might forgive me, too.

I set aside the Amstel. The thirst born out of a need for escape had vanished.

Joanne leaned her head against the passenger window and stared at the blur of pines. Blake drove without speaking, and each mile of silence spoke his disappointment as loud as a shout.

She glanced at him, aware that his gaze was fixed forward, focused only on the highway. He'd changed. Or had he? Was she only now seeing him as the manipulative freak that he had always been?

She'd cared for him once. And momentarily thought she might again, but in the last few days, she'd seen something else. Any appreciation for his supportive friendship had melted. He'd crossed a line and now fear replaced respect.

All she wanted was to get home and find some sense of normalcy again.

"Did you puncture my tire?"

He looked at her, his mouth agape.

"You know, when I had the flat, did you leave something under my tire so you could rescue me?"

"I wanted to be close to you again."

She wagged her head in disgust. She'd been too flattered to see how convenient his rescue was.

Her mind raced ahead, heartbeat chasing after it. "Did you

make the prank phone calls? How about my window? Did you break that to scare me back into your arms?"

He stayed quiet. Answer enough.

"You betrayed my trust."

"I'm sorry. I only wanted you to see that I could be the one to save you again."

She sighed. "Go save someone else."

She looked away and whispered the next phrase into the window, so that a fleeting fog was the only evidence of her communication. "I'm taken."

A few minutes before ten, Blake called Tricia Morgan's cell.

"Hello."

"She won't bite."

"Blake?"

"Yeah." He sighed. "I've tried everything," he said, lifting a bottle of Jack Daniels to his lips. "She doesn't even want my friendship."

"Too bad. I suppose she's still enthralled with that waterman."

"I suppose."

"She always has had a weakness for needy men."

"I wanted you to know I tried."

"I just wanted her to be happy. She doesn't realize how happy she could have been with you."

He turned up the bottle and let the liquid burn his throat. Then he clicked off the phone and cried.

POLICE OFFICER PAUL Letchford looked up at the old house in the Fan district of Richmond and sighed. There was an 867A and an 867B. He knocked on the A door first.

No answer.

Then he tried B.

A elderly woman answered. "Hello, officer. May I help you?"

"Is there any trouble here tonight, ma'am? We got a call about a possible death."

She put her hand to her mouth and ran her tongue along her top denture plate. "A dead body?"

From inside her husband called out. "Who is it?"

"It's the police."

A moment later he appeared behind his wife, cane in hand.

"Do you know who lives next door?"

"A doctor. He's real nice," the woman said. "Blake Swenson."

"Is he home?"

The man pointed. "See that car? Not too many of those running around. He must be."

"Thank you," the officer said.

He turned his attention to apartment A. When there still wasn't any answer, he headed around back.

He let himself into the backyard through a gate in a white

fence. He ascended three steps to a small back deck and tried the door. It was unlocked.

He drew his Glock handgun and pushed open the door. He first entered the kitchen. It was an old house, but you wouldn't know it by the kitchen. It looked to have been recently remodeled. There was an open bottle of Jack Daniels on the white counter. The curtains were all drawn, the place quiet and dark.

He flipped a light switch and walked into the dining room. On the table was a handwritten note. He glanced at it, raised his eyebrows as he read it, then moved on, certain of what he would find. "Dr. Swenson?" he called.

The house remained eerily silent.

Paul raised his voice, "Dr. Swenson?" He walked into the back bedroom. There on the dresser were multiple bottles of prescription medication. Thorazine. Valium. Vials of midazolam were stacked next to a ziplock bag of syringes. A poster of a red Ferrari had been tacked to the wall above a waterbed, an old solid-side style. He pushed his hand down on the mattress, sending a wave across the top. The door to the closet was ajar. The officer lifted his handgun.

He found a man in the bedroom closet, hanging by a rope around his neck. The skin of his face was pale blue, the body unmoving.

He touched his wrist, feeling for a pulse. Nothing.

Paul knew better than to disturb the scene. He backed out, feeling slightly nauseated. He lifted his radio from the holster on his belt. "Dispatch, I've got an apparent suicide at 867A Park Avenue. I'm going to need a forensics team and the ME."

An hour later Blake Swenson's place was crawling with interested police personnel and the local ME. From the body temperature, the time of death had been recent, approximately two and a half hours previously.

John Jaster, a Richmond PD detective, frowned and looked at Paul Letchford, who was holding up a note. "Looks like a suicide note. It's addressed to a Joanne and signed, 'Blake.'" He paused, "Any idea who Joanne is?"

"Not a clue." He lifted a photograph. I found this on the mantle over the fireplace," he said. "If this is our victim, it's possible this woman is Joanne."

"Have you searched the rest of the house?

"I found one other thing," he said, holding out a second slip of paper. "Looks like a lab test. Says that a Rachel Conners is blood type O and Blake Swensen is blood type AB." He gestured toward the stairs. "Haven't looked upstairs yet."

Jaster nodded and walked to the stairs. "Then you're not sure that this isn't a murder/suicide, are you?" He climbed the stairs, letting his heavy footfalls speak his disappointment in the officer's failure to search the remainder of the house. At the top of the stairs he paused, letting his eyes adjust, and searching for a light switch. The first door to the right was a hall closet. The next door was what interested him. There was a padlock hanging from a metal latch so that the door could be secured from the outside.

He knocked on the door. There was no response.

Five minutes later he closed a bolt cutter on the padlock, snapping it open.

Once inside the room, his eyes widened. A small girl lay in the center of a double bed with an IV hanging from a curtain rod next to the window. Clear fluid dripped through a tube into her arm.

She had blond hair and appeared to be sleeping. He looked around the room. There were scattered remnants of McDonald's Happy Meals and a plate of half-eaten instant mac and cheese on the bedside stand.

He touched her shoulder. She didn't move. He shook her

more vigorously and called for the ME. "Dr. Besley, I need you up here immediately!"

Dr. Besley, in his twenty years as a medical examiner in Richmond, Virginia, had seen about every different variety of man's inhumanity to man that he could imagine. But he hadn't seen anything quite like this. He bent over the small girl and mentally ran through the ABC's. She had an adequate airway. She was breathing. She had a pulse. He pinched the skin below her clavicle.

The girl made a slight grimace.

He shut off the IV. "We don't know what's in here. Likely something that's keeping her asleep." He looked at the detective. "Get an ambulance crew here. We need to get her to a hospital."

Jaster nodded.

The ME straightened. "Now!"

Joanne Conners loved her work in the emergency department at the Medical College of Virginia. It wasn't the hours of routine, but the moments of terror that had addicted her.

She looked around the trauma bay and took stock. They'd lost two gunshot victims just that shift, the victims of a robbery gone wrong, and a Quick Mart owner who'd taken the law into his own hands after his third holdup in as many months.

He and his would-be robber were both dead, their still bodies lying on the stretchers amid the bloody evidence of the fight to save their lives.

She pulled the curtain and walked away. *Such a waste.*

Ten minutes later the automatic doors parted. She looked up

to see a familiar sight. A rescue unit rolling in a stretcher, another victim of accident or illness. Someone with a story.

She stood and walked toward the crew. "Hi, Evan. Give me the bullet."

She didn't hear his answer. She felt her heart in her throat. The busyness of the ER clamored around her, but in that moment she could not think. She could not respond. She stood numbly staring at the little girl, her newest patient, and gasped.

Could this be real?

She shook her head. Shock and disbelief assaulted her world. With her hand to her mouth, she tried to speak. "Ra-Ra-Ra—"

Another nurse looked at Joanne. "Jo, what's wrong?"

Joanne's hands begin to tremble. "That's my daughter!"

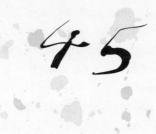

JOANNE STOOD AT the side of the stretcher and kissed the face of her daughter. *Could it be true?* "Rachel, Rachel."

Rachel's eyes opened.

Joanne couldn't believe her eyes. "Rachel!"

Her daughter twisted and stretched.

Evan Thomas, paramedic, looked at her. "You know this girl?"

"She's my daughter."

Tears streamed down Joanne's face, her vision blurring. "I need the police! Now!"

Nurse Donna Snyder slid a firm arm beneath her shoulders. "Calm down, Jo. Tell us what's happening."

Joanne spoke haltingly through sobs. "I thought she was dead. She's been missing since July seventh." She grabbed the sleeve of the paramedic. "Where did you find her?"

"Police responded to a nine-one-one report that a dead body was at a house over in the Fan. When they got there, they found a suicide victim and the little girl. She was locked in a bedroom with an IV running. She was very sedated. She started coming around once the ME disconnected whatever was in her IV bag."

"Suicide? Who committed suicide?" She felt her knees weaken, and Donna helped her find a seat on a vacant stretcher. She raised her voice. "I need the police."

She looked into the faces of her coworkers and the ambulance crew. The expressions were the sympathetic ones you offered a patient out of touch with reality. "Please," she pleaded. "Someone obviously kidnapped my daughter."

The paramedic stepped back and lifted his two-way radio.

She stood and wobbled to her daughter's side. "Oh, Rachel, Daddy was right all along."

She stroked her daughter's face and thought her heart would fail. Her cries erupted again. "I . . . thought . . . you . . . were . . ."

The words of the paramedic began to register. She looked up at the young man. "You said suicide. You didn't tell me who."

Evan shrugged. "Don't know."

"Where did you say it was?"

The paramedic said, "Park Avenue."

"Where?" She was practically screaming. "Exactly, where?"

He looked at the clipboard in his hand. "867 Park Avenue."

Oh, dear God. Not Blake!

She turned to her daughter, held her hand, and stroked her forehead. "Rachel, it's Mommy. Talk to me, sweetheart."

Rachel yawned. "Mommy?"

"Oh, my baby, my dear, dear Rachel."

Rachel sat up and leaned into her mother's embrace.

I was frying a hamburger on the stove when the phone rang.

Joanne's words tumbled out in excitement. "David, are you sitting down?"

"Hi, Jo. No, I'm standing up." I looked around my new kitchen and smiled.

Jo's voice was edged with excitement. "Sit down, honey."

I chuckled. "Jo, what's going on?"

"It's Rachel. She's been found. She's alive."

My throat threatened to close. "A-a-alive?" Everything closed inside me began to open up. I thought my heart would burst with joy. "Where?"

"They found her locked in a room at Blake Swenson's place."

I gasped. "Blake? She's alive?"

"Yes, David," she practically shouted. "Rachel is alive!"

"Why was she at——"

"David, are you listening? Our daughter is alive!"

I stood, speechless.

"They found her at Blake's house." She halted. "David, he committed suicide."

"How do they know it was——"

"Blake left a suicide note and called nine-one-one."

The news was horrible. But I couldn't stop smiling. I could hardly believe it. "Where is she now?"

"Medical College of Virginia Hospital. Evidently, Blake kept her drugged. She was sedated and doesn't remember where she's been. The pediatric team wants to watch her for a while."

"I'm on my way. I'll be there as soon as I can."

Thirty minutes later I was traveling west across the Chesapeake Bay Bridge-Tunnel, barely able to believe that Rachel was alive.

I called Richmond PD on my cell and left a number for the detective to call. "I'm the father of the girl who was found at 867 Park Avenue. Could you have the detective handling the case call me?"

Ten minutes later my cell phone sounded. "Hello."

"Dr. Conners? This is Detective John Jaster. I understand the little girl we picked up in the Fan may be your daughter."

"Most definitely," I said. "She's with my wife."

"I've spoken with Joanne. You knew Dr. Swenson?"

"Yes. He was an old friend. What can you tell me?"

"Only that he left a note addressed to your wife."

"A note?"

"Apparently he was quite obsessed with her and the idea that the little girl was his daughter."

I sighed. *Oh, Blake.*

"How'd he die?"

"Hung himself in his bedroom closet."

I groaned. I gathered myself enough to ask, "Tell me about the note."

"I'll show it to you when you arrive at the hospital."

Two hours later I sat in a hospital bed holding my daughter. Rachel squirmed. "Daddy, you're . . . squeezing . . . me . . . too . . . tight," she gasped.

I grinned and squeezed her even tighter before releasing my life-grip. "Sorry." I looked up in response to a knock at the door to see a man wearing a dark suit. "Dr. Conners?"

I stood to greet him, holding out my hand.

"I'm Detective Jaster, Richmond PD." He motioned with his head toward the hallway. "Could we speak?"

I turned to kiss Rachel's forehead for what must have been the thousandth time and slid her back onto the bed. Joanne led the way into the hall.

He held out a paper to Joanne. It was sealed within a clear plastic bag. "You asked to see this? Careful," he said, "we haven't examined it for fingerprints yet."

I slipped my arm around her and read the letter. The suicide note.

> Joanne,
>   I dreamed that one day we could be together, that one day we could be a family, you, me, and our daughter, Rachel. I took her only because I thought it was the only way I could be with you. It was no longer tolerable for me to allow another man to raise my child. I believed that

without Rachel, you and David would fall apart and I
could fill the void. Then, I'd show you how happy we
could be. But you never responded the way I wanted.

Now I realize that I've been so wrong. The blood test
finally convinced me. Rachel isn't mine. So sorry for the
confusion and misery I've caused.

Love, Blake

I looked at him. "Tell me about the blood test."

"Well, I'm not an expert on these things, but from what the
ME told me, his blood type and your daughter's blood type were
incompatible with him being the father." His eyes flickered between Joanne and me.

"Do you have my daughter's blood type?"

He flipped open the folder in his hand, then shuffled
through a few papers until he found what he was looking for.
"Yes, here it is. She's type O."

My heart skipped a beat. "Type O?" I looked at Joanne who
hadn't taken her eyes off the note in her hand. "Are you sure?"

"I'm holding the lab test results right here. Blake Swenson
was type AB and Rachel is type O. The ME tells me that the children of a person with type AB blood will be A, B, or AB, but
never O."

"Yes, I know," I said, feeling the blood rush from my face.

"Dr. Conners?"

I couldn't speak.

My blood was type AB.

I TRIED TO cover up the emotional blow. "Let me see the note, Jo," I said softly. She handed it to me. I read it again. Inside, I put aside all the questions in order to focus on what didn't seem right. Blake was irresponsible. Manipulative. And certainly not above trying to win Joanne's heart.

But suicide? That didn't seem like something Blake would do.

I looked at the officer. "It's from a printer. Anyone could have written this."

The detective nodded. "We've taken a laptop we found in the apartment. The forensics team is there too, looking for evidence that someone else might have been involved."

I felt Joanne tremble beneath my arm. "He was crazy in the end," she said. "He snapped. He finally realized that no matter what he did, I wouldn't come around."

"He was a lot of things, but Blake thought too much of himself to do this."

Jo shook her head. "Not if he realized the insanity of his little plan." She pulled away and faced me. "His efforts to win me over became more and more desperate, David. He had taken Rachel, thinking she was his daughter, believing all along he could recapture my heart when our world fell apart." She handed the note back to the detective. "When his plan crumbled, so did he."

Detective Jaster looked as though he agreed.

I stayed quiet, but couldn't deny my suspicion. *Did Blake feel trapped, thinking he would be found guilty of kidnapping?*

Or did someone manipulate Blake and set him up to look guilty?
My next thought chilled me even more. *Was this murder?*

It took three days for Rachel to physically return to normal. And despite my gentle prodding, her weeks without us remained locked in a drug-induced haze.

For three days I played a game of cat and mouse with Joanne to see if she would tell me the truth about Rachel's biological father. But she couldn't or wouldn't crack. The keys to the lock on her heart were solely in her possession, and she wasn't sharing them with me. When she was ready, I knew my role. I'd be there to forgive.

Every day a clearer picture of Blake emerged: a man obsessed with the daughter he couldn't raise and the only woman who had spurned his offer of marriage. In his house they found not only a variety of photographs of Joanne and Rachel but enough mind-altering pharmaceuticals that Rachel didn't have a clue that she'd been away for so long.

But my doubts about him remained. I'd known Blake a lot longer than Joanne, and I doubted that he would ever end his own life. But the police never found any other evidence of foul play, and the case seemed destined to go down as a suicide, something I would always have a nagging suspicion about, but nothing I could ever prove.

It was a Saturday morning when I sensed a subtle quietness around Jo. I knew something was on her mind, and all I needed to do was respond with a gentle embrace and she would likely dump the entire load. I put my arms around her and kissed her.

I'd thought through the fatherhood issue a thousand times. My conclusion was always that whoever Rachel's biological father was didn't matter. From the time I was on the scene, Jo had been my gal. She arrived in my life during a troubled summer, and as it turned out, she wasn't only troubled about her relationship with Blake—something I was glad to rescue her from—but she was troubled *and* pregnant. I had no idea then what amount of craziness I had swept in and taken over when I asked her to be a permanent fixture in my life. As I thought it through, I still didn't.

But that was before Rachel. She'd been a daddy's girl from the time she was placed in my arms, and nothing could break the bond we had.

Should I be angry? Bitter toward Jo for keeping such a secret? Or had I been directed down a difficult path to teach me that revenge and bitterness would do nothing but make me and the recipient of my venom miserable?

I held her at arm's length and whispered. "I love you."

Her breathing seemed to catch in her throat. "David, there's something I need to tell you."

I raised my eyebrows as she struggled to formulate the next words.

"About Rachel?"

She nodded. I put my index finger over her lips. I figured she wanted to tell me about Rachel's blood type. I wanted to assure her that it didn't make a difference.

"Don't," I whispered. "It doesn't matter now." I smiled and brushed back a tear from her cheek. "All that matters is that we are together as a family."

"But I—"

"Shhh," I said. "I learned some important lessons while Rachel was gone. I learned how to forgive." I shrugged. "So let's not talk about it."

That afternoon I escaped to my study and called Amina. I wasn't sure what was in her mind, but I knew that when I next visited the shore with Joanne, I didn't want there to be any confusion.

She answered after the first ring. "Hello."

"Amina, it's me."

"David," she said.

"I wanted you to know that Rachel has been found."

"I read about it in the paper."

Of course. I cleared my throat. I pressed on, my heart racing like a junior-high school boy trying to talk to a girl on the phone for the first time. "My wife and I are back together."

She was quiet for a moment. I listened to her breath, whistling into the phone. "We are friends," she said. "Nothing more."

Was she trying to convince me? Or herself?

"Of course."

"My father is talking about moving. We have relatives in Minneapolis." She paused. "Since the *Beautiful Swimmer* is gone."

"Oh—I, well, good luck with that." I halted. "I mean if you move."

"Mahadsanid." Somali language for "thank you." She'd taught me that much.

"Good-bye," I said.

"David," she said, her voice steady. "I'm glad for you. About Rachel."

I tried to read between the lines. *But not about Joanne?*

"Good-bye," she said and the phone line clicked.

Rachel sat staring out the front window, watching a car drive past, an odd look on her face.

"What's wrong, honey?"

"I remember getting a ride in a car like that."

"Like what?" I asked.

"An old car. A red one that didn't have a roof."

"When, Rachel?"

"When I was gone from you."

The thought chilled me. I remembered the three angry men in a red convertible.

Maybe she was remembering. I wondered how much else she would eventually have to relive if memories started coming back.

I hugged her against my chest, not sure if I wanted her to remember.

She wiggled around and laid her ear against me. "How's your heart, Daddy?"

I smiled. "Just fine." *Now that you're here.*

"Can I ride my bike?"

"Sure. But will you stay in the cul-de-sac so that I can watch?"

"Okay."

Rachel scampered off, and Joanne joined me in watching from the front porch.

It was there I verbalized something that had been percolating ever since Rachel had been returned. "Did you ever wonder if Blake's death was a cover for what really happened with Rachel?"

I watched as Jo's eyes seemed to glaze over for a second before she offered a smile. "What on earth do you mean?"

I shrugged. "The whole thing is just so convenient. Rachel disappears. Your father sponsors moving legislation to help kidnapped and missing children. His poll numbers soar. The balance of the Senate is likely to shift with the next election." I waited a moment for the words to sink in. "All because our little girl disappeared. What if Blake didn't take her at all?"

Joanne leaned over the railing, keeping her little girl in sight.

I continued. "Blake doesn't seem like the type to take his own life."

"So you expect me to believe that there's a secret group

behind my father's Senate bid that is capable of using a child like a pawn in some political chess game and setting Blake up for the fall?"

I wasn't sure what to say.

Joanne started laughing.

It did seem unlikely. So I started laughing, too.

I smiled and walked into the kitchen where I grabbed a bottle of corn oil. Then I searched in the garage until I found what I wanted.

What I needed was to relish the joy of ordinary life. Breath. A heartbeat. A sunny Saturday afternoon with my family. I lifted a blue sled from where it leaned against an upright freezer where I'd cast it aside on a day that changed me forever.

There were things that mattered in life. Things I knew to be true. Others would always hide in the shadows, beyond my caring. One thing I knew. I remained a prisoner, bound only by an act of my own will. Love held me to two women as certainly as iron bars. My crime was only that I had fallen too hard in love, and I would give my all to serve out the life sentence I'd been issued. Love bears all. Believes all. Forgives all. And in that prison, my soul was free.

And for me, that was enough.

I stepped onto the front porch, eyeing Jo, knowing I would proceed with her eager approval.

"Rachel," I called, lifting the sled in the air. "Want to go sledding?"

Epilogue

ON ELECTION NIGHT Gary Morgan won a landslide election. However, Joanne, Rachel, and I stayed out of the public light at our newly renovated house on the Eastern Shore. Fortunately for me, the county sheriff convinced the district attorney that I had suffered enough with Rachel's abduction, so he decided I wasn't worth prosecuting for helping Riley escape the farm.

For Gary Morgan, the sympathy vote may have paved the way to victory. For many, it seemed like a falling-dominoes cascade. A new party was in power in Congress, the majority determined by one seat, my father-in-law's. The president had promised reform and had the backing of his own party to push forward with a new agenda. Energy and oil were the real winners, with promises from the Oval Office that would keep America indebted to an oil-based economy for years to come. If I'd had some sort of business sense, maybe I'd have invested in ExxonMobile.

Rachel sat on the edge of the pier swinging her legs over the water. She looked so innocent and free. The irony didn't pass without my recognition. The world was different today because of one little innocent girl.

Joanne touched a glass of wine against mine as we sat in the gazebo next to the pier. "Why don't we move here?" she said. "Richmond is wearing me out."

I raised my eyebrows. "Really?" This wasn't the woman I'd married. "You're running from something." I studied her for a moment and couldn't quite dispel the feeling that an invisible weight still burdened her soul. Or maybe it was just a bit of melancholy due to being onstage most of her life.

She laid her head against my shoulder. "Maybe here I can be something other than the senator's daughter."

"Doc Larimore is looking for someone to take over his practice. I'm sure he'd love to have a local boy."

She sighed in contentment. "It's weird."

"What?"

"I've come to love this place."

"Or do you hate Richmond?"

She stayed quiet. "Love, I think."

"Gets in your blood." I sipped from my glass. "They're looking for a head nurse in the ER at Nassawadox Community Hospital. I'm sure they'd be delighted to see your application."

"Let's do it."

In a ballroom at the Marriott in downtown Richmond, the Morgan victory celebration was running full tilt. A jazz band, dancing, an open bar lined with men in tuxedos, women in sequined dresses, and waiters balancing glasses of champagne helped Tricia Morgan savor her husband's victory.

She was standing near the edge of the room when she heard a familiar bass voice behind her.

"Congratulations, Tricia."

She startled at the sound. She tilted her head toward his voice but didn't turn, preferring that anyone watching not appreciate their conversation. The man was of imposable size. But it was not his mass that determined his power.

She saw him without looking. In her mind, he loomed, a man not easily lost in a crowd. Tuxedoed, he would be impressive. She imagined the glistening of sweat above his full lips, the squareness of his shoulders, and the way his stomach pushed forward, entering the room before him and announcing his arrival. He may not have had his fingers on all the dominoes, but he certainly worked for those who did.

"You shouldn't be here." She shivered. "I did what you asked."

"Is that any way to treat the ones responsible for your little victory?"

"You promised to leave my family alone now."

"But we made such a great team."

"We are not a team."

"Oh, that's where you're mistaken."

"You came to gloat." She took a deep breath and lifted a champagne glass in front of her lips. "Unless you're coming to collect on your victory."

"Contrarily, I'm here to thank you. I wasn't sure you could pull it off."

She forced a laugh. "I can be resourceful."

"Evidently." She sensed him moving closer. She glanced at him. He was staring away from her with a cell phone lifted to his ear.

He talked to her, but pretended to speak into the cell. "So the girl is back home again. Shame on that awful doctor for stealing her away."

"Did you have to kill him? That wasn't part of the deal. I didn't agree to that."

"Sure you did. You needed a job done. We did it."

She tried to keep her lip from trembling by pressing the glass to her mouth. "I never want to see you again."

"But I need assurances."

"Assurances?"

"Assurances that the good senator will push forward with the president's agenda."

"Of course. That was the agreement."

"I still have a backup plan."

Tricia felt her stomach tighten. The powerful ones always did.

"The girl looks happy now. I saw her playing at her new house at the Eastern Shore."

"You're watching her?"

"We're always watching. We intend to help you remember your end of the bargain."

She steeled herself against showing the fear now gripping her soul. She should have known this wouldn't be the end.

Tricia gulped the champagne and set the glass on a passing waiter's tray. She saw her husband nearing the stage where he would make a victory speech. It was time to move forward. She glanced at the fat man. He stood facing away, tuxedoed and proper. She took a deep breath, pasted on a winner's smile, and strode across the floor toward the senator.